THE LONELY HEARTS TRIVIA NIGHT

THE LONELY HEARTS TRIVIA NIGHT

A Novel

LAUREN FARNSWORTH

alcove
press

Copyright © 2024 by Lauren Farnsworth

All rights reserved.

Published in the United States by Alcove Press, an imprint of The Quick Brown Fox & Company LLC.

Alcove Press and its logo are trademarks of The Quick Brown Fox & Company LLC.

Library of Congress Catalog-in-Publication data available upon request.

ISBN (hardcover): 978-1-63910-829-9
ISBN (ebook): 978-1-63910-830-5

Cover design by Alexandra Allden

Printed in the United States.

www.alcovepress.com

Alcove Press
34 West 27th St., 10th Floor
New York, NY 10001

First Edition: June 2024

10 9 8 7 6 5 4 3 2 1

For my husband James—
my first reader, my biggest fan, my best friend.

And for my dear Dad—Barry Douglas Farnsworth, 1954–2023.

"Next to trying and winning, the best thing is trying and failing."

—L. M. Montgomery, *Anne of Green Gables*

CHAPTER ONE

PUB QUIZ TEAM-MATES WANTED

Thursdays, 8 p.m. at the Five Bells on Westow Hill. Team of four or five will do. Big money! Last pot £50. Only clever clogs need apply (joking!). Email Donna at . . .

Bryony had read Donna's ad on the "neighborhood events" forum and had waited until she was alone to answer, deleting and retyping her reply with a ragged thumbnail held against her bottom teeth. And now, hesitantly crouching at a golden-lit window of the Five Bells, peeking inside over a crest of yellow winter pansies, she wasn't entirely sure she didn't regret it.

In the spirit of preparedness (because Bryony never committed to anything without it), she hoped to glimpse whoever else might be there to meet her tonight. Inside, broad-backed men in plaid shirts stood shaking their heads and shouting over each other, their pint glasses dripping froth over their fingers, and a sleek, ponytailed woman sat with another, her eyebrows riding high as she pointed and gestured with a wine glass over some atrocious tale that needed urgently to be told. They belonged—they probably had their "regular" tables, the barman knew their orders—and they would cast furtive glances over at Bryony when

I

she entered. Who was this woman? Was she lost? And why were her clothes so hopelessly drab?

Outside, a lone girl in a fleece-lined suede coat stood on the other side of the entrance doors, blowing solemn curls of cigarette smoke into the December night, her delicate profile in a critical squint, but she turned away, her arms hugged tightly to her waist; she didn't look as though she was here to meet anyone.

At home, Bryony had allowed herself to imagine the pleasantly rowdy table at Donna's pub quiz: the warm, chestnut smells, the wide, laughing smiles of interesting people all around her, a chilled glass of wine at hand. And as the suspenseful voice of the quiz host would rise and fall, her teammates would cry out in awe of Bryony's quick, unfaltering ability to know or intelligently guess the answer to question after question ("You've got it, Bry!"). Donna would have stylishly cut hair and neat, clean clothes. She would sip from a frosty cocktail and wink at Bryony like a coconspirator over the rim of her glass. "Bry," she would say, "I'm so glad you came." Bryony had been able to hear her warm voice at home in her small, cluttered living room.

She could see now this was delusional. They would sniff her out in a minute—the tedious people pleaser, her hair never tidy enough, who would only blink in panic when asked about that latest podcast episode or the new exhibition up town or whatever else it was she was missing in the world.

She stepped away, under the winking Christmas lights strung between the lampposts of Westow Hill, the shabbiest side of the Crystal Palace Triangle—folded cardboard boxes for tomorrow's trash pickup lined a darkened charity shop, and a hazardous buzz kept a neon Domino's sign half lit. And then she thought of sliding into her front door in tiptoeing shame, having failed, and having everyone know about it.

She took a steadying breath and pushed her way inside the doors. "Hi," she muttered. "Hi, I'm Bryony. So nice to meet you. Can I get you a drink?"

* * *

Standing in front of the dusty living-room mirror, with its listless draping of tinsel, Jaime applied a wobbling slick of eyeliner.

"You nearly ready?" she said.

2

"I was thinking," Luke said from inside the bedroom, and his voice sounded as though he had rehearsed what to say next. "If it's not my thing and I'd rather . . . well, would you mind if I sort of ducked out early or . . ."

Jaime's gaze came to rest on the reflection of her powdered bottom lip. "Or what?" she asked.

"I don't know."

"Well, we have to go in . . ." Her watch read almost seven-thirty. "For God's sake, we have to get going, and I haven't even—look, this Donna booked the table for seven. Can't we just see how it goes?"

"I thought the quiz started at eight."

"Yes," she said, her voice a little too loud. She expelled a hard puff of air through her mouth that untidied her fringe. "But we all want to meet first, right? And what if everyone's there before us, and we're stuck at the end of the table, not talking to anyone?"

"We could talk to each other."

"That is the exact opposite of the point. The *exact opposite*."

"I was joking. It was a joke."

"Well, it's not . . ." She caught sight of her startled eyes in the mirror, and wondered why it should be a joke that they should have each other to speak to. "Funny," she finished.

"Well," he started again, "what do you think about . . . what I just said?"

"Look, I'm nervous too, alright? But let's just—let's just do our best."

"I'm not 'nervous.' Who said anything about being nervous? I'm just not sure it'll be my thing."

"I mean, it's not exactly fun for me if I'm forcing you into it," she said. She snatched up a lipstick and dragged the dark plum color across her bottom lip. Pressing her lips together, she felt the sticky snags of dried skin that she then attempted to pry off with two pinched fingers.

All she could hear from the bedroom was Luke's sigh.

"Well, thanks for sort of ruining it for me," she said, to prompt a response. "One night out with actual people, and you can't even do that."

He still didn't say anything, and she knew the silence was supposed to fill her with guilt. He'd be sitting on the bed with his hands folded in

3

his lap, awaiting a tentative finger tap on the door, for her to say, "Sweetie, it's OK. We don't have to . . ." She could sit beside him on the buttercup-print duvet and rest her chin on his shoulder. But they had been there before, and she wasn't sure it made either of them feel better.

Jaime applied a second smear of lipstick, but, against the bright polka dots of her sweater, it made her mouth look clownish. Her face was too white against the heavy curtain of her copper-bright hair, and her cheeks were too childishly plump to convey any real sense of world-liness or sophistication. She had the sudden impulse to pick up her phone and cancel the whole thing.

Luke emerged from the bedroom, pulling the hem of a maroon T-shirt over his pale belly. He was neither short nor especially tall, with silky fine hair, growing too long now, that was not quite blond but not dark enough to be called brown. Even his clean, rimless glasses, almost invisible in certain lights, left the impression that he might not be wearing glasses at all.

"Whatever. Let's go, then," he said.

Sometimes Jaime wasn't sure if the tender quality of his pink skin had changed since they were children.

"You look nice," she said. She tried to smile, but had to disguise the odd shape she could feel her mouth making by turning away.

*   *   *

The Five Bells was the only pub on the Crystal Palace Triangle that hadn't yet been gentrified. The mahogany doors, increasingly stiff on their hinges, were scuffed by two decades of feet kicking them open. The green-glazed tiles that clad its exterior were now milky with dissolved graffiti and tacky with sloshes of drink. You could even still buy a pint of Ruddles beer for £1.69.

Donna stood lingering over the end of a cigarette. She'd pulled the fleece collar of her suede coat up to her earlobes to keep warm. As she breathed a long stream of bluish smoke toward the entrance, a young couple approached. The girl hurried slightly ahead, one hand clasping the opening of her parka and the other finger-combing her thick, red fringe. The boy followed, mouth and nose buried so deep in a tightly

4

wound scarf that the lenses of his rimless glasses perched on its woolen edge instead of his cheeks.

Donna made an enthusiastic attempt to wave away the smoke. "Sorry," she said, but the girl either didn't hear or ignored her. She shouldered open the doors, and the two of them disappeared inside.

It was probably them. They looked nervous, as if they were running late—but they were awfully young. And that other woman, peering surreptitiously in the windows, bent in an anxious crouch, had finally gone in too—she might have been another of them. And yes, Donna was running late too. It was bad manners as their host, but for God's sake, she was tired and was even starting to regret the whole, stupid thing.

She stubbed out her cigarette and flipped her mobile phone screen to the front-facing camera, picking at the ends of her disheveled top knot, which now, she realized, resembled the fronds of a pineapple. She pulled the hairband out and attempted to tousle it into some sort of carefree arrangement.

There was nothing left to do but go inside. She had to: it seemed like all of her friends were making excuses lately, to either cancel plans or not makes plans at all. It was time to make new and better ones, or, honestly, she just might die of boredom.

* * *

Harry's pint of Magners cider was chilled and sweet. The crisp flow of it over his tongue and down his throat delivered a spread of relief from his collarbones to his navel.

Behind the jewel-colored bottles of spirits, in a smoked mirror on the wall, he could see a sepia image of himself, framed by blinking Christmas lights. And, from this distance, it revealed an arresting portrait. And if he turned his head just so, an attractive shadow was cast across his cheekbones. Since he'd lost his job, he had taken to wearing his hair a little long (why bother to have it cut?), and sometimes, if he gave his head a quick sideways shake, a lock of curling hair would tumble over his forehead. In those moments he would feel just like James Dean. Even if he wasn't entirely sure what James Dean looked like or whether he'd seen one of his films, he was confident that it was a good thing—an excellent thing—to have hair just like him. The only thing wrong with his reflection now was the half-filled pint glass (a tumbler of some iced amber liquid would have been better) and the fine-boned hand that gripped its base. However striking his face might be, his hands, as slender as an adolescent's, had always let him down. He took those hands now and buried them deep into the crooks of his elbows. He was thirty-one years old, with hair like James Dean, so why did he feel as if he were a teenager about to grapple with a bunch of grown-ups?

The other dilemma was that he had not changed position for ten minutes and now wasn't sure how to. He knew the table behind him (*Reserved. Donna. 7 p.m.*) was most likely occupied by two or three people by now, and it had become a matter of increasing importance to disguise that he'd been predrinking at the bar alone. Best to try for some languid twist at the hips that would allow him to catch someone's eye, raise both his eyebrows and say something like, "Oh, hi! You're here!" in an appropriate, easy-going tone.

He wiped his fingers over his cold mouth and performed the twist, only he had raised his eyebrows too soon and immediately met the startled gaze of a dark-haired, heavy-browed woman seated alone at the table.

"Oh, hi!" he said. He couldn't seem to relax his eyebrows into their natural position, and the realization of this seemed to cement them in place.

"Hi? Are you . . .?" The woman pulled back her chin in suspicion. "I'm Bryony. Are you . . .?"

"Harry. I'm Harry. Sorry, I was . . ." His face finally relaxed into a smile. "I mean, I didn't realize anyone else was here."

Bryony didn't smile. "Getyadrink?" she said suddenly.

"Sorry?"

"Can I get you a drink?"

"Oh, I . . ." A half-moon of white froth was clinging to the bottom of his empty glass. He wondered when he'd finished it. "Please, let me."

"No, it's fine," Bryony said, already standing and rummaging in an oversized shoulder bag. "Sit down—what can I get you?"

"Oh. A cider, thanks." He hunched his shoulders, feeling small and childish as he sat in the chair opposite hers and waited to be brought his drink. He pulled at the front zip of his blue windbreaker to take it off, but then thought better of it in case dark spreads of moisture had formed under his armpits; he was sweating. He started to check for any offending smell, but then Bryony was striding back to the table, holding aloft a glass of white wine and a half pint of cider, which she set down in front of him. A *half* pint—what sort of joke was this?

"Cheers," he said. "So."

"So." She placed her glass on the table so heavily that it sent the surface of the wine rocking precariously close to the brim. Annoyance or tension creased her forehead. He wondered how old she was, and he almost asked her before remembering that you weren't supposed to do that.

"You live nearby?" he ventured instead.

"I'm down by Anerley station."

"Anerley?" he said, sounding more delighted than he had meant to. "Nice."

"Is it? Wrong side of the tracks, some might say." Her humorless face dipped into her glass, giving Harry a view of the scattered, greying hairs down the length of her parting. The rest of it had been swept back into a ponytail as though she didn't have time for such things. He took three long, cold swallows from his glass and saw afterward that it was already half empty.

"How about you?" Bryony asked.

"Oh, live round the corner, always have. Went to school here and everything. Good at pub quizzes, then? You can say no. I won't tell anyone." He poised himself to take another drink but lowered the glass in time, before furiously licking his sweetened lips. Jesus, he better slow down, but the problem was there was nothing to do with his hands. "Pretty shit, myself," he said.

"Then why come?"

"Don't know. A laugh, I suppose." And he was pleased that it sounded plausible, and less alarming than the truth: that since his ex-girlfriend had left him, he wasn't sure he could spend another night alone in his flat without slowly losing his mind. In fact, it might have already started to happen. Some days, when he woke up to silence, he didn't know whether the glowing "6:00" on his digital clock meant morning or evening.

7

"Didn't really . . . well, didn't do too well at school," he said. "Enough to get by. Didn't get to university or anything like that."

The little crease between Bryony's eyebrows fell away. "Oh. Neither did I. What sort of work do you do, Harry?"

"Well, I'm—I mean—I *was* an estate agent. Up on Westow Street. I'm sort of—what do they say? Between jobs right now. You?"

"Oh, I'm—I'm just a mum." She licked her bottom lip. "A stay-at-home mum."

"Nice. How old are your kids?"

"Eleven and thirteen."

"Crikey. Must've been a teenager when you had them."

"Yes. Well. So do you want to stay in that line of work? The property business, I mean."

"Haven't really thought about it."

"Well, you should find something you love doing. Otherwise what's the point?"

Harry knew the alcohol was working around his system now—how many pints had come before this one? Had it been two or was it possibly three?—because heat gathered behind his eyes, and he swallowed a knot of gratitude.

"Well, I just need to pop to the—to the restroom," Bryony said, and she rose in an unsure, timid stiffness from her chair. He could only hope she didn't think he was a complete loser.

CHAPTER TWO

Question: *Name the 1963 American epic war film starring Steve McQueen, James Garner and Richard Attenborough.*
Answer: The Great Escape

In the dim, pine-scented restroom of the Five Bells, Bryony filled the stained sink and brought handful after handful of cold water over her squinting face. Oh, this was horrible. Who was this drunk guy she'd been saddled with? Where were all the other people?

She ripped three paper towels from the dispenser and held them over her dripping face, and when she brought them away to see her flushed reflection in the mirror, her wet hair clinging to her forehead like cobwebs, she knew it was time to get on with it. She pulled the plug from the sink and crouched under the weak stream of hot air from the hand dryer.

She stood up, blew her nose and raked her frizzing hair back into its ponytail. It was time to face him again, except . . . what was this? Something small and stiff passed between her fingers at the back of her neck. She had left the shop tag attached to the label of her cardigan. She snapped it off and punished her reflection with a look of withering contempt. Shouldering open the door, back into the sharp, bright noises of the pub, she saw two others were now at their table: a red-haired girl with a youthful, round face and a pale, soft-looking boy, who was gripping a pint and looking over his shoulder. His head tilted upward, causing his glasses to flash fearfully in the ceiling lights.

With an apologetic duck of her head, Bryony took her place at the table.

"Hi, sorry. Hi, I'm Bryony."

"Hi!" The girl waved timidly with both hands. Her dark lipstick accentuated a smile that was distorted by nerves. "I'm Jaime, and this is Luke . . ." She hesitated. "My boyfriend." Appearing uncertain of what to do with her still-waggling hands, she laced her fingers into a tight, anxious package and let them fall into her lap.

Luke gave Bryony a look of such regret that she wondered if he could possibly know about the shop tag on her cardigan. Harry blinked up at her, apparently surprised to see she had returned. "Bryony, this is Jaime and Liam," he said, leaning back in his chair, holding a fresh pint glass tenderly to his chest. "They're from Cumbria—originally, I mean," he said, and—did he just wink?

"Cumbria? That's certainly very . . . well, very far. But it was Luke, I thought?"

Luke's face stiffened like a small, startled animal. "Yes, that's right."

Harry buried his mouth in the frothy brim of his glass and mumbled something that might have been, "Oh, sorry, sorry."

"I've been so nervous today," said Jaime, spinning one of the many rings on her fingers. "Has anyone else been nervous? It feels like . . . well, it feels like a first . . . *date*." She immediately seemed to regret using the word "date." Her chin dropped and her heavy fringe hid her eyes.

"Oh, absolutely," Bryony assured her. "I was just going to say that exact same thing." She might have added that she'd never been on a first date—not a real one—but it was probably too soon to start saying personal things like that.

And as she started to wonder when you did start saying things like that, and whether it would be obvious, Donna entered the pub—the girl in the fleece-lined suede coat who had stood smoking outside. It might have seemed implausible to the others that Bryony could have known this was Donna (her profile picture online had been of the back of her slender torso as she sauntered down some gritty, residential street), but she knew, absolutely, that it was. And she was right.

With the sharp clip of her heeled boots echoing above the babble of the pub, Donna strode directly to them and sat down at the head of the table, flanked by Jaime and Luke, as if she had only dashed quickly to the restroom and back.

"Hi. Sorry I'm late."

There was a flurry of talk as she shrugged off her coat, artfully organized the drooping shoulders of her white knitted sweater and arranged and rearranged her golden wheat-colored hair.

". . . such a good table . . ."

". . . Can I get you a drink?"

". . . Always book this table, it's closest to the—Oh, yes, thanks, I'll have a gin and tonic . . ."

". . . So nice to meet you, thanks for . . ."

". . . Honestly, I just lost track of . . ."

She couldn't have been older than twenty-eight or twenty-nine, with narrow shoulders and a notably small, fine-jawed head. But with each dramatic laugh at jokes that weren't particularly funny—a laugh that displayed the slight crookedness of her bottom teeth—she commanded the table with an intoxicating overfamiliarity. She touched Harry's forearm with her fingertips as he offered to get her a drink, and then admired a silver charm bracelet around Jaime's wrist with more volume and enthusiasm than necessary ("Beautiful. *Beautiful!*"). Bryony wasn't at all sure that she liked Donna, but at the same time didn't know exactly what it was she disliked.

Luke, silent and unsmiling on Donna's right, had reared back in his seat, so Bryony leaned forward to catch his eye.

Then Donna spoke loudly to Jaime. "Gosh, you're very young, aren't you? What're you—twenty-two?"

Jaime's eyes flicked between Donna and Bryony, as though searching for the right answer. "I'm twenty-four."

"Christ, I'm twenty-nine. You're practically a child. And you must be Bryony," Donna said. "Can I just say . . . and, alright, it might sound silly, but I knew—I *knew*—from the moment you emailed me you were going to be one of the most intelligent people here."

Bryony became conscious of Jaime, that she had begun to nervously pull on one earlobe, perhaps wondering if there was something about her own email that made her seem notably stupid.

"Oh," Bryony said. "I can't even remember what I wrote. But that's—you know—nice of you to say."

"I knew you'd say that. You're too modest," Donna said. Harry placed a tall, fizzing drink with a bobbing lime in front of her. "Oh, thanks, love. I'll get the next one—you just say the word."

"I suppose everyone has intelligence in one form or another, though, don't you think?" Bryony said, adding a smile to convey her lightheartedness.

Donna's eyes flashed to one side, their whites a little bloodshot. "What a nice thing to think of people. Oh, look." She leaned forward, resting her chin on her knuckles. "That's Jude. Here we go."

*　　*　　*

Jaime tightened her hands on the table's edge. A broad-muscled bartender with a complexion of dark freckles made his way from table to table, handing out sheets of paper and calling for attention. She hadn't taken off her coat. They hadn't even picked a team name—wasn't that something you were supposed to do?

There were nervous silences for the first two questions of the first round (Capital Cities)—what if they got them wrong? But then Bryony answered without hesitation for the next three questions in a row, and their laughter and insistent whispering took on the tone of true camaraderie.

"What is the capital of Belarus?"

"Minsk," she whispered, scribbling, with the tip of her tongue held against her top incisors.

". . . Morocco?"

"Rabat, I think. Yes, I'm sure of it."

". . . Croatia?"

"Zagreb."

They chose a team name—the Red Hot Quizzy Peppers—which was probably not as funny as their fits of self-conscious laughter suggested it was, but the room was warm and alive with the buoyant sounds of easygoing, like-minded talk. Their drinks were full, and, from a distance, they could easily have resembled real friends.

Round two (Sports) caused such a scurry of talkative indecision that Jaime found she could hardly keep up.

"In Formula One, who retired from racing after being dropped by Jordan following the 1999 season?"

"Trust me. Damon Hill. I absolutely guarantee . . ."

"Who hosted the 1992 summer Olympic games?"

". . . No, wait. Wasn't it Barcelona . . .?"

"What sport is Eddy Merckx known for?"

". . . No, no, that's the cyclist who . . ."

"In what match did Diego Maradona's 'Hand of God' incident take place?"

". . . Well, what year was that, then?"

Jaime nudged Luke's knee at two other motorsports questions he surely should have known, but he shrugged and sipped at his beer. She guessed he didn't feel like answering.

The microphone cut out in round four (Anagrams), causing a flurry of quiet giggles, and then when Harry unwittingly shouted the answer to question ten across the room—"Yosemite!"—Jaime laid her forehead on the table, shaking with laughter so intense it almost upset Luke's bottle of Estrella. And by round five (Pop Culture), they had even acquired enough knowledge of each other's expertise that they could confidently slide the answer sheet to the person who would, no doubt, have the answer.

"In what movie did Irving Berlin's song 'White Christmas' make its debut?"

"Bryony—you love old films, don't you?"

"What is Batman's real name?"

". . . Oh, whatshisname? Harry, go on—you'll know this."

"Which artist creates iconic balloon dogs constructed of stainless steel?"

"Jaime! Here, pass it quick."

Everything looked to be pointing toward a successful evening, but then, as round six (American Presidents) came to an end and a ten-minute break was announced, Luke rose from his seat.

"Get some air," he said, and weaved through the clamor of people flocking to the bar until he was gone. Jaime considered the possibility that this really wasn't his "thing," but then what was? Was scrolling through Twitter his thing? Was watching hours of old Formula One footage his thing? Was driving his girlfriend to want to claw her face in desperation his bloody thing?

"Drinks?" Donna enquired. "Harry, I'm getting you some water; you look awful. Do you want some chips? I'm getting you some chips."

Harry's eyes had taken on an unfocused glaze, his pint glass empty once again. He put a fist to his lips as he swallowed what might have been a hiccup or burp, and Donna and Bryony smiled down on him with affection. Harry was someone who had undoubtedly sailed through life, burping or hiccupping or whatever else he was doing, on the merits of his beautiful face—his long, straight nose, his white teeth, and his luxuriantly thick, curled hair.

Then, when Donna wandered away to the bar, a stiff silence fell over the table. Harry kneaded his eyes with his thumbs and stared drowsily off into the distance.

Bryony gave Jaime a conspiratorial smirk and said, "Is Luke alright?"

"Oh, I suppose so. It's sort of stuffy in here."

"So, you said you worked in an art shop?"

Jaime blushed with pleasure. "Yes. In Norwood. But it's just a print shop—PrintPro? Not that we print anything. You know those god-awful photo canvases of shells or roses people put up in their houses when they don't have any actual art to put up? That kind of thing."

Too late, she realized that those god-awful shell or rose canvases might be exactly the kind of thing Bryony put up on her own walls, but Bryony apparently either didn't or had too much grace, or maybe shame, to say so.

"Did you study art?" Bryony asked.

Jaime nodded. "At uni in Cumbria. But I'm just . . . well, I'm just on the till."

Donna arrived back at the table, clutching four over-spilling glasses, and, after a round of thanks, she launched into an explanation of how tonight had come about. She'd stayed up until three in the morning after posting the pub quiz ad, she said, having watched a string of late-night gameshows.

"And I thought, well, wouldn't it be fun to create the most formidable team? Who are all those ridiculous, middle-aged people who go on those shows anyway? But look, I did start to worry—what if I'd only managed to round up a bunch of dim-witted . . . well, anyway, I've done this quiz with some friends before, but they all just lost interest." And now she was repeating the compulsive action of pulling strands of her hair from root to end. "Everyone's so flakey these days, don't you think? Everyone just comes up with excuses, but whatever." She took a long sip from her draught Amstel lager. "Oh look, Harry, here're your chips . . ."

In the warm sounds of friendliness—exchanges of history, fetching each other drinks and snacks—Jaime's tight spine began to relax. Everyone was so *nice*. And why couldn't Luke be that way? It may be shyness or awkwardness, but it came across as plain rude, and it had plagued him since they were seventeen. She could remember all the way back to Keswick Academy, most often in the overcrowded, greasy kitchens of sixth-form house parties, how a few short seconds after starting to say whatever it was he was saying, he would rub one clenched fist with his other palm and his chin would drop to his chest, defeated. Those around him would be left blinking stupidly in the dimmed overhead lights, wondering if they'd missed whatever had gone so wrong. But then six or more overconfident voices would begin talking all at once, and Luke would be forgotten. Back then, Jaime may have taken his clammy fingers to squeeze in her hand, but over time she had begun to hide her mouth with a cupful of whatever she was drinking and suck on her teeth until it was over. Why was it that other, stronger, better people could say what they mean and mean what they say?

Now Luke had exchanged fear of socializing with an indifference to it, and if she wasn't careful, that would poison them both. And where was he, anyway?

"Scuse me a minute," she said.

Outside, she found him concealed between two of the flower-filled window boxes, sipping at his beer. The wind had picked up, with a light rain beginning to spatter the pavement. The sweet smell of earth and decaying leaves rose from the flowers.

Jaime clutched her arms around her stomach. "Luke, it's raining. Come on."

He blinked at her behind his rain-speckled glasses.

"Come on," she said again.

He stepped out from between the window boxes as a gust of chilling wind sent the heads of the pansies straining sideways, exposing their pale-yellow undersides. "Do you mind if I head off?" he said. "I'm really tired."

"Oh, don't start with this again. And you know what, Luke? It's rude. You taking off without even—what time is it, anyway?" She inspected her watch. "It's barely nine. What am I supposed to tell these people?"

"You don't have to 'tell' them anything. I'm not feeling well, is all it is."

"So which one is it? Are you tired or are you not feeling well?"

"I don't feel well because I'm tired."

"I knew you'd do this to me. You're a selfish, ridiculous—"

And now there was no stopping them. He was selfish. He was ridiculous. He'd keep them alone and friendless forever if he had his way. And she was overreacting, Luke hissed. She needed to calm down. And she'd better not start crying out here in the street, as if this whole business wasn't embarrassing enough. The argument was the worst they'd had in months. It had them snarling, desperately gesturing into the rain, and it pulled their faces into distorted shapes of resentment. At one point, as Luke tried to walk away, it led them to the front of a darkened tattoo parlor, where an embracing couple saw them and hurried away, sending them startled backward glances.

"I had friends in Keswick," Luke was saying. "What do I want to come down here for and spend time with a bunch of pretentious—"

"Oh, your friends? Your friends in Keswick? Your friends who smoked weed in Stratten's garage every night and—"

"Oh, for the love of—Are you going to hold that against everyone for the rest of their *lives*?"

"And what are they doing now? What's Stratten doing? What's Mikey and Robbie and Phil doing?"

"I wouldn't know, Jaime. Because I'm down here being swallowed by—"

"Oh, 'swallowed.' Give me a break."

"Yes, swallowed. Swallowed by this place and swallowed by *you*." He jabbed a pointed finger at her chest, and his hand trembled when he pulled it back. He spun on his heel, his hands deep in his pockets, and took off toward the corner of Gipsy Hill.

Jaime stood breathing hard outside a brightly lit fried chicken shop, in the hot smell of wafting grease. The dancing, chirping sounds of the opening bars of "Let It Snow" came floating from a nearby car window. Most of their arguments could be traced back to beginnings or endings like this—outside nighttime venues, drink-fueled, under the bewildered stares of happier people.

The rain had stopped, but she was soaked; her hair and clothes clung to her skin. Her collarbones stung in the cold, after she'd clawed them in the urgency to demonstrate to Luke the acute pain he was causing her.

Back at the entrance to the Five Bells, Bryony peered round the entrance doors, her dark eyebrows knitted together with concern.

"Jaime? Are you alright?"

"I'm sorry. How embarrassing." Jaime wiped at the edges of her inflamed eyes with the heel of her hand. It came away streaked with black eyeliner.

Bryony reached out hesitantly to touch Jaime's elbow. "Is everything OK?"

"Yes. No. Luke just left. We had an . . . argument."

"Oh. I'm sorry. Do you want me to—do you want a glass of water or anything?"

"I'm fine. I suppose I need to go now. I'll get my things."

"Let me go with you. We can walk up the hill."

The pub was so warm that all her blood rushed into her throbbing fingers. At their table, Donna and Harry were turned toward each other with their knees touching.

"And the stupid thing is," Donna was saying, "I started this job a whole six months before she did—Oh, Jaime. Are you alright?" Her arm was propped up on the back of her seat, allowing her head to lull attractively into her hand. "Jude's just about to announce the winner."

Jaime swallowed the remainder of her watery Jack and Coke. "Luke isn't feeling well. I need to be off."

"Oh. Poor guy," Donna said with her small mouth forming a concerned pout.

"Hope he feels—you know—better," said Harry.

As Jaime threaded her arms through the sleeves of her parka and folded Luke's jacket and scarf over her arm, Jude called for attention. He ran through the rankings, adding glib jokes between the poor performers and the better ones. The Red Hot Quizzy Peppers had ended up in the forgettable middle—had it been sixth or seventh place?

"Pfft," Harry exhaled. "Reckon they googled everything anyway," he said, referring to the team who had won by a clear seven points. He used his index finger to mop up a sprinkle of salt from the bowl in front of him.

"Now, listen," Jude continued, raising his voice. "Pretty exciting news—pretty exciting indeed—the Five Bells will be the host for this year's London Pub Quiz League's annual tournament . . ."

As a chorus of "oohs" rose up across the room, Harry leaned onto the table. "What the hell is that?"

Donna held up a finger. "Shh."

"Next Thursday we'll begin with the preliminary phase for the South London division. The first matches will run until the middle of January. The quarterfinal, semi, and final will take place next spring and summer. The winning team will take home—are you listening? Ten thousand pounds."

Jaime winced as shrieking whoops and hollers rebounded around the pub walls. A laughing, skeptical voice heckled Jude from somewhere in the room: "You joking, mate?"

Jude flipped through a stack of glossy paper in his hands. "Flyers on the bar here—rules are on the website. Ten quid entry fee per team member. Hope to see some of you next week."

Donna whipped round to them, her eyes bright and her face alive with frantic movement. "Oh my God. We have to enter. I mean, don't we?"

Bryony gave an uncertain, tittering laugh as she buttoned up her coat. "I don't know, it sounds sort of serious, don't you think? Isn't this just meant to be a bit of fun?"

"Ten thousand quid." Harry gave a low whistle.

"I'll pay the entry fee for us," said Donna. "No problem."

"You can't do that," Bryony said. "I mean—thank you, but that's too much."

"Why don't we let that be my business?" Donna said. "Besides, I started this whole thing. I'm responsible."

And as the argument wore on—What sort of time commitment could they expect? Would they embarrass themselves?—Jaime lowered herself into her seat and allowed the others to decide for her. It hardly seemed to matter; the whole night was ruined.

"I think we should all—you know—make sure we're happy to be involved first," Bryony said. "Jaime should probably speak to Luke, and then we can—"

"Oh." Donna waved a hand dismissively. "I'm sure he will."

"I suppose," Bryony said, "it's nice to have some sort of goal, isn't it? A motivator?" With her coat buttoned up to her chin, her cheeks pink with pleasure, she resembled a tirelessly plucky schoolteacher.

It was agreed—the Red Hot Quizzy Peppers would enter the tournament. Jaime and Bryony said their goodbyes to Donna and Harry, clumsily kissed their cheeks, squeezed their shoulders and made promises to see them again next week. "We'll start a thingy," Donna said. "A group chat." And they left Donna and Harry speaking too loudly into each other's laughing faces.

Looking ahead onto the wet, shining slabs of pavement as they walked to the crest of Gipsy Hill, she found herself telling Bryony about the argument with Luke. There was no need to tell her how Luke felt "swallowed," but she tried to paint an unbiased picture of the matter at hand.

". . . And that's essentially the problem," she was saying. They stopped at the corner of Gipsy Hill and Westow Hill, outside a pink-fronted hairdressers, where a light-speckled view of central London and the illuminated tip of the Shard glittered in the distance. The 432 bus to Brixton clattered past, and they stepped back from the curb as the wheels sent a brown puddle showering over the pavement.

"We left Keswick to make a go of it here. London's always been it for me, you know? I knew I'd meet all the right people and start doing all the best things. And Luke wanted to come—really, he did—but now we've been here for two years, stuck in that awful flat, and we still know absolutely no one. That's why I thought this pub quiz thing would . . . I thought if I . . . oh, I'm being silly. You've got to be getting home."

"Well, do you think Luke will be up for this whole thing? The tournament, I mean. Perhaps he'd enjoy it."

"Oh, I suppose. I don't know."

"Listen, what time is your lunch break at the shop? Why don't we meet for a coffee tomorrow? I don't have many—you know—many friends either."

CHAPTER THREE

Question: *What branch of science involves the study of the composition, structure and properties of matter?*
Answer: *Chemistry*

"Well, Bryony was alright, I suppose. A little up herself though, didn't you think? And Jaime was sweet, but she didn't answer more than two or three questions the entire evening. And what was with her funny little boyfriend? He hardly said a word and then he just upped and left. What was his name again?"

In the stale bedroom of Harry's flat, a cramped Victorian conversion with a tight galley kitchen and high living-room windows that faced the leafy southeast boundary of Crystal Palace Park, Donna sat upright in his rumpled bed and talked and talked.

"Luke, I think," said Harry, remembering calling him something else and having Bryony correct him.

At some point, Jaime and Luke had left, although he didn't remember when or why—and had that come before or after the chips someone had bought him? Jaime had been nice enough, but with a tendency to duck away from eye contact and hide her timorous face behind the bright fall of her hair. And he scarcely remembered Luke's face at all, only a silent, bored presence sitting in one of the chairs. Bryony had been more memorable—an unsmiling, aloof woman who had softened eventually, in the revelation of scoring a string of correct answers in the first round.

Thankfully the ending memories of the night appeared to be intact. There hadn't been a need to smile amiably into Donna's pale morning face while he tried to remember the exact events that had led them there.

Their knees had been touching beneath the pub table and, before he knew it, Donna's head had been falling onto his shoulder as she'd laughed at something he'd said, her sweet-smelling hair splayed over his nose and mouth. She was one of those cool, beautiful girls who laughed easily and generously, that you usually only caught glimpses of across the room at a party or bar, surrounded by a swollen-chested gaggle of competing men. You could never normally get near them.

But "I mean it," she'd told him. "You're one of the funniest people I've ever met."

And wasn't that one of the nicest things he had ever heard? And could burying his nose in that hair, maybe even into her neck, bring about some relief from being dumped? So when the bell for last orders had rung, the obvious move had been to ask her to come back to his flat for another drink. She'd lowered her eyes and said, "OK, sure."

Harry had considered leading her back through the moonlit park (it might be romantic). But it wasn't moonlit, as the rainclouds had gathered, and he wasn't entirely sure "romantic" was what he should be going for. There was also every possibility it might come across as creepy. Instead, they had walked the perimeter of the park, down the sobering stretch of Anerley Hill, braced against the cold wind. And when they had stopped outside the brightly lit Tesco Express, where Donna suggested buying more alcohol, Harry recalled being struck with fear that if he had any more to drink then he wouldn't be able to perform.

He'd had a vivid mental image of them stumbling backward through his front door while kissing, of urgently stripping each other of their clothes. But that hadn't happened. They had walked quietly and awkwardly up the stairs and sat on his bed in their coats, with Harry wondering how exactly you went about the business of transitioning from cold, tired drunkenness to delirious passion.

They had got there eventually. When Donna had started talking about work again, Harry had made a clumsy lunge for her constantly moving mouth, more out of boredom than lust. Then they were underneath the covers and Donna was gloriously on top of him, making small moans of desire and breathing so heavily that he felt as if he must be the most attentive lover in the world. But at the peak of that feeling, when he had risen over her with the intent to have her crying out in his arms, it had all fallen to pieces: he had lasted for fifteen gratifying seconds before he came (and he was reasonably sure that she hadn't); then it was over.

"That was nice," she had said politely, once Harry had rolled off her. And he knew that "nice" was the most unlikely thing a girl would say if it actually had been. It would have been better if she'd said nothing at all.

Now, in the gauzy morning light of his bedroom, he became aware of Donna talking again. He needed a glass of water.

"Oh God, and the Yosemite thing," she was saying, holding her hands to either side of her face. She started laughing so hard that her words came out in pieces. "And you were so proud of—oh God, ha!—so proud of knowing it." Her laughter died away. "Oh, that was funny. And when the microphone kept cutting out. Poor Jude."

"Who's Jude?"

"The bartender—the quiz host. Honestly, he's such a flirt."

"How many times you been to that thing anyway?"

"The quiz? Oh, I don't know. Couple of times. The people I was going with—some friends—they just sort of got bored of it."

"You done this league thing before? The tournament?"

"No. It sounds like fun though, doesn't it?"

"Oh, I'll be useless." He then chanced wearing the joke too thin—"Yosemite!"—but it still won an earnest little laugh out of her.

Harry wondered what they were supposed to do now. It was Friday. It was eight-thirty a.m. Surely Donna had a job to get to, but she wasn't making any move to leave. She appeared completely at ease, nestled in his yellowing pillows against the headboard. Maybe he could take her for lunch or—no, wait, he didn't have any money. He could make her a cheese toasty with a dollop of pesto to make her think he was cultivated—but how long had that pesto jar been in the fridge? He knew one thing:

there was no possibility of them having sex again. Not this morning. He didn't trust that he could. Best to test the waters first, before committing to toasties.

"Do you want a cup of tea or something?"

"OK. But look, I should be getting to work soon."

And from the way Donna flicked her hair from behind her ear so it fell to shield the side of her face, and the way her mouth drew to the side in a clamped little bud of withdrawal, he knew there would be no impromptu day of lazy toasties, a walk around the park. and of talking so much and so freely that they might discover they were made for each other.

"Oh. Right. OK. I'll be right back. Why don't we go into the, uh . . . to the living room. What time do you start work?"

"Oh, no special time."

At some point during the night, Harry had had the foresight to put his boxers back on, so he was at least spared the humiliation of hobbling naked around the bedroom in search of them.

In the living room, he nudged the mouse of his desktop Dell to wake the screen. He clicked through to his email, hoping one of the job applications from earlier in the week might have come through, but none had. Once in the kitchen, filling the kettle with water and searching for a clean teaspoon, he heard Donna move into the living room; she was wearing his T-shirt.

"Who's this?" she asked.

"Who?"

"The girl on your screensaver." And if she was asking out of jealousy, he wouldn't have known. Her voice sounded wholly unconcerned.

"Oh. That's my ex. Vivienne."

"Recent?"

"Few months ago."

"She's very pretty."

"She was. She is. Now she's with a guy I used to work with at Kingsley—the estate agent up on the corner?"

"Oh. Shame."

"That was after I got made redundant though, thank God."

"Why'd you break up?"

24

Harry scratched the back of his scalp. Vivienne had been clever and independent and full of bright laughter—and oh, God, had she been beautiful. And now she was living in Streatham, spending her nights in the toothy-grinned company of Ashton Taylor-Phipps and his cheap pinstripe suits. Not only was he the newly promoted assistant manager of Kingsley & Co. (Harry had checked his LinkedIn), the guy even had these huge, tanned, large-veined hands. It was enough to make him sick. Still, it was nice to say Vivienne's name again. The few friends he'd retained since losing his job had quickly grown bored of listening. They all had girlfriends, wives, and even squirming, pink newborns of their own; no one had time to nurse a freshly dumped man through a second adolescence.

"Oh, I don't know," he said. "I wasn't adventurous enough, I guess. She wanted to go live abroad and—you know—she wanted to go do something like that."

"And you didn't want to?"

"Didn't see the point."

"And did she go? With the guy from Kingsley?"

"No. He's still working there. Same as I was. So maybe it was just me after all."

"Oh, don't be so self-pitying, Harry."

"No, but what you have to understand about Vivienne is that she's— well, she's just about the most extraordinary girl you'd ever meet. Don't know if I've ever met anyone as clever. She was interested in politics and international . . . well, you know—all that stuff. Would've done great at the pub quiz. And she was funny. She'd come up with these terrific one-liners out of nowhere. And, wow, could she turn heads. You'd walk into a room and—*pow!* There she was. Even remember what she was wearing the first time I . . ." He became aware that he had only heard the sound of his own voice in a long time. He cleared his throat. Well, he'd killed it now. What girl wanted to go out with someone who talked so endlessly of his ex that he forgot for how long he'd been talking?

Bringing two mugs of tea into the living room, he found Donna standing in front of the computer screen with her arms folded, studying Vivienne's smiling image, as if deliberating whether she was worth all that trouble.

"Ran out of milk," he said.

"Oh no, that's fine, love. Thanks." And after one delicate sip, she set the mug down and started to wander around the living room, touching the tips of her fingers to things she presumably found of interest: a hanging acoustic guitar that was gathering dust, a stack of used scratch cards, a hanging print of an abstract figure in blue.

"You like Matisse?" she said.

"Who? Oh, that? Not particularly. My mum got it for me."

Her eyes lost focus. "That's nice. You close to your mum?"

"Oh yeah. See her every week."

"Well. She's got good taste."

"Don't think she knows what it is, to be honest. Picked it up from the charity shop or something. She said I was living too—you know—that the place was too grim or something."

"Hm. Well. Mums worry, don't they?"

"What sort of work do you do, anyway? You said something last night about 'campaigning'? Like, political?"

"Oh no. I run marketing campaigns, for an agency. And before you ask if it's my passion or anything—it's not. What I really want to do is . . . well, the thing is I'm not sure. I tried out fashion design at uni, but it was all just . . . well, frivolousness, I guess. Nothing *meant* anything, you know? So I tried to switch to law. It's so amazing to do something that makes a difference, isn't it? A *real* difference, I mean. But my A Levels were a bit of a mess because I—Well, anyway, I didn't get onto that course. And then all I could do was a late application and ended up on some stupid little Communications degree."

"Oh. Well, it sounds—you know—fun."

"It can be. The people are a bit of a bore, though." She shrugged. "You live nearby?"

"Maberley Road. With a flatmate."

"That's nice. You friends?"

"Not really. I guess it's time I got going. Can I use your shower?"

"Oh, sure. Through there. Let me—wait, let me get you a towel."

Donna was in and out of the shower within ten minutes and didn't even finish her tea. Then, at the open door with her suede coat slung over her arm, she tilted her head to him. It took a moment to figure out what was different about her face—she'd scrubbed off all her makeup.

"I'll see you next week, then? For the Quiz League? I'll enter us this evening."

"Sure, yeah. But just so you know, I'm not very . . . clever or anything."

"Oh, don't worry about that. And listen, Harry, I don't want a boyfriend. Do you know what I mean?"

"Me neither. A girlfriend, I mean."

"There's nothing to worry about, then."

"I guess not."

And then she was gone.

For the remainder of the morning, Harry sat in his day-old boxers and an egg-stained dressing gown. He might've scoured the job advertisements, but he knew that nothing came up on a Friday. And while it kept occurring to him that he ought to clean the flat (the kitchen was coated in breadcrumbs and the bathroom sink with shaved hairs and splatters of dried toothpaste), the effort seemed wasted; no one ever saw the place.

Except that wasn't true: Donna had now seen the place. And it wasn't that she hadn't been nice—though "nice" was the wrong word; "fun," perhaps—it was that listening to the sound of her voice and noticing the shape of her smile had brought about a fresh sense of loss for Vivienne. He'd hoped that answering Donna's ad may have led him into the flirting company of a girl, but instead he'd found himself wondering if Donna's hair had smelled as good as Vivienne's, or if her waist had fitted as neatly in the grasp of his hands. Or was he only thinking that now because she clearly wasn't interested? Who knew.

As the day drew on, he even became less concerned about the quality of the sex. Of course it hadn't been up to standard; of course he had been left with a heavy sense of failure. After all, how could sex be anything more than adequate if it wasn't with Vivienne? And by four o'clock, as the setting sun closed in and lengthened the shadows the furniture cast on the floor, he even became convinced that he had subconsciously sabotaged its climax, just to get the whole thing over and done with.

The memory of the dying throes of his and Vivienne's eleven-year relationship had not faded in the last four months. There had been the desperate, hand-wringing night where Vivienne sat him down to tell him she'd packed several bags and made arrangements to "stay with a friend," where he'd followed her from room to room, begging her to "Please just think about this, Viv." But it was clear to him now, even if it hadn't been at the time, that the relationship's true end had occurred several weeks before that.

She had arrived home from work with pink cheeks and a wide, white smile. She had still been clutching her Oyster card, perhaps too distracted to have put it away when she got out of the train station.

"You won't believe it," she'd said in a breathless rush. "You absolutely won't *believe* it." She must've hurried the whole way through the park to get home.

"Believe what?" he'd said. He had been sitting on the sofa with the television volume too loud, doing something that immediately put him in a weak position, like cutting his toenails or inspecting the hardened skin on the balls of his feet. And he had vague regrets that if he'd been doing something more sophisticated (reading a novel, maybe sipping a glass of red wine), then the whole thing might never have happened. It put him squarely in the role of the uninspired, tiresome boyfriend, and why would anyone put up with that for longer than necessary?

"Now don't freak out," she'd said, but he'd started to.

"For God's sake, what is it?"

She'd lowered her eyes, fingering the tattered edges of her Oyster-card wallet. "I've been offered a transfer to New York. To head up the logistics team. We could . . ."

His expression alone, the straight set of his mouth and the way his gaze had drifted away, caused all the color to leave Vivienne's cheeks and her smile to fall away.

He might've said anything then, anything at all to win her over, but he hadn't. Though now he'd imagined many revisions of the conversation in his head, he doubted if he could have said anything to repair it.

Instead, he'd asked her if she'd applied for this thing without even telling him. And her long, tired blink, before she'd turned her back on him and stalked into the kitchen to wrench open cupboard doors only to smack them shut again—well, it had told him everything.

Didn't his own life here mean anything? he'd demanded of her. How could he leave his mum? And how could she have applied without talking to him?

She had momentarily stopped smashing around the kitchen, making small mumbles about his "bloody mother," to fix him with a look of such devastating contempt that he feared he'd never forget it.

"Oh, Harry," she'd said. "Don't you know? It's because you never would have let me."

She had turned down the New York job in a half-hearted effort to "make things work," but it was clear, from then on, that things might never work again. She would chew her breakfast in resentful silence, her talk over dinner was small and restrictively polite ("Fine, thank you, and how was your day?"), and she rolled away from him in bed. A month later she was gone. She'd made quick, thorough work of cleansing her presence from the flat—her tailored work dresses from the wardrobe, the winter coats stored in boxes under the bed, her toothpaste. Even the scattered piles of black hairpins had gone from the bathroom cabinet. Her pillow lost the vanilla scent of her hair. He'd started sleeping in, arriving at work late, gray-skinned, and shouldering past his colleagues when they said "hello" or before they'd said anything at all. Then feigning sick days with vague flu-like symptoms that lasted anywhere from a day to two weeks, so he could lie undisturbed with sour breath in his unwashed sheets. It had come as no surprise when he'd lost his job at Kingsley. "Downsizing," the regional manager had claimed, mumbling under his twitching moustache, among other things of which Harry had only fleeting memories: ". . . significant loss of revenue . . . Brexit . . . generous redundancy package . . . sure you understand." But Harry knew—surely everyone knew—he'd done this to himself.

And Ashton, the wanker—the way he'd clapped Harry on the shoulder when he'd wandered into the kitchenette to retrieve his heavily stained mug, with its bright slogan I CAME, I SAW, I SOLD!

"Mate," Ashton had said. "Mate. It's a hard business, you know."

And if it had been necessary to stand there listening to Ashton's condescension, he only wished he could have been spared the indignity of the bright strip lighting that must have illuminated him so vulnerably, the consolatory glances of others as they came into the kitchenette, and holding that bloody mug in his weak, slender hands.

On his shoulder, the weight of Ashton's own hand had felt like it could crush his collarbone. And if Harry spent too long imagining that hand resting on Vivienne's thigh, tangled in her hair . . . Jesus . . . he didn't think he could make it through the day.

He went to the kitchen now to search through the drawer of takeaway menus. But by seven-thirty, his visions of Vivienne engulfed the whole flat, and he could not stop recalling her disappointed voice ("Oh, Harry. Don't you know?"). He plucked a cold can of Kopparberg cider from the rattling fridge and stood at the black-paned window in his kitchen, tossing his phone in his other hand. He could call his mum, check up on that leaking kitchen tap he'd sorted for her last weekend, but it was a weak reason to call, and she might only worry why he was home by himself on a Friday night. So instead he called his old mate Wes from school, if only to wait for the impulse to dial Vivienne's number to subside.

"Oh, Harry, hi." Wes's voice was thin with fatigue. "Sorry, just getting stuck into bedtime."

"Bit early, mate."

"Ha! No, no—Ruby. Ruby's bedtime."

"Oh, course. Yeah, sorry. What is she now—six months?"

"Almost one, mate."

"Christ."

"Yeah." Wes sounded hesitant, perhaps contemplating whether if he said nothing else then Harry would hang up the phone and go away.

"Caught up with anyone lately?" Harry said. "Matty? Nathan? Anyone like that?"

"Well, it was Francesca's first birthday party last weekend, so we got together then."

"Oh. I didn't realize."

"Sure he would have invited you, mate, but . . . well, soft play—kill me now, right?"

"Right."

"So, how's . . . things? How's work?"

"Well, I was let go, Wes. You know that."

In the silence that followed, Harry could almost see Wes's blank, blinking face as he tried to think of how he might recover. But then he appeared to give up and just said, "Hope things pick up soon, yeah?"

But there was no need to hang on to resentment. There was no reason both of them couldn't get back to old times.

"Listen, after—you know—the whole bedtime thing, come out to the pub. Haven't seen you in months."

"I would, mate, but Ruby still keeps us up half the—wait, let me get my—just got my calendar up. I guess we're pretty slammed till after Christmas. How about March? You free?"

Harry trailed a path through the window's condensation with his finger. "Sure. March."

"Great. Send me some dates. Looking forward to it."

Wes ended the call with relief in his voice, but not before saying, "Give my love to . . . well, you know—hope you're keeping well, mate." He'd been about to say "Vivienne," Harry was certain of it.

Harry tossed his empty can into the sink. There was no infiltrating this inaccessible life of people more mature and successful than him. No one wanted an unemployed thirty-one-year-old sulking on the fringes of their dinner parties or kids' birthdays, and why should they? And this pub quiz group would probably be no different—they had all levelled up already.

The impulse to call Vivienne had not passed at all; if anything, it had become more urgent.

His hand trembled as he held the phone. What if Ashton answered? What if no one did? Worse still, what if it went to voicemail after only a few rings, making it clear she had declined the call?

But then, after a click that seized his heart, her life-giving voice answered.

"Hi, Viv? It's me. It's Harry. I just thought I'd—What was that? . . . Wow, yeah, wow. It's nice to hear your voice too."

CHAPTER FOUR

Question: *Which song from Pink Floyd's 1979 rock opera, was the band's only UK and US number-one single?*
Answer: *"Another Brick in the Wall"*

Between the wide, thriving junctions of Old Street station and the leafy canopies of Regent's Canal lay the soulless stretch of City Road. Past the regal front of Moorfield's Eye Hospital, the road was bleached of color and character, where buses ambled forward under the abandoned construction of a shimmering glass high-rise, past squat office blocks and row after row of algae-stained awnings that opened to unremarkable shops.

Donna appeared from the shadows of the underground station, holding her phone to her ear with a hunched shoulder as she threaded her fingers into woolen gloves.

"Hello?"

"Hey!" came a quick, too-bright voice. "Hey, Donna?"

"Who's this?" Her hand crept into her bag and started to claw at the cigarette packet that she now found was empty.

"It's Jacob? From Kick? Last weekend?"

She searched for a recent memory of Kick, the bar on Shoreditch High Street with its red Formica tables, and what might have happened before or afterwards. But nothing came.

"Hi. Jacob. How are you, love? Sorry, I didn't recognize your voice. Look, I'm just headed into work."

And who called on a weekday morning anyway?

"Sure, sure, sure," he said in a rapid spray like bullets. "How about later? Afterwards. After work."

"Oh. Well, maybe."

"I hope your shirt's OK, by the way."

"My shirt?"

"I spilled, like, an entire pint over you."

And the memory was there like a coin dropping through a slot. She'd tagged along to a colleague's birthday drinks. Jacob had been dark-haired, with a number of prominent moles on his clean-shaven face, and so remarkably tall that her sharpest recollection was of commenting on it a number of times ("You're so *tall*. Is your family tall? Were you some sort of six-foot twelve-year-old?"). They had only started talking because he'd spilled most of his draught beer into the lap of her jeans—not on her shirt—as he weaved and swayed from the bar back to his table of friends, who together had crumpled into judders of laughter and handclapping. What came after was a twenty-minute conversation circling around how sorry he was and how very tall he was, and the inevitable "Are you named after Donna Summer?" No. She had had to grit her teeth. No, she wasn't. And then, later, a hurried exchange outside on the damp pavement in a light spray of rain, where she must have taken his number. Any finer details were so hazy that she couldn't be entirely sure whether she was remembering whoever Jacob actually was or someone else.

"Well, no harm done," she said. "But I have to go now."

"Sure, sure. Later then?"

She could escape now, back into Old Street station, and be basking in Jacob's tallness and adoration by this afternoon in some orange-lit, leather-smelling bar for an early happy hour—him with an Old Fashioned, her with a Negroni. There might be a sweet, whiskey-scented kiss and strings of indecent messages the next day that allowed her to get through the hangover. Better not—she'd only get some nagging call from her boss anyway.

"I'll see what time I get out."

"Great, I'll wait to hear from you."

"See you."

It was already ten o'clock, but she headed into the wide, glass-fronted coffee shop on the corner.

Standing in line, squirming in the damp feel of the white sweater she had worn the previous night, she considered the exposed brick walls and whether she might remove the plaster on the chimney breast in her own living room. And, by the time she had reached the counter, it had become the most urgent task of the morning; she would google the details as soon as she got to her desk, along with purchasing all the necessary materials. They might even arrive in time to start on Sunday. So alright, she was supposed to go to that pottery class she'd booked herself into (or was that Saturday?), but she could reschedule, and—shit—wasn't there something else being delivered today? Maybe the reupholstery fabric or the terracotta planters—

"What can I get you?" the barista asked. His wispy moustache, probably painstakingly grown to make him look older, gave the unfortunate impression of adolescence.

"Are these walls original?"

"Sorry?"

"These walls. The brick. Are they original?"

"Original what?"

"Well, you know—to the building."

"Not a clue. Can I get you anything?"

Donna frowned. "White Americano, please."

The offices of Icon Marketing covered the fourth floor of a converted red-brick warehouse. With rows of tall casement windows, it might have been described as "grand" if it hadn't been so flat and otherwise featureless. The office itself was suitably trendy in an industrial way, with galvanized air ducts that spiraled around the high ceiling and glass-walled meeting rooms. But the furniture was cheap and not everyone dressed well enough.

In the lobby, the security guard, a stubbled, smiling man called Mo, leaned back in his chair at the wide concrete desk and laced his hands over his stomach.

"Donna, it's late, you know?" he said. "You look tired, sweetheart. You taking care of yourself?"

Donna laughed, but as the lift doors closed on her, she was faced with her ghostly image in the reflective doors. Her animated face fell still. She hadn't realized quite how late it was; time had the slippery habit of escaping her lately.

"Oh my God, and the Yosemite thing," she was saying later that morning to a timid junior desk editor with white-blonde hair as fine as milkweed. Her name was either Carla or Kayla, and they stood together by the whirring printer. "Suddenly he blurts out the answer to the whole pub. It was so funny."

"Oh, wow, he seems pretty cool though. This Harry guy."

"Oh, I don't know. I suppose." Donna had hoped to slip it in with more skill, but she became afraid the conversation would end without having said it at all, so she dramatically lowered her voice and said, "We did go back to his place, though."

"Oh my God, you *didn't*."

"It was just a bit of fun. And who has the patience for any of that business anyway? You know," she said, rolling her eyes. "A relationship." And then Donna walked away with her stack of copy, imagining the girl to be staring admiringly after her.

Harry had been cute: adequately tall and tousled, with benevolent features that could, in fleeting moments, take your breath away. And he was funny too, without even realizing it (she could tell by the way his eyes turned round in a surprised, blinking flurry any time she'd laughed with him). She usually found laughter was something she had to forcibly generate and exaggerate, because laughing was the easiest way to get someone to like you when being nice didn't come naturally. But with Harry she'd found unpredictable swells of it coming from the pit of her chest. Her cheeks had ached. It was all silliness, and the indulgence of that silliness had carried her away, all the way back to his flat. But there had also been something too listless in the way he sat slouching into his chair, and in the way his shoulders came up with a little noncommittal shrug whenever it was required of him to give an opinion. And sure, maybe that was meant to mean he was "cool" or "easygoing," or any number of other things, but in the presence of his rumpled, dirty flat, where he'd openly mourned the loss of Veronica or Vivienne or whatever her name had been, it became clear he was another rapidly ageing thirty-something who couldn't get his shit together.

Donna took her seat opposite Steph, her newly pregnant coworker, who always had one hand or the other adhered to the mound of her belly, which was often draped in motherly, floral shirts, as though to remind everyone of it.

"I've been rumbled," Donna said, ruffling her hair.

"Hm?"

"By Carla."

"You mean Kayla?"

"Sure, Kayla."

Donna flipped the stack of copy in half, so it appeared as though she had got through more work than she had, and then moved a William Boyd novel to the front of her desk, to be more easily noticed by anyone walking past.

Steph folded her arms on the desk and leaned forward, keeping her voice low. "Listen," she said, looking troubled. "Tess is going to call you in."

"Fuck sake. When did she say that?"

"When it got to ten and you weren't in."

"Tess gets in late all the time."

"Does she?"

"I don't know. Anyway. I may have had an indiscretion last night with a guy at the pub. Of course I was late."

"Like a random guy?"

"Well, not completely. I'm doing a pub quiz thing. He's on my team. He's a . . ." What could she say? Unemployed estate agent? No, she couldn't say that. "He's in the property business," she said.

"What kind of business?"

"I don't know—investment? Does it matter?"

Steph was silent for a few moments as her eyes flickered across her screen. Her lips pressed together in a thin line of concern. "Wait, did you get those infographics out to Optex?"

"Sorry?"

"The Optex files—did you send them?"

"They're not due till the thirteenth."

"Today's the fifteenth."

"Look, it's fine. I'll send them now. Or no, wait—they must still be with the freelancer."

"Don't worry. Just let me . . . I'll just sort it out, OK?"

And Donna couldn't look at Steph's discouraged face as she went about the set of efficient clicks and taps that were required for "sorting it out." How was anyone supposed to remember anything in this stagnant, airless place?

Instead, she began to read the webpage she'd bookmarked: "How to Expose Brick: 9 Steps—*Inspect the condition of the brick you want to expose before you begin*" . . . Well, how were you supposed to do that if it wasn't already exposed?

"Hey, Steph, do you—Oh."

Tess O'Grady, the managing director, was suddenly there beside her desk, short but trim in her pencil skirt and with an untidy pile of graying hair atop her head. Donna clicked the webpage closed, but it was clear Tess must have already seen it, because her eyes remained on Donna's screen for a long time afterwards.

"Donna. Would you come into my office? I won't keep you long."

Donna followed behind the rhythmic sway of Tess's shoulders. She was the kind of woman who insisted on being "one of the girls" and who took up ample width wherever she stood by setting her hands squarely on her hips with her feet spread apart—a display of dominance spoiled by so often misplacing her glasses.

Tess closed the door of her office behind them, but what privacy was there to be found in a glass cube that faced an open-plan floor of people? They could peer inside at any time to see from the high set of Tess's shoulders and the downward turn of her thin-lipped mouth that things weren't going well. Donna crossed her legs and sat back in her seat, with a loose hand free to bring thoughtfully to her mouth when the motion might be required. Anyone who might be watching would conclude that she was thoroughly unconcerned about the whole thing.

"I'd appreciate it if you could arrive on time, Donna," Tess began. "It's not the kind of thing I should have to ask."

"Sure."

Tess slid a printed email, colored with several highlighted passages, across the desk. She patted the top of her head to locate where her wire-rimmed glasses sat. "I've been talking to Optex," she said.

"Oh?"

"They're quite . . . well, frustrated at the quality of work they've received from you." At the word "frustrated," Tess gave a small shake of her head that wobbled the loose flesh on her jawline.

"Well, I don't see how," Donna said. Though OK; the emails from Optex had grown increasingly brusque until the last of them had consisted of four abrupt words (*Confirm receipt of this*).

Tess lowered her glasses in position and read from the email. "You underdelivered on their social media campaign. You misquoted pricing for the brochure—it completely threw out their costing. You approved copy that left them open to libel—do you know the implications of a thing like that?"

Donna didn't. Not entirely. But the best thing was to remain silent and let Tess say everything she needed to.

"I'd like Steph to finish up the Optex campaign by herself." Tess leaned forward and clasped her papery hands together on top of the treacherous email. "But with Steph starting her maternity leave in June, it leaves no room—no room whatsoever—for any member of the team to be . . ." she drew her mouth to one side, an expression Donna had come to think of as her "mean" look, "working under capacity."

Donna wished Tess had stopped there, so she could leave her behind in this glass prison. But now Tess was leaning back in her chair with her fingers laced in her lap, and Donna was reminded of Mo downstairs as he'd asked after her welfare. And sure enough, fine creases of sympathy began to appear between Tess's eyebrows.

"But tell me, Donna," she said. "How have you been? Did your time off in the summer help the way you'd been feeling?"

Donna sat for a moment and became aware of the hot stream of air hissing from a heating unit that Tess permanently had switched on; she was beginning to sweat.

"Oh, you know. It was just overwork, I suppose."

"Are you feeling overworked now?"

"I guess not. Things are pretty . . . good."

And she was already thinking ahead to lunch, of sitting in the bright corner café across the road, where she would recount the entire exchange to Steph with as much dramatic emphasis as she could. *What did this woman want from her?* she would demand of Steph over the table. *What sort of bullshit, amateur therapy session was this supposed to be?*

"Good," Tess said after a while. "You need only let me know."

Donna nodded, assuming it was safe to get up and leave. "You need only let me know" was exactly the kind of fake compassion that Tess liked to come out with when she had you trapped and overheating in that office, whose glass walls seemed only to exist to reflect and expose all of your shortcomings.

She had told Harry this wasn't her "passion," so what was she even doing here? Since graduating from her tedious Communications degree program, she had spent eight years leaving one job for another—there was that PR firm where the receptionist had slurped her coffee with such persistent volume that one day Donna had walked out and not returned, or the one after that (or had it been before?) for an exhibitions center where she'd felt such a hopeless sense of inadequacy that she'd handed in her notice before they could discover it for themselves. She could always get another job—she'd proved that—so if Tess wasn't careful, Donna would have no problem in walking out of this one too.

Talk about stagnant. Talk about airless. Everything about this place was tedious and menial and pointless. How could anyone in their right mind ever be expected to be creative or inspired, or at the very least productive, in this lifeless failure of a place?

She and Steph did go to the corner café for lunch. And if Steph was annoyed about having to rescue the Optex campaign, she was doing a good job of not showing it. She forked through her cheese omelet and sipped on a mug of decaffeinated tea underneath the steady whir of the ceiling fans that circulated the thick smell of frying food.

"And the real issue is," Donna said, after she had drained the bitter remnants of a black coffee, having left her eggs and buttered toast untouched, "it just shows an utter lack of integrity, you know? That whole project has been a nightmare from the beginning and I—" and here she held a splayed hand over her chest, "I have done nothing but carry it for her."

"Hm. You want some of this omelet?"

"No. No, thanks. And it's draining, is the main thing. It's draining me emotionally."

Steph set her fork aside. She let a few moments of silence gather before she licked her lips and said, "How've you been feeling lately?"

From the next booth along, above the clatter of dishes and scraping of knives and forks, Donna heard the conversation between two muscular, balding men in paint-splattered clothes (". . . so I say, love, you ain't getting it up them stairs unless I cut it in *half*. . ."). Outside the window, miserable, scurrying people ducked their heads against the gray rain, and a small old woman in a beige coat, waiting at the bus stop, clutched a plastic shopping bag.

"Everything's fine," Donna said. "Everyone needs a break sometimes. I don't get what it's got to do with this. And anyway, I'm allowed to be vulnerable, Steph."

"Fine," said Steph. "Hey, I brought my scan pictures in. Did you see?" And from out of her bag she produced five or more grainy black and white images for Donna to admire.

Donna thumbed through them politely and mumbled all the required things—wow, was this part an arm? And how about this, a leg?—all the while not being sure which formless, speckled patch represented the baby or some other part of Steph's insides. She handed them back almost as quickly as she'd taken them.

"Tell me about the guy then," Steph said. "The pub quiz guy."

And Donna was more than happy to let her eyes drop modestly while her hands shredded a paper napkin into neat strips. The problem was, Steph was always so much harder to impress than people like Kayla. "Oh, I don't know," she said. "He was alright, I suppose."

"Will you see him again?"

"Well, I'll see him at the quiz next week, but I don't know about—you know—anything else. I'm trying to work on myself right now, you know? To get to a place where I feel complete self-worth. I was listening to this podcast about the spiritual connection one has with the self and . . ."

But as Steph quietly sipped at her tea, her gaze began to wander around the room; Donna was losing her attention.

She cleared her throat. "If I'm honest, the sex was kind of bad, or, well . . . mediocre. And he's still hung up on his ex."

Steph's attention came snapping back. "Really?"

"He still had a picture of her as his screensaver."

"Oh, yikes."

"I know. Anyway . . . Hey, listen, do you have any exposed brick walls in your place . . .?"

It wasn't until later, on the swaying, dimly lit tube-carriage home, that she recalled all the reproachful mentions of how she'd been "feeling", and wondered for how long that question would follow her.

And not only that, she realized with a flash of fear; she wondered how long it would be before she forgot the frightening betrayal of her mind this past summer and, if she were honest, the summer before that too. The succession of endless mornings where she had found herself in tears over the arrival of each pale dawn, not knowing how to move through each day spent in the grip of an unbearable anxiety and hopelessness. Even the ringing of a phone had had her twisting her fingers in dread. It soon came to a point where Tess had called her into the glass box to tell her that she seemed "terribly stressed" and to take as much leave as she needed. And, for what seemed like weeks after that, she had circled her room in fear, hiding from her flatmate and ignoring phone calls from her mother and sister, who pleaded with frightened voices for Donna to just let them "help" her. But help was out of the question; help meant digging around in the tender parts of her mind, where any number of terrifying things might be lying in wait to be unearthed. So what else could she do but wait for it to subside? And gradually, the sun peeking through her curtains began to seem more inviting, and the smell of her flatmate's brewing coffee and toasting bread didn't turn her stomach. She tentatively stepped out of her room, daring to believe it was over, and for some weeks after that, before she began to relax, she had skittishly believed it would soon creep up on her again. But it hadn't yet.

She didn't see why everyone was so determined to have her remember it. It scarcely seemed to matter to anyone that now—now that she

41

was better—she could easily spring awake at six in the morning or even earlier, her brain seized with a buzzing fusion of new ideas and senses. These glimmering crevices of her mind could keep her from sleep until the early hours of each morning. It was intoxicating. Could Steph claim that, with her decaffeinated tea and cheese omelets?

At least people like Harry and the others who came last night had never witnessed her swollen, tearful face, or the time she had smashed a full glass of water in the office kitchen because she couldn't bear for anyone to come near her. And so what if there'd always be people like Tess and Steph in the world who would never be on her side? There were plenty of others out there who thought Donna March was extraordinary. It was fate—wasn't it?—that the Quiz League had come along at the perfect time to prove that.

CHAPTER FIVE

Question: *Which pastry, inspired by the Austrian* kipferl, *takes its name from the French word for "crescent"?*
Answer: *Croissant*

When Jaime had let herself into the flat last night, after the solemn walk back from the pub quiz, it had been dark and silent. In the bedroom, Luke had fallen asleep with a lone hand escaping the duvet, flung to one side. In bed next to him, she had run through reenacted versions of the fight in her head, where she had said better, cleverer things ("No, *you* listen, Luke. I'm tired of coming second place to your nostalgia."). And so robust was this improved rendition of the argument that she had found her lips were moving with relish in the dark.

She woke before seven the next morning, squinting and smacking her dry mouth, and Luke wasn't beside her. Perhaps he had wanted to rise first as some sort of example of superiority.

She came tiptoeing out of the bedroom, feeling self-conscious in her tea-stained dressing gown with the bear ears on its hood. Luke was sitting, fully dressed in a pair of jeans ripped at the knees through wear and not purpose, at the two-seater table in their kitchen, a room that felt thick and humid no matter what the season.

43

"Hi," he said. "I made croissants—well, I put the frozen croissants in the oven."

"Oh. Thanks." Jaime sat down, pulling the fleecy cuffs over her knuckles.

The passing of a clattering bus down Gipsy Hill, outside the kitchen window, filled the room with a vibration that set the cups on the mug tree tinkling against each other.

"Hey, listen," Luke said. "Seriously." He set down a shriveled croissant and laid his palms on the tabletop, as if to let her know how serious he was. "Last night was sort of awful. Want to take a walk before work?"

Jaime took enough time in their small, white bathroom, with enough makeup, to disguise how tired and unhappy her face looked in the mirror. But anyone passing them on the walk to Crystal Palace Park could easily see they were two people trying to divert a crisis. Luke buried his hands deep into his pockets with his shoulders riding high and Jaime tucked her chin into her chest, watching the rhythm of her Converse trainers on the pavement.

"You're hounding me," Luke had told her on a similar, agitated walk around Derwentwater back in Cumbria, when they'd hoped the sunlit beauty of the lake and the hazy blue hills could offset the turbulence between them. "I'm not 'hounding' you," she'd insisted, following close behind him. "London would be good for you—for us."

Now, after they'd wandered through the carefully planted terraces and headed deeper into the park, they stopped near a headless, lichen-mottled statue of a seated woman. Nearby, a slab of frost-covered stone on the ground sufficed as a bench.

"That Donna's a character, huh?" Luke said.

"I suppose." Jaime toed a moist clump of moss that was matted into the grass. "Which reminds me, she's roped us into this—this thing. This pub quiz tournament thing. There's like a prize—a big one."

But Luke wasn't listening. "Do you want to talk about what happened?"

Jaime's lungs constricted. When had he ever been so keen to "talk about what happened"? Next he might say something like, "Let's just discuss this rationally," or worse, "like adults."

"I don't know what you want me to say," she said.

"Why don't you say what you think?" He crossed his legs at the knee and laced his fingers around one shin, a gesture so similar to how she would imagine a patronizing psychotherapist that it set her teeth on edge.

"Alright. Well, I thought you were incredibly hurtful, and I—I'm fed up of coming second place to your nostalgia."

"My what?"

"Your nostalgia. We're not teenagers anymore, mooching round Keswick and living with our parents. It's time we took things seriously. Bryony had two kids by our age, and—"

"Who?"

"Bryony. From last night. She's married with two kids."

"*Jeeee-sus*, Jaime." A long stream of misted breath flowed out of his mouth.

"Don't you want that for us? Don't you even think about it?"

"The fact is I'm very unhappy; that's the truth of the matter."

Jaime stood up. Behind the statue, distant traffic shuddered down the A212, passing a row of darkened restaurants. Even without her head, with her crossed ankles and her hands folded listlessly in her lap, the stone woman looked slumped and cheerless, adrift in a world of Ford Fiestas, honking buses and shuttered cafes.

"The fact is" . . . "The truth of the matter" . . . Those were also not things Luke would normally say. Clearly he'd been preparing for this all morning—getting dressed while she'd slept, placing a row of frozen croissants on a baking tray.

"OK," said Jaime. "So what does that mean?"

He took a breath and adjusted his glasses, as though it would make the suggestion more sensible. "I want to go back to Keswick. And I think last night it hit home for me, you know? I don't fit in, that's all. People look down on us, Jaime, because we're—you know—because we're northerners. And so . . . yeah, I want to go back to Keswick."

If the announcement had come as a surprise, at least then a period of shock might have allowed some time for him to come to his senses, but she had known he was going to say that. And now he had said it out loud, the blood drained away from her hands, leaving them numb. London was supposed to be their savior, and he just wouldn't—he *refused*

45

to—be saved. She might have nodded in understanding. She might have said something like, "Well, it's something to consider, if you're that unhappy." But instead, with distress creating deep, ageing creases over her forehead and twisting her fingers at her waist, she said, "You want to leave me?"

"Well, it's my job for one thing. It was meant to be a stopgap. Three months, six months—"

"What's wrong with your job? You make OK money. You like it OK."

"I don't *want* 'OK.' You think I want to work on a reception desk in the sports center the rest of my life? I was so bored this week I started counting the tiles in the lobby."

"I didn't assume you ever wanted to be anything."

Luke opened his mouth, then shut it again.

"Luke, I can't . . . I'm opening the shop. I need to get to work."

"Alright, but we need to talk about this later."

On the trembling 432 bus to West Norwood, Jaime couldn't remember what she'd said back to him before she walked away. It might have been "OK" or "If you want" or even "Fuck you." She only remembered feeling so sick that she had to take several deep, lung-chilling breaths through her mouth as she stalked across the frozen grass to the bus stop. It was only when a dark-haired woman with two little boys boarded the bus that she was reminded she'd agreed to meet Bryony on her lunch break today.

Perhaps Bryony, with her insightful brown eyes and her calm, methodical way of speaking, might help her.

*   *   *

While he rubbed his ears dry with a towel in their bedroom, the solid shape of his shaved head reflecting a gleam from the overhead lights, Glen asked Bryony about the pub quiz and "how it had gone."

She folded the hem of her oversized night shirt in her lap (did other women wear seductive, silken slips to bed every night?). "Yes. Alright," she said, tentative on whether she felt one way or the other. Jaime was the sort of girl who, in her painfully shy isolation, was ready to get along with anyone. But who was Harry, other than a handsome, easygoing

46

drunk? And who was Donna, with her flicks of her hair and overconfident talk? And Luke . . . well, he was the most enigmatic of all of them.

Glen tossed his towel on the bed. Beads of water freckled his chest and shoulders. "Bit strange, though, don't you think? People don't advertise for a pub quiz team. They take their—you know—their friends. Their actual friends. Me and Jonesy once did the quiz down the Rose—it's just a bunch of mates."

"Well, anyway, it's nice to use my brain for a change."

"Not rocket science, is it?"

Bryony wasn't sure she liked him when this superior tone crept into his voice. What would he know about it? She read a lot. More than him. Maybe not as many books as she should, but articles—and good ones, too. Only last weekend, even as Lydia thundered on her bedroom floorboards (she'd lost one of a pair of silver earrings), she had finished a four-page feature from the *Sunday Times* in one clean run—"How Mesopotamia Became the Cradle of Civilization"—enjoying the speed and rhythm at which she easily absorbed paragraph after paragraph, before her cup of coffee had even cooled.

"Wait," Glen said suddenly, his face coming alive as it popped out from the neck of a fresh T-shirt. "I know." He left the bedroom and she heard the tread of his feet on the stairs. When he reappeared, he was thumbing through a fat, brightly colored paperback—*The Big Book of Family Trivia*—biting the tip of his tongue and frowning into its pages.

"General knowledge?" he enquired.

"Oh, come on. Look, it's gone eight o'clock. This is silly," she said, but sat up straight against the headboard. She felt a small chill of anticipation.

"Ready?" His knees spread wide, Glen sat down on the bed with an elbow on each thigh, holding the book between his two, large hands. He moistened his thumb with a wet flick of his tongue as he turned each page, leaving the corners smudged and crinkled.

"What is the capital of Venezuela?"

She thought for a moment, feeling an unexpected shyness, though she knew the answer. "Caracas," she said quietly.

"In bowling, what is the term given for three consecutive strikes?"

"Oh, a . . ." she shook her head. "I don't know. A hat trick?"

"A turkey—come on, I knew that. What nuts are used to make marzipan?"

"Almonds."

"In what year was Joan of Arc burned at the stake?"

"Fourteen thirty-one."

"How'd you know that?"

"I don't know. How did you know turkey?"

"Everyone knows that."

Before she could point out what was wrong with this, he was turning the page with another swipe of his moist thumb and gathering his breath. "Which country invented gin?"

And with the bouncing flow of her answers—"Holland . . . Catherine Parr . . . Red—no, wait, orange . . . The Brothers Grimm . . ."— she found she had curled her fists so tightly in her lap that her fingers had started to ache. And while Glen had begun with impressed little nods of his head, a small crease had now appeared between his eyebrows. He had started to look bored, or maybe vaguely annoyed.

"Let's stop," she said. "I need to get the kids going."

Glen rubbed his fingers over his upper lip. "No, no. What land was called Caledonia by the Romans?"

"Scotland."

"Ah ha." He bounced his heels. "Nope. Colchester."

"You didn't even check the answer page."

"I don't need to."

She folded her arms. "It's Scotland."

With a tolerant sigh, he flipped to a back page of the book. His lips twitched as he silently read, and then he shut the book with a slap.

"Suppose you think I'm pretty stupid," he said, his eyes downcast. He bunched a pillow into a soft ball to clutch under one armpit.

"Well, now you're being ridiculous." She took the book from him and slid it under the duvet where it could not be seen.

"Yeah, well." He got up to shuffle through the hangers in the wardrobe.

She wondered if there'd been too much ease or arrogance in her answers, and whether she should have claimed not to have known one or two, or even answered incorrectly. No, she decided. And what sort of childish game would that have been anyway?

"I'm going back next week," she announced. "We're entering a sort of tournament—did you know there's a London Pub Quiz League that puts on these things? And I'm meeting up with one of the others who came. For a coffee. Today. She seems sort of—"

"You bored with us or something?"

"What do you mean?"

"I don't know. All this. Pub quizzes. Tournaments. Coffees."

"What do you think I do all day?"

"I don't know. Stuff for the—I don't know."

"You go to the pub all the time."

He rolled his eyes and turned his back on her. "Yeah, but that's with *Jonesy*."

"OK, so yes, I get bored sometimes. So what?"

"Nothing. Forget it."

And Bryony did forget it, or at least she tried to. But the image of his rolling eyes when he had said "Jonesy" and the little quivers of the soft, protruding flesh of his pectorals as he walked back and forth between the wardrobe and the bed kept setting her teeth on edge while she went through the task of arranging the breakfast things. It was the last day of school before Christmas.

Glen disappeared into the back garden, where she caught glimpses of him through the window, crouching on the balls of his feet and caressing patches of rain-soaked lawn with a tender, sweeping hand. Behind her, the door opened and Lydia came into the kitchen, the hems of her pajamas rolled at the ankle. She was thirteen and short for her age, and as a result had developed the habit of walking on her toes. She opened the fridge door, pulled out the milk and filled a glass to its brim.

"Mum, have you heard of a pixie crop? Like Cara Delevingne? I want a pixie crop like Cara Delevingne."

"But you've got such lovely hair."

Lydia opened a cupboard and knocked down a bottle of chocolate syrup on a high shelf with the tips of her fingers. She proceeded to squeeze a steady stream of it directly into her open mouth, before bringing the milk glass to her lips and drinking deeply.

And then Arthur, who was eleven and taller than Lydia (a fact that caused her untold sorrow), came into the kitchen with a *Horrible*

Histories book held up to his nose. He hoisted himself up to sit on the dining table, crushing a stacked pile of envelopes and rocking a small, potted fern. "You'll look like a boy," he said. "Mum. Hey, Mum. Hey, listen, Mum." Arthur placed his book face down on the table as he spooned up a dripping heap of Rice Krispies. "Did you know Henry VIII beheaded two of his wives? Anne Boleyn *and* Kathryn Howard. I mean, he didn't do it himself—obviously the executioner did it. And Anne Boleyn's head was hanging on by a bit of skin and she went running all around the scaffold trying to hold it back on. *Blee*ding all over *every*one."

Lydia made a noise in her throat. "Don't be stupid. That didn't happen."

"Yes it did. Mr. Broderick told me."

"I hate Mr. Broderick," Lydia announced, breathless from a swallow of milk. "I hate his stupid curly hair and his . . ." and here Lydia's small hands came up into claws and shook as if wringing an imaginary neck. "He's a *dickhead*!"

Bryony threw a dishtowel into the sink. "Lydia—"

"And he never listens to me. And just because I missed the . . . well, I didn't mean to miss it, I just forgot. He said—he said in front of everyone—that I was the stupidest person in the whole class."

"I'm sure he didn't say that, Lydia."

"He did. Why are you taking his side?"

"You probably *are* the stupidest girl in the class. Mum—Mum, listen—she doesn't even know who Thomas Cromwell is—"

"You're just a disgusting little boy!" Lydia spun around to him in a deep blush, tipping over the open milk carton. The white puddle glugged onto the floor, seeping into the gaps between the floorboards where it could never be cleaned. Both Lydia and Arthur fell silent.

Bryony's chest tightened with such suddenness that she wasn't sure that her voice would come out at all when she started to speak.

"Can't you just—can't you just for once—go and get dressed."

"I didn't even—"

"School. Now. We're going to school *right now*. You can sit in the library until—No, I don't want to hear it. Go and get dressed. Go—and—get—dressed."

As Lydia and Arthur shouldered past one another in an effort to be the first out of the kitchen, Glen came in through the back door to the garden. He was whistling.

"Derek next door. Got that—what-d'you-call-it—Rota-Power Three Hundred? Says it's got five cut heights. Gonna make an absolute show of our lawn come spring if I don't get it together—is that milk?"

"Can you get the kids to school? I've got to clean this up. They're driving me in*sane*."

"Fine." And then he dug in his pocket for his keys as Bryony crouched on her hands and knees with an unravelling roll of kitchen paper. "Don't get too bored today, eh?"

Soon enough the kids had been taken, sullenly, to school, and Glen was gone, into the damp-smelling interior of his van, where he drove from client to client, grinding out tree-stumps, raking out topsoil, rolling out turf and whatever else he did all day.

Bryony retreated onto the sofa in their tinsel-strung living room to chew through a slice of buttered toast, where their Christmas tree tilted in the alcove and stripes of pale sunshine leaked through the Venetian blinds. And her throat closed when she saw that the hand that held her toast was cracked and red-knuckled; without knowing it was about to happen, she began to cry. She was thirty years old, her hands were ugly and her husband was annoyed at her for knowing the answers in a stupid quiz book. And there was no one to call to tell them about it.

She thought of a decade ago, hauling three-year-old Lydia and one-year-old Arthur to playgroup or the park, when there had never been any free time. Of how much older all the other mothers had been, how they had looked at her with judgmental pity; she hadn't known how to talk to them. And then, much later, in the long afternoons when both the kids had started school, of how the continual sense of feeling lost had her vacuuming and revacuuming the over-trodden carpets and looking for new ways to make the arrangement of their cheap furniture look, if not elegant, then at least interesting. And now, most recently, of the quiet early nights, beside Glen's velvety snores, in a room next to children who no longer called out her name when they woke in the dark. Shouldn't things have somehow got better by now? Later Glen would return home smelling of earth and stale deodorant, smeared in grass stains, and the blowing of his nose would often reveal a tissue full of dirt-colored mucus. She didn't know how to talk to him.

In the early afternoon on the bus to West Norwood to meet Jaime, Bryony noticed a dried splash of milk on the knee of her jeans, and as she sat swaying with each rumbling swerve of the bus, she tried several ways of arranging her hands over her knees or crossing her legs so the stain would not show.

On the high street on Knight's Hill, Bryony stepped off the bus against a gust of rain, between a graffitied Pizza Hut and a limestone, columned church, enclosed by a foreboding barrier of spear-topped railings. And inside a cafe called the Jackdaw, which turned out to be a plain, functional place with leather seating and laminate floors, Jaime sat at a table for two, spinning the rings on the fingers of one hand. Her eyes were wide and round as she stared about the small, winter-dimmed room.

"Oh, Bryony, here!" Jaime stood up in a half-crouch, waving her over.

As Bryony draped her wet coat over the back of the seat and combed her damp hair back into its ponytail, Jaime sat down, still fiddling with her rings, the other hand clutching at the buttoned edge of her cherry-print cardigan.

After making a short, awkward order with the teenaged waitress, during which both of them were too embarrassed to order any food ("Oh, just a cappuccino for me, thanks"), they exchanged a few further pleasantries. Wasn't this place nice? When did Jaime have to be back at work? Did they think Harry and Donna had kissed after they'd left them at the Five Bells? (Yes, they were both certain of it.) Then they relaxed enough to get down to the business at hand.

"I hope you and Luke made up," Bryony said once the waitress had set two frothing cups down in front of them.

Jaime ducked her head. "Not really. He told me he wants to move back home. To Cumbria."

"Oh. Well, that's . . . What do you want?"

"I want to stay here. I want *him* to stay here. I don't even know if he's coming to the quiz next week. And then Donna will be annoyed at us and—"

"I wouldn't be concerned with Donna. Maybe he just needs more time to—you know—cool off."

"I don't think so. He seemed so sure, you know? Like he'd been thinking about it for a while." Her eyes began to shine. "I'm sorry," she said, looking down into her lap while she pinched the bridge of her nose.

"No, no. It's OK." Bryony handed her a clean napkin. One already lay by Jaime's cup and saucer, but it seemed there wasn't anything else Bryony could offer.

At the age of sixteen, after meeting at school, Jaime and Luke had been what Jaime described as "pretty much dating." Luke adored Formula One—he still did—and he'd built a popular fan website, which, Jaime said with a hardening face, was the most passion she'd ever seen him apply to anything. He'd lived with his parents and worked as a fairground operator while she went to university and commuted from home. "And he'd hated it," Jaime said. A kid had vomited on his shoes after stumbling off the Waltzer and he'd quit—"They were new Vans, and he was fuming." By the end of her second year she wished she'd studied Graphic Design and not Fine Art—"Where did I think Fine Art was ever going to get me?" She spent her evenings watching Luke play Mario Kart with his friends from their old sixth-form, smoking weed and eating cold saveloy sausages brought home from someone called Stratten who worked at the chip shop. As her third year drew to a close (she'd left with a C average and a heavy sense of regret), she told Luke she was moving to London.

Jaime folded her hands into her lap and lifted her chin. "I knew this place would open up a whole world for us, you know. Culture and diversity, away from all the small-minded . . . Anyway, I said, well, come or don't come. I was going to go anyway, and he could do what he wanted."

Bryony smiled down at the puddle of foam on her cappuccino. She knew that probably wasn't true, and that Jaime had probably spent weeks, if not months, convincing him to go with her. "So what if he goes back to Cumbria? Did you discuss what that would mean?"

"I haven't—I don't know."

"Sometimes people just . . . grow apart. You know?"

Jaime's blinking eyelashes trembled the edges of her fringe. "But he's my *person*," she said.

And Bryony had to quickly force her face out of an expression of distaste. How she detested that phrase and how delusional it was, how destructive.

"He just needs to find another job," Jaime said, bringing both her hands up to her temples, as though it were all just an exercise in logic. "Something that gives him more . . . I don't know . . . purpose."

"Sure, maybe."

"I could send him some job ads. I'm sure he finds it overwhelming."

"You could try that."

"I just, you know . . ." Her hands came together so she could spin her rings once again. "Love him."

"Oh, of course you do, Jaime." And Bryony would have reached for her hand if she wasn't unsure whether it was still too early in the friendship for that sort of thing. "I'm not saying you shouldn't. I'm not saying you don't."

"I don't know how I'd—how would I ever meet anyone else?"

Jaime swiped at her eyes and sat straighter in her chair, apologizing for "going on and on." And Bryony did feel sorry for her. There was too much pain and fear in her poor swollen eyes not to. But, God! All that choice. Jaime was so young. She could buy a plane ticket to New Zealand tomorrow if she wanted to. She could hitchhike to the Isle of Skye and live gazing out at the ocean.

"I hate to sound like a segment on *Woman's Hour*," Bryony said, "but being in a relationship isn't—"

"What's *Woman's Hour*?"

"It's a radio program on—never mind—I just mean not having a boyfriend isn't the end of the world. You could live anywhere. Do anything. Rent a studio with a couple other artists, backpack across Europe—"

"Oh, I couldn't do that. My mum would kill me."

"All I'm saying is, you're twenty-four and the world is your oyster." And Bryony knew that later she would admonish herself for saying something so clichéd.

Jaime gave a thin smile, and just when Bryony thought her argument might be having some sort of leverage, when she thought Jaime might look shyly up at her and say, "You know what I've always wanted to do?", she actually said, "It's so wonderful, though, to think two people can stay together as long as you and your husband. You know—childhood sweethearts. Marriage. Kids. The whole thing." She hadn't been listening.

"Sure," Bryony said. "I mean, sure. But it's no fairytale. Marriage is hard. Kids are hard."

"You don't think getting married makes someone more willing to stick it out? You don't think it proves that someone loves you?"

Well, OK, Bryony wanted to say, but what did that have to do with anything? Being married didn't stop you grinding your teeth when they'd clogged the toilet, stacked the dishwasher nonsensically or stolen the best years of your life.

Then, inevitably, the talk turned to Bryony's family.

"Wow, and they're both in secondary school? You must have been so *young.*"

Bryony looked down into her cooling coffee. "Yes—seventeen. It wasn't the plan, obviously. But life doesn't always go according to plan."

This was how she always explained it, with what she hoped sounded like being worldly enough to accept these things. But then the question always followed: what nerve did she have to blame "life"? There'd been no injustice; they'd been teenagers and had got carried away. And what a self-deceptive excuse "carried away" had always been, too. As though they'd been stranded on a boat and at the mercy of the tide.

And even if it was acceptable to get carried away once, what about when it happened again? When Lydia was a year old and Bryony found herself pregnant for the second time, she could only point to their own inability to have thought it through. And if she were honest with herself—and why shouldn't she be, now, eleven years later?—she knew there had been another reason: that a second baby would prove how content and happy they were with the first one.

"Wow," Jaime said. "That sounds tough."

Bryony propped her chin into her hand. "We just got on with things, I suppose. I didn't get my degree, and I guess that's the main—you know—regret, but Glen got an apprenticeship with a land-scaping firm. Then, when Lydia was born, my mum and dad lent us the deposit for the house."

She might have mentioned that the deposit had been her university fund, that her parents had saved for years only to helplessly watch their aspirations fall away, but she was still too ashamed to say so.

"Oh, but you should."

"Should what?"

"Get your degree. Why not?"

"Oh, I don't know." Bryony was stricken but pleased. "That's a lot of . . . the kids are still young and everything."

"But you could do part-time or online. It's so flexible nowadays."

Bryony shook her head. "It's a lot of money."

Perhaps uncomfortable with discussing finances, Jaime gave an amiable little shrug and changed the subject. "So where did you get married?" she said dreamily. "Was it lovely?"

"Oh, just a quick thing at a registry office."

"So he supported you completely? Glen, I mean. Financially?"

"More or less." Then Bryony eyed Jaime carefully. "It's not glamorous," she said. "And Glen is not 'my person.' I mean, I love him and everything, but he's just *a* person. And that's just what happened."

Jaime's eyes widened before she quickly looked away.

"Maybe I could pick up a few extra hours at PrintPro," she said after a few moments. "Give Luke some—you know—financial space. Or do you think he could get an apprenticeship? Like Glen did? What's involved with something like that?"

But then inside Bryony's pocket, her phone started to vibrate. "Sorry, one sec. It's the kids' school—hello? Yes, speaking . . . I see . . . She said what? . . . Well, that's—I hope you know how out of character that is for . . . No, I understand . . . Yes. Yes, I'll see you at three and we can . . . Sure, see you then." Bryony clicked off the call and kneaded a pounding spot between her eyebrows. "For God's sake."

"What's happened?"

"My daughter just called her history teacher a dickhead."

CHAPTER SIX

Question: *Which song, released by Mariah Carey in 1994, topped the Christmas charts in twenty-six countries?*
Answer: *"All I Want for Christmas Is You"*

Donna completed the online entry form for the London Pub Quiz League Championship, and an automated reply had asked her to ensure the whole team arrived at the Five Bells no later than seven-thirty the following Thursday.

The weekend had brought a vicious disagreement with her flatmate Bernadette ("Don't call me, Bernie, OK?"), a tall, spindly "financial wellness coach" who was proving to her father (some big shot in hospitality) that she could live an authentic life by slumming it in southeast London, while also spending her weekends at Loft, a private members' club in Mayfair.

Donna had laid down a dust sheet in their small living room, surrounding the chimney breast, and had begun tapping experimentally at the plaster with a brand-new chisel and hammer.

"God, Bernadette, calm down," Donna had said, squinting through eyelashes full of dust when Bernadette emerged frowning and questioning from her room.

"Are you a builder, Donna? Did you ask our landlord?" She gesticulated at the plaque of chipped wall with her dark ponytail swinging angrily. "And for God's sake, wear some goggles!"

"It's a renovation, Bernadette. He'll thank us." Donna had whirled round, waving the chisel in a full arc, at which Bernadette jumped back, squealing and skidding over in her socks. And the girl wouldn't shut up until Donna had agreed to email the landlord or the letting agent, or whoever else it was that took care of these ridiculous bureaucratic things.

And then it was Monday—the last week at work before Christmas. Tess was bright and cheerful (though perhaps too much so), and Donna found a tolerable existence could be found in sifting through her inbox in between periodic visits to the photocopier, where Kayla could be relied upon to provide all the right kinds of exclamations of delight and silly laughter. And then at a secondhand market stall on Whitecross Street on Wednesday lunchtime, she had found a remarkable book—*The Mindset of the Winner*, by Dr. Jay Jenison. It was full of insights that had her nodding her head in silent agreement as she read it at her desk (if she lay it open to one side of her computer, Tess couldn't see it). *Top performers understand that the journey is the destination . . . A winning mindset doesn't allow the shortsightedness of others to deter them from being great . . .* Donna would find herself gazing at the author photo on the jacket flap—this man, with his dignified silver beard and intelligent eyes, would be the answer to all of their concerns.

That evening, Jacob from Kick had called again, but Donna had ignored her vibrating phone in annoyance until it fell silent. Wouldn't the guy leave her alone? By Thursday morning, she was in a fidgeting sweat anticipating the first match of the Quiz League. And as she fumbled with the clasp of a necklace, with a frothing toothbrush hanging from her mouth, her phone rang again! She spat out her toothpaste and, without paying attention to the phone's screen, she answered.

"Listen, Jacob—can't you take a hint?"

"Donna?"

"Oh. Mum."

"Who's Jacob?"

"I'm just about to leave for work."

"I thought I'd caught you early enough."

"Well, I can be quick."

"I was just thinking about Christmas."

"What about it?"

"Well, whether you were coming, Donna. Isn't that obvious?"

"I haven't decided yet."

"It is next week. You do know that, don't you?"

"Yes, of course I know that."

"Are you spending it with this Jacob instead? Why don't you bring him down to meet us?"

"Look, Mum, he's no one, alright?"

"Is he a vegetarian? I can always—"

"No, I mean there is no Jacob. Not in the—you know—There's no one, alright?"

"Well, alright. And are you—well, are you feeling OK?"

Donna braced one arm against the sink, looking down into the dark plughole. She could see her mother now: pacing the living-room carpet, her gray eyes wide in suspense as she clutched and fondled at her collar. Her voice would dissolve into a high-pitched shrill of worry if Donna said no, and she wouldn't believe her if she said yes.

"Good days and bad days, I suppose."

"And you will let us know, won't you? If that . . . changes."

"Course. Listen, I'm running late now."

And the sound of an appeased little sniff let Donna know she was satisfied.

"Will you speak to your sister?"

Donna let go of an audible sigh. "Alright."

And Lottie didn't even say hello. "Who's Jacob?"

"For God's sake—*no one.*"

"Listen, when are you visiting Dad? You haven't been down to Meadow Hall in months."

"How do you know I haven't?"

"Because he *told* me."

The accumulation of squat, red-brick buildings of Meadow Hall—the inpatient mental health unit, designed to neither be attractive nor particularly functional in their maze-like interiors—sat on the outskirts of Worthing. And in a serviceable room that smelled of instant coffee and the ever-recent vacuuming of the polyester carpet, sat Donna's dad. The solid magnitude of him—his large-jawed head, even his earlobes, thick as meat—somehow shrunken in a chair. He wore a rotation of velveteen dressing gowns, purchased by Lottie, and stared out of the window, revolving through an endless sequence of boredom and hostility.

It had come as no great surprise, when Donna was sixteen and Lottie twenty, when he had been diagnosed with bipolar disorder. For years they had witnessed his overwhelming feelings of worthlessness, resulting in their mum soft-footing down the stairs with a finger held to her lips ("Shh, your dad's not feeling well"), or being bundled into the car for a last-minute stint at an aunt or cousin or grandparent's house. And then that was gradually replaced by the distressing cycle of his feverish energy. He would not eat. He barely slept. He was full of "important plans." He quit his job to buy a secondhand taxi but failed the driver's application process. He brought home an upright piano to give Donna daily lessons, only to swipe her away in irritation when she mixed up her arpeggios. And because neither crying or quietness or red-faced outbursts had any effect on her dad's unpredictability, Donna began to punish her mother with sourness and blame instead—why couldn't she *do* something about it?

And even after the divorce, when she had escaped the seaweed-smelling drizzle of Worthing for university, when she was arguably old enough to know better, she still found herself prone to unforgiving disdain for how her mother had handled the whole thing—why hadn't she divorced the man years ago, saving them all that trouble? Why, in fact, had she married him in the first place?

The other inexcusable wrong that her dad had committed was to name her Donna ("All his idea," her mother had said). She could barely meet anyone without them asking if it was after Donna Summer, the beautiful, sultry Queen of Disco, following which she was forced to endure the same tedious conversation, over and over again.

"No, actually. Donna Douglas."

"Who?"

"She played Elly May Clampett on *The Beverly Hillbillies*."

"Oh."

And every time she would find herself thinking, *You see, you idiot, you couldn't even do that right.* Was there any way in which he hadn't failed her?

"So they did allow him some excursions last month," Lottie was saying now. "And he seemed to be—you know—enjoying the change in routine and everything. We had a couple of walks on the beach that were quite calm."

Donna allowed the sound of Lottie's voice to fall away as she studied the frothy pool of spat-out toothpaste in the sink and the thin vein of blood running through it from brushing her gums too hard. Lottie— she should have been an ally, but she didn't give Donna a break. She only asked continuous, unanswerable questions, her frowning, freckled face in a resentful pout—well, why hadn't she visited Meadow Hall lately? When was she planning to go again?—and gave herself over to these long, pensive monologues, detailing their dad's "condition." That was another reason to resent her mother: she'd been able to free herself.

Donna was supposed to be the little sister—she was supposed to be sheltered from this—but nevertheless she'd grown up (and she had ensured she'd done so quickly and efficiently, by learning to emulate the things Lottie and her mother said and the way they said them) with the obligation of displaying her own self-sufficiency. "I'm afraid my father's not feeling at all well," she'd tell acquaintances, with a mature squint. "Sorry for all the fuss," she'd assure the neighbors when they came to investigate his shouting voice, "but really, we're quite alright." And perhaps that was why nobody had thought she needed taking care of. She was an eight-year-old, then a twelve-year-old, then a seventeen-year-old who could plainly take care of herself.

"I have to get to work, Lottie. I don't have time for this now."

There was silence on the other end of the line, and then when Lottie's voice came back it was terse and accusatory. "So you're just going to stay in London by yourself all Christmas?"

"Maybe. What's wrong with that?"

"Jesus. You're just like him."

Well, alright, maybe I am, Donna wanted to say. But if they thought they could lock her up in somewhere like Meadow Hall then *they* were the crazy ones. All she had to do was hold on to those golden parts of her mind before they tipped over into misery and chaos. The only problem was, seeing him—seeing any of them—always hit her with the reality that it might not be possible.

And as though Lottie could hear this thought through the tinny reception of the phone, she gave a loud and fretful sigh, saying, "If you're not careful this will all blow up in your face, you know."

* * *

Jaime walked into the Five Bells with Luke trailing behind her. The rapid approach of Christmas Day saw the pub strung with glinting foil garlands, some crumpled and torn, and the Christmas songs playing over the speakers had people swaying and bopping at the bar.

It had been a week of broad silences; she and Luke had not known how to talk to each other following Luke's revelation ("I'm very unhappy, that's the truth of the matter"). But the bright beacon of Thursday at the Five Bells had calmed her when she could feel her quick breathing becoming out of her control, signaling a day when she could talk to someone who wasn't a customer at the shop. And over breakfast this morning, she had at least been able to establish that Luke was coming to tonight's quiz, or rather infer it from the way he grunted behind a mouthful of cereal.

A wide area in front of the bar had been cleared to accommodate two separate sets of tables and chairs. Jaime saw Donna and Harry perched together on bar stools, smiling and leaning unnecessarily close into each other's bodies. She felt a twitch of envy; was it really so simple to find someone who made you smile like that?

"Hey," Harry said when he saw them. "Welcome to the set of *University Challenge*."

Donna hid a burst of laughter behind her hand, as though it had surprised her. "Oh good, you're here," she said. "I'm getting us a bottle of wine. Dutch courage and all that. Have you been practicing?"

Before Jaime could admit that they hadn't, Bryony came in through the double doors, blinking rapidly and clutching at the strap of her big, lumbering bag. "Is that where we're supposed to sit?" she asked them. "In front of *every*one?"

They all stood regarding the table set-up with poorly concealed horror. A knot of nerves was pulsating low in Jaime's stomach.

"Jaime didn't explain this very well," Luke said.

Jaime pressed her lips together. Why was it her responsibility? "Well, it was sort of confusing," she said.

"OK, listen," Donna said, smoothing down the scalloped collar of her expensive-looking work blouse. "Has everyone got a drink? OK, good—I've been reading the—you know—the rules, and it's really quite straightforward . . ."

Two teams would play against each other, she explained. Coin toss for who starts. Each player would be asked a question in turn—you could either answer for two points or pass to another member of your team for one point. No conferring. Get the question wrong, and it would go to the opposing team. The first team to fifty points would win.

"And listen," she concluded, "don't answer straight away. Not even if you think you know the answer. Not even if you're *sure* you know the answer. Say the question again in your head, and then you can answer. You should do that before passing to anyone too. It's the ethos of winning."

Jaime blinked. "The what?"

"The ethos of winning. It's in a book I've been reading called *The Mindset of the Winner*. It's by this terrific guy called Dr. Jay Jenison and he—"

"You've read a book about winning the pub quiz? Since last week?"

"Why shouldn't I? We want to win, don't we?"

"Well, listen," said Harry, "don't worry about it. It's just a bit of fun, alright?"

"But we can't *settle*," Donna insisted, staring round at their unconvinced faces. "Don't you see how self-limiting that is?" She splayed all ten of her fingertips out on the bar-top. "It's all about motivation, see? You either fear failing or crave the prestige of the reward. You either really want something or you're scared of being without it. It's simple."

"So, wait," Jaime said, frowning and clutching the top of her head, having lost track in Donna's monologue. "You mean we have to answer questions by ourselves? Not like a normal pub quiz?"

Harry sniffed. "They're allowed to confer on *University Challenge*."

Donna sighed. "It's all on the website. I can't help it if you didn't take the time to read it."

"And what if you keep having to pass?" said Jaime. "Everyone'll just think you're stupid."

Jude appeared beside them then with an official-looking blue clipboard that he'd probably bought especially for the occasion and that made him feel important.

"You a team?" he asked. "Name?"

"The Red Hot Quizzy Peppers," said Donna.

"Original." Jude smirked. "You're on first, with the . . . uh . . . the Nomads. Starting at eight, OK? You can sit down if you like. And can you stick on these name tags? Makes things easier." He lingered over Donna's sticker. "Don't see that name often. After Donna Summer?"

Donna clutched at the sticker with a protective hand. "Donna Douglas, actually."

"Well, that's . . . different. Anyway, good luck." He winked.

Perspiring under the orb-like lamps, plastered with the white labels that bore their names in black marker, they took their seats. Soon enough the Nomads joined the spectacle on the adjacent table.

Donna looked across at them, pulling at the front tendrils of her hair. "This is a sure thing," she said, once she appeared to have finished inspecting whatever qualities she was looking for.

How could Donna tell? The Nomads consisted of two women and three men, all middle-aged, and all so strikingly similar that they could be siblings. The women had brassy blonde ponytails held back by ice cream-colored scrunchies, and all three men were at varying stages of baldness, with receding lips and brown muscular arms. Why was it a sure thing?

At Jaime's side, Luke was still. She asked him if he was nervous, but he only shrugged and said, "Not really." He was no help at all.

The audience assembled in a horseshoe around them, muttering loudly behind their drinks, perhaps debating which of the two teams looked the more promising. And then Jude, looking cool and devilish, hoisted himself up to sit on the bar in front of them. He brought the microphone to his mouth.

"Hi, folks!"

Jude repeated the rules, and let them all know that any disputes or instances of foul play would be adjudicated by the president of the London Pub Quiz League, Priya Hirani, who sat to one side of the audience, smiling benignly with an iPad laid neatly on her lap. Jaime tried to catch Bryony's eye for reassurance, but she was peering forward, her face grave with concentration.

"And now," Jude said, as he reached into his pocket and drew out a fifty-pence piece, "let's find out who'll begin. Red Hot Quizzy Peppers—heads. Nomads—tails. Are we ready?" And the audience pantomimed noises of suspense as the coin flickered and glinted as it spun in the air before landing neatly in Jude's closing fist. He opened it to reveal tails.

"Ah, shit," Harry muttered.

Donna grabbed his shoulder. "Come on, you'll psych everyone out. Look at Jaime—she's about to pass out already."

Jaime's face flamed, but Donna may well have been right.

Jude slotted the coin into his shirt pocket. "Nomads, are you ready?"

"Ready, mate," answered one of the hulking Nomads. He lifted a dripping pint to his mouth and drank deeply before wiping the froth from his upper lip.

"First round—Movies. David, which British actor died whilst still filming his supporting role in Ridley Scott's *Gladiator*?"

"Oliver Reed."

"Correct. Caroline, *The Godfather* was released in 1972; who played the title role?"

"Marlon Brando."

"Correct. Jenny, what is the name of the villain in the first *Superman* movie, played by Gene Hackman?"

"Oh . . . uh." Jenny lifted her fingers to her chin. "Pass to David."

David folded his arms. "Lex Luthor."

"Correct."

And it seemed as if their streak would never end: "Damian Lewis . . . Bobcat Goldthwait . . . Dirty Harry . . . Will Smith . . . Roots . . . Christopher Lee . . ."

"Nikos, who played James Bond in *For Your Eyes Only*?"

"Pass to Jenny."

"Sean Connery?"

"Incorrect. Nomads, you have fourteen points. Red Hot Quizzy Peppers, the question passes to you—Donna?"

Donna cleared her throat. "Pass to Harry."

"Oh—me?" Harry said. "Roger Moore?"

"Correct. Round two—History. Harry, in which month of which year did the Japanese bomb Pearl Harbor?"

"Pass to Bryony."

"December 1941," Bryony answered clearly.

"Correct."

"Bryony, whose rebel army threw the Spanish out of Venezuela in 1821?"

"Oh . . . uh . . . Bolivar. Simon Bolivar."

"Correct." Jude rounded on Luke. "Luke, which US President gave the Gettysburg Address?"

"Abraham Lincoln."

"Correct. Jaime, during which World War did the Battle of the Somme occur?"

"World War . . ." Jaime froze. "Pass to—"

"I'm sorry, you can't pass if you've started to answer."

"World War . . ." Donna was going to kill her. "World War One?"

"Correct."

Jaime wilted onto the table.

"Donna, who succeeded Hitler on his death in 1945?"

Donna sat back. "Pass to Bryony."

"Admiral Donitz."

"Correct . . ."

And with the rhythmic ease of Bryony's answers, as they all swiftly passed their questions to her (". . . Kuwait . . . 1815 . . . Mount Vesuvius . . . Warsaw Pact . . ."), they earned eighteen points before she finally faltered.

"On 19th August 1968, Soviet tanks rolled into which country?"

"Slovakia?"

"I'm sorry . . ."

Under the held breath of the audience, in a silence so complete that the hacking laughter of a man passing the pub could be heard outside, the two teams frowned and bellowed and grappled with the answers. When David from the Nomads was one year off the correct date of the Battle of the Little Bighorn, he slapped the tabletop with such ferocity that he received a stern glare from Priya. Harry tore off his sweater ("Aren't you hot? It's so hot in here") and Luke so nervously buffed the lenses of his glasses on the hem of his shirt that they tumbled out of his fingers across the floor. After the History round came a brutal round of European Politics, which won both teams only two points apiece. The Quizzy Peppers gained a respectable sixteen in the Sports round, but then the Nomads tore forward, scoring an astonishing twenty in the Music round, which the Quizzy Peppers could not seem to wrestle away from them.

And then, for both teams, fifty points came within reach.

"OK, then." Jude licked his lips. "Nomads, forty-seven. Quizzy Peppers, forty-six. Round six—Art. Quizzy Peppers: Bryony, which seventeenth-century Spanish artist painted *The Rokeby Venus?*"

"Pass to Jaime."

Donna twisted in her seat to stare down the table at her, and Jaime, caught still and astonished in a puddle of light from the lamp above her head, could not seem to inflate her lungs with any air at all. In her scruffy coat and with her apple-round cheeks, she must look like the most unconvincing of all of them.

But she knew the answer. She gave her head a little quiver as she cleared her throat. "Velázquez?" she said, her voice thin.

"Correct. Luke, which English painter was renowned for his depiction of horses?"

"Pass to Jaime."

"Stubbs." Her voice rang clearer.

Now it was Jaime's actual turn. If she could answer without passing, earning them two points, they would win.

"Jaime, who painted *The Body of the Dead—*"

"Holbein!" she called out, a bubble of conviction rising in her ribcage.

"And the Red Hot Quizzy Peppers win!"

Donna struck the tabletop with two fists, causing them all, sitting in high-shouldered stiffness, to jump. An earnest applause rose up around them and then quickly died—drinks needed replenishing, ciga-rettes needed to be smoked and bladders needed relieving.

"We won?" said Jaime. She whipped around to Luke, whose stunned, uncertain face was a mirror of her own. He might have clasped her knuckles, his face splitting into a wide grin, or shaken his head in wonder, saying something like, "That was brilliant, Jaime." But he didn't do either of those things. Instead he gave a curt, close-lipped nod and said, "Well, that's that then," and excused himself for the bar. Nothing had changed.

*   *   *

Warmed in the flattering glow of their excellence, they collapsed around a table to recover, to congratulate each other and to finish a third bot-tle of Pinot Grigio. Except for Luke, who, in a seemingly restless or bored fidget, kept getting up to wander aimlessly to the bar or toilets by himself.

Two further sets of teams had faced off, some visibly more pale and shaken than others, and Donna noted that things looked somewhat dif-ferent from the audience. Hadn't the lights been brighter and the room been warmer? Hadn't Jude barked the questions more impatiently? Hadn't the audience been more prone to heckling and sniggering sips of their drinks?

And while everyone seemed relieved it was over, they were happy to relive every moment of turmoil and every squirming mistake.

"God, that Battle of the Somme question—I could've *killed* myself . . ."

"Did you see that David when he smacked the table? So aggressive . . ."

"Slovakia! It was *Czecho*slovakia, for crying out loud! What was I thinking? . . ."

And Donna should have been euphoric—why shouldn't she be? But the warm surge of it was steadily pushed aside for other, more somber thoughts: who were these funny little people she had gathered online? And what was this shitty little pub in Crystal Palace? And then, in a sudden grip of bleakness—what was the point in any of this?—Lottie's hard voice filled her head: *You're just like him.*

"Are you alright?" Harry asked, catching her in a long moment of silence.

"Oh, yeah. Yes, of course."

"It's cool you made us do this, you know? It was fun. And who cares if we don't win?"

"Of course we have to win."

But Harry just gave her a half smile and turned his attention away. "But I mean, seriously, Jaime," he said, shaking his head in wonder. "That last round—Jude didn't even finish the question."

Jaime bobbed her head in embarrassment. "Oh, you know . . ."

"Aren't you so proud of her, Luke?" Donna said.

Luke's eyes were startled. "Well, sure."

But he didn't look proud; he didn't even look interested. If Donna had asked him what he had been most proud of, he probably would have shrugged and said something like, "Oh, you know, all of it really." What use was he?

"You still keep up with it all?" Harry asked Jaime. He tipped his head self-consciously. "The art world, I mean?"

"Oh, a little. I just love the National Gallery—I *love* it. And the Tate Britain too. It's so wonderful to have it on your doorstep—not like in Keswick. And I like to look at the online auctions too. You know—Sotheby's, the Dorotheum."

Donna sat forward. "How does that work, then?"

"Like a fancy eBay, really—you bid online. I like to guess how much pieces will go for. It's just a silly game."

"No, it sounds fun." On her phone Donna bookmarked the webpages for the Dorotheum and Sotheby's—she would investigate them both later tonight.

When they shrugged on their coats and said goodbye, wishing each other happy Christmases, they promised to "brush up" on the weakest of their knowledge (what exactly *was* the difference between Luge and Skeleton in the winter Olympics?). The next match would take place in the second week of January.

Bryony, Jaime, and Luke shuffled out, but Harry lingered, adjusting the collar of his shirt beneath his windbreaker. Was it possible he was waiting for her?

"Do you want another drink?" Donna said.

"Oh." He looked down at the table. "I would, I've just got a . . . I'm meeting up with a friend in Streatham."

Her lungs turned heavy with disappointment. "Oh, sure. That's fine."

"Look, it's not—"

"No, no, really. It's fine."

And it was fine. She'd told him she didn't want a boyfriend, hadn't she? Everything was fine. But then why was she saying "fine" so much? It was no good getting into anything like that.

She was glad—relieved even—that growing up with her dad had stunted whatever romantic or carnal endeavors she may have sought out. There was never the time or freedom of silliness to giggle about boys with the other girls at school, and there was never—*never*—the opportunity to bring one home for sugared popcorn and a film and a fumbling snog under a blanket. Lottie had learned the hard way, when her first boyfriend (Dylan? Daniel?) had come for dinner, only to witness their dad, in his week-old pajamas, crying in front of the open fridge door, a spill of yellow light illuminating his pink, broken face. Dylan or Daniel had not called again and Lottie had shut herself in her bedroom, where the swell of Toni Braxton's "Un-Break my Heart" filled the landing and leaked under Donna's bedroom door. Thank God, she had thought, I can spare myself this.

Safely escaped to university, she thought she might try again. There had been one or two encounters there—a mawkish veterinary student called Martin who would lie on Donna's pillow, lazily picking at the strings of a tuneless guitar, and ask her things like, "So, have you ever been in love?" And then a surprisingly well-read rugby player called Tony, whose crooked nose had been broken in a scrum, and who Donna assumed to be safely lacking in emotional depth. She didn't feel like sharing the tragic intricacies of her life with either Martin or Tony. She didn't want to see their eyes glaze over in alarm when she revealed the circumstances behind the ruin of her parents' marriage, or how she sometimes lay awake in the early hours of the morning, promising herself she would never end up like either of them.

Except one night, having made their way through the best part of a cheap bottle of Icelandic vodka in the halls' common room, with Tony's hulking arm draped over her shoulders, Donna had found herself telling him all of it.

". . . And I haven't really seen much of him since," she had concluded, looking down into her lap where her bloated, over-warm hands twisted anxiously.

"Wow," Tony had said with an awkward sniff, "that's fucked up," leaving Donna to say nothing and never call him again. But when she'd caught glimpses of Tony after that, in the dim student bar or on the green at end-of-term picnics, she told herself that he'd probably been right—it *was* fucked up. Plenty of people had only sparing relationships with their families anyway; what was the big deal? There was nothing to do but move on and leave it behind her.

Since then, other than one or two drink-fueled one-night stands and phone numbers briefly exchanged and then discarded, there hadn't been anyone else. But then there had been Harry, who wasn't flirtatious or fumbling or interfering or anything like that. His easy smiles and permissive brown eyes had allowed her to believe she was normal, whatever that might mean. There may have even been a small stab of jealousy while she listened to him lament over his ex-girlfriend in his flat. But what was the point? And who had the time or patience for anything as trivial as "jealousy" anyway?

CHAPTER SEVEN

Question: *Which food, known in Italy as* cipolline sottaceto *is an essential garnish on a Gibson Martini cocktail?*
Answer: *Pickled onions*

Harry took an Uber to Streatham, too anxious that the bus would run late or that he'd end up sitting next to someone who'd spill curry sauce on his trousers. The back seat smelled of pickled onions and the journey had him compulsively buttoning and unbuttoning the neck of his shirt, trying to decide which looked best. When he tried to look at himself in the rearview mirror, the driver caught his eye, and attempted to draw him into a conversation he didn't want to have.

"Someone special, mate?"

"Well, you know, sort of."

"You look good, mate. She'd be lucky."

No one had ever said that Vivienne was lucky to have him; it was the opposite. They had met in the awkward years after school, at nineteen, when everyone was a little bit spotty and their clothes a little too contrived, and hanging out down the local pub was the most grown-up thing they could do. Vivienne was there one evening, with her immaculate teeth and long eyelashes, flashing him a withering look from across the bar when he was trying, too loudly, to make his mates laugh. She was there a night soon after that too, when Harry's rowdier friends had drifted away to other parts of London to start "proper jobs," leaving him solemn and brooding, which she presumably found more attractive because she had come to speak to him.

"You're in here a lot."

"Oh . . ." He had switched his eyes from side to side. "Me, you mean? Yeah—live up the road."

"I'm from St Albans, but I just got into a flat here on Dunmow Avenue. I'm at City University."

"Oh right. Nice."

"Economics." She had said it and held out her slim, pale hand for him to shake as if it had been her name. "I like your hair. Are those curls natural?"

And the conversation had gone well enough into the evening that she had eventually asked him, "Well, are you going to ask me out then or what?"

That had been that, and Harry had been certain a more miraculous thing might never happen to him again.

"Bloody hell, mate," Wes had said with a low whistle, his backpack slung fashionably low over his buttocks. "You got balls made of gold or something?"

He should've known all along that it was too good to be true. Maybe it was cool, back then, to date a slobbish, mumbling boy, if his hair was good enough, but that couldn't last forever.

He and Vivienne had often come to this Streatham pub in their excited flurry of first living together. They had sat here talking quickly and laughing loudly in the need to let each other know how wonderful they thought the other was, and later, too, when the ease of making conversation started to elude them. The problem was the rising sense of nostalgia and regret about the place. Here were the tall windows, piled high with the sun-faded boxes of board games they'd lazily played on weeknights. There was the cozy, pillow-strewn corner bench where they had discussed the schooling of their future children ("You can't rule out private school on principle, Harry. You'd be some kind of reverse snob").

And there she was, at a table for two on her own, with a glass of red wine, a bottle of Old Mout cider and a tattered Ludo box in front of her. Harry pulled off his windbreaker because it wasn't quite clean. He should have worn that double-breasted wool coat from John Lewis she'd bought him last year, but what had happened to that thing?

"Viv."

"Harry."

She stood up, arms outstretched, and Harry thought he might cry in the clean-smelling warmth of her fuzzy pink sweater and the feel of her solid body underneath.

"Oh, Harry, you look wonderful," she said when she released him.

"Oh, well, thanks. I mean, you too."

"Have you been eating pickled onions?"

"No, no. It was the cab."

She picked at the peeling edge of the name sticker on his shirt. "What's this?"

"Oh." He tore it off to get it out of sight. "Just a silly little—I'm doing a pub quiz. With some . . . friends." Christ, he couldn't get a sentence out.

"Oh—fun! You were always quite good at that—what was that show with all the disappearing squares?"

"*Catchphrase.*"

"*Catchphrase.* That's right."

They sat down and she pushed the cider bottle across to him. "I took the liberty," she said. "And, you know . . ." She patted the Ludo box. "I thought we might need an icebreaker."

She looked remarkable. And he didn't know if this was better or worse. He might have been heartened if she'd grown thin, gaunt, and anxious, or terribly dull and frumpy. But no: her face was alive with a faint blush, her black, bobbed hair shone, and her painted nails and selection of delicate gold jewelry all gave the impression that she was taking care of herself, that life was good. But how much sex was she having? How good was *that* side of things? He'd have to find some way of edging it into the conversation. If she said something like, "It's not better, Harry, it's just different," he might well ball himself up on the floor, right here in the pub.

"So," he said instead.

"So."

"How's things?"

"Alright, I suppose. What's new for you?"

"Haven't found a new job yet, if that's what you're asking."

"I wasn't asking."

"Seemed like you were." He took a long, cold drink and wiped his mouth. "How's Ashton? Can't imagine he's too happy that you're here with me."

She pulled a face that he couldn't decipher and began to unpack the ludo box. "Do we need to do this?"

"Do what?"

"*This.*"

"Suppose not."

"If you must know, he's out with the boys."

"OK. And how's—you know—things with him?"

"They're great. He takes good care of me."

"Oh, I bet."

"This isn't the conversation I wanted to have with you, Harry. I'd hoped we'd all moved on from this sort of thing by now."

And why did she get to decide that? Wasn't it entirely reasonable to still be hurt—to still be fuming—over something like this? It was easy for her; the one holed up in a love nest with a meaty-handed, pinstriped slab of a man. There would be no asking how much sex there was now. She might walk out, leaving him with the shameful task of finishing his cider and packing away the board game, all under the pitying scrutiny of the other people in the pub.

"Listen, Harry, I did want to talk to you about something. About Ashton and me. If I'm honest, a large part of why I wanted to meet you tonight . . . well, I want to know that you forgive us."

And now he had to be careful. If he went ahead with what immediately sprung to mind ("Are you fucking joking?"), he could ruin this for good. Forever.

"Well, Viv, I may not have been the best boyfriend, but that's between you and me. And, you know, I still—I miss you and everything. But Ashton? I don't think so."

"Ashton didn't do anything wrong."

"Course he did."

Vivienne folded her arms.

"You know," he said. "Bro code."

She turned her face away, her mouth pinched. "I think you're being very immature. We're all adults here."

But there was nothing—*nothing*—mature about Ashton Taylor-Phipps. Not the way he'd chew the lid of every office biro, not his *Simpsons* socks, and not the way he'd sneeze into his sleeve and wipe the contents of his nostrils onto the underside of his chair. But he could see in telling her this he'd come off as bitter. What, after all, did he have to offer? A flat of missing teaspoons and an egg-stained dressing gown.

Instead he began to set up the bright Ludo game board so he didn't have to answer. Ludo was logical; it would be her turn and then his turn. Someone would win and everyone would understand why, and there would be no hard feelings, no unbearable need to go back and erase your mistakes. Even the way Vivienne played was pretty—the elegant shake of her fist as she neatly threw the dice. And it was sexy too, how, when waiting for her turn, she would lean her neck into her hand and display the smooth tilt of her jawline.

"You know," she said eventually. "Ashton might be able to help you out. On the job front, I mean."

Harry made a noise in his throat. "Now he's the big man?"

"Did you hear that regional manager left? What was his name—guy with the moustache—Keith?"

"Kevin."

"Kevin, right. Well, turns out the 'downsizing' was a bit of a shambles. But, you know, it was his hill to die on."

It struck him that "his hill to die on" was exactly the kind of phrase Ashton would use, and he would bet that was where she'd heard it. Curled up on the sofa one night, Ashton would have come swaggering through their front door—"Viv, babe. Want to hear about Kevin? Guy lost his job today over the downsizing fiasco. But whatever; it was his hill to die on."

"Well," said Harry. "Too bad for Kevin."

"My point is, Harry, that they're refilling positions. And you were only let go because of their dumb little 'last in, first out' policy."

"I was let go because I . . ." But wait, she didn't know about the acute lovesickness in his heart and lungs that had forbidden him from getting out of bed. "Never mind."

"What's it been now—three months? Have you even had any interviews? And wouldn't it be nice—wouldn't it be wonderful—to start the New Year off in a better place?"

He didn't trust himself to speak straight away. How, by any stretch of the imagination, could she think he would go back to working with Ashton again? But all those job applications that he had sent into the chasm of the internet, only to never receive a response . . . all that scrolling through the job sites with the deluded impression that they were looking for somebody just like him—it was all lies; they weren't. The state of his bank account too—his breath came more rapidly every time he used the cash machine and was faced with the "check your balance" button (which he hadn't pressed in some time).

She tilted her head to one side. "And don't you want your mum to stop worrying about you? Doesn't she want you back on your feet?"

She'd done it now. She would have known that would slice into his gut. "What makes you think Ashton wants anything to do with me?" he said.

"Don't be like that, Harry. He feels awful, just *awful*. You can keep things professional, you know. You don't have to be best friends with the people you work with."

"Viv, he stole my girlfriend."

"He did not steal me, Harry. We'd already broken up. And anyway, I'm perfectly capable of making my own—"

"Yeah, yeah. OK. Fine. Talk to him then." It occurred to him that if he declined, he might never see her again.

"Really? Oh, he'll be so pleased. He's been so—well, too ashamed to message you."

And now he had some vague sense of having satisfied her, he took a long drink and let her do the same, before he said, "Just tell me one thing, Viv. What's it like? Is it better?"

"I don't know what you mean."

"Yes, you do, Viv. Come on. How is he—you know—compared to me?"

"Oh. *That*. It's not really appropriate to ask me that, Harry. Does it bother you that much?"

"Yes. Yes, it does."

"I don't know. It's just diff—"

"Yeah, yeah, OK. It's different. I get it."

And then there was nothing else to do but to finish the game of Ludo. But as the play went on and the pieces continued to creep across the board in Vivienne's favor, Harry remembered how much he'd always hated this particular game. There was no skill involved, no competence; it all hinged on the throw of the dice.

* * *

Jaime arrived back at the flat with a renewed certainty that all could be made well. As they'd left the pub after the victory of the Quiz League's first round, she tried to preserve that golden feeling of ease—for the first time in her life, she had been held in some sort of high esteem. And OK—while she and Luke hadn't walked home holding hands or falling against one other in helpless laughter as she'd hoped they might, how invigorated she felt—how full of life! How pretty the lights from the vista of central London looked as they crested the hill, and how sweet Luke looked bundled up in his scarf and coat. Was there any more need to agonize over what Luke had said? No: it could all be dealt with as triumphantly and competently as winning the quiz match.

Luke settled onto the sofa without taking off his jacket or turning on the lamp, and switched on the NASCAR highlights program. Jaime perched on the edge of the coffee table, sitting on her hands to stop herself pulling at her earlobe, unable to see Luke's eyes behind the flashing reflection of the television on his glasses.

"Wow, wasn't that great?" she said.

"Sure. It was fun."

When it became clear he wasn't going to elaborate, when he expelled a low whistle at a sudden screen full of flying car debris, she gathered her breath.

"Listen, Luke, I know it's been a pretty awful week, but I've been thinking a lot about what you said. And, look, I know I didn't react very well when you told me you wanted to—you know—when you told me how unhappy you were, and I'm sorry for that. I think I—Are you listening?"

"Hm?"

"Can you turn that off for a minute?"

He lowered the volume.

"I said I've been thinking a lot about what you said."

"What I said about what?"

"That you wanted to go back to Keswick."

"Oh. OK."

"Well, I was speaking to Bryony and—"

"Who?"

"For God's sake, Luke. *Bryony*. From the *pub*. We were just with her. What is wrong with you?"

"Sorry. OK. You were talking to Bryony."

"She just—she really made me think, you know? Her and her husband, they haven't had it easy. They had their first kid when they were *seventeen*. They didn't have jobs or a place of their own or—"

"What's this got to do with anything?"

"Well, they didn't have choices. And we do. And we could—*you* could—do anything you wanted. And I realize I've sort of been ignoring that." She began to wind a lock of hair around her finger. "You just always seemed sort of 'whatever' about it. But I think if you had the time and space to—you know—" and here she ducked her head in embarrassment—"*find* yourself, then you'd be a lot happier. It's not because people look down on us or that we don't fit in. I think you just—maybe you just don't know who you are."

She worried, suddenly, that she'd gone too far, but his shoulders slumped and he said, "And how am I supposed to do that?"

She stood up, laying her fisted hand lightly in the other. "I think you should quit your job—No, wait a minute, just listen." She brought both her hands to her chest, in order to convey to him completely her sense of ownership, her sense of duty. "I'm going to get a second job, outside of PrintPro. I mean, what do I do with my time anyway? I already asked about twilight shifts at the supermarket. I could pay the rent on the wage they pay. Easily."

And now Luke turned off the television and held the remote in a limp hand, letting a full minute pass.

"Well, listen," he said, leaning forward onto his knees. "This will need some thinking over. First of all, you'd be exhausted. And what's a twilight shift anyway?" But there was no mistaking a glint of excitement in his eyes.

"Nine till one. I could get back by six from the shop, have dinner. You could—you know," she added shyly, "maybe cook me something if it wasn't too much bother. And it's not like it would be every night. Just a few times a week. Plus, if we win this Quiz League prize—"

"Well, we can't count on that."

Then he started to move around the room, apparently aimless. He ran his hand along the frame of the mirror, inspected his fingernails, then he stood for a long time, consulting the dark windowpane and absent-mindedly touching the leaves of a potted spider plant on the sill; perhaps all with the aim of discovering an answer among the crevices of their possessions.

And she had to be honest (even if she wouldn't say it out loud)—she was disappointed. She had expected more gratitude from him, more recognition of her sacrifice. What sort of reaction was this?

"Well, what would I do, Jaime?" he said eventually. "Seems like we'd only be replacing one type of stress with another."

There was genuine fear in his voice, and Jaime wasn't sure what to tell him. She'd had vivid images of herself arriving back home—her feet sore, her fringe damp in a hard sweat, in a sort of happy exhaustion—to a rested, contently smiling Luke. He might shyly reveal his laptop screen, where he'd been working on some sort of motorsport journalism project, or perhaps the application process for primary school teaching. But no, saying anything like that would only put pressure on him.

"That's the point," she said. "You would figure out what you want to do."

"Well, OK. Look, it seems we'd better start a spreadsheet or something. Figure out the—you know—financial logistics of this."

Jaime was more than happy to hurry to get the laptop. And there on the sofa, with their thighs pressing against each other, they hammered out "the financial logistics of this." It wasn't easy; more than once Luke would bring his hand to his temple, frowning, and say, "I don't know, I just don't see this working," and both of them—when faced with the indisputable, black and white numbers onscreen—had to make more suggestions of "trimming" than Jaime had expected.

". . . Well, what about the broadband package? That seems like an awful lot, don't you think?"

". . . so it would have to be four nights a week. That's the only way to—you know—break even—"

". . . Did you cancel that *Motor Sport* magazine subscription?"

". . . No one *needs* a holiday abroad. It's a middle-class privilege. And anyway, there's always camping . . ."

But when they'd finished, the plan in front of them resembled something sensible. It was so reassuring that Jaime wanted to print it out, to keep it folded on her bedside table, there to reach out and unfold when she woke up feeling sick with worry.

Then they were both grinning at each other, and Jaime couldn't remember the last time that had happened. And so what if there was a slight tightening in her stomach and who cared if something in her decided she wouldn't be divulging all the details to her parents? If you couldn't do this sort of thing at twenty-four years old, then when could you?

CHAPTER EIGHT

Question: *Which large bird, in the genus* Meleagris, *is native to North America?*
Answer: *Turkey*

"OK, here we go," Jude said, and Bryony held her breath. "Red Hot Quizzy Peppers, round three—Fashion. Donna, what French luxury leather goods company has a jockey riding a horse as their logo?"

"Longchamp."

Bryony's shoulders rode high in dread. She wouldn't know any of these.

"Harry, what is Coco Chanel's real first name?"

"Uh . . . Jessica?"

Donna raked her fingers over her scalp. "Really, Harry? *Jessica* Chanel?"

"I'm sorry," Jude said. "Over to the Banana Splits. Rhiannon?"

"Gabrielle."

"Correct. Aishling, what nationality is model Gisele Bündchen?"

"Brazilian."

"Correct."

The Banana Splits swept through another three correct questions ("Donna Karan! . . . Christian Louboutin! . . . Burberry!") before, to her astonishment, Bryony managed to snatch the round back from them.

"Luca, what is the name of the dark green precious stone which is carved to make ornaments?"

"Emerald."

"I'm sorry. Red Hot Quizzy Peppers—Bryony?"

"Oh . . . jade?"

"Correct!"

"Now hang on, hang on." Luca, with his swept, sandy hair, stood up to lean his knuckles on the table. "Surely 'emerald' is a perfectly acceptable answer?"

Priya cleared her throat. "'Carved to make ornaments' is the crucial element of this question . . . Luca, is it?"

With that settled, and with Luca tamed back into his seat, two more lucky passes to Donna ("Cravat! . . . Sweden!"), concluded round three with the Quizzy Peppers eighteen points ahead. But there was barely even time to take any cooling swallows of their drinks before Jude was gathering his breath again.

"Alright, round four—Sport. Donna, which country won the first ever football World Cup?"

"Pass to Harry."

"Argentina?"

"I'm sorry, no—over to you, Banana Splits. Rhiannon?"

"Uruguay."

"Correct. Aishling, who is the oldest out of Serena and Venus Williams?"

"Serena?"

"Incorrect—Quizzy Peppers, Harry?"

"Well . . . uh . . . Venus, obviously."

"Wait, wait, wait." Aishling, with a long, swinging plait and over-sized glasses, spread her arms out wide before her neighboring team-mates, as though to hold them back from attacking. There was a bored-looking girl who repeatedly inspected the cuticles of her nails and another man, who, from his loose bottom lip and slow-blinking eyelids, appeared unsure of where he was or what he was doing.

"Is that even allowed?" said Aishling. "I mean, there's only two answers."

"That's certainly something we can take up with Priya again. Take a breather, folks."

As Jude and Priya inclined their nodding heads toward each other, whispering as Priya gestured to the screen of her iPad, Donna released a groan.

"That's the second time they've kicked up a fuss about something," she said, jabbing the tabletop and stiff with annoyance. "They're trying to throw us off."

"We're sixteen points ahead," Harry said, folding his arms with a confident swell of his chest. "Don't worry about it."

"Well," Bryony said, thoughtfully rubbing her earlobe. "I suppose it's a valid dispute. By getting it wrong, Harry can't lose. There's a—"

"*Bryony!*" Donna's eyes narrowed as she leaned over Harry's lap and dramatically lowered her voice. "Do *not* let them hear you say that."

Bryony sat back to await Priya's ruling. There was no point in trying to convince Donna of anything. With the Banana Splits trailing behind, somewhere in the low thirties, if they could hold on to this Sports round until its end, they could make it to fifty. But still—you never knew. Sometimes rounds came out of nowhere, enabling the other team to snatch the thread and unravel your lead as fast as you'd achieved it.

Outside, a fine, wet snow dappled the windowpanes. It was January; since the first match in December, Christmas had reeled Bryony in with its flurry of midnight present-wrapping and food shopping. She had stood in line at department stores with the balls of her feet aching. Stale cake sat on forgotten plates in various crevices of the house and strips of sticky tape could still be found clinging to the table edges. And after Boxing Day, after the bewildering, dateless stretch of days, the festivities had spat her back out again into the first, cold, hard day of the new year. Pull down the lights, drag the browning Christmas tree onto the curb and sweep up its shedding needles. But then the Quizzy Peppers group chat had fluttered to life.

Crikey guys, match two, we ready?

Happy New Year!! Oh my God!!

I hope you all had great Christmases. I'm feeling very nervous.

Quizzy peppers gonna slay team let's go let's go!

Now Jude ambled languidly back to perch on the edge of the bar. Priya crossed her legs in prim importance, her lovely face as placid as ever.

"The question," Jude announced, "will be allowed." And Aishling threw up her hands.

"Bryony, which six countries make up the Six Nations Championship?"

"England, Scotland, Wales, Ireland, France, Italy."

"Correct. Luke, what is the name of the cyclist who was famously involved in a doping scandal?"

"Lance Armstrong."

"Correct . . ."

Before its conclusion, the round skittered back to the Banana Splits for two brief questions—"Mark Selby . . .", "Correct! . . .", "Greece? . . .", "I'm sorry . . ."—before it came rebounding back to the Quizzy Peppers.

"Jaime, Jenson Button won the 2009 Formula One World Championship driving for which team?"

"Pass to Luke."

"Brawn."

"Correct. Donna, in which sport do teams compete to win the Stanley Cup?"

"Pass to . . . Harry?"

"Hockey."

"Correct. Harry, the Chicago Cubs and Boston Red Sox play which sport?"

"Baseball."

"Correct. Bryony, in bowling, what is the term given for three consecutive strikes?"

"Oh! Turkey! A turkey!"

"And that's fifty! Ladies and gents, the Red Hot Quizzy Peppers win and head into round three!"

Jude was clapping and Priya was clapping, her iPad wobbling on her lap, and the room suddenly filled with noise. Somewhere behind Bryony came the sound of a drink sloshing to the floor and someone's apologetic cry. And then four sets of warm, joyful arms reached out to encircle her shoulders, her neck and even the top of her head. There was a tremendous shouting in both of her ears—"Yes, Bry, *yes!*" A swell of tears blurred her vision; she wasn't sure if she'd ever been this happy.

*   *   *

On Friday night, Harry alighted the bus at Thornton Heath train station, on the way to his mother's house. A utilitarian, sixties office block, bearing no less than seven "To Let" signs in its rusting metal-framed windows, gave way to a boisterous negotiation of zebra crossings and roadworks.

On Melfort Road, in a terrace house with a grubby white door, a peeling latticework gate and a browning hedgerow, Harry's mum had cooked him a late dinner of turkey curry. She shuffled around him in her slippers, clearing magazines and empty water glasses, exclaiming that the place was "Oh, such an awful mess!" Above a hissing gas fire, a collection of Harry's school photos lined an unsteady shelf, still in the brown, gold-foiled cardboard frames they had arrived in, twenty or so years prior. Here he was in his primary school red sweater, and then the bottle green of the local secondary comprehensive. His hair moved from freshly cut to overgrown, and his overbite could be seen disappearing as his face matured to accommodate his adult teeth.

"How's the turkey?" she enquired, as she sat down next to him at the plastic-covered table in her living room, propping her chin in her hands.

"Fine. It's nice."

"Just frozen leftovers from Christmas. Don't know what to do with it all, do I? Still—have to get a crown at least."

Harry's mother was an apple-shaped woman of sixty, with a close crop of dyed mahogany hair and eyebrows expertly drawn (but perhaps sitting a fraction too high) on the shallow slope of her forehead. Harry's dad had packed a suitcase and left when Harry was eleven, while he had sat on the beige-papered landing, clinging to the stairway spindles. Sharon hadn't cared, she'd insisted at regular intervals after it had happened— "Honestly, I'd expected him to die first anyway. His cholesterol was sky-high." And although he had not seen his dad since the few brief and scattered visits that took place in the six months after his departure, the memory of the strong, able hand that gripped the oiled leather handle of his suitcase would never fade. He'd told himself back then that he would step up, be the man of the house. He would pick up his dirty socks and food-smeared plates and vacuum under the sofa. Who else would take care of his mum now? But the world had scared him with how brutal it could be, and he'd only retreated into immaturity—bunking off school and slouching around the house eating potato waffles straight from the toaster. A father could leave his son and never think of him again, a betrayed mother had to take two or three minimum wage jobs to meet the rent and put fresh vegetables in the fridge, and, when she couldn't afford the year nine trip to France, the teacher would frown and lecture her about the importance of "enriching activities."

"Where's Vivienne?" his mum asked. She was wearing a lilac terry cloth dressing gown and fussed with its straggling, knotted rope. "Don't tell me; she's working."

"She's busy, Mum. She got a promotion."

"She looking after you? What's she eating when you're round here for dinner?"

"I don't know. She just grabs something from—Look, just leave it, yeah?"

"She didn't even come at Christmas."

"She went to see her family—I told you."

"Well, why didn't you go with her, then?"

"'Cause I wanted to see you, didn't I?"

Vivienne wouldn't have come for Christmas anyway, despite him revealing to her that, ever since his dad left, he'd promised himself he'd never let his mother spend Christmas alone. But across the years, Vivienne had let him know, in so many words, that she found his mother's house distasteful. ("Well, it's just not very Christmassy at Sharon's, is it? She doesn't even do a cheeseboard.")

In his mother's disgruntled silence, as she gave a long, exasperated blink, Harry rapidly forked through his microwaved rice; perhaps it was a mistake—a big mistake—not to have told her that he and Vivienne had broken up, but it had seemed easier at the time, and sometimes still seemed easier now. There were ample excuses available for someone as young, busy, and vibrant as Vivienne—she was finishing up a big project at work; she was babysitting her niece; there was a bachelorette party in the Cotswolds. Then he didn't have to console her through an unending succession of worries about "how he was coping" or doubts of whether he'd ever find someone as wonderful as Vivienne again.

"I'm in a competition, Mum," he said now. "At the pub. Like a pub quiz? Might be some money in it." He waited for her cheerful approval—perhaps a "Oh, isn't that nice?"—but it didn't come.

"Shouldn't you be spending less time at the pub and more time getting a new job?"

"Christ, Mum. I'm hardly at job interviews at eight o'clock at night, am I?"

"Have you tried dropping your CV round the shops?"

"That's not—people don't do that anymore."

"Oh?"

And he thrust down his knife and fork with more clanging force than he meant to. There were so many things she would never understand—not redundancy or job applications or heartbreak or anything else. She would stay here in her dressing gown, sheltered by the yellowed net curtains that hid her windows and the hedgerow that blocked out the sun. He picked up his knife and fork and took a steadying breath.

"Any pudding?" he asked.

"It scares me, Harry. All these young men without work. They wander the streets all day, all night. They haven't got anything to get up for, they haven't got anything to do."

"What's your point, Mum?"

"I don't want you to end up like them."

His throat closed with guilt and tenderness. "What are you . . . Mum." He took her cold, papery hands in his own. "Why would you worry about something like that?"

"I hear them outside the windows. They're always shouting something—all of them—shouting at each other, shouting for no reason. They drop their cigarette butts over my gate. They could set the garden on fire with those things, Harry. *And* they steal my packages."

"Mum, they don't."

"I should sell up. Bugger off to Tenerife like Barbara from number twenty-eight."

Harry's heart turned cold. So everyone would leave him—all thanks to Ashton Taylor-Phipps and Barbara from number twenty-eight. And then what?

"Anyway, listen," he said, "how's that tap I sorted for you?"

"Oh, it only started dripping again."

Wiping his lips, he started out of his seat. "Take another look," he said, but she tugged his arm down again.

"No, no. I got a plumber out. It's fine now."

"Oh. Well, what plumber? Where'd you find him?"

She folded her broad, freckled arms on the tabletop, her lips thin. "I'm not useless, Harry."

"No, I know. I know that."

"Well. I've got apple crumble."

He allowed her to take his curry-smeared plate and sat wiping his mouth on his sleeve. With oven gloves she brought in steaming bowls of crumble with sticky rivulets of custard sliding down the sides. She warned him not to touch; they were too hot. And then she smoothed away the curls on his forehead and dabbed a dribble of sauce off his bristled chin.

CHAPTER NINE

Question: *Which nineteenth century French artist created the commercial poster,* Reine de Joie, *or* Queen of Joy?
Answer: *Henri de Toulouse-Lautrec*

Four weeks after Bryony was first called into Lydia's school about what she and Glen had come to call "Dickheadgate," they were still no closer to solving what Lydia's head of year, Miss Twitchett, described as "issues with defiance and aggression."

"What you may find, Mrs. Ward," she told Bryony now in her heavily perfumed office, while furrowing her large, black eyebrows, and chewing on an apple, "is that your own behavior may affect a situation like this—a situation in which Lydia is . . . uh . . . responding negatively to authority. It's important to be a good role model for your child."

"I'm afraid I don't understand what you mean by that."

"Well," Miss Twitchett continued, "by trying to maintain a calm and peaceful presence at home." And here she used her apple core to emphasize the phrase "peaceful presence," by letting the hand that held it bounce with each syllable.

And why did this have to be happening now, when the third match of the Quiz League—the match that would see them into the quarter-final—was only four days away? Didn't she ever deserve a little time for herself? And why couldn't Glen go to the school or get the phone calls and listen to the teachers?

* * *

"Well, I don't understand," Donna was saying down the phone on Tuesday morning. It was ten-thirty and she stood in a toilet cubicle at the office. "A buyer's what?"

"The buyer's premium," said the pleasant yet vacant-sounding voice of whoever it was that picked up the phones at the Dorotheum in Austria. "I am afraid it is added to the hammer price, Miss March. So with the shipping option you have chosen . . ."

Donna had won the online auction for a Toulouse-Lautrec lithograph (*Mary Hamilton*, 1895—a large-nosed, jacketed woman in scratchy pencils) for four hundred and fifty euros, after three weeks of losing out on other works to anonymous, richer people. What a thing to be able to say to people when they came over—"Oh, that? Just a little Toulouse-Lautrec piece I picked up at auction. Are you familiar with his work?" But now it turned out that wasn't the end of it; there was this "buyer's premium" and then the shipping, the handling, the insurance—all of which exceeded the price of the thing in the first place.

With the voice on the other end of the phone sounding increasingly troubled, she paid the entire balance—if only to get the voice to stop talking. But after she'd hung up, it hardly seemed to matter. She'd have her split of the ten-grand Championship money—they would win it, she was absolutely certain of it.

And then, before she put her phone away, a message from Bernadette lit up the screen.

Are you clearing up this mess, Donna? The dust!

Why couldn't everyone chill out?

* * *

Breadcrumbing. That's what they called it. Harry discovered this on Wednesday morning, sitting on a bench overlooking the island of dinosaur statues in Crystal Palace Park, on his second Diet Coke. Of course there was a legitimate, internet-verified description of what Vivienne was doing to him; she was so predictable. *The act of sending out flirtatious but non-committal social signals.*

"Ha!" he called, startling a passing woman with a pram. "Sorry, sorry."

He scrolled back over her messages since their evening in Streatham before Christmas, in response to his genuine enquiries over her well-being, "the job thing", and then his last couple of desperate cat GIFs.

> **Aw, good thanks. So nice to meet up. I've missed talking to you so much xx**
> **Christmas has been MENTAL, love, sorry. I'm on it, K? Don't you worry x**
> **Haha!**

And why had the kisses not only depleted but disappeared? He shoved his phone back in his pocket and drained his Coke. Perhaps Ashton was hanging around, looking over her shoulder. He had done that at work too, while the others typed out their emails. ("Mate," he'd told Harry more than once, "there's *two* 'm's in accommodation. Makes us look a bit crap, yeah?")

If only Vivienne could come to the Five Bells for the third match on Thursday. She would see him sitting confidently at the table, his face attractively lit from the overhead lamps as he lent an easy arm on the back of his chair, tossing out the answers with a smooth, controlled voice ("I think you'll find, Jude, that the answer is 'femur'"), with none of the usual apologetic little glitches and hesitations that littered his speech. Vivienne would become flushed with admiration, and there would be no question—no question at all—of how superior he was to Ashton in almost every way. She may even plant a soft kiss on the corner of his mouth, her eyes gleaming with the promise of more to come. Everything in the world would be right again.

*　*　*

Jaime had already worked three twilight shifts at the supermarket—Monday through Wednesday—and late on Thursday afternoon, when

PrintPro was empty, she lowered herself onto her knees behind the till; inside her sensible-heeled black shoes, she had two blisters on each of her feet. The twilight work was the sort of routine, menial kind that anyone could do while half awake—wheeling stacked trolleys of produce down the squeaking aisles to be unloaded and shelved, setting aside dented tins, bruised peaches and crushed cake boxes to be repriced and hauled to the discount section. And it would have been perfect, too, to allow her mind to wander over more interesting things, as she wheeled back and forth and lifted and sorted and arranged (there was a certain pride to be taken when the tinned tomatoes all proudly faced in the same direction). But she hadn't accounted for the burden of doing it fast enough. There was a seasoned "twilighter" called Jan—a trim, constantly moving woman of sixty-two—who could complete her side of the aisle in half the time Jaime could. And as Jan efficiently trotted away, Jaime would be left under the surveillance of her hard-faced, dissatisfied supervisor, Miriam, whose dyed orange hair and pink lipsticked mouth flashed like a beacon of warning from the end of the aisle.

"Well, I don't get it," Luke had said that morning, as he dozed in bed while she carefully applied her makeup. He had finished working out his notice at the sports center, and he starfished his limbs on the mattress in the luxury of not having to get up. "Why pack so much into the start of the week?"

She had explained (and she was certain she'd explained before) that she wanted Thursdays free for the quiz and wanted weekends free to rest.

"Are you looking forward to tonight?" she'd enquired shyly. "Are you—you know—enjoying the whole thing?" He gave no recognizable hints of enjoyment and was always either too tired or too distracted to talk about it when they arrived back home. Though he had smacked Harry on the shoulder in celebration after their last win, his glasses askew and smiling, and there had been no further talk of how "very unhappy" he was.

"You know what? Yeah, I am," he'd said.

And his peaceful, sleepy face had looked so pink and content that she had climbed over the bed to kiss his warm mouth.

Now the shop door opened, and she got to her feet. A middle-aged, graying man in a business suit, jangling his car keys in one hand, circled the shop once before stopping and asking, "Do you have starry sky? A poster or anything?"

"We have *Starry Night* by Van Gogh. Could that be the one you're after?"

He had a prominent, flesh-colored mole on his brow that became buried in the folds of a frown. "How would I know? It's for my daughter. It's the one with the swirls. Starry sky."

Jaime showed him to the display rack and flipped through the Perspex-framed posters to Van Gogh's *Starry Night*.

"Hm. Yeah. That's the one."

And after Jaime had selected the corresponding rolled tube, rung it up on the till and slid it into one of the long poster bags, the man fixed her with another mole-burying frown.

"You shouldn't be on the floor like that when a customer comes in. It looks lazy."

"Oh. Sorry."

"Hm," he said. And then he left.

CHAPTER TEN

Question: *What is the former name of the Indian city of Mumbai?*
Answer: *Bombay*

Donna stood with Jaime at the bar, while Jude scribbled on his clipboard on the other side and Luke sipped on a pint of Heineken beside them.

"Are you nervous?" Jaime asked her.

"Not particularly."

"I'm so nervous."

Donna rumpled her hair with all ten of her fingers. Her eyes were so wide and unblinking, staring out at their table, that the lights and shadows of the room had started to dance in her vision. "It does you no good to be nervous, Jaime. Anxiety doesn't serve us in any way."

"No, I know. It's not exactly like I can help it, though."

"Of course you can. Remember that book—*The Mindset of the Winner*? It's all in chapter seven: 'Don't Feed Your Mind.' Well, anyway, look . . ." and she took hold of Jaime's upper arms, over the fluffy weave of her rainbow-striped sweater, so they were facing each other, "take a deep breath—no, not like that, in through your nose. You have to temporarily detach from your mind."

But Jaime stood high-shouldered, with her arms held stiffly at her sides, holding her chin back in an expression of doubt and meekness.

"Are you detaching?"

"Sure."

"Good. Oh, Bryony—over here!"

Her cheeks pink with cold, Bryony shut the double doors behind her, raising a hand in greeting. "Hi!—Hi!"

"Bry—oh my God, are you nervous?" Jaime twisted her fingers at her waist.

Before Bryony could answer, Donna had to stop this pointless sharing of fear. It would bleed into everyone. "Look, Jaime, we get it. You're nervous. But you're meant to be detaching. You have to put in the effort. You can't expect to—"

"I'm trying, OK?"

"Well, listen," Bryony said, with a calm and diplomatic smile. "Let's just enjoy ourselves."

And then there was no more time for feeling nervous or disagreeing about it, because Jude had hauled himself up on top of the bar. "Ladies and gents—hey, hey, *listen*—we're about to *begin*. Now let me remind you—the winner of tonight's match has a place in the quarter-final of the Championship in April." He paused to allow polite applause. "To my right . . ." he held out his hand, "we have Donna, Harry, Bryony, Luke, and Jaime of the Red—Hot—Quizzy Peppers!" More applause zipped through the audience, which, Donna noted, had grown in volume since the last two rounds. Someone called out a hearty "whoop!" Christ, did they have fans?

"And on my left . . ." he held out his other hand, "we have Kaldeep, Virdi, Sukdev, Aman. and Manjit—the Bombay Bad Boys!"

But the applause for the Bombay Bad Boys was considerably louder and more boisterous. Donna straightened her shoulders in annoyance and shook the hair away from her face. She peered over at the opposing lineup: each of the Bombay Bad Boys sat in a softly lit pool of their own smiling self-assurance, making cool gestures to smooth back their silken, swept hair or leisurely inspect their trim fingernails. What a bunch of cocky bastards.

"Quizzy Peppers, heads. Bombay Bad Boys, tails—ready? OK." With a skillful flick of Jude's finger and thumb, the glinting coin spun high into the air, but he missed the catch, and it clinked to the floor somewhere under his dangling legs. Both teams were on their feet and leaning forward over the tables.

"Heads!" Donna cried out, pointing. "Look, by the table leg—*there!*"

"Heads it is," Jude said. "Coin tosser wanted, CVs to me, please."

Laughter rippled through the audience. "He really does command the room, doesn't he?" Bryony said, and Donna rolled her eyes.

"OK, here we go. Quizzy Peppers, round one—London. Donna, which football club now play at the Olympic Stadium?"

"Pass to Harry."

"West Ham." Harry's voice was full of relief.

"Correct. Harry, in which year was Buckingham Palace built?"

"Pass to Bryony?"

"1703."

"Correct. Luke, how many capsules are on the London Eye?"

"Twenty?"

"That's incorrect. Virdi?"

"Fifty?"

"I'm sorry, that's incorrect. It's thirty-two. Back to the Quizzy Peppers—Jaime, which punk rock band had a hit with 'London Calling'?"

"The Sex Pistols?"

"No, sorry. Bombay Bad Boys—Sukdev?"

"The Clash. Obviously."

"Correct—"

"Less of the sarcasm, maybe?" Donna said. "I mean, honestly, Priya—it's a bit unsportsmanlike, wouldn't you say?"

"Oh, give it a rest," Sukdev said wearily, folding his arms.

"If players could refrain from commentary," Priya called.

Jude cleared his throat. "Let's crack on, folks. Bombay Bad Boys. Aman, where was the beach volleyball held in the London 2012 Olympics?"

"Horse Guards Parade. Good venue that, too."

"Correct. . . ."

When round two (Music) came and went, the Bombay Bad Boys held on to the round for seven straight questions, and Donna became more agitated with each passing "Correct!" They soared forward with twelve points to the Quizzy Peppers' eight, and the Quizzy Peppers could only wrangle it back to score two more, to ten points, before the Bombay Bad Boys wrenched it away again to score a further three.

Donna leaned forward onto her elbows, staring at Jude until her eyes began to sting, as if the force of her devotion could make any difference. The next round—Science—was no better for any of them; no one could seem to get anything right. "You need a flipping PhD for these," Manjit said with an annoyed shake of his head when asked, "What is the acronym for 'light amplifications by stimulated emission of radiation'?" But even though the Bombay Bad Boys had no opportunity to crawl further ahead, the grueling passes and incorrect answers sunk them all into a deep sense of tiredness. They began to droop their listless, leaning heads into their hands.

The next gratifying rounds of Current Events and Geography revived them. The Quizzy Peppers sprinted forward to forty-two points, to the Bombay Bad Boys' forty. But then Jude announced the round they had all come to dread: General Knowledge.

They shook themselves alert, taking deep gulps from their drinks and rubbing fatigue from their eyes. A General Knowledge round felt like a set of slippery stepping stones across treacherous water; you never knew how safe you were and there was no one person (Bryony for History, Luke for Sport, Jaime for Art) to guide you dependably to the other side. And the passes were the worst—in any other round, a pass proclaimed confidence in your teammate's knowledge, but to pass in General Knowledge was akin to flinging a lump of glowing coal to someone, in the urgency to get it away from you as quickly as possible. It could induce resentment and betrayal, weakening any previous bonds of trust you had formed.

"Donna, what is the most populated country in the world?"

"China."

"Correct. Harry, where are the Spanish Steps located?"

"I'm presuming not Spain?"

"Is that your answer?"

"No, no. Pass to Bryony."

Thankfully Bryony earned the point ("Rome?" "Correct!"), but Donna whispered furiously under her breath. "You were lucky Jude let you pass that," she warned Harry. "You want to lose us points?" Harry sighed and faced forward.

"Luke, what is the name of the longest river in Africa?"

"Oh, the Nile!"

Heads whipped around to the speaker—because it wasn't Luke who had answered. It was Jaime, who had shouted out and then immediately clamped a hand over her mouth, already turning pink.

"I'm sorry. I'm really sorry. It just came out. I'm sorry."

Bryony reached over Luke to squeeze Jaime's white-knuckled fingers, assuring her that it "doesn't matter."

Donna twisted round. "Yes, it *does* matter."

"I'm sorry." Jaime's lips shrank back in wincing disgrace.

"Your enthusiasm knows no bounds, Jaime," said Jude. "But unfortunately we'll have to pass to the Bombay Bad Boys."

Donna slumped back into her chair, folding her arms high against her chest and ignoring Jaime's soft, distressed apologies.

"Kaldeep, what is the name of the part of a river that meets the sea?"

"The mouth."

"That's correct. Virdi, which singing voice is the highest pitch?"

"Soprano."

"Correct. Sukdev, which is the highest mountain in Scotland?"

"Ben Nevis."

"Correct. Aman, what kingdom has the oldest monarchy in Europe?"

"Germany?"

"No, I'm sorry. Quizzy Peppers, Luke, since you didn't . . . uh . . . get your turn."

"Pass to Bryony."

"Denmark."

"Correct. Jaime, with which art movement is Claude Monet most associated?"

"Impressionism." Jaime's voice was weak with relief.

"Correct. Now, Donna . . ."

And she realized—from the silence of the audience, from the intensity of Jude's voice and the straining necks of both her teammates and the Bombay Bad Boys—that they were there. If she answered correctly, she'd earn the two points to win.

"Donna, what do the words 'Auld Lang Syne' translate to?"

Donna cleared her throat so that her voice would ring clear. "'Old long since'."

And over Jude's consolatory voice—"I'm sorry . . ."—Kaldeep emitted a high peal of laughter. "That doesn't even make sense," he said. "It's 'days gone by.'"

Donna was on her feet and shouting. "That question is ambiguous." She was shaking. "That is a basic translation. I gave the literal one. And it's not even your turn, Kaldeep, so you can't answer."

"Ah, Donna, don't be a sore loser." Kaldeep sunk easily back into his chair, stretching out his long legs so that the polished tips of his shoes could be seen protruding from the other side of the table.

Donna could feel all her blood rising to her face. Her ears were ringing with it. "Jude, they've been mocking us since we started—it's antagonistic. They should be disqualified."

Jude reached out his steadying hands. "OK, OK. Listen . . ."

Then Priya was out of her seat too. In the audience, small noises arose in a whispered and excited crossfire, relishing the prospect of a punishment.

Donna cast a triumphant look over to her teammates, but their small, downcast faces were contorting in what looked like embarrassment. Well, what was their problem? Did they want to win this match or not?

Priya's face was as serene as ever. "Donna, is it?" she said. "I'm afraid 'days gone by' is the official answer."

"I don't care what the 'official' answer is. The phrasing of the question is obscure. Don't you have anyone checking these things for you?"

Priya took a moment to compose her expression, but her features were growing tight. "Well, maybe we can have a further—Jude?"

Priya excused herself and Jude to "deliberate". A hesitant chatter resumed around the room, and Donna sat down, but remained stiff and upright, her knees knocking the underside of the table.

When Priya and Jude finally parted, Jude stepped obediently back to the bar, clasping his clipboard at this thigh, and Priya came forward. Pressing the tips of her fingers together in a display of diplomacy, she rose her resonant voice above the noise.

"We award two points to the Red Hot Quizzy Peppers for providing a satisfactory answer to the question—which may, indeed, be interpreted ambiguously." She displayed the downturn of her black eyelashes in what looked like regret. "And I believe that concludes this match."

In an uncertain applause, Harry, Bryony, Luke, and Jaime all exchanged quick glances with each other—a language Donna wasn't invited to understand. The Bombay Bad Boys silently left their table, sending the Quizzy Peppers malevolent backward glares.

Donna waited for the relief of the victory to spread through her limbs, but it didn't come; she was still in a fury. "I hope the other matches will be conducted better than this," she said before Priya slinked away.

"We do have penalties for unsportsmanlike behavior, Donna," Priya said, folding her arms. "Do bear that in mind."

"Is that a—" She had been about to say "threat", but suddenly Bryony was at her side, with a tentative hand held on her shoulder, as if Donna were a bomb about to detonate.

"Come on, now, Donna. That's enough, isn't it?"

Donna pulled back her hair from the clammy nape of her neck, shrugging away Bryony's hand. She told herself that they had won— they had won, for God's sake—and wasn't that the most important thing?

CHAPTER ELEVEN

Question: *Originating in New Orleans, what word is derived from coquetier, a French egg cup, from which a mixed brandy drink was served?*
Answer: *Cocktail*

"So you want to hear how I want the ground to open up and swallow me? I want the ground to open up and swallow me, OK? But that Kaldeep made me so angry with his stupid . . . Anyway. I can't do anything about it now, and that's just the way it is. You want to kick me off the team, then alright—I guess I deserve that."

Jaime watched Donna suck on her cigarette as they stood in line for the Ministry of Cocktails—some sort of bar or club that stood modestly in between a hairdresser's and a vaping shop, a hundred yards away from the Five Bells—with a sparse line of drunk-looking, swaying people.

"Look," Harry had asserted back at the pub, when most of the audience had dispersed for better things and the five of them had loitered around the bar, not knowing what to say to each other. "Look, why don't we all get out of here? Besides, we got something to celebrate. Well, don't we?" And then he said he knew "just the place." And even Luke had swiftly drained his pint, wiping his damp fingers on his wrinkled T-shirt, and nodded along with the rest of them. Jaime had given him a bright grin of encouragement, realizing, too late, that she was trying too hard.

"It's hardly a case of 'kicking you off the team,'" Bryony said now, hugging herself either against a chill or in the same self-consciousness Jaime felt about this bar (and could you wear a rainbow sweater in a bar like this? Or in any bar for that matter?). "If you want to know what I think, well—tensions have been running high; it's all been very stressful."

Donna had turned to face the row of stalled traffic on the road. The winking red brake lights lit up her cheeks and nose and tinged her blonde hair pink. "It's been wonderful. I get pretty bored of things, you know? But not this."

Once admitted inside by a bouncer who formed a sheer wall of shoulder and chest muscle over the entrance, they settled into a corner of black leather seating. And while Jaime, Bryony, and Luke perched awkwardly on the edges of their chairs, all squinting and raising their voices over the relentless, palpitating throb of a heavy bass speaker, Donna and Harry goaded each other into dancing to a vintage Kylie Minogue track. They flung their swaying arms high in abandon and linked hands to spin each other in dizzying, joyful circles, as Donna's chiffon skirt whirled prettily around her ankles.

When they returned with a wobbling tray of tequila shots, Harry announced, "To the Fab Four!," holding a dripping shot glass aloft. And their cheers and smiles and calls of affirmation were genuine, as they dutifully threw back their heads to swallow with wincing grimaces of thanks.

"Five," Jaime corrected him.

"Sorry?"

"You said 'Fab Four'—there are five of us."

"Oh, sorry," he said, and Donna let out a bark of laughter.

Jaime's spine loosened as she basked in the warm pleasure of sentimentality. Yes, she thought, these people are my friends. She put a hand on Luke's thigh; it was time.

"Well, as long as we're celebrating, we have some news," she said brightly, but her smile faltered.

"Oh my God, you're pregnant," Donna said, slamming down her shot glass.

"No, no. Nothing like that. No, we're—well, Luke, I mean—Luke has finished with his awful job at the sports center. He's a free man."

Bryony's eyes dashed nervously between them. "What do you mean?" Luke sat in an unmoving slump that wasn't anything like celebration. "Well, he quit."

There was a silence that Jaime had not expected, and she quickly hid her mouth with her drink.

Donna spoke first. "Well, Luke, I can't say it ever occurred to me that you weren't a free man to begin with. Did you get another job?"

"I took on some extra shift work," said Jaime. "Luke's going to find his calling." And she instantly regretted using such a supercilious little phrase, because, sure enough, Donna snatched it up.

"Oh," she said, and then smiled. "Oh, I see. His calling."

*   *   *

Donna had never heard anything so ridiculous, and the two of them—Luke and Jaime—looking at each other, holding hands and grinning like teenagers, made it all the more nauseating.

"So what are you going to do?" she demanded. "Paint? Write? Join a band?"

Jaime tugged on her ear. "Well, he's going to—"

"Why do you think it is," Donna interrupted her, "that you always feel the need to speak for him?"

Jaime looked into her lap, her round cheeks quivering in the wobble of her chin. Harry and Bryony began to protest all at once.

"Oh, come on now . . ."

". . . completely unnecessary, Donna . . ."

". . . Hasn't tonight been stressful enough?"

Donna laid her scarlet-tipped fingers on the tabletop to restore order. "All I'm saying, is that it would be interesting to hear what Luke has to say about the whole thing. I can ask a thing like that, can't I?"

"Well, I suppose it's not anything to do with us, anyway," Bryony said, but her steady face, held in a tightly composed grin, looked unconvinced. "We wish you all the best, Luke."

"Oh for—" Donna flung her hands onto her knees.

She'd done it again. Harry had started to look around the room, deliberately indifferent, and Bryony took an unnatural amount of interest in inspecting the chewed wedge of lime in her shot glass. Would she always be made to feel so unreasonable? And when would the whole world stop tiptoeing around each other? She was certain of one thing: if you were going to walk out of your job and let your girlfriend pay for it (and wouldn't they all be so lucky to be able to do something like that?), then you better have something to say for yourself.

And then Luke finally opened his mouth, looking around as if just becoming aware of them all. "The truth is, I don't know what I'm going to do, but I'm going to find out." He laid his hand on Jaime's knee, gave it a determined shake. "And with Jaime's help, I think we'll figure this whole thing out."

Jaime's face filled with hope as she covered his hand with hers. It was as though she was performing a perfect little demonstration of courage. Look, she seemed to be saying, look how doting and loyal I am. Look what I'm willing to sacrifice.

"And anyway," said Luke, "I'm not sure you can overestimate the value of getting out of a situation you're unhappy with—you know, mental health and all that."

Donna nodded, her smile serene. It might have been the most he had ever said. But oh, you little prick, she thought, what do you know about mental health?

* * *

As Donna, Bryony, and Jaime set about discussing the thing from a practical angle—what exactly would they do for money? Jaime had taken on a "twilight shift' at the super-market apparently—Harry leaned into Luke's shoulder.

"No, but really, mate," he said. "I'm happy for you. You're right: life's too short to hate what you do. Tell you one thing, though—unemployment isn't all it's cracked up to be."

"Yeah. No, I can see that."

"Just got to keep motivated. Wake up in the morning, have a routine—that sort of thing. You'll figure it out. And Jaime's happy, right?"

"Well, it was her idea."

"There you go then. That's the most important thing."

Harry hoped he had conveyed how necessary it was to keep Jaime happy at all costs. Because who knew? Late one night, Luke might look up from clipping his toenails to find that Jaime had lost all respect for him.

If he could rewind to the night Vivienne had come home to tell him about New York, he would have stood up (and he wouldn't have been wearing his dressing gown) and said something spirited and fearless—"That sounds brilliant. When do we leave?" What frightening things, lurking in New York, could possibly be worse than the way things were now? His stagnant, toothpaste-splattered bathroom; his distant, other-worldly friends; the silent gray dawn or dusk out the window—these were the most frightening things of all.

"Anyway," Luke said. "What's new with you? Any interviews yet?"

"No. Well, sort of. Might have something in the pipeline."

"Oh yeah?"

"Back where I used to work. Friend of mine says they're rehiring."

Luke exhaled, his breath producing a low whistle over the top of his bottle. "Didn't they fire you?"

"I wasn't *fired*. I was made re*dun*dant. And it's no fun not being able to make rent, mate."

Luke's smile fell away. "No, I guess it's not."

Harry wiped his mouth and felt a shuddering wave of loss.

* * *

Jaime's mouth was sour with tequila. Harry excused himself for the bar, where Jude from the Five Bells was perched on a stool, and Bryony and Donna were engaged in a replay of the quiz match.

"I thought they'd be happier for us," she said to Luke.

"Who cares? We're happy for us."

And while she supposed he was right, she couldn't dispel the gnawing feeling that she'd somehow done something wrong. And more than that—that they now looked down on Luke. It wasn't only Donna either. The others might be too polite to say so, but she could see it in the slight rise of Bryony's eyebrows, in how Harry drew his mouth to one side and sucked on a side tooth.

All her life she had told herself—usually while facing herself sternly in bathroom mirrors—that it didn't matter what anyone else thought of her, as long as she was happy. And that was fine and everything, but when did the "happy" bit start happening? It seemed as if she were always climbing a wall to it, making the necessary adjustments along the way—a different foothold here, a new handhold there, inching sideways for a better grip. Surely the summit had to be reached soon. Did anyone else feel this way? It didn't seem so—not in the way Donna effortlessly wore her clothes, not in the measured certainty of Bryony's voice, and definitely not in Harry's ability to make his jokes in all the right places.

"Listen," Luke said, patting his pockets until he located his keys. "I'm heading home."

"Oh, do you want me to come with you?"

"No, no. You stay. I'll see you later. And, look—I love you, alright? We'll be fine."

"OK. I mean, I love you too."

As soon as Luke left the room, Jaime pressed her hands between her thighs, her limbs all at once feeling as though they were adrift on water.

CHAPTER TWELVE

Question: *At what temperature does glass start to melt?*
Answer: *1400 degrees Celsius*

"I'm not saying you should marry him or anything," said Donna. "I mean, do what you want. I just think you're putting a lot on the line. And listen, women have been putting themselves on the line for men for centuries—and for what?"

Jaime pinched the bridge of her nose as she held a third dripping shot glass in her loose hand. "Donna, I just don't . . . I know what you're saying, but he's never even mentioned it—getting married, I mean. And look, I really can't afford these drinks."

Donna slid the top knot from her hair, shaking it free. She waved a dismissive hand. "A man isn't going to ask a woman to marry him when he's already getting all the benefits of having a wife. Why would he? He already has everything he wants."

"But that's a horrible thing to say. Because he loves me? Because he cares what I—"

"Well, but, Donna," Bryony said, full of reason, "that would imply no man wants to get married at all. I just don't think that's true."

"If he wanted to marry Jaime," Donna continued, "he would have asked her. Men are incredibly focused when they want something."

"I don't want to pressure him," said Jaime, but her attempt at conviction was ruined by a small whimper in her voice that revealed the need for reassurance.

"'Pressure.' For God's sake, why are women always treating men as if they're made of glass?"

"And it wouldn't be a surprise or anything nice like that."

"You've been together for—what? Five years?"

Jaime hesitated. "Eight."

"That ship has sailed, don't you think? Listen, Jaime. Don't be the cool girl. She's a myth."

"The what?"

"The cool girl. The girl who loves watching football and giving blow jobs and is totally fine with her unemployed boyfriend sitting round in his pants all day—because she's just *so cool*. She doesn't exist. And if she does, let me tell you—she's the most miserable girl in the world."

In a wobbling display of defiance, Jaime said, "Well, are you seeing anyone?"

"What?"

"I said, are you seeing anyone?"

Her mouth drawing into a small bud of reluctance, Donna's gaze strayed over Jaime's shoulder. "No. Why would I?"

"You just seem to know an awful lot about relationships for someone who doesn't have a boyfriend. When *was* your last boyfriend?"

"I haven't had a boyfriend—not anyone worth calling a boyfriend anyway. Why would I want one? All they do is tie you down until they find something or someone better, or let you down in whatever way they can. Most people are better off on their own, don't you think?"

"What about Harry?" Jaime asked.

Donna swallowed. "What about him?"

"Aren't you two sort of . . . you know."

"No. We're not anything. Look, why is this about me all of a sudden?"

Bryony, whose eyes had been flicking between Donna and Jaime, stood up abruptly. "Drink, anyone? I think I'm going to get a drink."

* * *

Having ended his shift at the Five Bells, Jude had joined them "to celebrate," and the man was beaming, his two freckled cheeks as hard and plump as apples. They were the only team, he said, to have made it to the quarter-final from the South London division.

"And you come from *my* pub," he said to Harry at the bar. "I've been doing this three years now, and no one's ever made it. And a year we're hosting too. Seriously, mate, I'm made up."

"No thanks to Donna." Harry made a noise in his throat. "Bloody mortifying."

"Oh, she's just—you know—a hothead. If she hadn't argued that question you might not have won."

"Yeah, OK. OK."

"Are you and her . . .?"

"Oh no, no, nothing like that. Not sure she's really after anything anyway. But truth is, sort of got complicated with my last—you know—my last girlfriend."

Harry sucked up the dregs of a syrupy, purple cocktail, and he had another lined up—they were, after all, cheap, but his tongue felt so thick and dry that the thought of more alcohol had him shuddering. He was already drunk, and all his thoughts were occupied by Vivienne. And now Jude was talking about something else, and Harry had no idea what it was. Thankfully, Bryony came up between them, tugging on the hem of her white fitted T-shirt.

"Bryony," Harry said, licking his lips. "Listen—Jude's very proud of us. Very proud."

"You're the only team," Jude said again, "from the South London division to have made it to the quarter-final."

Bryony ducked her head. "Oh no, well—you're really terrific out there too. I don't know how you keep track of everything."

Jude's wide smile showed all of his teeth as he gave his head a modest little shake. "Oh well, you know, it's nothing special."

"No, I mean it. It's very impressive."

"What about you? I've never seen you miss a history question."

"I'm sure that's not true . . ."

"Tell me something, Bryony," Harry said suddenly. "Tell me something. And—you know—don't beat around the bush or anything. I want you to be completely honest."

"Alright."

"What the hell do you people want from us?"

"I'm not sure I—"

"Women, I mean. Wait . . ."

He couldn't believe it. He kneaded both his eyeballs with his thumbs. At the far end of the bar was a small gaggle of Vivienne's yoga buddies from her Crystal Palace days. The one with the long brown ponytail was Melinda, and that other one was Jenny or Julie or something like that.

"'Scuse me a sec," he said, and lurched toward them.

*   *   *

Bryony watched Harry as he swayed up to a group of uninterested-looking women, who gave him small and uneasy smiles of recognition.

Jude gave a small chuckle of derision before turning his attention back to her. "I've not seen you around before the League started. You local?"

Jude was tall, muscled, and deeply freckled, and he had tried to disguise the thinning of his auburn hair by keeping it a little too long on top. Some sort of scar had deformed the outer edge of his left ear, leaving a bulbous fold of skin. She didn't know how such a small, strange detail could seem attractive, but it was—perhaps because it suggested a past on a scrappy rugby field or getting into teenage scrapes.

"Oh, I am. I'm just mainly home with my . . . with my kids. Excuse me . . ." She caught the bartender's attention. "Can I have a gin and tonic, please?"

"How old're your kids?"

"Arthur's eleven. Lydia's thirteen."

"You're having me on. What are you? Twenty-seven, twenty-eight?"

She smiled. "Bit more than that."

"Well, I'm forty-five. Can you beat that?" He sipped at his beer. "I have a boy myself. He's eighteen. I'm divorced, though." He looked distantly forward. "Coming up nine years now. Listen, that drink's on me, OK?"

*   *   *

"So . . . so she, like, never comes back for the yoga stuff or anything?" Harry was saying to the woman he thought was Melinda.

"I don't think so." Melinda inspected the gold rings on several of her fingers. "She found some new classes in Streatham."

"Well, she found a whole bunch of new things in Streatham, didn't she?"

And Melinda either looked intensely bored or sympathetic. The trouble was, the image of her had started to split into two wobbling, violet-lit portraits, and he couldn't be sure which one was real.

"Sorry," he said. "I'm sorry. I'm just trying to—you know—make sense of how a thing like that can happen. With him of all people. Don't you people have any standards?"

Melinda might have been nodding, but the purple image of her also might have been moving of its own accord.

"I don't know what to tell you, Harry. She seems pretty happy now. She's moved on. It's a shame you can't do the same."

*   *   *

And then Bryony was asking Jude what his son's name was (Dexter), and what he was doing with his life ("He wants to be a nursery teacher; can you believe that?"), and she wondered did the school years get any better? Because she swore Lydia and Arthur were turning into psychopaths. She noted how lovely it was when Jude shook his head and ran a finger over his top lip as he recounted a story of how funny it had been when Dexter said or did something or another when he was three or five years old. And how concerned he looked, his pale eyebrows drawing together, when he wondered if Dexter was making enough friends at college ("He's always been on the quiet side"). And before she knew it, he was buying her a second gin and tonic when she couldn't remember finishing her first.

*   *   *

"So what you mean is," Jaime was saying over a relentless bass note that was starting to throb painfully behind her eye sockets, "he doesn't love me?"

Donna shrugged. "How would I know? Do you think he does?"

"I know you're trying to help me and everything, but—"

"I mean, do what you want, Jaime."

"OK, OK. But—you know—you don't know anything about mine and Luke's relationship and I—"

"I don't need to. I've seen it a billion times before."

"Well, OK. But everyone's an individual, everyone's a—"

"He's a child, Jaime. And so are you."

*　　*　　*

"I just wish me and his mum got along better," Jude said. "You don't think they'll notice when they're little, but they do. And then suddenly they're teenagers and—Do you know what Dexter said to me the other day? He said, 'You don't know what love is.' It nearly killed me. And I'm thinking—did the divorce entirely mess him up?"

"Well, that seems a bit sinister," said Bryony. "My kids will be ruined if that's the case."

Jude drew his fingertips over his closed lips again, flicking his gaze intently from one of her eyes to the other. "You're divorced?"

"No, no. I just don't . . . I don't think me and my husband get along very well."

He nodded at her second empty glass. "Same again?"

"Yes. Please. That'd be nice."

*　　*　　*

"Just let me ask you one thing, Melinda."

"It's Maria."

*　　*　　*

When Jaime's shoulders started to tremble in tears, Donna felt the uncomfortable grip of guilt in her lungs.

"Well, alright," she said, trying to shield Jaime behind one of her shoulders in case Bryony saw her and came running over. "There's no need to get dramatic about it. It's just a conversation."

*　　*　　*

Over Jude's shoulder, Bryony made out the dim image of Harry, tilting on his heels while he jabbed a pointed finger into the air. The girl with the brown ponytail clutched her hands fearfully to her collarbones.

"Oh dear. I'm not sure if I should . . ."

Jude followed her gaze. "Looks like he needs to get out of here—but listen, can I get your number? No funny business. It's not often I get to talk about Dexter and everything."

"Oh, I—actually, Jude, maybe it's not . . . well, OK. Sure. Why not?"

* * *

Using the cuff of her sleeve to blot black-stained tears from her cheeks, Jaime took a shuddering breath. The problem was, she couldn't seem to meet Donna's eyes; she felt every painfully diminutive year younger and more foolish than Donna was.

And then, as the music faded between tracks, she heard a shouting voice at the far end of the bar. It was Harry. "And the crazy thing is," he was saying, "I bet *you* knew before *I* did."

* * *

Donna shouldered through a dozen people to Harry. There were three or four huddled women, casting pitying looks at him, and a broad-shouldered man with two gold earrings through his thick earlobes who stepped out of the shadows to defend them. "I'd watch your mouth if I were you, mate," he said.

Donna wrenched Harry away by one of his slippery hands. "Let's go home, love."

Harry shook her off, raking all ten fingers over his scalp as if to hold in his brains. "Yeah, yeah. Alright."

Back at their table, Bryony was crouching down beside Jaime, whispering something into the fallen curtain of her hair. Jaime lifted her face, her black-smudged eyes squinting up at Donna.

"You're a horrible, horrible person," Jaime said. And although it seemed as if the bass through the speakers should have ceased its thudding and the purple lights should have snapped off to allow them all a sobering moment, the Ministry of Cocktails persisted to pulse around them. People continued to drunkenly shout above the music and bottles; glasses and ice cubes continued to clink behind the bar.

Jaime's face was small and fearful, and it was all Donna's fault.

CHAPTER THIRTEEN

Question: *Which song by American pop rock band Sixpence None the Richer was first released in August 1998?*
Answer: *"Kiss Me"*

In the silence of her bathroom, Bryony brushed her teeth, swaying in tiredness. Jaime hadn't wanted to talk about it, so, with relief, Bryony had let her go, standing watch from the top of Gipsy Hill until Jaime's slouching, shuffling figure became too small to see.

Bryony inspected her hair in the mirror—had it been this frizzed and shapeless when she'd been talking to Jude? And to what extent had the dim lighting of the bar obscured the stray eyebrow hairs that needed plucking and the way her T-shirt emphasized the bulging lip of soft belly above the waistband of her jeans? With the frothing toothbrush dangling from her teeth, she swept her hair to one side and smiled as if she'd been told something delightfully funny; she brought her fingertips to her chin to appear deeply engrossed—and this is what she may have looked like through Jude's eyes. And wasn't it genuine—the way her pupils flicked around with interest? Weren't her teeth white and straight, and all her responses intelligent?

She spat out her toothpaste and blew her nose. Silly—she was being silly.

As she lay in her cold bed, the room began to swim in the dark, and Glen, turning over in his sleep, smacked his lips.

There had been a moment tonight—maybe two—when she had imagined Jude leaning over to kiss her. And, oh, perhaps that was wrong, but what was the use in feeling guilty when she knew it would never happen anyway? She hadn't even wanted him to, for God's sake. She had just wondered what it would have been like.

With a zip of pleasure that sang down the length of her spine and settled, buzzing, somewhere over her hipbones, she rolled over and tried to find Glen's face in the dark. And there were his lips, chapped by the cold, emitting a stale smell (had he brushed his teeth?). She lightly kissed him anyway and his mouth moved against hers until he let out a small grunt and scratched his jaw.

"Mm, my belly hurts," he said. "What time is it?"

"Almost one."

"Hmm."

"We won the match. We're in the quarter-final."

But he was on his back and snoring. Disappointment rolled up in her throat like a wave of heartburn or indigestion. If it subsided quickly, she might be asleep in a minute or two, but it crept higher, up into her prickling nostrils, and then leaked behind her eyes, until she had to cry, suddenly and vigorously, far on her side of the bed. When it became clear the tears were becoming a little too self-indulgent, she stopped and wiped her nose.

She checked the time on her phone (1:15 a.m.), and then opened a new message window.

It was good to chat to you earlier. Hope you have a good night.

It would be grossly inappropriate to add a kiss, so she didn't, and ridiculous to stay awake to wait for his reply, so she didn't do that either.

*   *   *

Jaime hoped the cold walk home would diffuse some of her anger. But her tears came faster as she tottered down the steep pavement in the dark, where curious passers-by sent her sideways glances of concern. A lone teenaged girl slowed her hurrying footsteps, perhaps to ask her if she was OK, but instead flicked up the hood of her sweatshirt and carried on.

Why did other, better women seem to have the dignified ability to hold back their tears? She was certain of one thing: Luke was not going to see her like this, and so she silently opened the front door and sat on the steps of the dirt-trampled communal hallway, waiting for the worst of it to pass. But then the ground-floor neighbor, a graying, middle-aged woman whom Jaime had scarcely met, peeped around the edge of her front door to investigate the noise of Jaime's crying. Jaime reassured her that yes, she was fine; no, she didn't want some tea; and yes, really, she was fine.

When her face had returned to its normal temperature and the painful hitches of her breathing had ceased, Jaime climbed the staircase and let herself into the flat. The grinding, zipping sounds of an F1 video game spilled out into the narrow hall, and Luke's muddied shoes sat tossed to one side and the other of the laminate floor.

Luke sat in the middle of the sofa, peeling a hard-boiled egg between his knees and depositing damp pieces of broken eggshell onto the coffee table, his glasses flashing from the display on the television screen. He muttered something under his breath as the car onscreen took a corner too widely and skidded over a stretch of neon green pixelated grass.

The worst part of all this—rather than the muddy shoes or the video game or the foul-smelling egg—was that he didn't even notice she was home. Could this man ever be expected to do anything an adult was supposed to do? Oh, Donna may be egotistical and malicious and maybe even crazy, but it didn't stop her being right.

"Hi," she said from the doorway.

"Oh, hi." He didn't break eye contact with the television. "How was it?"

"Pretty bad, if I'm honest."

"Oh yeah?"

She could have told him that she'd called Donna a "horrible person," but she was deeply embarrassed. He'd discover it eventually, but that didn't need to happen tonight.

"Why are you still up?" she said. "It's past one."

"I dunno."

"Shouldn't you get some sleep or something?"

"Yeah, I will. I just—Shit, that hairpin is insane."

"*Luke.*"

"What?"

She composed herself. "Do you, like . . . You do think about the future and stuff, don't you?"

Luke hit the mute button, the white wobbling egg held in his lap. "Sure I do. I mean . . . well, in what way?"

Jaime dragged her heels over the frayed laces of her Converses, pulling the cuffs of her sleeves over her hands. "Do you ever think about getting married? I feel like—don't you think that I'm putting a lot on the line here, to make you happy?"

And his white face looked so stricken that Jaime wasn't sure she would be able to forget it or ever stop wondering what it meant.

"I mean, yes," he said carefully. "Yes, I do."

"I know we're still finding our feet . . . but how does two years strike you?"

"Strike me for what?"

"Well," she said shyly. "For an engagement, obviously."

His blinking face told her there was nothing obvious about it. "Aren't these things supposed to be a surprise?"

And although she had used the exact same line of argument with Donna ("It wouldn't be a surprise or anything nice like that"), it suddenly seemed unacceptable. What was going on here? Was his "Yes, I do" an answer to wanting to marry her or thinking she had put a lot on the line? And shouldn't the answer be yes to both anyway? So she found herself using Donna's own line of attack, putting her hands on her hips for emphasis.

"After eight years, don't you think that ship has sailed?"

"I'm just not sure about it—the time frame, I mean. Shouldn't we be more focused on a house deposit or something?"

"But that would take ages."

"I don't know what you want me to say."

But it seemed as though anything—*anything*—he could have said would have been better than this.

"Look," he said. "We just have to have some—you know—trust in each other. Everything is heading in the right direction, don't you think? And that's the whole point of this thing, isn't it? This idea of yours—for me to 'find myself'—it's to get to where we want to be."

"Sure. Yeah, OK. I just . . . I felt like we should have the conversation."

"OK, good. Me too." And then the grinding volume of his beloved cars resumed.

She told him she was going to bed, and he said he would be there in a minute. And it occurred to her, as she went about the business of brushing her hair and shaking out her pajamas, that they had never defined what "finding yourself" meant.

*　　*　　*

Perched on the windowsill of a long-shutdown shop with Donna, between a brightly lit newsagent's and a darkened Nepalese restaurant, Harry's sinuses felt plugged with rubber. He consciously fought to keep his eyelids open, but they involuntarily drifted shut until he was drooping sideways into Donna's shoulder.

When his phone buzzed in his inside jacket pocket with a call, his loose, fumbling fingers dropped it into a stain of ketchup or barbecue sauce at his feet.

Donna picked it up. "It says 'Mum.'"

"Oh shit. Oh no." Harry took the full weight of his head in his hands. He could hardly hold his brains together, but then he heard Donna's clipped and assured voice.

"Mrs. West? Hi. This is Donna. I'm a friend of Harry's and—Oh, he's fine. Really, he's fine. We've just been out with some other friends and he's popped to the loo—Oh. Oh, I see." Donna held the phone between her knees. "She's been texting you since five," she whispered, before whipping it up again. "Honestly, he's absolutely fine. Men, right? I'll tell him off for you, I promise. I'll tell him to call you first thing . . . Absolutely . . . Well, you don't leave your mum hanging around, do you? . . . Exactly! . . . Alright. And please don't worry. Bye . . . bye now."

Donna dug through Harry's elbow and shoved the phone back inside his windbreaker pocket. "Well—you owe me. Poor woman. She sounded frantic."

"Yeah, yeah. Alright." His eyes ached. "I mean, you know, thanks."

"It's fine." She got up, dusting the seat of her skirt. "Shall we go?"

Once he'd consumed enough bottled water and Mars Bars from the newsagent's to restore a sense of normality, they were plodding the steep stretch of Belvedere Road toward Donna's flat, where tall Victorian villas—some decaying, others kept in freshly painted magnificence—towered high above the streetlights.

"Well, look, I was just trying to *help* Jaime," Donna was saying from behind the upturned collar of her suede coat. "But then she got all defensive and—did you hear what she said to me? It's not *my* fault if Luke won't commit to her. Honestly, if he had any sense of . . ."

And she said a great many things, seeming to flit between deep irritation and brushing the whole thing off as "just pointless and immature really—we all got a bit too drunk."

"And did you . . ." She started to laugh. "When you said 'the Fab Four,' did you forget about Luke?"

"No. Well, OK—yes."

"Oh, that's hilarious. I knew it. I like your moves, by the way," she said, and Harry couldn't help but tease out more of her bright laughter in a pantomime of his Kylie Minogue dancing until they reached Donna's red front door, in a tall, semi-detached Victorian conversion.

"Oh, this is me here. You coming up?"

The first sight of Donna's living room would have been unremarkable—a handsomely polished cabinet supported a cluster of potted plants and several framed prints hung in thoughtful arrangements on the walls—if it hadn't been for the strew of wrinkled, plastic sheeting encasing the base of the chimney breast. Several large chunks of pink plaster had been hacked off and lay crumbling on the floor, revealing plaques of yellow brickwork beneath. Was he supposed to ask about this thing or what?

"Scuse me a minute," Donna said, and she wandered past him into a small, white bathroom and shut the door behind her.

And then another door opened and a tall, dark-haired girl in short jersey pajamas came striding out to thump a curled fist against the bathroom door.

"Don-na! Don-na!" Receiving no reply, the girl whirled round to Harry, causing her long ponytail to whip her cheek. "Do you see this?"

she said, gesturing furiously at the chimney breast. "Four weeks. Four weeks and . . ." she slapped the flat of her hand against the bathroom door, "she thinks it's OK to keep us living in a construction site. Don-na! Don-na! Who are you?"

"Me? Oh, I'm Harry."

"Boyfriend?"

"Oh, no. I mean . . . no."

"You know she's crazy? It's the wall and the paintings and 'Oh, I'm going to sand the floor,' and the—You see these plants? She bought thirty of them and now they're all dead. And don't get me started on the bills. But of course it's 'Oh, Bernadette . . .'" she threaded her fingers together and brought them up to one cheek in simpering mock affection, "'. . . oh, let's open a bottle of wine and we'll be best friends now', and things are cool for a while, but do you think I ever see that bill money?"

The girl—Bernadette?—left a slice of silence, and Harry wasn't sure if he was supposed to answer.

"And then the sleeping and crying just start all over again. Oh, and don't think I haven't threatened to move out."

She strutted into the kitchen, where she opened several cupboards and clapped them shut again, muttering in another language. Then she strode back out into the room from where she'd come, slamming the door behind her.

It took several more minutes for Donna to emerge, after the sounds of a flushing toilet and a running tap. When she did, she rolled her eyes and gestured for him to follow her into her own bedroom. One bright blue wall dominated the other three white ones, and layers of luxurious clothing hung from the top of a pine wardrobe, some with expensive-looking tags of thick cardboard looped with ribbon still attached. Donna threw herself onto the duvet of the large double bed, among half a dozen cushions.

"That your flatmate?"

"Don't get me started," she said. "And she can afford the bills, you know—she's loaded. She's a member of Loft– you've heard of it? You know, that private members' club in Mayfair? Anyway, they've got all kinds of—I guess it started as a nightclub—you know, a seriously exclusive one; the guys have to wear jackets—and now, well, it's an *institution*. Yoga mornings, Christmas brunch . . . *you* know. Anyway, she's getting me a guest pass."

And since Harry could not make sense of most of what Donna was saying, or of what Bernadette had said about Donna (what was the sleeping and the crying and the not paying the bills all about?), he shrugged and said, "Alright."

Donna started to pad around the room, wiping off her makeup and unpicking various pieces of jewelry from her ears and wrists and from around her neck, and he lingered over the chaotic surface of her desk. Here were neon Post-it notes containing instructions or ideas or reminders: *Look up repointing*; *DIY cabinet doors*; *Half marathon? June?* And several thick books sat piled against the wall—*The Winning Mindset*, *Habits of the Happy*, *The Power of Now*—topped by a murky cup of cold coffee.

While rubbing circles of some white cream onto her forehead, Donna started to say something about "transforming your thinking" and "becoming more present" and "sort of a modern guide to spirituality," and he realized she was talking about one of the books.

A notebook lay open too, with a hasty list written in biro.

Matisse, Danseuse debout, accoudée —£1,000
Franz Ecker, various —£580
Chagall, Bonjour Paris —£700
Xenia Hausner, Red White Red —£750

"What do you think?" she asked from behind him.

"About what?"

"These pieces." She came up behind him to run a fingernail down the list. "Are you familiar with any?"

"Can't say I am."

She opened the lid of a laptop to show him a penciled image of a stocky dancer in a stiff, flowered tutu who leaned her pinched face against her hand, explaining it was a Matisse lithograph that she "had her eye on."

"Kind of pricey," he said.

She shrugged. "Don't you think art is an investment? Besides, I think she's beautiful."

Convinced he didn't possess the vocabulary to contradict her, it was easier to agree.

"You're quiet," she said.

"Well, listen—you were a bit full on tonight."

"What about you? Starting fights in bars. Who were those women anyway?"

"Friends of my ex."

"Oh, Harry."

"Alright. Leave it, yeah?"

She danced away to the bed. "We don't have to talk about such boring things, do we?"

"I'm not sure we should do this."

"Do what?"

He could not tell her, but his head was full of Vivienne all the time—of imagined conversations and reenacted encounters, of the flirtatious dart of her gaze and the soft fall of her hair on her shoulder. There wasn't room for anything else. He wasn't sure if he would ever feel at peace again without her.

Harry nodded at the bed. "You know."

Looking embarrassed (for him or herself, it was hard to tell), Donna snickered dismissively.

"I just think . . . you know," Harry continued, gesturing to himself and then to her. "I'm a mess. You're a mess. Maybe we should just sort of . . . not?"

Donna's head snapped up, the hard blue of her eyes accusatory. "I'm not a mess. *You're* a mess."

"Look, I just meant . . . Doesn't matter."

Donna's eyes turned suddenly round and unblinking. She sucked in her bottom lip. "Will you still stay with me? Just to sleep."

"Oh, I . . . sure, OK. But I mean, why?"

"I just . . . I don't know. Sometimes I feel a bit—Look, why not?"

"Alright."

She straightened her back and as she shook away her hair with a flick of her head, the vulnerability dissolved from her face. "I really didn't mean to upset Jaime, you know. I just—well, I didn't realize she'd get so—I don't want to upset anyone."

"Bit harsh, though."

"Alright, well, I said sorry."

But had she? Harry only nodded. "OK if I lie down? Think I just want to pass out."

"Sure, go ahead. I'm going to stay up for a bit."

Harry fell asleep on Donna's bed, but at some point he woke up in the semidarkness, smacking his dry mouth and pulling strands of hair from his eyes. A pale blue light glowed in front of him, and when he squinted into its source, he made out Donna, swinging listlessly on the swivel chair at her desk, her face illuminated by a YouTube video. On the screen, an image of interlocking yellow and blue hexagons blinked with black letters. A clipped voice was saying, ". . . three colors on the board—two blues and a white. And it's Peter picking the next letter . . ." It took him a few minutes to realize she was watching an old episode of *Blockbusters*.

"What are you doing?" he whispered.

"Researching," she said without looking round at him. "We're in the quarter-final, in case you didn't notice."

"Not till April. We've got ages. Don't you have work in the morning? Aren't you going to get any sleep?"

"I'm almost done with series ten. Don't you think this is more important?"

CHAPTER FOURTEEN

Question: *Among some Roman Catholics, who is venerated as the patron saint of hopeless causes?*
Answer: *Saint Jude*

For the remainder of January, all through February and the beginning of March, Bryony and Glen reached an unspoken understanding that if they didn't talk about their problems, then those problems ceased to matter.

And Lydia never missed an opportunity to seethe at Bryony.

"I'm going to make brownies and blondies and rainbow cakes—"

"For what?"

"The end of term bake-off."

"How about cake pops?"

"You're so out of touch, Mum. No one does cake pops anymore."

And so what if Bryony had kept up a steady pattern of messaging Jude? And who cared if she sometimes misled Glen as to who it was that kept her so occupied?

"It's Jaime," she might say in an even voice, as she turned the screen of her phone away.

"What's there to talk about all the time?"

"If you must know, she's going through a horrible ordeal with Luke. The poor girl doesn't have anyone else to talk to."

Besides, it was true; sometimes she *was* messaging Jaime. So it didn't seem to matter. She couldn't help it if Jude was easier to speak to, if she could use half the number of words she had to use with Glen simply to be understood. When Arthur had come home with the shoulder of his school shirt ripped open one time, Glen had been as obtuse about it as possible.

"Do you think he's being bullied?" Bryony wondered.

"Well, by who?"

"How would I know? But do you think he is?"

"Because of his shirt?"

"Well, yes, Glen. Why else?"

But in a simple exchange with Jude:

Arthur came home from school today with his shirt ripped.
Poor kid. Speak to the teacher?

She wondered if parenting was supposed to be this confusing or whether it was because she was doing it with Glen. And if being friends with Jude made her happier, and if it made her less stressed, then what was the harm?

The trouble was, she wasn't entirely sure that Donna hadn't started to notice. One Thursday in February, when they had gathered at one of the ordinary quizzes to practice, Bryony had lingered a little too long at the bar with Jude after her drinks order had been filled, and Donna had narrowed her pale eyes as Bryony lowered the tray of glasses onto their table.

"You looked awfully cozy over there," she had said.

Bryony's face had turned warm as she'd busied herself with the handing out of drinks. And later, alone in the toilets, she had pounded her temple with two jabbing fingers, furious with herself.

And then suddenly it was the middle of March, and before Bryony knew it, it was the last week of school before the Easter break, and time for Lydia's parents' evening. And while it had always seemed like something to have to sit through—nodding pleasantly, injecting attentive queries when it seemed necessary ("And so that's when you transition to key stage four, is it?")—this particular evening became the source of a tension headache which grew sharper as the day wore on.

Bryony and Glen sat waiting on a row of classroom chairs in the school hall, among the echoing, politely hushed voices of a hundred or more teachers and parents. They were both tired and aching from the concentration the evening entailed, exchanging bickering remarks.

"Well, who understands verb tenses and—what-d'you-call-it—conjunctions anyway?" Glen said, looking down at his loafers.

"What do you mean? *I* do."

"What I mean is, it's hardly like you use them in the real world. It's not a practical skill."

"It's certainly a practical skill if she ever wants to come across as intelligent, Glen."

His nostrils flared. "Oh, I see, so I don't come across as intelligent. I see."

"Oh, for God's sake."

And now almost every one of Lydia's teachers had been sat down with, nodded at, empathized with and thanked, and the only one left to meet was Mr. Broderick—"the dickhead."

Bryony closely analyzed his conversation with the set of parents ahead of them. Mr. Broderick was startlingly young, with a pink, greasy complexion and an unfortunate sweep of fine, curling hair that stood up at all angles from the roots of his scalp and suggested the beginnings of baldness. He had the habit, too, of curling his lip contemptuously before starting his replies, as though he were continually having to explain something of a tedious nature.

Like an athlete studying the characteristics of their opponent, exposing all the ways they might be beaten, Bryony hoped that Mr. Broderick might be conquered this way.

Within another minute, he was beckoning Bryony and Glen forward.

"So," he began, straightening the cuffs of his thick flannel shirt, something which may have been purchased in a shop selling "country casuals," with an efficient little jerk. "Lydia. Lydia, Lydia, Lydia."

Did this funny little man have anything else to say?

"Let me be frank with you, Mr. and Mrs. Ward. If truth be told, we've had a very hard time with Lydia this term."

Bryony lifted her chin. "We know Lydia's no saint."

Mr. Broderick's lip curled up. "Lydia is disruptive, unmotivated, poorly organized . . ."

And the list continued, until Bryony started to wonder if a teacher was even allowed to say these things.

". . . failed to maintain even the lowest—"

"What do you think," Bryony said, finally having to interrupt him, "Lydia finds so challenging about your class? Is it not your role to motivate your pupils?"

"Well, now, listen, Bryony," Glen said, coming forward over the small desk to slice one of his hands between her and Mr. Broderick, as if to suggest something unreasonable might be taking place that he felt compelled to stop. "This is one of Lydia's *teachers*. I mean, we're not around, are we—during the lessons and whatnot? And Lydia's been pretty . . . well, rebellious lately. We all know that, don't we? There's no point in pretending otherwise."

"I believe Miss Twitchett had some recommendations about Lydia's home environment," Mr. Broderick continued, and out of the corner of her eye, Bryony could see Glen nodding his head rigorously.

Mr. Broderick leaned back in a smug little posture of satisfaction and Bryony felt her neck and cheeks grow hot. This man was only here to prove she was a bad mother; there was no other purpose for him—so why was Glen agreeing with him?

"She did," Glen confirmed. "That's what you said, wasn't it?" He turned to Bryony. "And I have to say, things haven't been plain sailing."

"Well." Bryony straightened in her chair. "Yes, I did tell you she said that, but I didn't necessarily *agree* with her."

But Mr. Broderick was nodding at Glen, smoothing back an unruly tuft of eyebrow hair. "I see it frequently, Mr. Ward. When there is conflict at home, the anxiety will naturally overspill into the classroom."

"Anxiety over what?"

"And I think she just needs to control her temper as much as anything," Glen was saying. "She can really—you know—really fly off the handle sometimes. If only she could calm down and *listen* to what people are saying. And if she doesn't get the best example of that at home—managing conflict and all that—then where else is it going to come from?"

"Well," Bryony said. "But 'managing conflict' is surely only part of—"

"Well, sure," Glen said. "But what I'm trying to get at is that Lydia's not developing the right skills to manage her—you know—her emotions."

"Seems like you've given this some practical thought, Mr. Ward."

"Oh, well—I'm no expert. No one gives you a parenting manual, do they? And as you all know, Bryony and I were only teenagers when we—"

"Well, alright!" Bryony stood up with such suddenness that her chair tipped precariously on its two slender legs before it clattered backwards onto the parquet floor. She was aware now that several other islands of teachers and parents, all with expressions of wide-eyed alarm, had turned round to look at her.

She had begun the evening with a plan of such control, but now it had evaporated, and if there was no opportunity to reclaim any dignity, then it might be more dignified for her to just go. There would be no arguing with these men—these proud, self-important men who only wanted to hear the sounds of their own voices.

She turned and strode out of the hall, taking pleasure in the efficient, unapologetic clicks of her heeled boots on the floor, under the astonished eyes of the other parents, whose mouths all seemed to form the same small "O." The problem was she'd forgotten her coat, but she couldn't weaken her exit by trotting back to the desk to retrieve it.

In the darkness of the car park, she found Glen's white van and sat in the silence of the passenger seat, taking gulps of air that smelled and tasted of damp earth. She put a cold hand to her forehead and tried to regain some control over her hammering heart.

Oh—oh, what had she done? The way all the other parents and teachers had looked at her. Images came to her of Lydia as a sweet two-year-old: her glossy dark head, the petal-soft plumpness of her cheeks and belly, one of her front milk teeth chipped from when she had fallen in the bath. What had taken place in the years between that two-year-old and the tiptoe-walking, angry, syrup-drinking teen? And as much as she might try to deny the influence of any "home environment," why was it that the other kids in Lydia's class weren't calling their teachers dickheads? Were their parents the sort that danced together in the kitchen as they made their lasagna dinners? Did they hold hands in public and sit thigh to thigh as they watched television on the sofa each night? Was Lydia absorbing all of the sarcastic, exasperated, corrosive bile that was exchanged between Bryony and Glen each day?

Bryony had been newly seventeen when she discovered she was pregnant with Lydia. The prospectus for Durham University still lay on the sitting-room coffee table, a pleasingly thick and luxurious booklet lovingly handled by her mother. She would run a fingernail over its silken pages and say things like, "See? Look what an exceptional life you will have here."

In her parents' bathroom, just beginning to come alight with the pink morning sun, Bryony had looped a meter of toilet paper around the used pregnancy test with steady, accepting hands, but there had been no disguising its shape—about the thickness and length of a dinner knife. She had tiptoed silently down the stairs and out through the back door. The chill of the early morning seeped up the fleece sleeves of her dressing grown and birdsong flittered to and fro above her head across the pale sky. And after pushing the bundle of tissue paper deep into the rubbish bin, her whole torso, from bowels to collarbones, had been gripped in a shudder that left her vomiting onto the grass.

She still recalled the conversation in her shadowed bedroom, four weeks before that, with seventeen-year-old Glen—who came from the local comprehensive sixth-form and not the grammar school Bryony attended. She had met him at the cinema, when his face had been full of tender pimples and Bryony's mouth had been full of braces. Bryony's mother only reluctantly tolerated him.

In the acrid heat from their bodies, he had tossed back the blanket, letting in a splash of cold air. "I don't—wait, *wait*," he had said. "I don't have a—"

"Oh, for God's sake, it doesn't matter."

"Are you sure?"

"Yes."

"I don't think—"

"It's *fine*."

How could she have ever explained to Glen the heart-seizing fear that seemed bound into the pages of the Durham University prospectus: that she would soon turn into the same mild-mannered, obedient adult that she had been as a child. She'd simply had to do something about it. But she'd lost that gamble.

Quickly after that—after the secret had been confessed and her mother had cried—a doctor's appointment had been scheduled and Glen's own parents consulted. Bryony would keep the baby, not necessarily because she was sure she wanted to, but more because she didn't know what to do and was paralyzed with the risk that she'd make another mistake. And then came the arrangements of where Bryony and Glen would live.

"Well, you can't stay here forever," her father had said, walking in circles around their living-room rug. "A growing family needs a space of their own. Besides, Glen needs to feel like—you know—the man of the house."

Bryony had studied for and passed her A Levels at home, knowing they might never be used, and when Lydia was almost a year old, Glen had been accepted into a landscaping firm's apprenticeship in South London and the deposit had been paid on their three-bedroom terrace in Anerley ("Well, it will do for the time being," Bryony's mother had said). On the day they moved in, Bryony had swayed in bewilderment through the empty rooms, touching doorframes and radiators and the appliances, thinking, *This is my house. This is my washing machine and my door frame and my radiator*, willing a sensation of pride or pleasure that stubbornly refused to come.

"Once you get your furniture in," her mother had reassured her, "some pictures on the walls, a few cushions, it'll feel just like home right away."

But though the furniture, curtains, and rugs (secondhand or inexpensively purchased by their parents) stopped the terrible echo that reverberated through the floors and walls, every item sat awkwardly in its new surroundings, reluctant to offer any feeling of comfort or homeliness.

Glen had done his best, she supposed. He had changed the nappies and prepared the baths and toddled Lydia in circles around the kitchen. Bryony just wasn't sure if she—if either of them—had the sense of anything other than the obligation of having to be there. She couldn't detach herself or Glen from the relentless trudging of parenthood. All that had come before—the cackling in cinemas, warming their hands in each other's pockets, fumbling on their bedroom floors instead of doing their homework—had been pressed down into the rubbish bin with that bundle of tissue paper.

And lately she had not been able to get Jaime's suggestion of getting her degree off her mind (even if Jaime was only trying to be nice). The thought, fizzing with promise, would dance into her head while she was spooning out a tea bag, pricking the roasted vegetables or straightening bed sheets. It was the first time since she was seventeen that anyone had proposed that she could be more than she was.

Now Glen's shadowed figure loomed in the driver's seat window, and he wrenched open the van door.

"What was that?" he whispered furiously, stealing glances left and right at the other departing parents. Once he had shut himself inside and finished grappling with the seatbelt, he held the steering wheel with two white, gripping hands.

Bryony folded her hands in her lap. The rain-spots on the windscreen flickered in the light of passing cars. "You completely stabbed me in the back."

"All I was trying to say was that things hadn't been ideal at home. We're meant to be able to work with them, aren't we? We're meant to be able to trust them."

"You hardly needed to start airing our dirty laundry. All that stuff about not getting a good example at home—you were insulting me, Glen."

"It's not all about you, you know. Lydia called the guy a dickhead. In front of her whole class—"

"Oh, I know, thank you very much. I was the one called in by the bloody head of year and had to sit there listening to all her—and you know what? Actually, I would like at least *something* to be about me sometimes—"

"But now you've just gone and shown him that you're a complete—"

"A complete what, Glen? Go on—a complete what?"

Neither of them spoke for a number of minutes.

"Do you think we would have stayed together," Bryony said into the silence, "if I hadn't got pregnant?"

"What?" came Glen's stabbing response, but she could not look at him. "What am I supposed to say to that?" And she knew, because she had always been able to peel back the surface layer of his voice like a ripe satsuma, how deeply hurt he was.

She had to give it to him: what was he supposed to say? But she couldn't sit in this van any longer. She opened the door.

"I'm going to walk home. I think we both need to calm down." And it scarcely seemed like she had finished shutting the door before the engine erupted and the van sped away.

She strode out of the school car park, reaching into her pocket to retrieve her phone, and opened her chat with Jude. Everything was awful, she wrote. How were they supposed to help Lydia if they couldn't even have a conversation? And she was tired—oh so tired—of always fighting somebody.

To her alarm, while waiting for his reply, her phone began to ring.

"Oh, hi, Jude. You didn't need to call. I'm fine."

"Well, you sounded pretty upset—what's happened?"

Then an account of the evening was spilling out of her—mostly accurate, she was sure—but she claimed Glen had sworn at her in the van, when she wasn't sure if he had. She also found herself saying that Glen hadn't even wanted to come to parents' evening in the first place, which might not have been true either. And all the while, Jude emitted all the right little sighs and mumbles of sympathy.

"Listen," he said, "you did the right thing. That teacher—he shouldn't be anywhere near children. Speak to the head. Speak to the governors."

"Do you think so? God, I could've . . . strangled him."

"Lydia is lucky to have you. All you do for your family, it really—it makes me furious for you, Bry."

"Oh, well . . . thank you. I don't—no one ever tells me that."

"Are you close by? I've got a shift at the Bells in half an hour. We could—"

"Oh no. No. I have to get home. You know—speak to Lydia."

She wished him a good night. Anerley Road was strewn with office workers scurrying home: people in the light coats of early spring, still in scarves for the evening chill, their tired eyes averted from the glare of oncoming traffic. All the inevitable landmarks of the journey home drifted past her—the shuttered pharmacies and the poster-covered newsagents: OYSTER CARDS, CONFECTIONARY, NATIONAL LOTTO—as she slowed her pace to prevent the arrival coming sooner than it had to. And also to have time to mull over the phone call, committing to memory all the heart-racing things Jude had said ("Lydia is lucky to have you . . .").

When she came to the door and let herself into the hallway, pushing her index fingers into the aching sockets of her eyes, it smelled of damp umbrellas and mud. She saw a hunched figure on the stairs in the blue dim light, and, for a flicker of a moment, she didn't recognize it as Arthur, reading a book balanced on his kneecaps. Who was this gangly, dark-haired kid whose jaw was already turning angular in maturity? Surely Arthur was chubbier than this, with smaller hands and no emerging chisel of cheekbones?

"I wanted to wait for you," he said, perching his chin on the book's edge. "Why didn't you come back with Dad?"

"Why aren't you in bed?"

"I wanted to wait for you. You might not've come home."

Guilt rolled in her ribcage as she sat on the stair beside him, draping a hand over the protrusion of his shoulder blade. She asked if he'd had anything to eat, whether he was tired, whether he wanted her to tuck him in bed (yes, yes, and yes, even though Glen insisted he was too old for that now).

"Alright. I'll be up in a minute then."

Arthur knew how to love someone. His love wasn't contingent on anything other than a steady supply of library books and being tucked into bed, and he would always forgive her, whether she deserved it or not.

CHAPTER FIFTEEN

Question: *Which vegetable gained its name from the capital of Belgium?*

Answer: *Brussels sprout*

Chest lifted, head held high, her hands propped on her hips and her feet planted solidly apart, Donna stood facing the mirror in the bathroom of Icon Marketing.

"It's the Superman pose," she said to Kayla. "To boost confidence. I saw it on a TED talk."

Kayla came hesitantly beside her, steadying her feet in a limp, distrustful version of the pose.

"You nervous?" she asked.

Donna returned Kayla's gaze in the reflection of the mirror. "No," she said.

In twenty minutes, Bernard Cope, founder of Mr. Sprout, one of the first vegan brands in the country, would be sitting in one of the deep-seated leather chairs of the conference room; Icon would be pitching for his business. On any other day, she would have relied on Steph's efficiency and composure, but Steph was away at her anatomy-scan appointment and wouldn't be back until tomorrow. This day, for Donna, had been both dreaded and desired so acutely that she'd woken up at 5:00 a.m., unable to swallow down any breakfast. But she had dressed carefully in a loose navy jacket and high-waisted chinos, to assure everyone of her capabilities.

Since January, time and focus had slid away from her. She'd found her work increasingly unmanageable: on some days anything on her computer screen would swim in her vision, and she couldn't keep any one idea straight in her head before it became formless and obscure. The only solid footing she found was in the details of the Quiz League—the League tables on the website were updated with a captivating array of performance statistics and the names of each team's members. It was easy to find them on social media too, and gratifying to see profile pictures of distinctly average people—a dopey smile with a Labrador, someone chugging from a pint glass, a white grin on a rocky beach. Surely these were the type of people only reliably able to answer questions about celebrity gossip and football? She would look up from her screen to see that an hour or more had unknowingly passed on the clock.

One Thursday night at the Five Bells, the only respite of the week, Jaime had approached her in a hand-wringing apology about the night at the Ministry of Cocktails—"Listen, we'd both had a lot to drink, and . . . well, I guess I didn't mean to upset you or anything. So—look, I'm really sorry is what I'm trying to say." Donna had given her a noncommittal sigh of weariness and said, "If you say so, Jaime." She had known she should just put Jaime out of her misery, but the problem was she always found her heart hardening at times like this, and it was easier to accept this was simply the way she was than to ask herself why.

But the meeting with Bernard Cope today had to occupy all her thoughts. And as the old man wobbled into the conference room and lowered himself into his chair with the aid of his two trembling hands, Donna felt all the tension in her shoulders float away. He was massively wrinkled and frail, in a V-neck sweater that was neither professional nor particularly clean, with a weak, sunken jaw, large, tufted ears and baby-fine white hair. And as he took Donna's hand (he was the sort of man to shake a woman's hand by clasping its palm as though he was about to kiss it, and then enclosing it with the other), he smacked his lips in greeting and strands of fine spittle clung to the corners of his deeply lined mouth.

"Donna *what*? Donna what was that? *March*?" he said loudly, looking around the room.

"Yes, that's right," she told him.

"Ah. After Donna Summer."

"Well, no. Donna Douglas, actually."

"*What*? What was that?"

"Yes, yes. Donna Summer, that's right."

Tess got into it with surprising swiftness, and for all Bernard Cope's frailty, he appeared to be listening attentively with rheumy-eyed brightness. Icon was digital-focused, Tess said, which was exactly what was needed now veganism was the choice of the younger generations—a serious lifestyle choice, most commonly entered into by young twenty-somethings. Icon combined behavioral insight, storytelling, and technology to amplify sales and brand trust. And with each of those sincerely spoken words—"insight, storytelling, technology"—Tess lightly pounded a closed fist into the palm of her other hand.

And Donna found herself echoing Tess's mannerisms—keeping her back straight, her chin high and tensing the muscles in her face in a way that began to make her temples ache—in the hope that she could inspire the same respect from the old man. She even found her hands twitching in her lap in rhythm with Tess's pounding fist. It was like mimicking Lottie and her mother all over again, twisting her expression and voice to conform with theirs, in ways that she knew made her look and sound more mature than she was. If you didn't feel capable, at least you could pretend that you were.

"Take your VLT burger," Tess said, sitting back in her chair, now the hard sell had been delivered. "It's bringing back customers that haven't been in the meat substitute market for some time. We can capitalize on that in the younger age bracket."

"Hmm," he said. "Yes, it's a tasty one. And did you like the name? Ha! Like a BLT?"

"Ingenious," Tess agreed.

"Mr. Cope?" Donna enquired. "If I might propose something?"

His tottering head followed her voice with a benign smile. "Of course."

"I was wondering if you'd ever considered a . . . well, a tweak to your brand name?"

"A tweak? Well, no. It's been our name for sixty years." The proud lift of his chin displayed the folds of his crepey neck.

Tess eyed Donna warily. This, after all, had not been on the agenda.

"I think we should consider dropping the 'Mr.,'" Donna explained. "Simply . . ." and here she fanned out her hands, as though inviting everyone to envision the name studded with lights, ". . . 'Sprout.'"

"First of all, Miss March, there is no 'we,' not as yet anyway. And no," he said, with his loose cheeks quivering, "that is not something I would consider."

"Don't you think there's the wrong touch of machoism in there? Did you know women are about twice as likely as men to be vegans? 'rMr.' isn't appealing to the largest demographic."

"Are you calling me sexist?"

"Well, no. But—you know—it's a fast-changing world, and it's worth exploring why you feel wedded to such a masculine identity. Now, I've looked into increases of sales in brands that switched names due to misogynistic connotations, and—"

The old man let out a noise of horror.

Between them, Tess leaned far over the table, as though to create a blockade. "Shall, we . . . uh—"

"It's just for comparison," Donna said. "Now—"

"Listen." Bernard Cope's hands clenched, yellow-knuckled, at the table's edge. "Listen here. My father—God rest his soul—did not lay down his life for Mr. Sprout to be labelled a sexist or anything else. He was feeding six of his children already on what little he had before I even came along. He was a businessman. He was a *great* businessman, and he never had any help from anyone."

Donna focused on the laces of her heeled brogues to stop herself fixing Bernard Cope with a hostile stare, which would only make it worse. The meeting, and with it her ability to impress anyone, was sliding away, too rapidly to claw back. Perhaps appealing to this old man's archaic devotion to "family" might salvage something.

"Not even from your mother?" Donna said finally, lifting her head. "By raising his seven children and allowing him to run his business?"

In the silence that followed, the thick grip of dread filled the room and pressed into her lungs. She'd fucked it up.

With alarming swiftness and strength, Bernard Cope's fist came down on the glass-topped table. Donna flinched and Tess spilled a loose-leaf folder onto the floor, where its contents scattered under their chairs.

"Thank you for your time, Ms. O'Grady," he said to Tess, and then rose stiffly out of his seat.

In Tess's glass box, for forty-five minutes, with the heater cranked up high enough to bake her eyeballs, Donna absorbed the torrent of Tess's fury. What in God's name was wrong with her? Tess demanded, making wide, sweeping arcs with her arms as she stalked left and right behind her desk with loose strands of hair escaping her hair clips. Could Donna not understand how grossly inappropriate that had been? Could she not see how she had ruined Icon's chances of landing Mr. Sprout as a client?

Donna found herself in a hunched paralysis, jumping a little with every incredulous drawing of Tess's breath. None of the old tricks of appearing unperturbed would have any effect. Anyone could see and hear that Tess was shredding her to pieces; the walls could well shatter under the force of her voice.

Finally, Donna was dismissed ("Just, please, get out of my sight"). She strode back to her desk, but the effort to keep her head high in defiance was thwarted by a hot swelling in her throat that closed all its edges. She started to cry.

Kayla came up to hesitantly touch her shoulder, and she allowed herself to be led into the bathroom where only two hours before they had posed before the mirrors. As Kayla hurried to gather tissues, other members of the team wandered in to ask if Donna was OK. Usually she found that crying at work could be pleasurable and wonderfully self-indulgent, that it could elicit pained expressions of concern from people and let them know how wronged she had been. But as she sat on the cold lid of the toilet, her eyelids pink and sore from the rub of scrunched tissue paper, she just wanted all of them to leave her alone. It wasn't only pity in their eyes, it was something else too; something that looked an awful lot like a fearful trepidation of what she might do next.

In the yellow lamplight of Kick in Shoreditch, rapidly sipping at her third or possibly fourth margarita, Donna was finally alone. A scattering of small groups sat around the bar, which smelled of ketchup and griddle-fried food, talking loudly over their burgers and happy-hour drinks. A few others played foosball under a wall-mounted television screen tuned to a sports channel. A peg letter board announced "CAN YOU KICK IT? YES YOU CAN."

"Oh, I don't know," Kayla had said, slipping on her jacket when the day was over, when Donna was trying to convince her to come out on a night of abandon. "I think I better just get home. Get an early night. Sorry." Though her weary face did not look sorry at all.

But it didn't matter—a woman could go out alone now, couldn't she? At least she wouldn't have to talk herself into exhaustion, until her voice was hoarse, trying to convince Kayla that they were being crushed in Tess's corporate grip. She only wished there was something to be done about the iron stiffness in all of her limbs; the margaritas were doing nothing against it. She thought of calling Harry—his warm, easy voice might lull it away—but it might only make everything more complicated. And with that idea rejected, she suddenly felt the loss of all her options: no friends she could talk to—*really* talk to—no family worth the effort, no job worth selling her soul to. Why not get away from here? To somewhere free of gray drizzle, paralyzing emails, and sour-mouthed flatmates? Maybe after the Quiz League—wasn't that the only reason to stay? Besides, she could use the prize money.

And then, by the window, Donna could see who she was certain was Jacob—pint-spilling-too-tall Jacob who had called her so obsessively—sitting with a woman. Of all the deceptive, cowardly, rotten . . . Who did this guy think he was? Prowling for unassuming young women, to sniff them out, to hassle them, and then to . . . Who the hell did he think he was?

The woman with him was petite with incredibly long braids, the ends of which touched the bench she sat on. Jacob leaned attractively over the table, smiling and chatting into her attentive face, with modest little darts and sways of his head. As Donna descended on them, it was clear from Jacob's expectant smile that he thought she might be a waitress.

"Jacob."

"I'm sorry, I—"

"I'm pretty surprised to see you here, and on a date?" And his date's mouth was set in a small pout of bemusement. "He's still calling me, you know," Donna told her. "Trying to get me to go out with him. I just think you have a right to know that."

"Look, Miss," Jacob said. "I'm sorry, I have no idea who you are, OK?"

"Oh, sure. Sure you don't." Donna stepped closer, her arms folded as she leaned in. "Donna? From Christmas? We met here. You spilled a pint on me."

Jacob opened his mouth silently and his eyebrows rose in recognition. "Now look," he said, bringing his palms up in front of him, "I haven't seen you in . . . since the night we met. And I haven't called you in . . . I don't even—"

"You know what?" Donna tapped the toe of her shoe. "I get so tired of people like you, thinking you can treat women like they're on some sort of supermarket shelf, waiting for you to pick them up or put them down."

There was a flicker of wariness in Jacob's expression before he squared his shoulders. "Hey, listen, why don't you—"

"And now you think you can treat me like I'm crazy? I haven't been picking up the phone, Jacob, because you've been ha*rass*ing me." She addressed the woman again, who was now clutching at her coat and bag. "That's right, your boyfriend's been harassing me."

Jacobs's date shook her head. "Look, I—"

Jacob stood up. All six-foot-six of him. The spiced scent of his deodorant washed over her. "Donna, is it? I haven't called you since before last Christmas. I started seeing Jada a few weeks ago. Now, I don't know what you're on, but it's about time you left us alone."

It came to her suddenly, under Jacob's and Jada's hostile stares, that she had not been bothered by Jacob—she had been bothered by her mother and sister asking who he was, and if she was "bringing him down" to meet them—indeed, all the way back before Christmas.

"I . . . I think I might . . ." Jada's face was tight with embarrassment. Donna had ruined her night.

And now, some staff member from the bar placed a kind but firm hand on Donna's shoulder and she was led away. "Come on, now, love. I think it's time you got yourself home, don't you?"

CHAPTER SIXTEEN

Question: *Which Ancient Greek goddess enacts retribution against those who succumb to arrogance, extreme pride, and dangerous overconfidence?*
Answer: *Nemesis*

"Harry!' Ashton bellowed down the phone. "It's been too long, mate. How's it going?"

Harry, sitting in front of the television in the late morning light in his dressing gown, let the phone hang loose in his hand for a full six seconds before he accepted that he had to reply.

"Oh," he said. "Hi." He quickly turned off the talk show in case Ashton could hear it. Nobody rang anyone's phone anymore, not unless they were trying to make some sort of point. And Ashton's was clearly trying to catch Harry in a moment of weakness: at home, alone, on a weekday morning, watching daytime television in his wrinkled, day-old underwear.

"I'm actually about to head out," Harry lied.

"Oh, of course. Of course. But I said I'd ring and, well, here I am. Sorry it's taken so long. You know how things are. Busy, busy."

The gall of this guy! Harry got up to pace the floorboards, flexing the fingers of his free hand. *How do you sleep at night?* he wanted to ask. *How do you sleep at night, you piece of . . .?*

"Anyway, listen," Ashton went on, and there were distant voices of urgency somewhere in the background. "Listen . . . yep, one sec, mate . . . sorry, Harry, absolutely slammed here. I thought we might get together. Tonight. You free? Grab a bite to eat. Hash out the old job situation."

"Oh . . . well, sure. I mean, sure I can find some time. Where?"

"Won't make you travel, mate. Know money must be tight. How's about that Vietnamese place? You know, on the corner. Let's make it early. Six o'clock."

"OK. See you there."

"Good."

And then, later, even before Harry had recovered all his ringing nerves, Vivienne called too, and her sweet, excited voice was trilling in his ear.

"Harry! Honestly, listen, this is going to be *such* a good thing."

"Viv! Wow, it's great to hear from you."

"And I know Ashton calling came out the blue. I *told* him to message you first, but you know what he's like. Are you terribly annoyed at me?"

"No, Viv. No. I just . . . well, never mind. No, not at all."

"I'm so excited for you. But look, I wanted to . . . well, to check in, I suppose. I've missed talking to you."

"That's . . . well, that's nice to hear."

Feeling like a devil of a man, swinging the rope of his dressing gown, he assured her that he was doing great—he was getting out and meeting people . . . yes, his mum was doing fine . . . yes, he was eating alright . . . no, not drinking too much. And for a long time after he'd hung up, as he went about the task of preparing for his dinner with Ashton—ironing a shirt, spending too much time in front of the bathroom mirror in the realization that his hair was far too long—he took a secret thrill in knowing that Ashton likely didn't know that Vivienne had called him today, that she "missed" talking to him. He could walk into the little Vietnamese restaurant, into its smell of steaming vegetables and boiling chicken stock, assured that no matter what Ashton was providing for her—vintage bottles of wine, reservations at the Shard, even adequate sex (because it wasn't better, it was different)—there was evidently something about Ashton that left Vivienne unsatisfied. And hey—he couldn't help that.

At six o'clock, Harry concealed himself in the nook of a side alley across the road until he'd seen Ashton arrive, look at his watch, and walk into the restaurant. Harry composed himself with a tweak of his collar and followed. Jesus—his hands were shaking.

Ashton opened his arms wide in welcome and clapped Harry hard on the shoulder, then sat down, taking care to keep the ironed crease of his suit trousers in place.

"Mate, good to see you. Christ, you've had that jacket since I've known you. Some things never change, eh? Sit down, sit down. Let me get you a drink—two more Hanois here, please, thanks. No Merlot to be seen in this place, mate, know what I mean? So, what's been going on?"

The small room, filled with rickety wooden furniture, was overly warm. Spotlights glared down on the grease-stained tabletops and sticky pots of chopsticks and napkins. And under their feet, in the basement kitchen, what must be an industrial dishwasher rattled the stripped floorboards and filled the room with a distant yet incessant vibration that you could feel in your teeth.

Ashton's big, blond, rosy face did not stop moving. It smiled, revealing an astonishing row of large, white teeth; it talked quickly with little flicks and wiggles of his eyebrows, his protruding bright blue eyes dancing in glinting arcs, and his plump lower lip rolled out whenever it was required of him to listen or mull something over.

"Oh, well, you know," Harry said. "Bit of this, bit of that. You?" He slid off his inferior jacket, wishing he could stash it under the table and out of sight.

"Let me tell you—insane. Guess you heard about Kevin? Got the axe in November. Left the operation on its absolute knees with the redundancies. On its *knees*. Still, poor bastard—and right before Christmas too. But you know what—and I've been saying this to everyone—it was his hill to die on. You make a decision like that—a big decision—well, you've got to take the fallout."

"Things've been pretty rough at Kingsley, then?"

"Mate." Ashton sat back and shook his head as if Harry wouldn't believe it. "I've been up there seven til seven for weeks now—viewings solid til nine some days, and don't get me started on Saturdays. Open houses are the thing now—get some orange juice, some biscuits, maybe a little prosecco, start a buzz, you know. But still, mate, I want to be home with a beer, you know what I'm saying?"

They ordered quickly from the laminated menus, and when Harry's chicken pho soup arrived, a tremendous bowl of steaming liquid and hot slippery noodles, he instantly regretted it. Now he would have to find a dignified way of eating this thing, while Ashton efficiently shoveled in forkfuls of his lemongrass grilled pork.

"So what's say we get down to business?" Ashton said, wiping his mouth on a paper napkin.

Harry had almost forgotten the way he talked—"How's about we do this? . . . What's say we do that?" The sound of it, merging with the juddering hum of the dishwasher, began to make his temples ache. He spooned his noodle soup into his mouth, dipping his face close to the bowl and catching the small dribbles of soup with a napkin that was soon sodden and ruined.

"Now, listen." Ashton settled his elbows on the table with his large, well-veined, superior hands free to gesture and point. "First off, yes—there's something there for you. Maybe not what you were doing before, but there's something there. What we're lacking is support staff. You know—your typical trainee post."

"I'm not a trainee, Ashton. Was working at the place for seven years before I—"

"I know that, mate. I *know* that, but look at it this way—it's all about getting your foot in the door again, right? Couple months, you'll be flying as high as you ever did."

"Go on."

"So it's the basic stuff. Stuff you can do with a hand tied behind your back: get the photography sorted, update the online feed, get all the—what-d'you-call-its—health and safety bits—the gas certificates."

"You think I'm desperate?"

Ashton languished back in his chair, draping one crooked arm over its back, and fixed him with a look of pitying tolerance, like a parent whose tantruming toddler had dropped his ice cream on the pavement. "As a matter of fact, yes I do. Now, do you want to convince me otherwise?"

Looking down at his half-filled bowl of soup and the soaking, beige ball of his napkin, Vivienne's hopeful voice came back to him ("This is going to be *such* a good thing"). He couldn't face her next phone call if he walked away from Ashton now. Her voice may well revert to the weary tones of defeat that had filled their last days together ("Oh, Harry, don't you know? It's because you never would have let me."). Or worse: there would be no phone calls at all. Tonight she might curl up on the sofa with Ashton, her ankles tucked up underneath her, and rest her head on his muscled shoulder. "Arrogant little bastard," Ashton might say. "Don't know how you put up with him." And Vivienne might nod her head in agreement, replying with a disappointed sigh, "Oh, I couldn't agree more. So ungrateful."

If it hadn't been for that, Harry would have stood up, thrown a ten-pound note onto the table and told Ashton where he could shove his lemongrass pork.

"Fine," he said eventually. "Alright."

Ashton clapped his hands together, delighted. "So, I'll talk to Darren. You know, sweeten him up. He'll call you in. Shall we leave it like that, then? Yes? Good man. But listen—no moping around like last time. Things are a little different around the old office lately. I mean, don't get me wrong, it's fine—it can even be fun—but I don't want to be stuck there after hours. I've got a life, you know what I'm saying? I want to be taking Vivienne out and . . . Oh, sorry."

And the way Ashton let the silence gather in the pause of his solemn face was a little too theatrical.

"Don't worry about it," Harry said. "I'm glad you and Viv are—you know—getting on alright."

Ashton hunched his shoulders in feigned compassion. "Look, mate. I'd be gutted if I lost Viv. She's a top-notch girl. Top notch. I don't blame you for being . . . well, depressed over it. But you've got to move on. We all have."

"No, I know. Alright if we sort of don't talk about it, though?"

Ashton said that was fine; of course it was fine. And then his clammy face came back to life with little anecdotes and sketches of "the boys" back at the office. Jensen, who'd hidden a gherkin in Ollie's drawer for a month; Andre, who'd slept under his desk after a heavy one at the Rose . . . Harry started to tune out his voice, and a repeating loop of one thought spiraled around his head: it wasn't fair. It wasn't fair that Ashton had won Vivienne. But, again, he could already hear Vivienne's proud voice in his head—"He didn't win me, Harry. I'm perfectly capable of making my own—" She would have said "decisions," but he hadn't let her finish, because he hadn't wanted to hear it.

When a waitress placed the bill between them, they both made a grab for it, and Ashton held up his hands with a white, flashing grin.

"Hey, mate," he said. "If it makes you feel better, go for it. And listen—one thing—get a haircut before you come in, yeah? Makes us look sloppy."

CHAPTER SEVENTEEN

Question: *What idiom derives from the practice of using red ink to denote debt or losses on financial balance sheets?*
Answer: *In the red*

On the walk back to her flat after her twilight shift, having left the warehouse where galvanized tin pans of raw, thawing chicken were piled high, Jaime could not dispel the rancid odor of the stuff. She imagined its slimed, milky juice permeating her polyester uniform and hair, and had to swallow a wave of nausea.

Tonight Miriam had "placed" her on warehouse unpacking, and Jaime was reasonably sure that "placed" had become code for "get rid of." All the twilight staff worked two-by-two down their aisles, but tonight Jan had taken a single aisle by herself, strutting jauntily up and down with her trolley. "The warehouse is short," Miriam had said, fingering the fine strands of her wispy orange fringe. "You'll be of much more use over there." Except when she'd got there, the warehouse supervisor didn't seem to know what to do with her. She'd been hustled into a darkened corner, pricing discounted washing detergent bottles, where the discarded pans of chicken and the dusty smell of crushed cardboard boxes filled her nose and throat with the decaying smell of rejection.

After three hours in the unheated, echoing chamber, her spine had stiffened into the crouching, bent position of her work and her frozen hands had turned white. She'd noticed that all the other warehouse staff had been wearing fleece-lined, nylon gloves.

When she was finally released onto the empty high street, her eyes stung with tiredness. Most shops were darkened, some spilling their sterile white security lights onto the pavement, and there was the estate agents where Harry used to work, its violet lettering—KINGSLEY & CO.—lit in a painful neon blaze.

Behind the flat's front door came the zip of racing engines; Jaime pressed her forehead against its surface, not wanting to go inside. In the dark living room, the walls flickered with the blue light of the television, illuminating the sleeping figure of Luke. He lolled on his back on the sofa, his glasses askew and his mouth open, a packet of prawn crackers balanced on his belly. The salty, oily smell of a Chinese takeaway leaked from four or five open containers on the floor. She might have woken him up, insisted he clear up the mess, but she knew if they got into an argument now she would never get to sleep.

On the kitchen table, among a slew of opened envelopes, Jaime saw her pay slip from the supermarket and opened it to reveal its meagre total. Logging onto her bank account on the laptop revealed she had already been paid by PrintPro, but the rent had not yet left her account, nor had they done the weekly food shop, and she had already tumbled into her overdraft.

She pressed her fingertips into her eye sockets, and then she was up and staring wild-eyed into the flickering gloom of the living room. How much had that Chinese takeaway cost them? How could she have allowed him to keep the subscription for the sports channels? And how much was this zombifying television set racking up the electricity bill? She could have switched it off with the remote, but for dramatic emphasis she lurched around the back of the unit and fumbled and yanked at the leads until finally the screen fell black.

The noise had woken Luke, who stretched and scratched his neck. "Oh, hi." He squinted at her. "You're back. What's that . . . you smell like meat or something."

"I can't do this anymore," she announced. "There's just—there's no money and I can't do it. And will you remember to turn off that fucking TV?"

Back in the kitchen, as she swiped through the envelopes, Luke eventually appeared in the doorway.

"Wait, wait," he said, his frowning eyes closed. "What?"

"I mean, seriously, hasn't this gas tariff gone up?" She shook the bill in front of him. "I could've sworn it wasn't anywhere near this. Did you put in the right meter reading? Well, are you sure? Because look—we need to look at some things here."

He yawned widely, leaning against the door frame. "OK. Well, calm down. Look at what things?"

"First of all, the sports subscription. I'm sorry, but—"

"Are you crazy? It's the start of the F1 season."

"And the takeaways. I mean, look at this . . ." She strode over to the fridge and wrenched it open, setting the glass bottles in its door rattling. "I left pasta for you. Why couldn't you eat that?"

"Well, I just—"

"And I don't think we should have a joint account while all this is going on," she said, sitting back at the laptop and scrolling through the statement. "I can't keep track of—what's this? eBay—twenty-two pounds?"

"I needed a new joypad, my buttons are glitchy. It's not like I bought a *new* one."

"I'll just have to give you some sort of monthly allowance or something."

"You mean pocket money? I'm not ten years old."

Well, alright, but if this "man" couldn't be trusted with his takeaways and toys and racing cars, leaving her to sink into the slippery-walled trench of her overdraft, then what did he expect? She stabbed a pointed finger at him. "You don't pay the bills anymore. If you don't like it, you'll just have to get some sort of job again. Just some little—Why not some shifts at the supermarket? Two a week? Three?"

"I knew it would come to this." He looked down forlornly at the television remote, cradled in his hands. "All that talk about 'no pressure,' 'find yourself.'" And now he glared up at her. "If you really want to save money then stop with the pub quizzes—do you know how much we spend on drinks at those things?"

"We can't do that. They're our friends. They're counting on us."

"They're not our 'friends.' We barely know them."

"*You* barely know them. I will go mad here, Luke, if I have to spend one more second by myself. Do you understand me? Do you understand what I'm saying? I will go *mad.*"

"Listen, listen." Luke crouched beside her chair. "We need to look at this long term," he explained patiently. "I thought you wanted better things for us? I thought you wanted to get married?"

There was a dizzying moment, as she flittered between rattling panic, surprise and hope, before she convinced herself she had heard him correctly; it was the first time he had said anything of its kind.

"We just need to think about this logically, OK?" he said. "Look, I'm sorry about the joypad. I'm sorry about the takeaway. I won't spend money on anything like that anymore, alright? And I'll—I'll start to consider . . . the marriage stuff."

Jaime was too tired. "OK," she said.

"Are we alright for this month? I still have that voucher my nan gave me for Christmas. I can ask her for the cash instead . . ."

"Oh no. Don't do that. She'll only worry. Look, go to bed. I'll just sit up for a bit and have a look at . . . well, everything."

And she did—at the interest on her overdraft (no losing that one), their energy bill tariffs (a saving of a few pounds), at exemption for council tax (no luck there)—but there were no other solutions to be found. How could their carefully prepared spreadsheet have failed them so quickly? If she insisted Luke get another job then he may well pack a bag and head back to Cumbria tomorrow. Oh, he might say it was "just temporary" or they just needed "some space," but she'd know the truth: if he left now it would be over. And if she followed him back to Keswick, she could even imagine the pointless, desperate conversation they would have on the doorstep of his mother's house—"It's better this way, Jaime. You love London. Go back. We've grown apart."

Two years ago, when they'd piled into the backseat of Stratten's car (he had agreed to drive them to London for fifty pounds and an indefinite number of Snickers bars along the way) with their scant, packed belongings, they'd been filled with a kind of thrilling terror. The drive would thread them through densely packed motorways and confusing junctions to spew them out onto this same sunlit street, in front of this same shabby flat. And it might be worn and single-glazed and full of inadequate furniture, but it was theirs, and they'd been poised to experience the best of life with the most accomplished and brilliant people the world had to offer. Perhaps Luke hadn't been as earnest as she had been—in scouring the internet for parts of London that seemed "edgy" and "convenient" and "affordable"—but he wasn't a planner, so that had been fine. And even when she'd asked him time and again if he wanted to go, and he'd said something minimal like, "Well, sure" or "I guess so," that had been fine too. He'd always been a person of few words.

On their first night, after Stratten had left to "hit some gigs in Camden" before he'd inevitably spend the night in the backseat of his car, they had nervously ventured out onto the streets. They'd ordered fish and chips from their local chippy, then stopped in at a newsagents to purchase a bottle of cava. And under the hanging naked lightbulb in their living room, they'd spread a gingham blanket on the floorboards because they'd had no table, eaten their humble dinner out of its paper wrapping because they'd had no plates, and clinked an impassioned "cheers" with their mugs because they'd had no glasses. They'd convinced each other of how brave and courageous they were. And even if not everything about London had lived up to her expectations—not the sirens that flashed down their street at three in the morning, or the stifling haze of the roads that left the mucus in her nostrils black, or the sightless, mindless people who shouldered past her as she walked the endless, gray pavements—at least they'd had each other.

Now she was on her feet and pacing the bright kitchen in feverish circles, spinning the rings on her fingers until her knuckles were red. Her eyes ached and the numbers on the microwave's clock danced; it was 2:00 a.m.

Wilting in her chair again, she hastily googled "fix money problems" and "how to make more money" and "get money fast," clicking through the webpages presented to her—credit card eligibility calculators, bank loan offers, payday loan companies. A credit card was too dangerous and a bank loan was terrifying—they'd be stuck with the repayments for months, if not years to come. No, the obvious choice, to get out of this as quickly as it had started, was a payday loan—it could be paid off as neatly and tidily as it had been taken out. And all the websites were so joyfully simple, with photographs demonstrating that normal, smiling people did this sort of thing all the time.

So at "We Pay Today"—whose website sported a tranquil green background and a laughing blond couple who each confidently clutched a debit card—she applied, and was approved, for a five-hundred-pound loan.

After the money zipped into her account ("We pay FAST"), the warm relief that spread through her limbs had her wobbling to the bathroom, where she brushed her teeth, and then collapsing under the bed covers where Luke peacefully snored. She'd been awake for twenty hours and had four hours to sleep before her alarm would summon her to begin another day.

CHAPTER EIGHTEEN

Question: *What rare variety of plant is traditionally thought to bring good luck?*
Answer: *A four-leaf clover*

Upon receiving the news that Darren Johnson, manager of Kingsley & Co., would be "calling him in," Harry had used it as an excuse to call Vivienne to thank her for setting up the whole thing, and she had urged Harry to "replace that dreadful suit."

"Well, it's important to make the right impression, isn't it?" she'd said over the phone on Thursday afternoon. "Why don't we go to Westfield together? It'll be fun. I can meet you there at five, OK?"

Harry was due at the Five Bells at eight for their usual quiz night practice session, but he could hardly believe his luck: she wanted to go shopping with him. And if he could make something as mundane and tedious as suit shopping fun, then it might lead to any number of other date-like opportunities.

But in the white, echoing fluorescence of Westfield, as Harry allowed himself to be shuttled through the doors of BOSS, Ted Baker, and Armani Exchange by the pull of Vivienne's hand, the sales assistants had dragged their eyes up from his Adidas trainers to his windbreaker in curled-lip disdain.

"Of course they're not looking at you funny," Vivienne said. "You're imagining things." But she had finally relented and they had compromised on John Lewis, where Harry now stood in front of a mirror in the curtained cubicle in a navy suit selected by Vivienne. And he had to admit that it looked pretty sharp, even if the price tag did make him suck on his teeth. The jacket squared his shoulders and lengthened his short torso, and the smart, clean cuffs, with their branded four-leaf clover buttons, even gave the impression that his hands, dangling beneath them, were as capable and robust as any other man's.

"Are you coming out?" Vivienne called.

He emerged into the hushed, upholstered area beyond the cubicle curtain that smelled of both clean linens and sweaty socks, and Vivienne made a meticulous little show of circling him to straighten the hem of the jacket, adjust the lapels and dust off the shoulder seams, all with snappy gestures of her hands.

"You don't look well, Harry. You're all skinny and gray. Have you caught up with Wes or Matty lately? Any of the old gang?"

"Well, you know, they're . . . busy. Kids and all that."

"Did you send Francesca a first birthday card?"

"No."

A little line of disappointment appeared between Vivienne's eyebrows. "Make an effort, Harry. Alright?"

"Been a rough few months."

"Oh, I know. But listen, you shouldn't keep these things to yourself. Talk to people. Talk to me. Just because things didn't work out between us, it doesn't mean we can't be friends. Besides, it's not all roses for me either."

"No?"

She shrugged. "No one's life is perfect." She wandered away to a high-backed velvet seat, and after a minute of silence, during which she inspected the clasp of the gold bracelet on her wrist, she said, "Sometimes Ashton is so . . . cold."

There it was—the nugget of her dissatisfaction he'd been waiting for. A bubble of pleasure rose in his diaphragm, and he had to force his face into an expression of concern. He nodded solemnly to show he was listening, hoping he looked handsome and reliable in this expensive suit, until he realized his T-shirt underneath and the graying socks on his feet must spoil the effect.

"And OK," she went on. "I know he works long hours, and he's tired, and that's fine. It's just . . . well, he never used to be so aloof about everything . . . so distant."

"Well, what kind of things?"

"Oh, I don't know." She shifted her gaze uncomfortably to the other shoppers, who were quietly chatting, pulling at the collars and hemlines of new clothes. She got up to adjust his suit lapels again. In the prettiness of her half-moon eyelashes and wistful pout, he could have kissed her, but she wouldn't have let him.

"Like at the weekend," she said eventually. "I was on the phone to my dad and—oh, you know how my dad can be—he asked me what exactly I was doing with my life and why was I wasting time at a little independent outfit—he actually said 'outfit,' can you believe it? I was like, 'Dad, you're not in the army.' Anyway—and that I need to get into a more corporate environment, because that's where the money is. I told him my company is an international leader in . . ."

And Harry had to admit he was zoning out now. She may well have been talking to herself as she wandered across the vacuumed carpet, but it was important to maintain his sincere, attentive expression until Vivienne got back to the part about Ashton being "cold."

". . . And so I get off the phone, and of course I'm a little annoyed about it—not just annoyed, I'm sad, you know? So Ashton asks me what's wrong, but not in a way like he's really interested. Like a 'So what's wrong now?' sort of way. So I told him, and he was like, 'Well, OK, Viv, seems like the sort of thing you should just get over—who cares?' So I told him—I said, 'I care! And why are you being so—so heartless?' And then he just sort of rolled his eyes and was on his phone or whatever."

"Wow, yeah. I mean, sounds pretty hurtful."

"It *was* hurtful, Harry. And I was sitting there thinking, how am I meant to carry on living with someone if they don't even care what I'm feeling?"

What Harry wanted to say next would either go one way or the other. But the hell with it—Ashton was "cold" and "distant" and "heartless," and Harry was standing across from her while she arranged and smoothed his jacket with all the attentiveness of a lover.

"You know what, Viv. Honestly? I can't say I'm surprised. I spent a lot of time with Ashton before you—you know—you got together or whatever, and he's always been an emotionless bastard."

Too late, he realized the "bastard" may have ruined everything, because Vivienne gave a sobering little roll of her eyes and huddled her arms over her stomach.

"I mean," Harry said quickly, "he's always been a solid guy round the office—took up the slack, fair about listings, stuff like that—but when it came to anything personal, anything where someone might need a bit of extra—you know—sympathy or whatever—well, he just didn't care."

"Really? I mean, I know you don't like him and everything."

"Take the redundancies. Poor guy called Tom got the axe—nineteen years old, fresh out of sixth-form, carer for his dad who had MS—he was crying in the kitchen and everything. Ashton never even looked at him. Never even said goodbye or good luck or anything."

"God, that's horrible."

Harry nodded, slipping off the suit jacket; it was about time to head back to Crystal Palace. He wasn't entirely sure that Tom's dad had had MS, and he didn't recall him crying in the kitchen either, but still, the story served as a neat summing up of Ashton's true self.

"I saw Maria at the weekend—from yoga?" Vivienne said. "She saw you at that tacky little bar on the corner of Westow Hill back in January. She said you gave her a bit of an earful."

"Oh. Yeah, that was . . . Sorry about that."

"Apparently some girl took you out of there. Tall, blonde hair, a bit gobby."

"Oh. That's Donna. From the quiz thing."

"Are you . . . close with her?"

Harry caught a glimpse of his stricken face in the large communal mirror. Would it make her envious if she thought of Donna as some sort of competition?

"You've gone all red, Harry. Maria said you looked pretty close."
Vivienne lowered her eyes in what he was sure was disappointment.

But it was best not to go in too decisive—there was every chance it
might scare her off. "Well, you know—she's fun and everything."

Vivienne took the suit jacket to thread back onto its hanger. "We
had a lot of fun, didn't we? Before things got sort of awful."

"Yeah, we did. And I don't think things got 'awful' either."

"Maybe not. I wasn't very happy, though. You never wanted to go
anywhere. You never wanted to do anything."

"No. Well." What could he say? It was true. It was wretched and
tedious and senseless, and it was true. He could have spun Vivienne
round dance lessons. They could have folded handmade ravioli
together in Italian cookery classes. They could have gone to Glaston-
bury and got off their faces on drugs. But he'd stayed at home, night
after night, eating beans on toast and picking his nose. "And I'm sorry
about that. I suppose I was . . . I don't know what I was doing. But
that's why I'm doing this quiz thing, to—you know—get out, meet
people."

"So what is this pub quiz exactly? You keep talking about it."

And then, once Harry had changed back into his clothes, he was
telling her all about the London Pub Quiz League in an effort to impress
her. They drifted the cool aisles of John Lewis until they found the till,
where Harry winced again over the price of the suit and accepted the
neat package of it from a smiling, well-groomed sales assistant (he'd
never owned a suit carrier before, and he liked the important, grown-up
weight of it in his hand). He told Vivienne how the quarter-final was
only three weeks away, and how Donna had advertised for teammates
on the internet—"I mean, who knew what crazy people she'd get
answering?" And he couldn't tell, from Vivienne's blinking, immobile
face, whether she was interested or bored, so he ended it there, rather
than explain that the Quiz League had become a refuge from a complicated and ungratifying life where he never seemed to get anything right.
The world of "grown-ups" may well have rejected him, but the Quizzy
Peppers never did.

"Well, anyway. It's just—you know—a bit of fun."

"No, Harry, that's . . . interesting."

As they passed over the glass-walled bridge that led them back to Stratford station, Harry wondered what he'd said wrong. She wasn't impressed after all.

"I just worry you're not taking life seriously, Harry."

"Oh, I am, Viv. And, listen, I know I have you to thank for all this. The interview, I mean. I really appreciate it, especially after everything we went through. My mum's really been . . . Well, you know how she worries. She'd have a weight off her mind if I could just—"

"Still attached at the apron strings, I see."

"No. No, nothing like that. She just—"

"Yes, OK, OK; she worries. Fine."

He wanted to clarify himself—couldn't she see? It wasn't that he was attached at the apron strings; it was that he'd disappointed his mum so profoundly. Her life had already been disappointment enough; the least she could have expected was a son who could get a job. Couldn't she see that at all? But he didn't dare press it further.

Vivienne stopped him at the foot of the bridge. "I do miss you, Harry. I'm not sure where it all went . . . Anyway, it doesn't matter."

"No, I know what you mean. I don't know where it went wrong either."

CHAPTER NINETEEN

Question: *What informal World War I arrangement between
Great Britain, France, and Russia meant "friendship and
understanding"?*
Answer: *The Triple Entente*

Jaime thought the practice quiz had gone better than any of them
could have hoped. How composed they had been, how self-assured and
quick-witted.

"Now listen," Donna had said, staring at them around the table.
"We're treating this like a match, got it? And for God's sake write your
answers down—Harry, I'm talking to you; no calling them out, OK?—
write your answers down or pass, just like normal. Everyone
understand?"

And it was as though tonight's quiz had been devised especially
for them.

Francisco Franco, Bryony had scribbled madly at the History round.
Triple Entente . . . The Hindenburg Disaster . . . Martin Luther King. Two
points, four points, six points, eight points. Donna insisted on using the
scoring system of a Quiz League match. ("Well, it's not practice if it's
not accurate, is it?")

Rococo, Jaime had answered. *Constructivism . . . Raphael.* Ten points, twelve points, fourteen points.

Jude had eyed them with intrigue as he reeled off each question, and they bent their heads studiously over their answer sheet. "What singer holds the record for most Grammy nominations? . . . What is the longest movie ever made? . . . How many husbands did Liz Taylor have?"

And so irrefutable had been their answers, so intelligent their guesswork, that it had come as no surprise when, in the gathered silence of the room, Jude announced that the Quizzy Peppers had the highest score of the evening.

"No wonder they're our quarter-finalists," he'd added, as they'd lifted their glasses and spoken over each other in their smiling eagerness to assure one another of their own brilliance. Then the five of them had sat back in their seats, stretching knots from their shoulders as if a great athletic feat had been achieved there tonight.

"You seem . . . I don't know . . . a little happier after yesterday?" Luke said to Jaime, after they'd left the Five Bells, reached the crest of Gipsy Hill and begun their descent. They were holding hands, and it created a discordant rhythm to their walk; the feel of Luke's fingers threaded through her own felt foreign.

She did not look at him. "I was tired, I guess. I sort of shifted some things around money-wise. I'm not worried anymore." And while that may have been true, the feeling of airy cheer in the pub could no longer be held aloft after she'd walked out of the double doors and was alone with Luke. She'd found it sinking, anchored by the weight of his hand in hers.

"That's good," he said. "Anything I can help with?"

"No, I don't think so."

"Listen." He pulled her in to stop at the entrance of a looming sandstone church tower that, from the top of the hill, dominated the skyline. When the sky blazed orange-pink in the sunset over central London, the light passing through its tall gothic windows made slits of fire, topped by the silhouetted crown of its four pointed spires. But it wasn't a real church anymore. Like everything else in this place, it had been sold, gutted and stripped—converted into the private home of a millionaire.

They stood in the shadow of a tall box hedge. "Listen," he said, and took her by the shoulders. "I appreciate all this. I do."

"OK. That's fine. Can we sort of go home now?"

"No, look—I mean it, OK? I know how tired and fed up you are. And I know you're putting on a brave face for the others because . . . well, because I know they don't think much of what we're doing. And—listen, I want to marry you, OK?"

"Alright. Well, look, we talked about this. I know you do. We'll get there."

"No, I mean—I'm actually . . . Will you marry me, Jaime?"

His face, vulnerably lit by a pale light from the church tower's wall, was serious. Jaime wasn't sure what she expected next. For a small velvet box containing a ring to emerge from out of Luke's coat pocket? For Luke to kneel on the gravel and take her hand? None of that happened. From somewhere, an open window leaked the sounds of a radio ad jingle ("Your teeth will be whiter and your smile brighter!") and engines hissed on the road beside them.

"What are you talking about?" she said.

"You heard me."

Oh, she'd heard him, and the delay in her response, she knew, had nothing to do with surprise—surprise in itself could be a wonderful thing. It was because she was waiting to feel something, but nothing would come. And none of this was right—not standing on the roadside, not wearing her woolen beanie hat and a parka with an oil stain down its front—none of it. But maybe that was all ridiculous and sentimental; maybe, as Bryony had said, life didn't care about your plans. He had asked her and it was time to answer.

Luke scraped the gravel with the toe of his trainer. "I don't really want to kneel on this stuff."

"No, it's OK. You don't have to. Look, I mean—yes. Yes. I will."

"Alright. Good."

His face stiffened with fear then, because she'd arranged her expression into an open-mouthed gape of elation and tossed her arms out wide to swoop around his neck—all because she thought she ought to. He let out a small grunt as the force of her embrace jolted him backwards.

"I can't believe it," she said into his ear. "We're engaged."

"I don't have a ring or anything."

"That's alright. We can get one later."

And it *was* alright. She was in shock; she was tired. The feelings would arrive. Maybe tonight as she lay in bed in the dark and told herself she was an engaged woman. In the morning she would comb out her hair and wash her face and finally start feeling all the things she was supposed to feel—settled, secure, happy. And even if there was no money for a dress or a cake or a DJ or anything like that, it would still be alright.

She realized they were still clinging to each other when a clomping set of footsteps from the pavement moved passed them and the slurring voice of a teenage boy cried, "Give her one, mate!" and the snorting, convulsive laughter of his friends trailed after him.

Luke pulled away. "Hey, listen. Let's keep it to ourselves for a while, OK?"

"Oh. Why?"

"I don't know. It's nice if we get to celebrate just us for a while, isn't it?"

*   *   *

"You know everything," Jude said to Bryony. "I don't know how you do it. You just know everything."

The members of the Quizzy Peppers had trickled away after buttoning and zipping their coats, foregoing their hats and scarves now the bitter snap was out of the air.

But Bryony hadn't left. She had gone to the toilets and spent a long time over her reflection in the mirror, pinching pink into her cheeks and shaking her hair from the roots as she hung her head upside down. But that didn't achieve the flushed, breathless sparkle that it did on other women—her hair didn't land with the softness of spun sugar, it only accentuated its liability to frizz and tangle—and her brow started to sweat under the lone ceiling bulb.

As much as she tried to pretend she didn't care, she'd wanted Jude to ask her to stay for another drink, and he had—"Time for a quick one?"—and she'd slunk onto one of the bar stools, sipping a white wine spritzer while he went about the business of locking the doors behind the last shuffling, stumbling customers at closing time. He'd gathered up bundles of clacking glasses with his fingers and polished each table-top to a high sheen, all the while sending her snippets of conversation. "You got a busy one tomorrow?" No, she didn't. "Kids on Easter break yet?" Not until next week. "You had your hair cut?" No, not for months. "Really? Well, it looks nice."

"But tell me honestly," he said, as they slouched in a corner booth with a fresh set of drinks now they were alone. "How'd you get to know all that stuff?"

"Oh, it's just things you sort of pick up here and there. It's hardly anything—"

"No, I mean it. What did you do before staying home with the kids? Teaching, something like that?"

"Well, no. I had Lydia when I was—when I was seventeen. I never really did anything."

Jude stumbled over a gulp of his wine. "Oh, right. Wow."

"Only now they're older, and I suppose I don't know what to do with myself."

And what would Jude say at this notion of hers that she might yet go to university? Donna, Harry, Jaime—they were all so young and carefree. But Jude was more practical; she could tell. And why not explore this thing from a practical angle?

"I could always go back to university and get my degree."

"Oh yeah?" Jude gave her a strange little smirk and swallowed the last of his wine. "You think that sort of thing's worth it?"

"How so?"

"It's all a bit . . . wanky, isn't it?"

"No, I don't think an education is 'wanky.'"

"Well, look. I mean, there's an education and there's an *education*."

She might have asked him what he meant, but she didn't want to hear it. He would start talking about things like "book-smart" and "street-smart," and she'd never had the patience for that sort of conver-sation. And besides, she felt overly warm and embarrassed.

"Anyway, Glen is still furious with me over all that Lydia business."

"Hey, look—you were standing up for her."

Bryony shook her head. "I don't know. I think I made it worse."

Jude came forward and took Bryony's wrist, and she stared for what seemed like a full minute at the shape of his solid fingers and his brown, freckled knuckles. "You're an incredible mum, Bry. You want to know what I think? Glen doesn't appreciate you."

"Well, you know—he's always worked a lot and everything. Bread-winner and all that."

"OK, but what I mean is, he's never really had to parent, right? *You've* been doing all that. You've been bringing up Lydia and—instilling her with values or whatever . . . and now he fancies throwing his weight around."

"Well, yes, there might be an element of that."

"And does he ever tell you what a good mum you are? That you look great? That you're doing a terrific job with the Quiz League?"

"Oh, he doesn't care about the Quiz League. It just annoys him."

"But it's important to you."

"I know. I know that." And she didn't know what had happened, because suddenly she was crying, and Jude's sturdy arm came around her shoulders in an unembarrassed embrace. She sank into the hot cavity of his chest, with her nose pressed into the malty smell of beer on his soft plaid shirt, and stayed for a moment in mortified pleasure. How warm and solid and . . . well, restorative this felt. He was practically a stranger.

"I'm sorry," she said eventually.

And as she drew away from him, his fingers slid into her hair and dragged against her scalp. His hot, roughened mouth came down onto her own. And so insistent and assured was the act, that for a dizzying flight of seconds Bryony was glad—was relieved—to be under the strength of his resolve. And then some small, blundering mistake was made by one or both of them—their teeth clacked together or a shift in their positions made the angle too awkward—and the suspenseful enchantment of the kiss fell into something clumsy and vaguely unpleasant.

Bryony ducked her head as she pulled away, so she didn't have to look at him. She didn't want to see his face, whether it be dopey and dreamy-eyed or tense with regret.

"That wasn't—that wasn't a good idea," she said, as she gathered her things and slipped on her coat. "I have to go now."

And by the time she found the courage to look up at his face, it must have recovered, because the placid set of his mouth and the way he lazily scratched his bristled chin displayed a thorough indifference to the whole thing.

"Sure," he said. "Let me unlock the door and you can—you can get going."

* * *

Harry cut through the park with Donna on the tree-lined gravel path that passed the floodlit athletics stadium and the stone-clad walls of the park farm. As they crossed the wildflower verge to the dinosaur sculptures, the sour, grassy smell of animal dung was ripe and the soft bleating of sheep punctuated the night. Harry was tipsy on cider, with hands in his pockets, as they brushed shoulders and elbows, swaying against each other.

"Do you think Bryony and Jude are flirting?" Donna asked, out of breath.

"Are you joking?"

"Oh, I'm deadly serious. Don't you ever notice? They're all like . . ." and she gave a seductive jiggle of her shoulders before she bent over in laughter. "Oh, look," she said, stalking up to the severed stone head of a dinosaur, which looked more like a dragon, sitting in a ring of brick on the grass. "I love this thing." She slapped the top of its head before perching on its snout. "So, what's that?" She nodded to the John Lewis suit bag.

"New suit."

"For what?"

"An interview."

"You're being deliberately evasive, Harry."

"You'll think it's a bad idea."

"Well, alright. Tell me anyway." Donna looked well-meaning enough, pleasantly sleepy and content.

"They're rehiring at Kingsley."

"Oh." Donna faced the lake. "That *is* a shit idea. Is this the place with the guy—your ex's new boyfriend?"

He winced. "Might be my new manager," he said.

"You're hung up on your ex-girlfriend who's with your ex-work colleague . . ." An outbreak of laughter stopped her from speaking. "And now he's going to . . . now he's going to be your boss. Oh God, that's funny."

In the ripple of her laughter, he slumped next to her on the dinosaur head. Alright—maybe it was pretty ludicrous when you said it out loud. "OK," he said. "Want to hear something really funny?'"

Donna faced him, bright with anticipation. "What?"

"I never told my mum—Jesus, this is embarrassing—I never told my mum that me and Vivienne broke up."

Donna's eyebrows leapt in delight. Her hand slapped against her mouth. "You what?"

"She still thinks—" and now Harry couldn't stop laughing either— "she still thinks we're together."

"Oh my God, stop it."

"So every time—every time I see her," he said, breathless, "I have to pretend she's at work or something."

They were both silently shaking as wave after wave of convulsive laughter gripped their stomachs and then when a lone sheep bleated mournfully into the silence, it set them off again.

Recovering, Donna stemmed her watering eyes with the heels of her hands, whimpering helplessly. "Just make sure they treat you decently," she said.

"Yeah, yeah. OK."

"No, I mean it. You allow people to treat you quite terribly, Harry. And why? You're funny, you get on with everyone, you're not bad on the eye. Everyone likes you. All of us."

His faced turned warm. He couldn't remember a time when anyone had said anything like that to him; the vulnerable honesty in Donna's blue eyes and the uncharacteristic shy curve of her mouth was too much. She blinked and gave an imperceptible shake of her head before her gaze turned hard once again, like a camera shutter snapping closed.

"I mean," she said, "you wouldn't catch me dead going back to somewhere that sacked me."

"I wasn't sacked. I was made redundant." He shook his head. Why couldn't anyone understand that? Did he seem particularly sackable?

"What's the difference?"

"Oh, for the love of—I've been trying to find another job. You *know* I have. And my mum—"

"I'm sure your mum would rather you be happy, Harry. Not have a job you hate."

"Why wouldn't it make me happy?"

"It's because you're obsessed with Vivienne, isn't it? You want to keep tabs on her and the boyfriend."

Stunned, Harry said nothing. The suit bag hung stupidly from his limp hand as he opened and closed his mouth, trying to formulate some sort of rebuttal.

"Do you not know how to live your life without her?" Donna carried on. "Are you so terrified of being by yourself?"

And what would she know about it? All she ever did was stay up all night watching *Blockbusters* and pissing everybody off. He was full of the night in her flat after the disastrous third match of the Quiz League, of her goading Jaime, of her shutting herself in the bathroom as Bernadette beat her fists against the door, of the piles of bullshit books and the crumbling disarray of the mutilated chimney breast.

"Alright. Alright—yeah, so I don't want to be by myself. So what? And I don't want my mum to know any of it ever happened. Because she'd be ashamed of me. I'm meant to take care of her and I can't even take care of myself. Happy?"

He saw an embarrassed swallow roll down Donna's neck, but he hadn't yet delivered his final blow.

"And being by yourself works out so well for you, doesn't it?" he said.

Her chin jerked back. "Excuse me?"

"You don't care about anything—your job, your flatmate, pissing away all your money. Where're your family? The quiz is the only thing you care about—so much that you scare everyone to death over it. And what for?"

"For God's sake." She twisted away and began pulling at the ends of her hair. Her knees rapidly bobbed up and down. "Why bring all that up? Leave it. It's none of your business."

"And Vivienne is none of *your* business."

Donna stood up abruptly. Her arms clamped around her stomach as she spun on her heel. "See you at the quarter-final, then," she said over her shoulder, and she stalked into the darkness.

CHAPTER TWENTY

Question: *Eostre, the Anglo-Saxon goddess of spring, is said to have inspired which festive character?*
Answer: *The Easter Bunny*

Bryony used to love Easter: hiding chocolate eggs in the garden to be collected in a bright, ribboned basket, constructing Easter hats to be worn with both pride and embarrassment at school. Now Lydia and Arthur only wanted to sullenly chew on shards of melting chocolate in front of the TV, while outside the wet streets were swept by heavy gusts of wind for the best part of the school holiday. And on Good Friday, the first sunny day of the week, they were getting ready to leave for lunch at her parents' house. Bryony had fabricated a local event they "absolutely couldn't miss" for Easter Sunday, knowing that she wouldn't be able to bear the natural melancholy of a Sunday afternoon combined with a visit to her mother. But now they were running forty minutes late. The table would already be set with the "good cutlery" and the lamb resting in its swaddle of foil on top of the oven. And Lydia chose this moment to reach what appeared to be the pinnacle of her adolescent turmoil.

"I don't *want* to go to Granny Win's house," she whined, pink-faced at the threshold of Bryony's bedroom door, "I want to go to *Keesha's*."

Bryony frantically rummaged to find a pair of socks that didn't have a hole at the toe or heel. She held her breath for ten seconds and released it slowly, but it didn't prevent the prickle of sweat from forming between her shoulder blades.

"I'm sure Keesha is doing something with her family today too, Lydia."

"Well, she's not," Lydia hissed, "because she just asked me to come over, so she can't be doing anything else, can she?"

"Well, *we're* doing something else. And we're leaving in five minutes. So that's that."

"*Dad!*" Lydia's screech trembled with the pounding of her feet on the landing floorboards. "*Dad!*"

"Wha-at?" Glen's voice floated up from the living room, sounding bored.

"I want to go to Keesha's today."

"Nope."

Lydia released another wail and slammed her bedroom door with such shuddering force that a slender glass bottle of perfume on Bryony's dresser toppled over.

Downstairs, as Bryony stalked between the kitchen and the living room, balancing armfuls of discarded cups of tea, greased plates of toast crusts, apple cores, and banana skins, Arthur plodded in slow circles around the hallway, reading *Moby Dick*. In the living room, Glen held a folded newspaper on his thigh, penciling in a sudoku and biting the tip of his tongue between his front teeth.

It had been a week since she'd kissed Jude—or since Jude had kissed her, or whatever had happened. She had been able to forget about it for long pockets of time, when pairing up four separate sets of laundered socks or when Arthur had cried in frustration over his maths homework ("Simplifying Fractions"), which Bryony didn't understand either. But at other times it caught her with such breathtaking shame that she could only stand in complete stillness with a hand pressed against her ribs, while she waited for the wave of self-disgust to pass: she had cheated on her husband. Or if it hadn't been cheating, it was something remarkably close. Sometimes she would find herself staring at Glen's stoic profile while he sleepily watched TV. Oh, you silly old bastard, she would think, you don't even know.

"What's the matter?" Glen said suddenly.

"What?"

"Well, what are you doing?"

Her hands had been twisting the fabric tieback of the curtain into a tight rope.

"Oh, sorry."

"That's alright."

"We need to get going." Bryony went to the bottom of the stairs. "*Lydia!*"

"I'm not coming." Her voice thundered down from her closed bedroom door. "It's my holiday too, and you think you can make me do whatever you . . ."

But as Bryony climbed the stairs, ensuring her footfalls sounded heavy and commanding, Lydia's voice trailed away, replaced by the sound of soft whimpering and frantically shuffling feet. Bryony opened Lydia's bedroom door and didn't at first understand what she was seeing. Lydia had covered her head with her arms, facing Bryony with her two pointed elbows.

"Go away!"

"What—"

"Go *away!*"

The carpet was strewn with dark crescents. With catching breath, Lydia allowed Bryony to pull her arms down, and her defiant face crumpled as she exposed her violently cut hair. Unable to form words, Bryony touched the shredded ends—some around her jawline and others up by her ears—while Lydia's silently trembling face became striped with tears.

"Oh, Lydia."

The most shocking thing about it was how little surprise Bryony felt. She only felt fatigue. In fingering the blunt bristles of hair, Bryony found the sad memory of Lydia's soft downy toddler head. (Was some of the hair curling on the carpet the same hair Bryony had once brushed and plaited?) And now it would all go in the bin with the apple cores and toast crusts, and Lydia wouldn't ever look the same again.

"Well, do we have to?" Glen had questioned when Bryony insisted they were still going—that they were leaving *now*—while Lydia sat on the bottom stair with the hood of her coat pulled up and her head hanging over her knees. "Why don't you go ahead with Arthur, and I can try to have a—you know—a chat with her."

"I see." And Bryony didn't care if both children could hear her. "So she cuts her hair off to get out of something, and we just let her? What is she learning then? Other than that she gets exactly what she wants, exactly when she wants it? Even when she's acting completely crazy. What sort of parents allow something like that? Are we in charge or is she?"

As the car swerved and weaved through the holiday traffic of South London, as it dissolved into the leafy suburbs of Kent, Lydia rode in the back seat in a quietly hiccupping daze, having allowed the remains of her hair to be clipped back behind her ears. Even Arthur hadn't tried to provoke a response out of Lydia, perhaps restrained by his parents' stiff, angry silence and the way Glen turned the wheel a little too sharply. When they rolled onto Bryony's parents' driveway, even before the hissing of the gravel beneath the tires had come to a stop, Bryony was out of the car and pressing the brass doorbell. She held her breath as the blurred figure of her tall, trim, neatly dressed mother emerged through the stained-glass panel.

"Oh, sweet pea," Win greeted her, stamping a scented kiss on Bryony's cheek. She was the sort of gray-haired, high-cheekboned woman some might call "handsome." "We wondered when you'd ever come." She beckoned them all inside with a waving hand, into the hallway and the smell of cooking meat.

"Mum, listen. Lydia's had a bit of an . . . episode."

"Oh?"

"She's cut off all her hair."

"What?"

"And I need you to pretend not to notice."

"*All* of her hair?"

"A lot of it. Look, can we not make a big—"

"Well, she's got such lovely hair."

"I suppose my point is that it's happened now, and I need you to—"

"Well, I'm not sure I—Joseph!"

And then everyone was ambling into the hallway at once—Glen with Lydia and Arthur, and Bryony's father, a tall, thin, stooped man who insisted to everyone that they "Call me Joe," and whom everyone obliged except his wife. Joe polished his wire-rimmed glasses on the flapping hem of his plaid shirt before settling them on his nose and squinting at his daughter.

"What's going on?"

"Lydia's cut off all her lovely hair," Win said, with all her fingers held to her wobbling cheeks.

"Why's that?"

"She's acting completely crazy!" called Arthur as he barreled past all of them, into the wide, bright kitchen where the heaped dishes for lunch and a marzipan-topped Simnel cake sat on the polished worktop.

"Can we just—can we just sit down and not talk about it?" Bryony pleaded.

"Well, honestly." Win led them stiffly through to a sunlit, tiled sitting room where plump blue cushions sat at right-angles on the deep sofas, and a succession of glass doors opened onto the lush, green expanse of a tree-lined garden. The ceiling gave way to a wide lantern skylight into which a number of brimstone butterflies frequently fluttered; there they would overheat and die, falling to the tiled floor like pale, shriveling mint leaves.

As they all sat with chattering teacups and iced glasses of lemonade, Bryony clasped her kneecaps in a high-shouldered readiness to escape. Win recounted yesterday's trip to the garden center, where her favored clematis had been out of stock, while Joe ponderously nodded along, interjecting that the new shortbread in the cafe had been very good, however.

To one side a polished mahogany dining table awaited the uncomfortable formality of their Easter lunch, and after Win had ushered them over to take their seats and arranged the steaming meat and vegetables on the table, she sat down opposite Lydia and shook out her napkin.

They had been slicing their potatoes and chewing tough cuts of lamb for all of three minutes when Win said, "You do realize you look like one of those grunge people, Lydia."

Lydia's head drooped, which Bryony recognized as shame, but Win wasn't finished. "And don't you sit at this table looking sullen. It's not *our* fault you did this to yourself."

Joe cleared his throat. "I don't know. It's sort of funky."

"She wants to look like Cara Delevingne," said Arthur. "But now she looks like a broom."

Bryony forced brightness into the stumble of her voice. "Well! So, you know what I'd like your thoughts on? I'm thinking of applying to university."

Glen blinked at her. Win hurried to chew and swallow her mouthful of lamb. "Oh, sweet pea, that's a marvelous idea. Isn't that marvelous, Joseph?"

"It most certainly is."

"What a shame you can't go to Durham where you were supposed to go," said Win.

"First I'm hearing of it," Glen said. "First the pub quiz business, now this."

"What 'pub quiz business'?" said Win.

"She's entered a pub quiz tournament," Glen said.

"That's rather juvenile, isn't it?"

Bryony rested her tense wrists on the edge of the table. If she looked at Glen now, she may well kill him. "It's just a bit of fun, Mum. A way to make friends. And I really enjoy it. It's really sort of . . ." She swallowed. None of them would understand. "Anyway, the university thing—I haven't looked into it or anything. It would have to fit around the kids and everything like that."

"Well, with these two—" Win nodded to Lydia and Arthur— "about to start lives of their own, I think that's absolutely the right decision. Oh, and you will do history, won't you?"

"Yes, I thought I might."

"Well, look," said Glen. "I know history is what you're interested in, and if you want to go and do something like this then alright, we could probably make it work. But history's not very practical, is it? I mean, what can you do with it?"

"Glen, dear," Win said mildly. "This isn't something you'd understand."

Bryony's cheeks flushed intensely. If only Glen had put down his knife and fork with some indignation and (politely) put Win in her place, but he was caught by surprise, with a trailing string of asparagus dangling from his bottom lip. But still, Glen had surprised her; she'd had every expectation of him ridiculing the idea.

"Mum," she said. "That's ridiculous. Glen is perfectly entitled to have his own opinion on—"

"All I meant was that Glen was never interested in university, were you?"

From the tight sound of Glen's voice, he was pressing his teeth together. "Not really," he said.

"So he wouldn't understand your passion for it, sweet pea. But tell me, how would you manage the financial side of things?"

"A loan. A scholarship. There's all kinds of—you know—assistance."

Win laced her fingers together. "You will make sure, of course, that the children are out of any . . . well, difficult phases first?"

Bryony resumed cutting through a thick sinew of fat. "Well, yes. Of course."

"My concern," Win said with a long blink, "is that Lydia is obviously under some less-than-desirable influences."

Glen solemnly chewed with an elbow resting lazily on the table. "Come on, you never did anything crazy as a teenager, Win?"

"No, I did not. I respected my parents."

"It's just hair, Mum," Bryony said, forking forcibly through her food. "It will grow back."

"Oh well, then, if that's the case, why don't we let her get her nose pierced or shave her head completely, as if she's in prison or something?"

"We're perfectly able to—"

"Goodness! You were only children yourselves when you had her."

"I am here, you know," Lydia said suddenly. "I can hear you, and I can speak for myself. I didn't even want to come to your stupid lunch today." But her voice gave rise to hysteria at the end and a flush crept from her neck to her cheeks.

"What on earth has got into you, Lydia?" Win dabbed the corners of her mouth with her napkin. "I think you ought to go and compose yourself, don't you? Go on—you can sit outside for a few minutes. It's not as if you've even touched your food."

Lydia pushed away from the table, and Win visibly winced at the sound of the chair legs scraping against the tiles. She stalked out into the bright sunlight with her arms folded and settled onto a wooden swing that hung from an old cherry tree. Maybe Glen had been right; Lydia should have stayed at home. They all should have.

"Now, listen, Win—" Glen began.

"Arthur," Win said, "out you go too."

"Oh, but I haven't finished my potatoes."

"You can take your plate out to the patio table."

Arthur got hesitantly out of his seat, and Joe followed after him, perhaps not caring to listen to what came next, having heard it several times before.

"Now *you* listen, please," Win said. "What exactly is going on here?"

Under her mother's steady, gray stare, Bryony, as she always did, began to shrink into herself, and Glen was bent over his plate in a docile slouch too. Having had Lydia when parenthood felt as alien to her as having a bank account, it had been natural to defer to Win as the mother who knew best and did better. And would that ever go away?

With her hands pressed between her thighs, Bryony lifted her chin. "She's thirteen. She's going through a—I don't know—a rebellious stage. What do they call 'it? Exerting her independence, pushing boundaries."

"Two-year-olds push boundaries, dear."

"You know, Mum, I'm closer to being a teenager than you are."

"Oh! Don't remind me! And it seems I'll be picking up after you and Glen forever. Do you know what worries me, Bryony—"

Bryony pinched the bridge of her nose. "Oh, please, not this again, Mum."

"What worries me is that neither you or Glen have enough experience—or maturity—to guide her. And now you're off down the pub every night—what sort of impression does that give? Young people need *guidance*."

"I am not off down—Look, we're fine, Mum. We're fine."

"Oh? Well, if you seem to know everything." And she picked up her knife and fork to primly slice and spear her Chantenay carrots.

Joe brought the children back in with a reassuring clasp on each of their small shoulders. They sat for the rest of the lunch in solemnly chewing silence, while Joe narrated a "fascinating" crime drama that had aired on the BBC the previous evening, taking his weary audience through a twisting convoluted plot until he ended in a triumph that none of them understood: "And she was in the car boot the *whole* time!"

"Well, Joseph," Win said when he had finished. "That's hardly appropriate for the dinner table."

After an hour or two of sleepy conversation back in the sitting room, where Arthur relieved the tension with an animated retelling of his school trip to Shakespeare's Globe, they were set free onto the gravel driveway once again. Win planted a dry kiss on Bryony's cheek and grasped her hand before she fled for the car.

"You will think about what I said, won't you?"

"Yes, Mum, I'll think about what you said."

But on the drive home through the fast-disappearing countryside, the atmosphere was no better. Arthur inserted his earbuds to listen to an audio book, and Lydia flipped up her hood to ignore them all.

Later that evening, when Lydia and Arthur were safely behind their bedroom doors, Glen shook out and refolded the newspaper on his sudoku page. He licked the nib of a ballpoint pen with the flick of his tongue before saying, "You always let her make us out to be failures."

"I hardly 'let her.' She does exactly what she wants. And telling her about the Quiz League didn't help, did it? Besides, you let her just as much as I do."

"She isn't my mum." Glen jabbed a finger into the hallway, as if Win may have lain in wait behind their front door. "Your messed-up mother—your job."

"My 'messed-up mother' got us this house, Glen."

He gave the folds of his newspaper a stiff little jerk before poising his pen over the page. His mouth was twisted in resentment. "I could have done it by myself. I never even had the chance. I was seventeen years old, for God's sake."

Well, she'd been seventeen too, and if they couldn't even find any common ground on that, then what hope was there? It was only eight o'clock, but Bryony could see nothing else to do but brush her teeth, pull on her pajamas and sink into the refuge of her soft double bed. And even when she heard a door opening on the landing, and Lydia's soft, tearful "Mum?," she burrowed her head into the pillows and told herself she had imagined it.

CHAPTER TWENTY-ONE

Question: *What is the world's most expensive country in which to buy property?*
Answer: *Monaco*

With freshly cut hair and in his new, pressed suit, Harry sat in the white, brightly lit client's lounge of Kingsley & Co. in a big, blue designer chair, about the same shape as an eggshell. With his feet dangling an inch above the floor like a child's, he could not find a dignified arrangement for his hanging legs, and his belt buckle was a notch too tight. He tried to loosen it, but a frowning woman sitting across from him, in one of the more sensible seats, eyed his fumbling hands suspiciously. Though it was the Saturday between Good Friday and Easter Sunday, the dedicated people of Kingsley saw not a moment to be wasted. Around him the loud, over-confident voices of "selling" rang above the clacking keyboards and ringing phones, punctuated with the polite, mumbled replies of harangued clients.

"And the best bit is, with your budget, you've got some of the best roads in Crystal Palace open to you—Belvedere Road, Fox Hill . . ." an agent called Charlie was saying to an amiably nodding couple.

"And this one is two doubles?" the woman asked, inspecting one of the property brochures.

"Yes, that's right. Two bedrooms."

"But are they doubles?"

"They both have double beds in them. Now, if you look at the . . ."

And what a power play it was to have him come in on a Saturday, as though they were testing his resolve. But Harry was here, as cool-headed as he could be and ready to make them believe he was indispensable, no matter what day of the week it was. The only thing that worried him was the fight with Donna; it kept pummeling into his thoughts. He should have called her.

In front of him a table hosted a fanned array of slick, stapled booklets—an internal publication called *Make a Move*. He used his dangling foot to nudge a copy to the table's edge, but the hand of the seated woman came forward and plucked it up; she gave it to him with silent disdain.

"Oh. Thanks—thanks very much."

Flicking through the familiar glossy pages, he found himself tutting and sighing. Christ, they still hadn't sold that four-bed on Millen Road. And it was horrendously overpriced. What it needed was a cash buyer, a developer, who could knock it into two flats and—

"Harry?" Darren, tall with a tight crop of coiled hair, came quickly around a corner of desks. He covered half the width of the room in three sweeping strides and, with what seemed an impossibly long arm, outstretched his hand to shake Harry's.

"Good to see you." He jabbed his thumb over his shoulder. "Shall we?"

Harry followed Darren around a sweep of computer-topped desks, where the agents sat peering into their screens or talking into their phones. Ashton, sitting in the middle of the cluster and appearing to take up more physical space than anyone else, caught his eye and pointed a finger at him, cocking his thumb as though to imitate a gun. He winked and clicked his tongue, saying something that Harry didn't quite hear. It might have been "Harry boy" or "Oi, Harry," but whatever it was, Ashton could fuck off.

"Let's get down to it," Darren said once they were enclosed in his office. He sidled into the chair behind a desk that was far too big for the cramped room. Harry edged onto a seat that was backed up against the wall. Darren took some time to adjust his rolled shirtsleeves, then took a glug of water while he side-eyed his computer screen and made a few important clicks of his mouse.

It was hardly a matter of a formal interview, Darren told him, but they should aim to establish the terms of returning. And it was no secret, Darren let him know, lowering his voice and dropping his chin, that Kevin and the "redundancy business" had left them "in a sticky spot—a very sticky spot indeed."

"Now, listen, we don't have the budget for another senior agent right now—I know that's disappointing—but will something else do nicely?"

"Well . . ." and Harry could hear the weakness in his voice, "suppose I have to hear what it is first."

"Ashton tells me you're not too keen on a trainee position. Can't blame you. But look, Harry, I don't want you to be unhappy. And Ashton's really looking out for you here."

"Oh. Well, that's . . . nice."

"So how's this? We can offer you junior agent on sales—shadowing Ashton. Your job will practically be the same in almost every way."

Apart from the salary, Harry wanted to say. This sort of bullshit might work on a school leaver, but Jesus—Harry was too old for this. And shadowing Ashton was completely out of the question.

"Darren, I—look, I appreciate what you're doing for me here, but that's not going to work. I was on my way to top sales person before I was—before the redundancies. I've been part of this place since I was twenty-three. Did my stint at the social housing group, finished up the apprenticeship. Doesn't that count for anything?"

"Look, mate." And Darren popped the top button of his collar open and loosened his tie, as though to demonstrate what a "mate" he was. "I know you and Ashton have had some sticky times. I get it. Not nice for anyone. But this shadowing business is just a formality. Besides, he's assistant manager now. You can learn a lot from him. No one wants to sell you short, mate. Least of all me. But—if I can be plain?—do you have any other prospects right now? I mean, please say so if you do." Darren laced his hands together expectantly.

Darren had him over a barrel. What leverage did he have? None. And why did he keep saying "sticky"?

"Three months, six months," Darren continued. "Let's get that profit margin up and we can talk again. Sound good? You'll have to start back on probation, of course—company policy—but the perk of that means you don't have to work notice. You know . . . if things don't work out. But I'm sure you won't be leaving us again, eh?"

It was almost a repeat of the conversation he'd had with Ashton over dinner. It was almost as if they had rehearsed it, to encircle Harry like two pinstriped velociraptors.

He could have said he'd think it over, give him a call later—but what would have been the point? He was offered a salary two-thirds of what he used to make and, feeling used, he shook Darren's clammy hand. Out on the office floor, clasping Harry's shoulder, Darren called for attention and made the announcement that Harry would be rejoining the branch. And Harry wished he hadn't, because there was a distinct lack of interest in their polite but tired smiles, and in the way their eyes wandered back to their emails before Darren had even finished speaking. And maybe it was because it was four-thirty the day before Easter Sunday and everyone wanted to go home, but what Harry really wanted to say was, "Well, OK. You think this is what I want to be doing with my life? I can't wait to be rid of the whole sorry lot of you." But then Ashton was lumbering over and wringing Harry's hand in the grasp of his gigantic fingers, his eyes protruding and his white teeth bared in a manic grin.

"Congratulations, mate. Good to have you on board."

Then it caught Harry's eye, in Ashton's other hand—a large white mug, bearing the slogan WORLD'S BEST BOYFRIEND. And Harry found his gaze wandering away from Ashton's face to stare it down, perhaps willing it to crack in half by the force of his jealousy.

And Ashton must have noticed, because he slid the mug onto a desk, saying, "Sorry, mate. I'm an insensitive bastard sometimes. You don't need to be seeing that."

"If that's what you want, then I'm happy for you," Harry's mum told him, when he called her on his shortcut home through the park to deliver the news. "And is it? What you want, I mean?"

Harry had expected a high cry of relief, a flurry of chatter and Thank God's, but he only heard a careful sense of uncertainty, and she was speaking too slowly. The birdsong in the park was more loudly enthusiastic than her voice. "What was that? Is it what I want? Well, you know—course it is," he assured her, having the sense that he was assuring himself too. "You're happy, aren't you?"

"Oh, of course I'm happy. I'm happy, love. I didn't mean to . . . Well done. Vivienne's relieved, I expect?"

And once he'd ended the vaguely disappointing call with his mother and called Vivienne instead, she *was* relieved.

"Well, that's fantastic!" Vivienne exclaimed in a shrill that made Harry's ear ring. "I mean, it sounds like it all went perfectly."

And he didn't have the heart to tell her that the position wasn't what he'd hoped for and that the salary was rubbish too, so he simply said, "Yep."

"Bet you can't wait to tell your mum. She can stop fretting about it now."

"Oh, I did. Just now."

"You called her first?"

"Well, I . . . Is that OK? I just thought—"

"No, it's fine. It's fine. I just thought you would have called me."

"You're right. I should've. All this—it's all down to you really, so—you know—thank you."

"Oh stop. You'll make me cry."

And the thought of her dampened, pink cheeks and her delicate, white fingers lifting up to blot the corner of one eye was enough to make his throat close in longing. He stopped at the railings surrounding the lake, where the dinosaur statues sat in their muddy water. A lazy gathering of white birds perched atop their stone heads, pecking and rooting at their feathers.

"How about a drink?" he said. "To celebrate."

"Oh, I . . . well, I suppose Ashton *is* out tonight anyway. Sure, then. Why not? Do you want to come over here?"

He didn't want to go to Ashton's flat; there would be no joy in seeing all the things that made him more successful than Harry—the leather three-piece suite, a seventy-five-inch television, probably one of those fancy coffee machines. But he couldn't deny the appeal of being in solitude with Vivienne, where there were no waiters to stumble in on their conversation to ask, "How is everything?," and no need to strain forward to hear her voice over the clash of knives and forks. And there was something definitely thrilling in Ashton being unaware of it too. Maybe he'd do something to mess with Ashton's head—hide all the teaspoons or his toothpaste. If you couldn't bring total destruction down on a man then at least you could bring small madness.

He made his way to Streatham Hill by train, to its high stacks of restaurants, flats, and offices that obscured the sky, and the tree-lined lanes of traffic that blared and trundled along its A-road. Outside on the pavement, Harry stood for a long time looking up at the art deco window arches of Ashton's flat. In a burst of inspiration, he jogged with his suit jacket and tie flapping to a small supermarket, where he purchased a drooping bouquet of tulips. And then he was standing, breathing hard, at the door to Ashton's flat again, pressing the intercom button. Over the speaker, Vivienne's shy voice told him to "Come on up," and an abrupt and obnoxiously loud buzz admitted him into the building.

Harry climbed the stairs, flattening the length of his tie. The fragrant scent of the tulips began to make him feel queasy. Well, why not just kiss her when she opened the door? That was what she'd really invited him round for, wasn't it? And his chance came when she swung the door wide, with both her arms braced to accept the weight of his body onto hers. With the tulips crushed between them and the crackle of cellophane in his ear, he foraged in the sweet warmth of her neck and then found her mouth, which tasted of mint and lipstick.

Oh, she was a marvel. She was a miracle. It was happening. It was really happening.

With a groping hand she closed the door and then they were stumbling into the living room, wrestling with the restraints of their clothing, fumbling with buttons and hooks and buckles and zippers. The tulips landed on the floor and Harry's shoe slid on the small puddle of water that leaked from their stems.

They broke apart momentarily so he could release his arms from the confines of his shirt, and he caught sight of two champagne flutes on top of a breakfast bar. Vivienne began to pull him toward a room that must

have been the bedroom, but in a mumbled protest against her mouth—
"No, no. Let's stay here"—he managed to get her onto the sofa. He
would've gladly had Vivienne on any surface available, but the thought
of Ashton's bedroom, where he snored and scratched himself and also
clasped and writhed with Vivienne in a breathless tumble, was so off-
putting that it threatened to ruin everything.

They freed themselves of the last of their clothing, but in the sounds
of their hot breath and the scrape of the sofa legs against the floorboards, Harry found an awkwardness in their blundering rhythm.
Should he be somehow holding her or was it fine to brace his arms
against the cushions like this? Could he ask her to scoot down a little to
stop the collision of his head with the sofa's arm, or would she be
annoyed? And also came small observations about Vivienne herself—a
whiff of something sour, like rancid milk, that he could momentarily
catch on her skin or breath or hair, and a dark, protruding mole on her
neck that sprouted a thin wire of curled hair.

Afterwards, they fell apart, taking pause to recover their breathing,
and then sat up on the sofa to pick up the clothes that had landed within
arms' reach. Vivienne held her blouse against her chest as she raised a
tentative hand to smooth the tangle of her hair.

"Well, I suppose that was unexpected," she said. The right side of
her face was red, rubbed raw from the fiction of his stubble.

"Yeah, I suppose it was."

"Scuse me a sec, Harry." She skittered away on her tiptoes around
the bend of the living room and disappeared into a corridor, and all he
could do was sit there in a stunned, clammy stupor. She was his again.
When he walked into the offices at Kingsley next week, he could laugh
softly under his breath at any of Ashton's condescending little jibes—
the best man had won.

When he had finished pulling on his clothes and rebuttoning his
shirt, Vivienne reappeared in a knee-length dressing gown that she had
belted so firmly that its fluffy collar closed around her neck.

"Well, this was for you." She touched the stems of the champagne
flutes. "Would you like some?"

"Sure," he said, so she went about the business of fetching the bottle
of champagne from the fridge and uncapping it, then wincing and

squealing in fright as she released the cork with a deafening pop and it shattered one of the kitchen spotlights. They toed around the kitchen tiles to clear it up, hurrying to restore some semblance of what the afternoon had promised them.

They sat at the breakfast bar and sipped at their champagne, making polite attempts at conversation.

"Well, here's to the job, then."

"Oh, thanks, and, you know, thanks for everything."

And when he had drained his glass, and after he said he'd better be going, they both made promises to see each other again soon, but he couldn't ignore how Vivienne looked slightly relieved. She may have been worried about Ashton coming home or she may have wanted to wander alone through the rooms of the flat, wondering what the hell she'd done.

"I want to hear all about it," she said as he pulled on his shoes at the door. "The job, I mean." And she gave him a restrained kiss on the cheek.

Harry swung down the stairs and into the blue evening, feeling a swelling pride in his chest. The honking traffic of Streatham High Road, the twilight birdsong and the pink setting sun all existed as a backdrop to his triumph, to the restoration of things to where they belonged. And he assured himself that any sense of awkwardness was only because they were out of practice. These things had a way of working themselves out; you could hardly slip back into it without any effort. It was only when he'd clambered onto a bus to Crystal Palace, after patting down his pockets and finding them empty, that he realized he'd left his tie somewhere on the floor of Ashton's living room.

CHAPTER TWENTY-TWO

Question: *What is the name of the oldest boat ever to have been discovered, found in the Netherlands and believed to be from the early Mesolithic Period?*
Answer: *The Pesse Canoe*

The voicemail left by Lottie on Easter Monday was three minutes long.

". . . and to not even come to see us at Easter when you missed Christmas. Do you have any idea how much you've upset Mum? By all means, go ahead and destroy yourself, Donna, but if Mum has to put up with anymore of your . . ."

Accompanying that was three missed calls, and the day only got worse when Bernadette sat her down to "have a talk."

"So I gave the landlord notice," Bernadette said. She had set the coffee table with a teapot and a plate of stale biscuits to break the news. "I only needed to give one month, but I gave three. I think that's fair enough, don't you?"

Donna became still under Bernadette's dark, apprehensive stare. "Well." She replaced her scalding mug onto the coffee table. "Why wait? Why not bugger off now?"

"We don't need to be hostile, Donna. Things don't always work out. It's fine."

"If you think I need you—if you think I need your money or your company or—well, anything, I don't. So as far as I'm concerned—just, whatever, OK?"

Bernadette's long limbs were bent like a cowering insect's, with her knees held to her chest. "Oh," she moaned, burying her face. "Look, I've told you. That's all I needed to do. Good luck."

"Wait—can I still have that guest pass to Loft?"

But Bernadette only let her slick tongue protrude in an exaggerated sigh, unfolded her legs, and went to her bedroom, shutting the door behind her.

Leaving the tea on the table to grow cold, Donna wedged her slipper-socked feet into her boots, crammed her trench coat over her sweatshirt and left the flat, slamming the front door behind her and almost tripping on the lichen-mottled path of broken mosaic tiles. She kicked out in annoyance at anything in her way—a discarded aluminum can, a child's scooter leaning against a garden wall. Well, whatever. Honestly, *whatever*. At least she would never again have to deal with Bernadette's cackling sisters who would stay entire weekends, or the empty bottles of mouthwash that accumulated around the bathroom sink—and what was a "financial wellness coach" supposed to be anyway? When a train sped past through the leaf-tangled wire fencing beside the pavement, she allowed herself a small outcry of anger, to be swallowed by its sound.

She entered Crystal Palace Park through the gold-tipped, speared gate on Anerley Hill. The dusty pebbled ground crunched underneath her boots as she hurried past the stone arches of the palace ruins. Smiling people sat picnicking on the expanses of green lawn, and the brick-red sphinxes rested placidly under the skeletal structure of the towering steel transmitter. She passed canopies of browning firs and solid oaks, and a gated fishing lake where only mysterious solitary figures were permitted to enter. Then the squat, mirrored sweep of the sports center and the jeering calls of the volleyball players outside on its sanded courts, until she finally came to rest, breathing heavily in a sweat, at the dark, leaf-spotted water of the boating lake. She joined the queue for the thirty-minute hire of one of the pedalos. She wanted to glide away, if only for half an hour.

"Shit," she said under her breath, clawing a cigarette out of her pocket and fumbling it into her mouth. She lit it and sucked deeply, cowering away from the other smiling people in the queue, with their white teeth and glinting sunglasses.

What was she supposed to do now? And who was she going to live with? Was she supposed to trawl those awful websites for strange, solitary people whose lives were in ruins? There'd be single, teary women whose boyfriends had broken up with them, who would either sit forlornly around the living room, agonizing over "what went wrong," or insist on going out drinking every night to prove how happy they were. Or worse: a perky, grinning couple requiring a flat share to "save for a deposit," who would lounge tangled-limbed on the sofa each night and merrily cook spaghetti together in the kitchen while tickling each other's waists or some bullshit like that.

So Bernadette hadn't been her best friend, but at least she'd provided a consistency to Donna's days; at least Donna knew what to expect when she opened the front door every evening. And for all of Donna's bluster about the superiority of being alone, the thought of coming home to the chilled, damp-smelling darkness of an empty flat, or to someone as unknown as any stranger on the street, was enough to knock the air out of her lungs. What if she started to lose it again? What if she couldn't scrape it back together again when Bernadette wasn't at least on the other side of the door? And then the image came—it always came—of a version of her future self, tangle-haired with a spiteful, downturned mouth, shuffling down the corridors of somewhere like Meadow Hall.

She swung back her foot and kicked the railing surrounding the lake, creating a reverberating sound—*dong!*—which caused a startled silence in the queue. A flare of pain shot up from her toe to her knee.

"Shit," she said again as tears sprang to her eyes. She pelted the cigarette into the water.

"Donna?"

She jerked up to see Harry in his greasy blue windbreaker, holding a can of Diet Coke and a Mars bar wrapper.

"Oh, Harry." She rushed at him, flinging her arms around his neck and burying her nose in the warm smell of his fragrant soap, before she remembered that they had not seen each other for over two weeks, since their argument in the park. She stepped back, mortified, scrubbing at her nose. "What are you doing here?"

"Coming back from my mum's. You waiting for a boat?"

Embarrassed, Donna hastily folded the edges of her trench coat over her torso. Her gray hooded sweatshirt, bobbled jogging bottoms and purple slipper socks, bulging out over the lip of her boots, had all been picked off her bedroom floor this morning, before she had even showered or washed her face. "I can do nice things, can't I?" she asked.

His lopsided smile was forgiving. "Want some company?"

Her instinct was to say no, but she bit it back, because she didn't want to be on her own, chasing her panicked thoughts around her head in solitude. There: she'd admitted it. And what was wrong with that? "Well, alright," she said.

They were led, swaying and wobbling, onto the seats of a hulking blue plastic pedalo, and Harry surprised her when he made a clammy grab for her fingers in a move to steady her.

"You been alright?" he said after a while.

"Yeah, well. Bernadette just told me she's moving out and I . . . well, never mind."

"How come?" Harry's voice sounded too flat, and he had hesitated a moment too long; he knew why.

"Oh, I don't know. Why does anyone do anything?"

Once they were settled into the lazy, ponderous rhythm of pedaling, Donna leaned over the edge of the boat, enjoying the soundless glide over the surface of the lake. She trailed a finger through the cold, black-green water, allowing straggled, blonde tails of her hair to dangle in front of her face. The water reflected rippling pieces of the white sky, over-hanging trees and the silhouette of her own drifting figure, on which twigs whirled in a lazy current and a hovering dragonfly stitched the surface.

"How's your mum?" she said, sitting up in the seat.

"Happy I got my job back. Well, I think she's happy."

"Oh, you did? Well done."

Harry made a noise in his throat. "You don't mean that."

Donna shrugged, sweeping the pedalo's tiller left to avoid a flock of geese. "Doesn't matter what I think."

"Well, thanks anyway. You see your family?"

"No."

Donna held her gaze firmly ahead at the skyline of trees. She let a few moments of silence gather, to allow the momentum of the conversation to wither and die, but tears were stinging behind her eyes. Her throat closed. She could hear Lottie's devastating voicemail in her head.

Harry moved the grip of the tiller away from her as another boat swept toward them. "What's the matter?"

"Nothing."

"OK."

"You're a great conversationalist, Harry."

"Doesn't seem like you want to talk about it."

"Well, I would. Most people just won't . . ."

"Well, go on then."

Donna closed her eyes. Orange light shone through her eyelids. She took a breath. "I don't like going home. My dad's a nutcase."

"What does that mean?"

"He's an inpatient in Meadow Hall in Worthing—the madhouse. The mental health facility."

"Oh. What's wrong with him?"

It was easier to imagine Harry as a disembodied voice. If she looked at his smiling eyes and stupidly handsome face, her nerve would dissolve.

"I don't know. Lots of things. And my sister says I'm 'just like him.'"

"Don't be daft."

"That's what she said."

The field of green water ahead of her, spotted with bright blue pedalos, shimmered under the sun—no torrential storms had come to sweep her away, no earthquakes had opened the ground to eat her up, the horsemen of the apocalypse hadn't come to claim her: everything was just as it had been a few minutes ago.

"He was . . . How do I even describe it? He was *electrifying*, he was impulsive, but when I was young that side of it looked pretty exciting—once he took me shoplifting and had me steal a bunch of cheap bangles from a department store. I thought he was so fucking cool. And I wonder—do I feel the same way he used to? I feel . . . I don't know . . . on fire. Like I can do anything. And I mean *anything*—get a promotion, start a business, win the Quiz League, learn Mandarin." She shot off all the possibilities with quick slices of her hand. "And everyone else drives me crazy with their tedious little lives—"

"Where'd you get 'tedious'? Come on. It's like with Jaime—you start off trying to help or whatever, and then you just go off on one. She's just trying to get by. Same as all of us."

"Well, I know that, alright? I know that. That's part of the problem. Don't you see? And do you know what the most tedious part really is? I can't stick anything out. I just chuck it all away. One day I'll wake up and things'll seem a bit shit, and it just gets worse and worse. I don't know why it happens, and all I can do is wait for it to get better again."

She didn't say anything for a long time after that.

"You could talk to someone about all this," Harry said eventually.

"Oh, I'm just being dramatic, I'm sure. And anyway, I'm talking to *you* about it."

"Don't the rest of your family want to help? Don't they know all about it?"

"Oh, I don't get along with them either. My mum just . . . I sort of blame her, you know? I feel like she could have *done* something— protected us. And my sister—all she wants to do is *talk* about him. Talk about how he's doing and what he's—and I just don't want to hear it. I don't want to think about it. I spent my whole *life* thinking about it."

"Well, how about a doctor or something?"

"Oh, Harry. Doctors aren't any good. All they do is send you off with some pills and stick you on a waiting list to get you in some little room with someone who tries to make you talk about all your feelings, or your fears—or worse, your 'triggers.' God, I hate that word. No, it's useless."

Harry silently pedaled for a minute—the rise and fall of his bobbing knees calmed her—and then said, "Did I ever tell you about *my* dad? He pissed off when I was eleven and me and Mum never saw him again."

"Harry, that's terrible."

"Yeah, well."

"I'm sorry."

Harry sniffed. "Long time ago. Always said I'd take care of her, make sure she was alright and everything. I don't know—made a right hash of all that."

"But you *do* take care of her, Harry."

"Nah. Cause her more aggro than anything."

"Well, if you want to know, I'm jealous. I wish I got on with my mum like that. And you know? You guys were better off without him—your dad."

"Well, I don't know. Sometimes I think about my mum sitting around all by herself every day—eating her dinner, watching TV alone, going to bed—you know. And it sort of makes me . . . well, a bit shit-scared, if I'm honest."

"But you're free, Harry." She held up the span of her silhouetted hands against the stark white clouds, indicating the wide world before them. "You're free from anyone letting you down, and ever letting anyone else down. Wouldn't it have been better if Vivienne never had the chance to break your heart? Wouldn't you have been happier?"

"*No.*" And he answered so quickly and incredulously that Donna could only roll her eyes.

"Well, I wouldn't worry. Someone like you will never be by themselves, Harry. You're too nice."

And I'm not, she thought. Which was exactly why being alone was the safest thing for her. But if that was true, then why was she so fearful of Bernadette leaving?

When their half hour was up, they steered back to the concrete dock in front of the boathouse. As Donna rose from the seat, Harry threw his weight from side to side with a teasing grin, setting the pedalo swaying and sending Donna into a laughing fit as she splayed her limbs out to balance ("Don't you dare!"). They scrambled off, the sobering boat ride successfully dissolved in the ring of their laughter.

And on Anerley Road, before saying goodbye, Harry suddenly said, "Wait!" and dashed inside the Tesco Express. He emerged minutes later, holding a brightly boxed Easter egg, which he gave to her with an abashed and youthful grin.

"Happy Easter," he said. "Let's not fight again, OK? Because I really . . . well, it would really suck if I couldn't talk to you." Then he gathered her up, pinning her against his chest.

She wanted to tell him it would suck if she couldn't talk to him either. Because . . . because, oh, Harry, she wanted to say, you're probably the only person I talk to *at all*. But a tightness in her jaw—from embarrassment or dignity or who knew what else—would not unclench. She allowed him to let her go, wave goodbye, and set off home.

|

CHAPTER TWENTY-THREE

Question: *What American sitcom, airing from 1985 to 1992, followed four older women who share a home in Miami, Florida?*
Answer: *The Golden Girls*

At the first Quiz League matches, when Jude had turned on her and said, "Jaime . . .," all the blood used to rush away from her fingers and feet, leaving them cold, while her stomach clenched and churned beneath her hammering heart. All those people, ready to curl their lips in ridicule or hide their laughing mouths behind their hands should she get it wrong. "How embarrassing," they might say. "Why is she even here?"

But tonight—the quarter-final—the pit of her stomach was a placid lake. She'd proved her worth here, hadn't she? She'd exceeded the low expectations of being "the young one" and earned her place among them. And so what if she still wasn't quite convinced Luke was enjoying the whole thing? They were engaged now. And even if engagement didn't yet feel like the goal it was supposed to, everything would settle down soon. Whatever "settle down" meant, anyway—it sometimes seemed as indistinct as the chaotic grinding of tires on the asphalt on one of Luke's motorsport shows, where every car looped in a circle until it was time to stop. Jaime had never understood the infinite laps of a race track, and she might not ever fully understand Luke either. But that was alright, wasn't it? Wasn't it a good thing to retain an air of mystery?

Her only disappointment was not having told anyone about the engagement. When were they going to tell their families? When were they going to set a date or get a ring? And OK, maybe they weren't in a position to afford that, but it didn't stop them being able to talk about it, did it? In fact, she had already planned to tell Bryony tonight; maybe even Donna if she was in a good mood.

And suddenly Donna snapped her fingers in front of Jaime's face. Jaime blinked—all the ice in her coke had melted. Bryony stood with them at the bar, while Luke and Harry loitered by the quiz tables.

"Are you listening?" Donna said.

"Sorry. Of course I am. Sorry. Go on."

Donna was chewing intently on a piece of bubble gum. "So, the Golden Girls—"

"Oh, I've never seen it," Jaime said.

Bryony sipped at a glass of white wine. "Oh, it's so good. It's about this group of single sixty-somethings—"

"No," Donna said. "Listen—the *team* we're playing tonight—the Golden Girls."

"Oh," Bryony said. "That a good name, though."

"What I'm trying to say," Donna said, using two sets of fingers to knead her temples in circles, "is that we can't assume they're a bunch of postmenopausal old women. We shouldn't get complacent."

"Do we know they're postmenopausal?" said Jaime. "Or old, even?"

Donna backed up against the bar, resting her elbows on its top and allowing her hands, nestled in the cuffs of a shell-pink smock shirt, to dangle down from her bent wrists. She popped her gum. "You don't choose a name like the Golden Girls if you're not. But, look, who we really have to keep our eyes on is the Mile End High Club." She took a wrapper out of the pocket of her jeans and folded up her chewed cud of bubble gum, before bending her head close to them and lowering her voice. "Read about them on the Quiz League website. They haven't dropped more than four questions in any match yet."

"That's impossible," Bryony said.

"Oh, it's true. Believe me."

"Well, how was your Easter anyway, Jaime?" Bryony asked. "Did you go home or anything? To Keswick, I mean?"

"Oh, no. The train fare's pretty steep. But, well—look, as I haven't seen you guys for a couple of weeks . . ." She let a few moments of expectant silence gather, arranging her face into an expression of glee. "Luke asked me to marry him. We're engaged!"

Bryony blinked and set down her glass. "Well, that's . . . Congratulations, Jaime. That's wonderful news."

Donna's distrustful gaze slid to Bryony and then back to Jaime. "I don't get it."

"Well, we're—what's there to 'get'?"

"We don't have to get it," Bryony said, smiling with her lips closed. She looped an arm around Jaime's back to squeeze her upper arm. Jaime stiffened. What did Bryony mean?

"So when are you doing it—getting married?" Donna said.

"Oh, well, no time—you know, not yet."

"So what's the point, then?"

"Well, it's the intent, isn't it? The intent for the future."

"Oh, I see. So it's symbolic. Well, listen, best keep it symbolic until he has a job, OK? I mean it, Jaime," Donna said, her face empty of any of its sarcastic quirks. "You're clever and hardworking and—well, all of it. He's got a lot of catching up to do. Do you understand what I'm saying? Anyway," she hurriedly carried on, "you wouldn't believe what Bernadette did."

And then she launched into a lengthy explanation of the imminent departure of her flatmate—something about the landlord and notice and the flatmate's sisters and somewhere called "Loft" that required some sort of pass—as though being so uncharacteristically kind to Jaime had embarrassed her.

Jude slid up to them with his clipboard, plucking a biro from behind his ear. "On in twenty minutes, ladies. You ready?"

Bryony coughed into her hand and muttered an apology. "Excuse me, I need to . . . excuse me," she said, and walked away.

* * *

Bryony held the cool palms of her hands over her burning cheeks. She went to stand with Harry and Luke, wondering if Jude was looking at her; the temptation to turn around and check made her scalp tingle. And why had he not even glanced at her when she had arrived tonight? He'd kept his head resolutely down where he stood at the bar, but he knew she was there. What kind of person did that? She was deeply irritated, but worse than that—she was hurt.

"And I said to him, mate, I was top sales person when I left," Harry was saying to Luke. "I don't have to take anything off of you."

"Oh right. So why did you? Take anything, I mean."

"Because it's a game. Don't you see? He makes me think he's doing me a favor. I come in there and prove myself—you know—indispensable. Then I have the power. Don't you see?"

Luke took a long drink from his pint glass, then wiped his mouth with the back of his hand. He looked white and squinting with tiredness. "I don't know. It sounds like a lot of unnecessary—Oh, hi, Bry. You alright?"

"Well, I hear congratulations are in order for both of you," she said. "Well done on the job, Harry. And, Luke, congratulations on the—you know—engagement." She lifted her wine glass in a toast, but it was empty, and she wasn't sure it was a convincing toast anyway.

Harry clapped Luke on the back with such a jolt that Luke's glasses dislodged and slid down his nose. "Engaged? Good job, mate—that's great."

"Oh, well, thanks," Luke said with a small cough. He cast a look back at Jaime, who still stood at the bar with Donna. "We were planning to keep it quiet for a while, until . . . you know. I suppose we've had a lot going on. And anyway, we haven't told our parents yet or anything."

"You haven't?"

"Well, we—I suppose—I guess we . . ." A sheen of sweat had appeared over Luke's nose.

Harry slapped an open palm down on his shoulder, saying, "You take your time. It's a big deal."

No one seemed to find that very credible, and in the silence that followed, Bryony tipped her head to drain the last of her wine before remembering her glass was empty. "I'm going to get some water and sit down now."

But as she poured a clear glass of water and a tumble of ice from the jug on their table, she heard Jude's voice behind her.

"Bryony?"

"Oh. Jude."

He took her elbow, and she jerked quickly away, as if from the accidental touch of a scorching pan handle. What if Luke and Harry saw?

"Look, I just wanted to say—I guess there's nothing to say other than, well, I'm sorry."

"You don't have to apologize."

"Well, it's nice of you to say that, but—"

"Look, it's not something we should be discussing now."

If he had approached her earlier in the evening, Jude may have found a calmer, more amicable version of Bryony. Someone who might have said, "It wasn't *your* fault, Jude. There's two people to blame in something like this." But it was too late for that now.

"I suppose not," he said. "I just didn't want—I don't want it to affect the way you perform this evening, alright? That's all I came to say."

Bryony's hand began to ache in the grip of her water glass. So he thought she'd wilt like a flower in front of him. He thought her poor flustered brain, under his charm, would fail to operate.

"I don't think that's a concern, do you?"

*   *   *

Harry and Luke took their empty glasses to the bar, where Jaime and Donna stood locked in an intense conversation.

"Jaime?" Luke interrupted them. "Can we talk for a sec?" And they wandered off together, until the mumbling dissent of their voices—the kind used by couples trying not to have an obvious fight in public— slipped away.

Donna shook her head, leaning back against the bar. "Those two are doomed," she said.

"Do you have anyone coming?" Harry asked Donna. "To watch us, I mean?"

"No. Do you?"

"No."

Harry had thought about asking Vivienne, but he hadn't quite been able to gather the courage. If she said no—or worse, if she covered her mouth in a smirk, embarrassed that he'd asked—he'd be crushed. Still, his fantasies of Vivienne standing aghast with admiration in the audience had grown progressively more vivid. He would lie in bed with his unblinking stare fixed on the ceiling as the jubilant scenes of their celebrations played out. But as the visions melted into the blue dim of his bedroom, his heart would constrict with dread. What if they lost? And worse—what if it was all his fault? He could hardly bear the thought of her gaze sliding away from him; the way she might drain the remains of her drink, shrug on her coat and slip out the door.

Now Jude told them it was time to take their places at the table. And then he was clapping his hands in a loud, enthralling rhythm, stirring the audience into an excited mass before it dissolved into chaotic applause.

CHAPTER TWENTY-FOUR

Question: *What year was the chocolate candy M&M's first introduced?*
Answer: *1941*

"Harry, what is the rarest M&M color?"

"Oh . . . uh . . . yellow?"

"No, I'm sorry. Golden Girls, Misha?"

"Brown?"

"Correct. Elena . . ."

What Donna found fascinating about the Golden Girls was that every time they correctly answered, they would collectively give a little stamp of their shoes and a shimmy of their shoulders, accompanied by a high-pitched little "Woo!" They all had the same haircuts, too—neat bobs with well-combed fringes, shot with silver—which would quiver and tremble in tandem with their shimmies, resting on the shoulders of their color-coordinated turtlenecks. And the crowd was rooting for them: the applause was longer and louder when they completed any streak of correct answers. When the Quizzy Peppers, almost out of breath with the effort, achieved a streak of eight—*eight!*—a pathetic round of clapping rattled around the room. And Donna, in disbelief, had almost thrown up her hands—what did these people want from them?

"Suppose they love an underdog," said Harry, who had slumped low onto his chair, always a sign he was ready to concede defeat. She had pulled him up by his elbow and rallied him to focus.

"Susan, what is the common name for dried plums?"

"Prunes."

"Correct!"

And at thirty-one points (now thirty-two . . . now thirty-four) to the Quizzy Peppers' twenty-two, it might not matter if they were postmenopausal or how much they Woo'ed and shimmied; they were soaring ahead.

"Gunita, what was the first soft drink consumed in space?"

"Lemonade?"

"No, I'm sorry. Red Hot Quizzy Peppers. Donna?"

"Coke?"

"Correct. Harry, which country invented ice cream?"

"Pass to Bryony."

"USA?"

"I'm sorry. Golden Girls. Una?"

"China."

"Correct."

"Woo!"

"Damn," Bryony whispered.

"Misha, which country consumes the world's most chocolate by capita?"

"Mexico?"

"I'm sorry. Quizzy Peppers. Bryony?"

"Germany?"

"No, sorry. It's Switzerland."

Donna writhed in silence, but Bryony, as composed as ever, faced resolutely ahead with her fingers laced in front of her.

"Right." Jude sighed. He appeared to be tiring. "Round three—Geography. Elena, what is the smallest country in the world?"

"Monaco?"

"I'm sorry, no. Quizzy Peppers. Luke?"

"Vatican City?"

"Correct. Jaime, Havana is the capital of what country?"

"Oh, it's . . . it's . . . uh . . . wait, wait. Oh, I know this one—it's . . ."

"I have to hurry you for an answer."

"No, wait. It's . . . oh!" She smacked both of her fists onto the table.

"I'm sorry, Jaime. I'm going to have to pass to the Golden Girls. Susan?"

"Cuba?"

"Correct."

"Woo!"

The crawl to forty points took the Quizzy Peppers through two more rounds. Five or more questions could pass unanswered before, with relief, a point was scored—"Ohio? . . ." "No, I'm sorry . . ." "Forty percent? . . ." "I'm sorry . . ." "Ben Nevis? . . ." "No . . ." "The Appalachian Trail? . . ." "No . . . No . . . No."

Donna leaned forward on her elbows with the table's edge slicing into her stomach, drumming her fingers on her temples, willing herself to pay attention. And the audience seemed to be losing interest too. Bored, whispered chit chat was simmering; Donna could hear it above Jude's listless voice.

Eventually Bryony lifted her hand in the air, as confident as a head girl at school, and demanded that "something be done about the noise, please." The audience's babble dribbled into silence, but that sort of thing would not endear them to anyone. Donna had a horrible vision of winning the match, only to find that all around them, while draining their drinks and getting ready to leave, the audience were making saccharine little declarations like, "Well, but the Golden Girls were the *real* winners tonight, don't you think?"

When the Geography round came to an end, with the Golden Girls on forty-two points and the Red Hot Quizzy Peppers on forty, Priya beckoned to Jude with a curling finger. Almost touching heads as they spoke quietly together, Jude nodded and came away, wearily swinging his arms—gone was his jaunty little jog.

"Seems like we're all a little tired here, folks," Jude announced. "We'll take a fifteen-minute break. Get yourselves a drink and we'll start back soon."

"Oh, thank God," Jaime said as she flopped over the table.

Luke and Bryony scooted their chairs back and the others turned in toward each other to form a tight semicircle. They scratched their scalps, pulled uncomfortably at their clothes, and all started to speak at once.

"Why is it so hot in here? Are you guys hot?"

"This is brutal . . ."

"What round are we even on?"

Donna sat back in her chair, her knee swinging side to side on the roll of her ankle. "This was always going to be difficult, but listen, the Golden Girls are having just as tough a time as us."

"They're just happier about it," Bryony said.

On the other table, the Golden Girls appeared well-rested and serene, perched attentively on their seats—refreshed, bright-eyed, probably having gathered in the bathroom to comb their little fringes and synchronize their shimmying shoulders in the mirror.

"So let's be happier about it," said Donna. "What did John Candy say about gold medals in *Cool Runnings*? If you're not enough without it, you'll never be enough with it." And she gripped her fist next to her heart, trying to hold her face in an imitation of wisdom and poignancy, until she and the rest of them collapsed in laughter. Priya, Jude, and the Golden Girls were all looking over at them, probably wondering if the strain of the evening had sent them all mad.

When the fifteen-minute break was up, they had scarcely caught their breaths before the game was away again.

"Round six—Animals. Red Hot Quizzy Peppers, Donna, what is the loudest animal on Earth?"

"Pass to Bryony."

"A howler monkey?"

"No, I'm sorry. Golden Girls. Misha?"

"A lion?"

"I'm sorry, it's a sperm whale."

Donna came forward in her seat. "Really? Are you sure?"

Jude eyed her warily. "Well, yes?"

She sat back again. "Alright."

"Quizzy Peppers. Harry, how many hearts does an octopus have?"

"Four?"

"I'm sorry. Golden Girls. Elena?"

"Two?"

"No . . ."

The progress of the round was no better than any that had preceded it. Both teams limped to forty-five points, and it appeared to Donna that no one in the pub cared who won, as long as someone did and soon.

"Bryony, what planet is the hottest in the Solar System?"

"Venus."

"Correct. Luke, how many teeth does an adult human have?"

Luke cast his tongue around the inside of his mouth. Donna could see the fleshy protrusion of it from beneath his cheek. "Thirty . . . thirty-two?"

"Correct. Jaime, what tissues connect the muscles to the bones?"

"Tendons?"

"Congratulations," Jude said wearily.

It came as a surprise to them all. Donna, hearing the sounds around her as though from deep under water, could not comprehend what he was saying.

"The Red Hot Quizzy Peppers win and will be heading into the semifinal."

They sat blinking stupidly for a full minute, accompanied by polite but unenthusiastic applause. Alright, the Quizzy Peppers' skeptical faces said: if you say so, we've won. And then Harry was on his feet, slamming his palms on the table-top. The rest of them followed, weak and stumbling out of the chairs, to find limbs and hands and shoulders to clench and hug and shake in a stunned relief. Donna's ears rang with their disbelief.

"Oh my God. Oh my God . . ."

"Wait—so that was fifty points? Are you sure it was fifty? . . ."

"We got it, we got it, we got it!"

"Jaime, you legend!"

CHAPTER TWENTY-FIVE

Question: *The name for which precious gemstone comes from the Greek "adamas," meaning "indestructible"?*
Answer: *Diamond*

On a cloudless and sweltering Saturday in June, when the air closed around them with the hot tang of petrol from the congested summer roads, Jaime and Luke stood over a glistening tray of rings in a jewelers on Church Street.

With his hands firmly in his corduroy pockets and his body angled away, Luke looked as though he were waiting for the arrival of a bus that he may or may not catch.

"How about this one?" Jaime shyly enquired. "Or this?"

"We're just looking, remember?" Luke reminded her.

"Absolutely. We're just looking."

And the congenially smiling jeweler ("Please. Call me Nigel"), with his bald, liver-spotted head and cloudy tufts of gray hair frizzing out from behind his ears, gave them both an understanding nod and a well-prepared little speech on the importance of taking their time. He concluded with a little subservient bow.

The shop was a twinkling sprawl of gold, silver, and winking diamonds, the walls clad in mirrors that frequently captured the startled expressions on Luke's and Jaime's pale faces: fleeting, fluorescent-lit portraits of two people who didn't know what they were doing, exacerbated by the appearance of their cheap, studenty clothes.

Just looking: it had been Luke's begrudging precondition, which was just as well, because even in this cage-fronted jewelers—practically a pawn shop (WE BUY GOLD FOR CASH)—the biro-scribbled prices were unaffordable anyway.

"And what would you say your day-to-day jewelry reflects about your personality?" Nigel asked her. "Are you a minimalist? Ostentatious? Quirky?"

"Oh, definitely a minimalist. Though maybe a bit quirky too? What do you think, Luke?"

"Oh, yeah. I agree. I mean, whatever you think."

The feud that had first taken root at the quarter-final in April had now spread beneath the footing of all the weeks that had come afterwards. Why had Jaime, when they had explicitly agreed otherwise, revealed the news of their engagement? And why was Luke so annoyed about it—was he ashamed or something?

"For God's sake, I'm not ashamed," he had said in the chattering center of the pub, as he'd fought to keep the volume of his voice down. "We just said we'd keep it quiet for a while, that's all."

"*You* said that. And, as usual, what you say goes, and everything's my fault."

"You didn't have to make such a huge deal about it."

"Oh, fine. Exaggerate everything like you always do. Go on."

And then Luke had said something that she couldn't argue with: "You know your problem, Jaime? You're never happy. Nothing makes you happy."

Oh, I'd be happy, she had thought. I'd be happy if only you'd let us live the life we're supposed to be living. This was what couples did—they got married, they moved into houses and decorated them and had children.

The quiz had commenced, and they had remained next to each other in silence until their victory had dissolved—or at least masked—their rigid misery.

The morning after, when the elation had worn off as it invariably did inside the bounds of their humid, makeshift flat, Luke was still asleep when Jaime had to stumble out of bed and brush her teeth in the painful, bright light of the morning. Then later that evening, her bus had been caught in a honking standstill of traffic, leaving her only enough time to hurriedly cook, chew, and swallow an unsatisfying dinner before she was shutting the front door behind her again, en route to her twilight shift. But before she had reached the supermarket, her heartbeats began to feel a little strange, as if there were either too many of them, or not enough, or they were happening in the wrong order. She'd had to lean against the trunk of a tree for a long time, with a hand clutching her collar, waiting for her heart to come to order. And she had remained feeling that way ever since. Luke appeared no closer to "finding his calling" than he had been back in January, and she was now paying off the interest of her first payday loan with a second one. She wasn't sure for how much longer she could remain quiet.

On this June Saturday morning, before the jewelers, she'd woken to the sound of voices. When she'd shuffled bleary eyed into the living room, it had turned out to be the preshow for the Canadian Grand Prix. Over his shoulder, around a mouthful of buttered toast, Luke had said he hadn't meant to wake her, but he still hadn't taken his eyes off the screen.

She'd gone through the silent motions of filling a cereal bowl and a mug of strong tea, of crunching and sipping in frosty stiffness. She'd taken a disproportionate amount of time to swallow her mouthful of cereal and to tongue out any stray pieces of food from her teeth before she replaced her bowl on the coffee table and asked him, "Do you still want to marry me?"

Luke's drooping eyelids had given way to a flare of blinking incomprehension. "What? Why would you even ask me something like that?"

She had stumbled over to him on the sofa, and he had pulled her onto his lap, where she'd perched awkwardly, with her socked feet dangling an inch above the floor.

"You never talk about it. You don't want to tell anyone. You want to keep it all a secret," she said in a wet, wobbling voice. She had pulled the cuffs of her sleeves over her hands and used them to hide her face.

His arms had been firmly looped around her waist, his fingers laced at her hip, but they fell away, releasing her to slide off his lap and sit next to him instead.

"Well, what is there to talk about?" he'd said. "We're still not in the position to—you know—do anything about it."

"It just—it doesn't feel real. It feels like we're pretending."

"This is about a ring, isn't it? That I can't afford to give you a ring." Hunched over his lap, his gaze had dropped between his knees, where both his hands hung slack. Look, he'd seemed to be saying, you see what a failure I am?

"Well, don't make it sound that way. And no, that's not what I meant."

"But it *is* what you meant."

Jaime had got up and moved to the window, where outside two ponytailed women were beginning their morning jogs in the bright sunshine. Their bouncing heads swept past the pavement below. "I'm not going to apologize for wanting the same things for us that other couples have," she'd said. "And it's not about wanting a ring; I suppose it's that being able to afford one would mean everything was . . . better."

"No, I get that. It's symbolic."

The unwelcome memory of Donna's voice had entered her head ("best keep it symbolic until he has a job, OK?"). "Yes," she'd said. "You're right. It is."

"Fine. Let's go have a look then—for later. When we can afford it. Will that make it seem more real? Isn't there a place on Church Road?"

"Yes, there's a—there's some sort of jewelry shop up there."

"It's just to look, though."

"No, I know."

"And let's be back by four. For the race."

And perhaps she should have declined; didn't it mean she was materialistic or something terrible like that? But what if she'd told him no? He might only repeat his earlier accusation that she was never happy; that nothing made her happy.

Now Jaime caressed the edges of the tray of rings, not entirely sure what this exercise was supposed to achieve. She felt embarrassed in front of Nigel, the sweet little jeweler, who was probably humoring them.

And while on the walk down here Jaime had been full of well-hidden excitement, the feeling had fallen and dissipated in Luke's persistent refusal to take an interest in . . . well, anything.

She may as well have been a little girl playing with the rings in her mother's jewelry box, stacking the things over her fingers where they would spin uselessly on her childishly small fingers. It made the overall message achingly clear: these things aren't meant for you.

During the last few minutes of the visit, Luke appeared to relent, because he came up behind Jaime, taking her elbow in his hand and said, "What one's your favorite?"

"Oh. Maybe this one." She pointed to a princess-cut solitaire. "I think it's sort of cute."

"Well, OK," he said, nudging her. "Now I know, don't I?"

Outside, under the cloudless blue sky, they walked briskly back to the flat in shy silence. The drone of the Canadian Grand Prix filled the rooms for the rest of the afternoon. Jaime dozed off in the armchair, and when she woke up it was almost time for dinner.

CHAPTER TWENTY-SIX

Question: *Founded in the eleventh century, and having been in continuous operation, which university is the oldest in the world?*
Answer: *The University of Bologna*

The glossy stack of university prospectuses on Bryony's kitchen table, each with its own little heartfelt slogan—"Seize the future," "Keep discovering," "Be the change"—had grown so perilously tall that one morning it had slid in a slick cascade off of the table, spreading the bright booklets over the floor. Bryony had been on her hands and knees, gathering them up, when Lydia and Arthur came trampling down to breakfast, creasing the covers underfoot.

She had thought it might be fun, nostalgic even, to have the prospectuses delivered. When she had first been looking at universities, before Lydia had shown up as a line on that pregnancy test, each fat envelope had landed on the doormat with a thump that would reverberate through the house, causing an excited gallop of feet across the landing and down the stairs. Either Bryony or her mother would pluck up the envelope and shout out its stamped post mark—"Manchester! . . . Cambridge! . . . Edinburgh!" And with their heads bent close together

they would flip its heavy pages, pointing out things of interest, sometimes seeming to compete with each other. "Did you see here? The
library has one-point-eight-million printed volumes. Astonishing!"

But there was nobody to read the prospectuses with now, and her
attempts to read them by herself had been overwhelming. How had they
come up with all this . . . stuff? And where had all the recognizable
subjects disappeared to? As she'd trail a fingernail down the contents
list, looking for "History," her vision would blur over the elusive streams
of course titles and descriptions: *Applied Public History*; *History and
Health*; *Western European Legal History*; *Magna Carta and its Legacies* . . .
until she'd flop the book shut, feeling stupid.

"Oh, Bry, please don't feel that way," Jaime said to her over another
lunchtime coffee in Norwood, when Bryony had gathered the prospectuses into a canvas shopping bag and spilled them across the cafe table.

"I can't remember how I ever got to grips with these things," Bryony
told her.

"I'll tell you what—let's go on an open day. It will be fun." Jaime
clasped Bryony's hand. "That's the only way to really—you know—get
a feel for these places."

Emboldened by Jaime's gentle encouragement, in the second week
of June, Bryony booked a campus tour of Birkbeck in Bloomsbury, her
voice hesitant as she spoke down the phone to the admissions officer.
Jaime took the Tuesday afternoon off from PrintPro to accompany her,
and Bryony met Jaime at the shop before they set off; it was a spotlit,
beige, stagnant place of dusty, sun-faded prints of the kind usually seen
on the walls of dentist offices and department store cafés. But Jaime was
cheerful—she and Luke had looked at rings over the weekend. "And he
was really quite sweet about it," she said. "But still, you can't expect a
guy to really be interested in all that, can you?"

At first look, the unassuming brown brick building of Birkbeck was
underwhelming. From the street, it could have been an office block or a
set of flats, or anything else, but inside, the cool, air-conditioned white-
ness, the chattering cafe and the slick, metal turnstile that admitted
them into the building with a beep of their guest passes, had Bryony
flushed with a sense of promise. The students looked purposeful and
intelligent as they strode the corridors and sipped coolly at their coffees

in the study rooms. The noticeboards were filled with opportunity—
Diversity Day! . . . Become a career coach! . . . Park yoga mornings!—and
the spotlit lecture rooms gave way to an impression of deep respect for
the art of learning itself.

"Well, but look," Jaime said, flicking through the prospectus as
they wandered the hushed aisles of the library, "some of these are short
courses, or separate modules or whatever; you want to be looking at the
bachelor's degrees—if that's what you want to do, of course."

She wanted it—oh, how walking these corridors and breathing in
the clean, wholesome scent of each room filled her ribcage with the
weightless sense of a future beyond stacking the dishwasher and
pairing up laundered socks. She would fit in here, with a rumpled
tweed blazer and set of mature, pressed blouses. But then she thought
about Glen, and how all this might put her on an island further away
from him.

"I'll see you on Thursday," Jaime said as they parted ways at Crystal
Palace station. "Can you believe we're in the semifinal? I mean, we could
win. Honestly, sometimes I swear I'm dreaming the whole thing."

And Jaime was so pink and smiling and hopeful, in her fresh polka-
dot summer dress, that Bryony stepped forward and slung her arms
around her shoulders, where the copper ends of Jaime's apple-scented
hair covered Bryony's nose. "Thank you for coming today."

"Oh, it's nothing," Jaime said, her hands gripping Bryony's shoulder blades.

"No, I really mean it." Bryony stepped back. "I'm really glad I met
you—all of you. Sometimes I don't know what I'd do if I didn't . . .
Anyway, we can win on Thursday. I know we can."

Jaime's eyes danced as she searched Bryony's face, as though she
were some arbiter of truth. "Do you really think so?"

"Yes. Yes, I do."

But after the ponderous walk to Anerley, at her front door Bryony
heard a long wail from Lydia coming from an open window. She had to
force herself to complete the turn of the key in the lock.

Inside the hallway, Lydia's sobbing words came from somewhere
upstairs. "And I—I asked if they'd let me come home myself and get
them and they said—they said I wasn't allowed—"

"Wait. Hang on, love," came Glen's gentle voice, and then he came trotting downstairs in his socks.

"Where have you been?" he asked her.

"Nowhere. What's the matter?" Bryony stepped out of her shoes, and even she could hear the sound of indifference in her own sighing voice.

"It was Lydia's school bake-off today. You were meant to deliver the cakes at two."

Bryony's heart froze, remembering Lydia's diligent mixing and beating and whisking on Saturday afternoon and the stacked Tupperware in the fridge. "Was that today?"

"She's devastated."

"Alright. Well, it's just a—"

"Just a what?" Lydia appeared at the top of the stairs in her crumpled school uniform, her eyelids pink and swollen. Her cropped hair, now more expertly cut by a skilled hairdresser, was decorated with several colored hair clips. "I spent hours making those things! I didn't get to do the fundraiser or anything. Everyone thinks I'm an idiot."

"No one thinks you're an 'idiot,' Lydia. Why do you always have to be so dramatic?" But Lydia had fled to her bedroom. Bryony chased her upstairs, where she was poised at her bedroom door, her hand fiercely grasping the doorknob.

"Mr. Broderick said it's no wonder I'm such a disaster at school if this is how forgetful you are. And everyone already knows about you storming out at parents' evening."

Bryony flushed. "I was defending you! Can't you even see a stupid thing like that?"

"You don't! Care! About! Anything!" Lydia whipped away, slamming into her bedroom. And when Bryony followed her and opened Lydia's door more suddenly than she meant to, it swung back on its hinges and smacked into the corner of Lydia's dresser, knocking over a wire display frame of dangling necklaces.

"Look, I'm sorry," Bryony said, tangling her fingers in the threads of chains and beads. "I didn't mean to—"

Lydia wrenched the necklaces away and threw them in a jangling heap onto her bed. "Don't *come* in here. I don't want you *in* here."

"You can't just scream at me when I get in the front door, Lydia. It was a mistake, alright? Why don't we sit down calmly, and—"

"What's the point? You never listen."

"Of course I listen. Why do you have to inflate everything? I don't know what's wrong with you lately."

But Lydia thrust out her chin, her little face hard and white with defiance. She jabbed her earbuds into her ears and flung herself onto the creaking bed and turned to the wall. Bryony stared at the shape of her tense back, where the rigid snake of her spine could be seen underneath her white school shirt.

"We'll talk about this later," Bryony said before she closed the door, even though Lydia probably couldn't hear her.

She retreated downstairs, where a squealing sound seemed to be coming from every room of the house; it might even have been coming from inside her own head. That's it, she thought, I've finally gone crazy. But as she chased the sound into the kitchen, she saw it was Glen in the back garden, pushing and hauling the lawnmower across the grass, his face in a livid red, crumpled scowl. And when he saw her through the open kitchen window, he lumbered toward it and peeked into the opening.

"You let her down," he said. "*Again.* And did you think you could get away with your little outburst at parents' evening without it affecting her?"

"If she hates Mr. Broderick so much then why does she care if I—"

"Ever since you started this pub quiz business it's like you're a different person—acting like a nutter at the school, and now this whole university thing. It's like you don't want anything to do with us."

"Why can't you do all these school things, Glen?" she hissed. "Why does it always have to be me? You really think you'd remember every single one of them? And the dentist appointments and buying new shoes and the haircuts?"

"We decided you'd stay home with the kids, Bryony. We decided that. You seem to forget that's a luxury these days."

"A lux—a luxury?" She could hardly speak in a grip of hysterics. "Oh God, that's funny. And you'd love to keep that status quo, wouldn't you? You don't want me to get my degree because you want to keep me trapped here."

Even as she said it, she knew it wasn't true, but the urge to hurt him had been too great, because if she didn't want to blame her children or herself, then who else was there?

"Don't be so fucking ridiculous. And don't you dare turn this into an argument about not working. This is about not being there for Lydia. It's your *job*."

"You don't think any of the other school mums do anything that's interesting? You think they're standing around doing the hoovering all day? Well, I'll tell you something: maybe they were doing all their interesting things when they were twenty-five, and then maybe they didn't mind when their lives became kids, kids, kids and house, house, house. I swear to God, Glen, I'm sick of this place. And I can't believe—I can't even comprehend—that I can't go out without this house descending into World War Three."

Glen's response was to shut the window with a slam and stalk back to the lawnmower. He proceeded to push and haul it over the grass with one angrily yanking arm as he pulled up the neck of his T-shirt to mop his face.

At the noise of a small, timid sniff, Bryony spun around. Arthur was sitting quietly on his own at the kitchen table. He was eating a sandwich, and his attentive, chewing face was looking intently down at his plate. But his mournful brown eyes looked a little too bright, and he had sucked in his bottom lip as he swallowed, in the effort to keep it from trembling.

* * *

"Have a seat, Donna. This is Mark—from HR." Rolling her chair forward to lean over the desk, Tess fondled the top of her head for her glasses. She pulled them down onto her nose and consulted a leather-bound notebook, on which indecipherable biro squiggles lurched across each page.

Donna acknowledged "Mark from HR" with a glum incline of her head. He was a dark-suited man, so unmemorable in his mousy features that each time she looked away from him, she found she forgot any details of his face.

Tess leaned forward, her palms together as if in prayer. "Now, Donna, let me be plain—we have found your attitude and your work ethic entirely unacceptable."

So it had come to this, had it? A prickle of sweat spread down Donna's spine. Her gaze flicked to the electric heater in the corner, where a wobble of hot air rose from the grate and an LED light stared at her like a red, confronting eye. "I'm sorry—can we turn that off?" she said.

"Turn what off?"

"The heater. It's very hot in here."

Tess reached behind her and thumbed the switch off. "Now," she said. "I'm aware there have been . . . difficulties in your emotional . . . stability, and we can't overlook that. I've been in touch with an organization that offers mediation for mental health support, and I—"

"For what, sorry?"

"For mental health support."

"Whose mental health?"

"Your own mental health."

Donna tilted her head all the way back, her lips open wide in a silent scream that must have looked like madness. Tess and Mark could probably see the wrinkled roof of her mouth and the underside of all her top teeth. But so what? Let them see every vulnerable crevice of her.

Tess continued. "An employment support officer will come in and speak with you about your needs in the workplace—your challenges, your . . . triggers. They will provide training for us to—"

"Now, wait." Donna came forward with her elbows on Tess's desk and swept back the wisps of her hair that months of compulsive pulling had withered into baby-fine down. Tess was moving fast, and Donna needed to keep up with her before she ruined everything. "I don't need to speak to anybody. What about more time off? That's what we did last year."

"You're more than welcome to take a period of leave, but we don't feel that alone would be—"

"Who's 'we' anyway? You and Mark?"

"Well, Mark's a representative from—"

"From HR. He's from HR. OK, I get it. Look, Tess, I just need a holiday or something, OK? I don't need to speak to anyone—"

"We *require* you to speak to someone." The breadth and dominance of Tess's voice bounced off the glass walls, but then she folded her hands and took on the tone of a doctor explaining the unpleasant details of a delicate diagnosis. This "employment support officer" (what, like a counsellor? Like a therapist?) would come in to discuss the "issues" she was "experiencing." They would speak to Tess and HR to "come to a consistent and comprehensive understanding" of the best ways to "support" her.

"I'm afraid if this isn't something you feel you can tolerate," Tess said, "then maybe you need to reconsider your future with us. Now, of course we appreciate everything you're—"

"I don't need you to appreciate it." Both of Donna's hands came up in an open-palmed barrier of defense and panic. "Look, can't you fire me, instead?" And she was aware that her voice now sounded as though it were pleading. "Why can't you just fire me?"

"I'm afraid that leaves us too vulnerable to legal repercussions. But if that's the way you feel, then why don't you hand in your notice?"

Because then, Donna thought, *oh, because then I can't blame you and it will be all my fault.*

CHAPTER TWENTY-SEVEN

Question: *Which Beatles song is the fifth track on their third album,* A Hard Day's Night?
Answer: *"And I Love Her"*

"Well, I suppose I could come," said Vivienne. "What day did you say it was?"

On Wednesday, during a hasty liaison on Harry's lunch hour, they lay in his bed. Both of the sash windows had been flung open, but they only allowed in more of the hot, oppressive air.

"Tomorrow, Harry said, "and it's the semifinal. The whole atmosphere should be—you know—great." He was sitting next to her but was being careful not to touch her. "Urgh, do you have to?" she had complained when, after they'd fallen away from each other, Harry had slung an arm over her shoulders, and she'd wriggled away. "You're all sticky; it's too hot in here."

The entirety of their two-month-long affair could be measured by Vivienne's tendency to either wriggle away from him or acutely crave his attention.

As soon as Harry had enquired after his tie, left somewhere on the plush carpet of Ashton's living room, Vivienne had turned aloof and critical.

"Well, I haven't seen it," she'd furiously whispered to him on the phone, where it became clear, from the sound of her voice, that she must be hiding in a cupboard or a bathroom. "And if you can't even keep track of your things, Harry, then I don't think it's a good idea for you to come over here anymore, do you?"

And the few times they had arranged an evening meet-up, when Ashton was either "with the boys" or working late, she had made it clear that any lingering to make them drinks or even use the bathroom was both unnecessary and hazardous. It had to be strictly transactional.

"Listen," she had once said as she lay underneath him, "could we sort of hurry this up a little?" And afterwards, after he had indeed hurried things up, when she was shuffling back into her clothes, he had asked what the plan was.

"What do you mean? What plan?"

"Well, are you staying with Ashton or not? Viv, I—isn't it clear that I love you?"

"Do we have to talk about this now?"

And thanks to the strictness of their time together, where their clothes had to be off and then on again in the space of forty minutes, having the time "to talk about it" never materialized.

Then there came another confusing period of time, when Vivienne would message him at all hours of the day—*Well, can't you sack off work for the afternoon, just this once?*—and she couldn't seem to care less should Ashton walk in, in plain sight of their entanglement on whatever piece of furniture they had ended up.

"Well, what time did he say?" Harry had asked her one evening as he attempted to lose his concerns in the taste of her neck.

"Oh, I can't remember now. I'm sure it's fine. Why are you worrying so much?" And the irritated pinch of her voice had let him know that if he asked again, the evening would be over.

"At the Five Bells, you said?" Vivienne said now. She waved her hand at an unseen insect which had flown too close to her face.

"Yep, that's right." He tried not to look too forlornly hopeful, but he could feel his eyes growing round in expectation. All his visions of having her there to witness his triumph, of a night where her love for him would surely have to dawn on her . . . it was all coming into focus.

"Well, I suppose I could tell Ashton I'm meeting some friends. You're lucky he never goes to that pub. That's the dingy one, isn't it? The one with all the graffiti outside."

There was nothing he could do about a venue she found "dingy" (she had always had high standards), but did that really matter when it was the spirit of the thing that mattered?

"Well, it's—it's not one of those fancy gastropubs, if that's what you mean," he said. "But it's a nice place, full of hardworking—"

"Oh, for God's sake, Harry. You're not saving the working class by boycotting gastropubs."

He stopped talking about it; it would only make things worse. In another ten minutes she had showered and was gathering her things. But no matter how many times she combed her hair or adjusted her clothing, the heat of the day kept her looking rumpled and damp.

"Stupid thing," she muttered, as her slippery fingers failed to fasten the back of an earring. When it fell out of her grasp and disappeared down the plug hole, she spent a long time with her head down, wearily contemplating the bottom of the sink.

When she was ready to leave, with her jacket slung over her arm, he stopped her at the threshold of the front door.

"Look," she said impatiently, "I'll try to be there tomorrow, alright?"

"I just wanted to say . . . well, I just wanted to say that I meant what I said a few weeks ago, Viv. I love you. I mean it."

Vivienne clutched her jacket tighter, shifting her weight from foot to foot. "That's very sweet, Harry, but you're getting a bit intense. It's like you're terrified of being without me."

And he was struck by the similarity of what Donna had said to him in their argument in the park ("Are you so terrified of being by yourself?"). Was he really so easy to read? And what was wrong with that anyway? Wouldn't everyone feel some degree of terror at being without the person they loved?

Under the looming shadow of a Victorian terrace on Woodland Road an hour later, Harry and Ashton waited on the rubbled path for a pair of clients. The ground-floor flat had been advertised and photographed as a two-bedroom, when the second bedroom was just a single bed that had been hounded into the corner of an overly wide and pointless hallway that connected the living room to the master bedroom.

The clients arrived, a couple in their early thirties, and Harry could size them up before they'd even reached the front door, their hands outstretched for Ashton's wringing handshake. This place wouldn't suit them without a substantial overhaul.

In the open-plan living space, three-quarters of which had been commandeered by a glossy black kitchen, leaving only enough room for a two-seater sofa and a small TV nestled in the corner, Ashton took to the floor. He shot the cuffs of his jacket before embarking on a speech to charm the socks off these poor people.

". . . double glazing, installed last year. New shutters; top of the range stuff, this. Sellers paid through the nose for it. Still, on the ground-floor flat, you need the security, right?"

"Oh. Have there been many burglaries in the area?" the woman asked, alarmed.

"Not to my knowledge, but it's peace of mind, isn't it? New boiler too, right here in the . . . uh . . ." He rapidly opened and closed the kitchen cupboards.

"It's through here," Harry said, leading them to the hallway bedroom, where a fitted wardrobe housed the boiler.

"Hot water tank is in the loft space," Ashton said. "Communal access at the top of the—"

"Well, no," Harry said. "This is a condensing boiler, so you don't have to worry about all of that."

Ashton cleared his throat and began on the hallway bedroom. What they had here, he claimed, was a very versatile space; it could offer them a bedroom, an office, a walk-in wardrobe . . .

"Well, I wouldn't want to walk through a wardrobe to get to the bedroom or the garden," the man said, and his folded arms said it all: no, no, this was not going to work.

And then Ashton was wagging his hands in front of the far wall to convey a vision they were unable to see—they could knock through here and make a magnificent master suite.

"Well, no," Harry said. "That's a load-bearing wall, see? Hard to take that out. But look, you could put up a partition wall here to make a narrower hallway. Cuts the room down a bit, but you'd be creating another functional room in its—you know—in its own right."

And then all their questions were directed at him, while Ashton stood with his clenched knuckles to his teeth. Did they need planning permission for something like that? No, they didn't! What about the chimney breast—could that be removed for more space? He'd check with the flat upstairs! Was the garden communal? No, it was entirely private; couple of nice mature trees back there, too!

On the sun-dazzled walk back to Kingsley & Co., Ashton kept his long strides ahead of Harry, who had to hurry in an awkward, fidgeting jog of inferiority, holding his suit jacket closed and keeping his tie from flapping over his shoulder. And for the entire journey back, Ashton emitted aggressive little snorts from his nose and throat, as though the fury of being undermined was accumulating somewhere deep in his sinuses. Everything got worse back at the office, when Darren emerged to announce that the young couple had already left a message to arrange a second viewing for later that week.

"And they want you to be their agent, Harry. Sound OK? No point doubling up. Sound good to you, Ashton?"

Ashton gave a curt nod, wholly engrossed in the screen of his computer, where some matter of importance required him to beat the keyboard with violent stamps of his fingers. And as the afternoon progressed, tension gathered around him like the pressured atmosphere of a planet. Those walking to and fro across the office gave his desk a wide berth, until he finally came to corner Harry in the kitchenette, in the rolling steam from the kettle.

Ashton breathed close to his face, his arm braced above Harry's head against the wall. "If you want to start showing off, mate, don't try it on me. You understand what I'm saying?"

And Harry might have retaliated, but instead he found himself staring at the cuffs of Ashton's suit jacket and the four-leaf clovers embossed on its row of dark buttons. They had the same fucking suit.

After work, at his mother's dining table, as they both cut and speared dry breasts of chicken, Harry tiredly tried to convey the point of the Quiz League tournament. At almost five-thirty on the dot, at the release from work or children's homework, his phone had started to ping with increasingly anxious messages about tomorrow.

Shouldn't we be practicing or something? I feel so out of it.
You can't study for it like it's an exam—it's just luck, isn't it?
Shit, I'm so nervous!!!
Remember what Dr. Jay Jenison says: find your wave, then ride it.

"So what is it? Some sort of trivia night? Is Vivienne doing it with you?" Tonight his mother had neglected to pencil on her eyebrows, and her softly tufted brow bone of colorless, downy hair gave her face a permanent look of astonishment.

"No, but she might come watch."

"Oh, it would be so nice to see her."

"She's just really busy with—"

"I know, I know. Busy at work. And how about Kingsley?"

"What about it?"

"Well, is it going OK?"

Harry shrugged. "Fine."

"Are you sure?"

"Don't worry about me, Mum."

"I'm not *worrying* about you, Harry. You just seem a bit . . ."

"What? A bit, what? Look, you wanted me to get a job, didn't you?"

"Nothing. Never mind."

In the scrape of their knives and forks, there was nothing else to talk about until she switched the television on to the news, where, in Liverpool, a festival was underway to celebrate fifty years since the release of the Beatles' *White Album*.

"It's wonderful to see,' said the broadcaster, "that the Fab Four are still very much at the heart of this community." Harry gave a small, snorting laugh, remembering when he forgot Luke and called the Quizzy Peppers the "Fab Four."

"What's so funny?"

"Nothing. Doesn't matter."

"Well, I think it's lovely." His mum grinned at the screen, with a wondrous shake of her head. "National treasures—all of them."

Under the dulcet tones of the news broadcaster's voice, Harry once again gave himself over to the fantasy of winning the semifinal. Vivienne's role had come to encompass more of it than the win itself; Bryony, Jaime, Luke, and even Donna were relegated to the background noise of celebration. And in the warm light of the bar, where the windows showed a sky beginning to deepen in the sunset, Vivienne would say something like, "You're just marvelous, Harry," and then, coyly, "What will you do with all that money if you win?" He would smile down at her and shake his head, as if they had both known the answer to that all along. "I'm taking you to New York," he would say, and there would emerge the full circle of their failings, now mended by his willingness to provide the things that she had always wanted. Their laughing faces, as they pressed their lips together for eager kisses, would let each other know that it was all going to be alright now. He had to make it happen; he had to.

CHAPTER TWENTY-EIGHT

Question: *Which duet is sung between Tony and Maria in the balcony scene of West Side Story?*
Answer: *"Tonight"*

Jaime had scarcely seen Luke since Sunday. There were so many things she had wanted to ask him since their visit to the jewelers—what did he think of the prices? Did he think sapphire might be more unique and a little cheaper? What if they both saved up for Christmas?—but all that had had to wait. He was asleep when she left home in the morning and either asleep or in a stupor in the blue light of the television when she arrived home, black-eyed with fatigue.

But in bed on Thursday morning, before her alarm sounded, she found Luke awake and lying on his back, gazing at the ceiling, his eyes making little darting motions over its surface, as though he was tracing the path of a moth.

"Morning," she said, and touched her forehead to his arm. "Ready for later?"

"What's later?"

She lifted herself up onto an elbow and brushed away the disarray of her hair. "It's Thursday. It's the semifinal."

"Oh, is that tonight?"

*　　*　　*

In the quietness of her kitchen, Bryony looked out at the green carpet of Glen's beloved lawn and the clematis she had planted last spring, whose leaves had succumbed to some sort of yellowing rot. She held a cooling cup of coffee in one hand and her phone in the other.

> Jude, I really think we should have a talk.
> About what?
> You know what. We didn't exactly leave things very well, did we?
> Alright. I'll see you tonight.

She had hoped their little liaison, or whatever it was, was over, but not talking about it was too open-ended. She felt nothing would alleviate her guilt until a decisive finish had been reached, one that would absolve her of all she had done wrong. What good would it be if Jude rejected *her*? No—this had to come from Bryony herself.

*　　*　　*

On her lunch break, Donna hiked up City Road under the hot blue sky to the rippling green water of Regent's Canal. She sat by the lock, crowded by the chatter of other office workers, their rolled sleeves and unbuttoned collars revealing their tender skin. They lounged on their elbows, their noses and cheekbones catching the glare of the midday sun and their starched shirts gleaming violently. With her legs dangling off the concrete, her white trainers bright against the dark water, and pretending the warmth of the sun felt like joy, she scrolled through the list on her phone screen.

> *21:30 LHR—8h 50m—10:50 +1 BOM*
> *18:50 LGW—9h 20m—8:40 +1 BOM*
> *11:25 LHR—13h 1 stop IST—04:55 +1 BOM*

She had to get out of here. Quickly. A direct flight was the best bet—under nine hours to Mumbai, too. She would see out the end of the Quiz League (because, she thought as the walls of her throat tightened, she owed them that much, didn't she?), and then she would make all the arrangements to disappear, not allowing Tess and Mark and whoever else to expose her. Alright, she wanted to admit to them, it's me: I'm the problem here. But why go through the humiliation? Why not just start somewhere new and resolve not to make any of the same mistakes? The sun would be brighter in India, the air full of warm and humid promise, and, best of all, no one would know who she was. But the problem was that she'd be expected to tell everyone, and they'd all wonder what was wrong; they'd all ask questions. They'd all be thinking, behind their inscrutable, placid gazes, that Donna was off on one again.

You're just like him.

Lottie's voice filled her head. And it wasn't scathing or petty or vengeful. It wasn't any of those things; it was simply true.

Behind her sunglasses, as she listened to the clacking lock gears turn, her eyes stung with the need to cry and all her blood felt like it was pulsating at the bridge of her nose.

She slipped her phone away and opened her book instead. For the duration of the week she had been rereading *The Mindset of the Winner,* carrying it around in her bag in the hope of absorbing some of Dr. Jay Jenison's brilliance in time for the semifinal, but his words had begun to read like a series of laborious instructions. More than once she had slammed it shut, feeling as though everything—*everything*—he said was overwhelming and insurmountable. It was of no help at all; it was a money-making scam to prey on the losers in life. So she closed the book and tipped it into the canal, thinking she might watch it, in triumphant contempt, as it sailed across the water. But instead it made an unceremonious splash—*plop!*—when it hit the surface, and sank like a brick.

CHAPTER TWENTY-NINE

Question: *What color are the flowers on the plant* Craspedia?
Answer: *Yellow*

"Well, Harry, this is all very—it's very busy, isn't it?"

Harry could hardly believe his luck when Vivienne came through the doors of the pub. In her light summer dress and a bright yellow headscarf, still perspiring in the afterglow of the evening sun, he could easily have thought she was conjured from one of his many imaginings. But she gave him a restrained kiss on the cheek and he took the opportunity to sweep her into an embrace. She made a damp package in his arms, and her hair smelled of cigarette smoke, but she was here, wasn't she? In all her loveliness.

"I don't even know anyone here," he told her.

"Well, that doesn't matter. It's very exciting. You should be very proud of yourself."

He had the sense that Vivienne may have practiced what to say on the bus or train ride over, that she may have sat swaying in her seat, mumbling well-meaning phrases until she found the right tone of encouragement. Except she wasn't delivering it as well as she could have—her face was held in stiff politeness, and her eyes switched furtively from side to side, making it clear that she wasn't at ease.

"No one's here from Kingsley, if that's what you're worried about," he said.

"Don't be silly. Now, listen, can I get you a good luck drink or anything?"

"No, no, you're alright. Let me grab you something—you want a wine? Why don't you come and meet my—you know—my friends. The team."

Her face betrayed a moment of panic and she stepped back from him, soon disguising it with a self-deprecating little laugh and shake of her head—"Oh, no, it's fine"—saying something about not wanting to distract anyone.

Well, what was the deal here? Did she want to be here or not? But he told himself she was probably nervous—maybe even intimidated at meeting his new friends—and he was supposed to be making her feel as comfortable as possible, wasn't he? It might not be the way the start of the evening was supposed to play out, but the night could still be salvaged. As soon as the quiz began and he gave the performance of his life (and hopefully he could manage that), there was every chance she would begin to relax and realize what a wonderful thing it would be, to be with him again.

*　*　*

"I mean, Senna was an incredible driver, for sure," Luke was saying. "But back in . . ." and he leaned back to squint at the ceiling and consult the depths of his memories, "1990, I think, he let Prost know that he was getting to the first corner first. He didn't care if they crashed, and he went for it. I mean, you've got to admire the audacity of the guy, but it's not good sportsmanship, is it? Not to mention dangerous . . ."

Donna fingered the loop of one of her silver earrings. She had thought allowing Luke to ramble on would distract her from the slosh of dread in her stomach, but it was making her feel worse. *Well, alright, Luke,* she wanted to tell him, *that's interesting and everything, but who cares?*

She sighed to show him how profoundly she disagreed. "Well, OK, but it sounds like he was a wound-up little show-off to me. They're in a very specialized car, going in circles around a very specialized track with very specialized—you know—a very specialized team. Seems like posturing to me, and everyone loves a rivalry."

Luke emitted an arrogant little chuckle, pushing his glasses up to the bridge of his nose before continuing. "No, that's not it at all. It's in the very nature of . . ."

And in the self-assured stream of his voice, it became clear that he didn't care if she was listening or not, as long as he could listen to himself.

Then she caught sight of Harry, sitting at a table toward the back of the room with a girl in a sunshine-yellow headscarf; the girl from his screensaver. Vivienne. His smile was wide, her face was as lovely as it had been on his computer screen, and Donna's chest performed an unwelcome little flip of envy.

CHAPTER THIRTY

Question: *What robotic rover, also known as MER-B, was active on Mars from 2004 to 2018?*
Answer: Opportunity

"It was funny because he was really furious with you, Harry," Vivienne said, relaying the discussion she'd had with Ashton about the viewing on Woodland Road. "But it's just his ego, you know? He can't stand it when anyone does better than him. Once it came across as strong and confident and . . . well, anyway, now I find it so completely unattractive. And do you know sometimes when he's giving a little rant about something or another, he'll look at himself talking in the living-room mirror? He actually *watches* himself talking, and I'll sit there and think, by God, he really does love the sound of his own—"

"One minute, Viv. Just nipping to the gents."

Harry breathed a sigh of relief as he escaped to the men's toilets. He'd thought he might never tire of hearing Vivienne describe Ashton's shortcomings, especially not when her annoyed face was turning as pink and spiteful as it had just now. But he had to admit he was growing bored. Couldn't they talk about anything else? And didn't she realize how her squinting eyes and downturned mouth, which created little creases of suffering over her face, made her look like the picture of resentment? And alright, maybe he was supposed to continually inter-ject with pitying phrases like, "God, Viv, you're a saint for putting up with him," but how much energy—how much sympathy—could you reasonably be expected to spend on something like this? She had her chances to leave him, and she hadn't yet budged.

Then, as soon as he walked into the empty toilet, all thoughts of Vivienne and Ashton vanished; his heart felt like it had stopped. Sitting on top of the hand dryer, as casual and unassuming as a discarded news-paper, was Jude's clipboard—complete with printed pages of questions and answers. And Harry was frozen, contemplating its humble, tattered corners and rust-spotted silver clip. It wasn't even face down, for Christ's sake. What had Jude been thinking?

Harry took the clipboard into a stall with him to get it out of sight and sat down on the lid of the toilet. He held it face down on his lap, weighing up what he should do.

Vivienne was finally here, as bright as the June sunshine, eager to watch him succeed. He had been plotting the joyous outcome of this night for weeks, and now fate may have provided a way to make it hap-pen. And even better—she had spent the evening griping over Ashton; it was the tipping point. He had her. He *had* her. And she may be worried he wasn't "taking life seriously," but how could she fail to be buoyed and carried by the inevitable atmosphere—him reeling off every answer with smiling ease; the raucous applause; the hearty shouts of his name. No man like that had to worry about eating his dinner alone, about going to sleep in a cold, empty bed or waking up to the solitude of another pale day. And even if a man like that had once been caught picking at his toenails, frightened off by the prospect of New York, that could all be forgiven. He could see off all his aching inadequacies, all of his under-achievements, and start again in a limelight of renewal and recognition.

And, more importantly, would anyone even know? Of course they wouldn't. One day in the future, cheating on a pub quiz could be a story retold as a hilarious little anecdote that had no moral bearing. ("Oh, that's marvelous, Harry! The things you got up to!")

"Oh, fuck it." He flipped the pages on the clipboard, furiously scanning each line, while the thump of his heart sounded in his ears, trying to memorize every word.

Which is the only American Football team to go a whole season undefeated? The Miami Dolphins . . . What is the name of the professional ice hockey team based in Toronto, Canada? Toronto Maple Leaves . . . What is the opposite of matter? Antimatter . . . Which marsupial is known for its bad temper? The Tasmanian devil . . . What fruit takes the scientific name Mangifera indica*? Mango . . .*

When he was finished, he let himself out of the stall and replaced the clipboard on top of the hand dryer. But as he moved among the pub crowd, passing the oblivious members of his team—their faces alive with anticipation—a surreal buzzing in both of his ears drowned out the babble around him; he felt sick. A heavy tide of shame gushed over him. He'd cheated. He was a cheater. And what way was there to get out of it now? Christ—what would Donna say? What would all of them say?

And then everything sank from bad to worse: as he neared Vivienne's table, he saw his mother, in a purple raincoat, standing over Vivienne; they were both unsmiling. His feet moved him closer to the table of their own accord, perhaps controlled by the disbelieving tick of his brain—this wasn't happening; this *wasn't happening*; there was somebody else in his mother's coat talking to Vivienne. And even if it was her, surely Vivienne had the delicacy not to talk about the breakup. No, with any luck, he might . . .

But as he came within earshot of the table, he heard Vivienne's distressed voice saying, "Sharon, honestly, I really have no idea what you're talking about—"

Her voice stopped; they had seen him. Vivienne's lip curled in distaste. And just as his mind started to spin with what he could possibly say, he felt a hand push him aside and Donna's blonde head was there at his shoulder.

"Sharon? I've heard so much about you. I'm Donna—we spoke on the phone that time?" Donna swung round to call back to the bar. "Jude! Jude, this is Harry's mum! I said, it's *Harry's mum*. Get her a prosecco or something, OK?—it's on me. Honestly, Sharon, you're the guest of honor. Harry? Harry? *Harry!* Why don't you take your friend to meet the others? Go on."

Vivienne stood up. "I'm alright, thanks. Actually, I need some fresh air."

"You didn't tell me," his mother said. And her trembling face, made up for this special night with her eyebrows executed magnificently and the red line of her lipstick disappearing into the fold of her mouth, looked terrifyingly close to tears.

"Sorry, Mum."

Donna came between them and took his mother by the elbow, and she was submissively led away. "Why don't you sit down over here and watch the—you know—the show?" Donna was saying. "It's the best seat in the house. *Jude!* Where's that drink?"

And then Harry was alone, staring helplessly after Vivienne's yellow headscarf as it floated away through the bobbing crowd of heads. But, for God's sake—hadn't she had months now to move back in with him and be rid of Ashton? His mum need never have known. If the guy was so "completely unattractive," then what the hell was she still doing with him? It was so unnecessary for any of this to have happened at all. Absorbed in securing her praise, he'd even been willing to cheat for her—and why?

And another thing was certain; there was no way he could go through with cheating now that his mum was here. How would he ever look her in the eye again? So he pushed his way through the tightening crowd until he reached Donna. He whispered into the fall of her hair, unable to look in her eyes.

"Men's toilets. Now. Bring the others."

*   *   *

"What do you mean you just found it in here?" Donna demanded. She rounded on Harry, whose stunned face was white and whose curly hair had been pulled into a tangle of panic. When they had threaded through the door, one by one, Donna had seen it first—Jude's clipboard, hanging in Harry's limp hand.

Bryony and Jaime stood back against the bathroom stalls—Jaime anxiously pulling on her earlobe and Bryony as defiant and stern-faced as a headmistress—while Luke crouched down on the floor with a hand held contemplatively to his chin.

"So come on then—out with it," Donna said.

"I told you. I came in here, and it was on top of the hand dryer. Jude must've left it."

"Well, have you looked at it?" Bryony wanted to know.

"I mean, a bit."

Donna clamped her hands down on her hips. Well, he either had or he hadn't—which one was it?

At her fierce expression, Harry's chest rose in an unconvincing defense. "I didn't realize what it was at first, OK?"

She didn't believe for a moment that he hadn't known what he was looking at—that bloody blue clipboard had been a fixture of the last seven months.

Bryony massaged the lines over her forehead. "This is completely unethical, Harry. We can't compete now . . ." Her voice sounded close to tears. "We simply can't."

"Well, no, hang on a minute," Donna said.

"We'd be cheaters," said Bryony. "Don't be ridiculous."

"Would you listen? We need to think this through."

"There's nothing to think about." Bryony folded her arms, pulling herself up to her full height, which was scarcely an inch below Donna's. "If you do this, I am out. Do you understand?"

"It's not like there's a buzzer," Donna said. "We take turns—the number of direct questions Harry gets is negligible. And as if he could have memorized every question on that thing anyway. I don't understand why we need to be so dramatic about it."

And then Jaime startled her. "Isn't the answer completely obvious?" she said, turning pink under the scrutiny of the others. "We play but Harry doesn't answer anything—he has to pass every time."

"I'll look like a complete idiot," Harry said.

Bryony shifted her weight from one foot to the other. "That *is* an option. We wouldn't be benefitting from it at all. But I don't know—it still feels dishonest."

"I hate to bring this up," Luke said. "But we've got ten minutes til start time. And Jude's going to start wondering where that clipboard is pretty soon."

"Alright," said Donna. "Are we agreed? Because we need to get back out there. Put that thing back where you found it. And let's not leave all at once, OK? We'll draw too much attention to ourselves."

With their heads hanging glumly, avoiding each other's eyes, they each gave terse little nods of agreement. And Donna knew it was useless—they'd never win now, and they all knew it.

"So, Harry," she said, "you're not to answer anything, alright? Just pass—you know—pass as best you can."

With his fingers hanging from the belt loops of his jeans in defeat, Harry lifted his chin. His bottom lip quivered before he could disguise it with a swipe of his hand. "Do you all . . . well, can you forgive me? I'm sorry."

And his face was so harrowed and lost that Donna couldn't find any malice to unleash on him. "Oh, Harry, look . . ." She pressed her fingers around his shoulder. "You're only human, OK? I'm sure anyone would have looked, and . . . well, you did the right thing in the end."

"Donna, I . . . you didn't have to—with my mum, I mean. Thanks."

Donna found it easier to focus on the mottled linoleum at her feet. "Don't worry about it. So, listen." Her head snapped up. "Bry, you come out last, OK? And then go and tell Jude that you've seen the clipboard in here."

Bryony frowned. "Well, what on earth do I say I was doing in the men's toilets?"

"I'm sure you can come up with something."

"Why me?"

"Because Jude won't want to disqualify *you*, will he?"

*   *   *

After the others had shuffled out of the men's toilet, Bryony counted to twenty before leaving. Jude gave her a wide smile when she came up to him.

"Jude—your clipboard, it's in the bathroom. Did you know?"

His eyes turned round in panic and he lurched toward the toilet door. He emerged clutching the clipboard in a desperate, protective embrace.

"Jesus Christ." He stashed the clipboard beneath the bar and hunched over to her with a haunted look on his face, his cheeks wobbling as he shook his head. "That could have screwed up everything." His face was full of fear. "You didn't look at it, did you? No, wait. Don't answer that. I don't want to know."

"I promise I didn't look at it, Jude."

And, in his relief, he didn't even seem to wonder what she'd been doing in the men's toilets in the first place. Perhaps he didn't care.

"You wanted to talk?" he said.

Bryony's shoulders tensed. "Yes. Well . . . what I wanted to say—I guess I just wanted to say that there's nothing to be gained from any of this. And I should have known better. I'd prefer it if we just went back to being friends."

"OK." And his still, blinking face was so passive, Bryony could have believed that he didn't have any idea what she was talking about.

"Or maybe not even friends. Acquaintances, maybe. None of it is really appropriate, would you agree?"

"Sure."

After all his affectionate and supportive words, his curtness was confusing. And what was it supposed to achieve? Was he supposed to come off as cool and aloof, while she was painted as some nervous wreck? She didn't know if she was furious or mortified: maybe it was neither; maybe it was both. If she let the conversation continue, he'd be saying something like, "You're overthinking this." Well, OK, let him think that; he wasn't the one that was married, was he?

She looked down at the entanglement of her fingers on top of the bar. "Well, I suppose that's that, then."

"That's that." And he retrieved his precious clipboard and wandered away.

*　　*　　*

Harry remained tense in his chair while Jude scrambled away from the bar to the toilets and back again. For a handful of terrifying seconds, Jude's wild eyes searched Bryony's face for answers, but soon it appeared as though they were talking about something else entirely, and then Bryony came away to take her seat at the table too. Harry tried to catch her eye, but she stared ahead, a small double chin forming under the miserable droop of her head. Whatever was wrong with her didn't seem to have anything to do with the clipboard; he'd got away with it for now.

He searched the audience. Vivienne was back—her bright headscarf was easy to spot, and beside her, an uncomfortable foot between them, his mother's purple raincoat. They offered no little smiles of encouragement, no heartening thumbs-ups—only their unforgiving, unsmiling faces. And, Christ—they didn't even know how bad this thing was going to get. He was going to have to pass on every question, revealing himself to be the most aimlessly idiotic person in the room. Under the table his hands tightened on his kneecaps, his fingernails burrowing through his jeans, making painful impressions in his skin. Well, you deserve it, you dumb little shit, he told himself. There would be no convincing Vivienne of anything now—any doubts she had would only be compounded. She would hurry home into Ashton's brawny arms, groped by his sturdy, capable hands, relieved to leave this "dingy" pub behind.

And to his mum—her downturned mouth and the deep creases it created either side of her soft chin—he hoped to convey a last apologetic glance. She sent him a brief nod and then cast her eyes down. Donna slid into her seat next to him, and he couldn't look at her at all. Then Jude's voice called for attention and a hush washed over the audience.

CHAPTER THIRTY-ONE

Question: *"Things without all remedy / Should be without regard: what's done is done"* *is a line from which play?*
Answer: Macbeth, *William Shakespeare*

"Quizzy Peppers. Harry, which is the only American Football team to go a whole season undefeated?"

"Pass to Luke."

Jaime tried to breathe evenly, only she kept forgetting how, and a pool of breath would end up painfully trapped in her chest. As soon as they'd sat down, and Jude's impassioned voice had begun, she had started to regret suggesting that they ever go ahead with this match. There was something suspicious about the speed at which Harry passed. Couldn't he try to make it sound more natural?

"The Red Sox?" Luke said.

"No, I'm sorry. Civil Servants. James?"

"Miami Dolphins?"

"Correct!"

"Aren't the Red Sox baseball?" Jaime whispered to Luke, and he swatted the table in annoyance.

"Graeme, what is the name of the professional ice hockey team based in Toronto, Canada?'

"The Blackhawks?"

"I'm sorry. Quizzy Peppers. Bryony?"

"Pass."

"Who would you like to pass to?"

"Oh—Luke?"

"I don't know," Luke said.

"Right.' Jude frowned. "So, Civil Servants. Taylor . . ."

Jaime pressed her fingers into Luke's thigh. "Couldn't you have at least guessed?"

"What's the point?"

Maybe she should have urged them to let Harry cheat after all. Wasn't winning the point? Their money problems would be eased, and they would have *accomplished* something. If they lost now, she and Luke would only go back to their dim, lonely little flat, no better off than they were before.

*　*　*

At thirty-five points to the Red Hot Quizzy Pepper's twelve, the Civil Servants, all handsomely young and disheveled in their shirtsleeves, were running away with it, and Bryony wanted to go home. It wasn't so much the loss of Harry as the destruction of morale. None of them seemed to have the energy for intelligent guesswork or for knowing who to pass to, and when a toss-up came between one answer and another, their intuition was always wrong.

At least, Bryony conceded, she would soon be able to announce to Glen that they had lost, that they were finally out of the running and he didn't have to worry about "the quiz business" anymore. But he wouldn't console her. He would never understand why she had done it all in the first place.

*　*　*

"General knowledge," Jude announced, and Donna almost threw her head down onto the table. Could this get any worse?

"Quizzy Peppers. Donna, in what year was the first-ever Wimbledon Championship held?"

"1915?"

"I'm sorry, no. Civil Servants, Jack?"

"Big tennis fan. 1877."

Of course he was a big tennis fan. Of *course* he was. The world had conspired against them to fill the opposing team with geniuses.

"Ali, which country produces the most coffee in the world?"

"Brazil?"

"Correct!"

And then, to their relief, the Civil Servants lost their footing and a blitz of easy questions came the Quizzy Peppers' way. Each of them sat up straighter in their seats, blinking their eyes into focus as though coming round from a trance.

"Bryony, globe and Jerusalem are types of what?"

"Artichoke."

"Correct! Luke, what is the capital of Spain?"

"Madrid?"

"Correct! Jaime, what is the painting *La Gioconda* more commonly known as?"

"*The Mona Lisa.*"

"Correct!"

They leaned forward on the table to hungrily absorb Jude's voice.

"Donna, what are the colors of the Norwegian flag?"

"Red, white and blue!" (And she hadn't even known it—she had blurted out the only combination to come to mind.)

"Correct! Harry, who discovered penicillin?"

"Pass to Bryony."

"Alexander Fleming."

"Correct!"

At twenty-eight points to the Civil Servant's forty-two, Donna began to allow herself to hope. And everyone else seemed to share that hope too. Even Harry, whose hands beneath the table were clutching and massaging his knees, appeared to hold his breath as the stretch of good fortune opened wide before them in the encouragement of Jude's voice.

But almost as soon as it had begun, it fell away again when Bryony tripped up on a question.

"Who is the Roman goddess of love and beauty?"

"Aphrodite."

"I'm sorry . . ."

Bryony winced and shut her eyes. Their chance was gone; the round passed to the Civil Servants and they snatched it up with relish.

Donna was so tired. What was the point in anything? What was the point in going to sleep tonight, only to wake up in the morning to face another day under the magnifying glass of Tess's office? Or a weekend stepping around Bernadette's packed boxes in the living room, where crumbs of pink plaster from her failed chimney-breast project still coated the skirting boards? She didn't even see the point in taking Kayla out to lunch and making tonight's loss seem somehow brave and courageous.

The motionless profiles of Harry, Bryony, Luke, and Jaime looked defeated; she'd probably never see any of them again.

*　　*　　*

For the last round they battled back and forth, until, cruelly, the question that landed the Civil Servants the victory fell on Harry. The elated sounds of the audience distantly rose and fell around him. Even Jude's voice became vague and obscure, and his broad figure, perched atop the bar, became blurred through an embarrassing and dangerous swell of tears.

"Quizzy Peppers. Harry, who is Arsenal's all-time top goal-scorer?"

Harry's throat closed. "Pass to Luke."

From the pause and the high wince from his throat, Harry could tell Luke didn't know the answer.

"Ian Wright?"

"I'm sorry, that's incorrect. Civil Servants—Graeme?"

"Thierry Henry."

"Correct! Ladies and gentlemen . . ."

They had lost. Jaime sobbed into the shoulder of Luke's shirt. Bryony forced a smile, clapping politely, but her head wobbled on her neck like a dandelion caught in a gust of wind.

Underneath the table, Donna found and clasped Harry's hand, silently mouthing something like "It's OK" or "It's alright."

He searched the audience for the sight of Vivienne's yellow headscarf, but it appeared she was gone. His mother was still there, bearing whatever shame she felt for him by herself. She's here, he tried to tell himself, she stayed. But what use was that when he didn't think he'd ever forget the look on her face—an old and tired woman who was resigned to the sort of son she had raised.

CHAPTER THIRTY-TWO

Question: *What book by Chinese military general Sun Tzu offers ancient wisdom on how to use skill, cunning, tactics, and discipline to outwit your opponent?*
Answer: The Art of War

Jaime did not have the opportunity to fully absorb the loss of the Quiz League. While getting ready for her day at PrintPro in the bright light of Friday morning, she repeated the mantra: Don't Think About It. Because if she did think about it, she would dissolve into tears. The mantra staved off the panic that crept up to startle her when she was brushing her teeth, inspecting her tired face in the mirror, or waiting for the kettle to boil and losing herself in the rolling steam.

Would the Quizzy Peppers ever want to see each other again?

Don't Think About It.

Bryony was probably relieved that she didn't have to spend another evening or lunch break hearing about Jaime's problems.

Don't Think About It.

Would Luke escape back to Keswick now it was all over?

Don't think about that either.

PrintPro was mercifully quiet, so she set herself the task of cleaning all the crevices of the shop that could not be seen—the shelves above head height, underneath the poster rack, the skirting boards hidden behind the stacked rows of sale prints. And in a satisfying sweat, as she climbed and crouched and reached, sneezing dust and squirming at the black bodies of dead flies, she began to think, well, what's the big deal? Wasn't it pointless to get worked up about a thing as silly as a pub quiz? It carried her through the twilight shift too; in replenishing the bare shelves with easy-to-stack cylinders and neat, symmetrical packages, she found a gratifying rhythm to her work and an optimism in her thoughts. It was no big deal at all!

By the end of the day, it was as though the whole thing had never happened, or perhaps had happened so distantly that the passing of time had erased any feelings of sadness and brought only a fond kind of nostalgia. Sure, it would have been nice if they'd won, and she guessed she felt sorry for Harry, who had left the Five Bells in a head-hanging shuffle, barely able to speak to any of them. But if she were honest, the whole experience had often left her sick with nerves. And it was a relief too, to no longer have to fortify Luke with her tireless cheerleading ("It will be so fun!").

The Quizzy Peppers group chat remained unhappily silent. Even when Jaime had sent a cheerful, self-deprecating note—*Well, it was a lot of fun anyway!*—nobody had replied. And that didn't matter either; everyone was entitled to the time it took to lick their wounds.

But when she woke up on Saturday with an aching dry throat (had she used her voice at all yesterday?), the sky outside her bedroom window was gray and oppressive; the forecast predicted a muggy day of rain. Where was the consistently joyous blue that had greeted her all summer? What was the point in having weekends off when you couldn't go outside and enjoy them? And what was the use in living in this gritty, foul-smelling, hateful city if you didn't have any friends to do it with? Winning the Quiz League would have cemented their friendships for years to come. They would have entered again next year and the year after that. They would have grown older together—as Bryony got her degree, as Luke "found himself," and as they all danced at her and Luke's wedding—able to look tenderly back on that first year, when they had scarcely known each other but had created something wonderful.

"You don't understand," she had told Luke that morning. "You never *cared* about it. It never *meant* anything to you."

But he'd sat on the sofa as benignly as an old man, sipping a cup of tea and making small adjustments to the position of his glasses, explaining to her why it didn't matter.

"Hundreds of people across London entered that thing," he'd said. "We weren't even very good. We were just lucky. You have to get over it."

So she spent the day trying to "get over it," and later they sat together in the early afternoon at Luke's laptop, at Jaime's insistence, redrafting Luke's CV.

"I'm not being controlling, Luke, but isn't it a good idea to have someone look these things over?" she said, while she pointed out small grammatical errors and areas that could be "embellished on."

"Controlling is exactly what you're being. I don't need someone to walk me through a CV. It's the easiest piece of—"

"But you haven't had any interviews!"

"I hardly have any qualifications, Jaime. I don't have any experience."

"And whose fault is that? Who was pissing about with Stratten when you could have enrolled in college? And didn't you say you were going to look into teacher training?"

"I need a degree for that." His tight voice sounded as though he was pressing all his molars together.

"There are top-up courses."

"I don't have the—you know—the . . . Oh, just leave me alone, will you?"

He got up from his seat, muttering that he was going down to collect the post, and as Jaime started to scroll through the search results for "teacher training scholarships," Luke came to stand in the living-room doorway, holding an opened letter.

"What is this?" The letter trembled in the grip of his hands. "Our client, Quick Cash 4U, has asked us to contact you regarding the above balance, relating to payments on an outstanding loan—"

"Why are you reading my things?"

"Never mind why I'm 'reading your things'—this is for six hundred pounds, Jaime. You took out a loan?"

"They're just dumb little short-term payday things," she said, but she could not meet his eyes. Was the balance really six hundred pounds? On just *one* of the loans? She swallowed, turning hot in the glare of the laptop screen. "It's what they're designed for," she said. "To tide people over when things get a bit rough. I get paid in two weeks. I'll just—"

He wagged the letter in front of her face. "This isn't a statement, Jaime; it's a debt-collection letter. They've passed it to an agency because you haven't been paying it."

She snatched the letter from him. "Don't be ridiculous. Of course I've been paying it."

But had it been possible that she had lost track? It had all got so complicated; there had been that first loan in March, and OK, that one had spun out of control, but she had settled it with a better deal she'd found on—or wait, had she settled all of it or just most of it? And had whatever had been left of that first balance still been accumulating interest? No, that couldn't be right.

"Wait—just let me log onto my . . . I could have sworn I paid that one off."

"How many do you *have*?" Luke came looming over her chair, grabbing the back rest and peering over her shoulder with his breath heavy in her ear.

"Luke, get out of my face—"

"This is my business. If you're too irresponsible to—"

"*I'm* the only one being responsible in this—"

"You're making a mess of everything. I should have known better than to—"

"It's *my* money."

Jaime stood up and took his laptop, pulling the charging cord with her as she backed into the window. "Get away from me," she said.

He made a lunge for the laptop—"That's mine. Give it here. That's my property"—and in doing so cracked his knee on the corner of the coffee table, causing him to erupt in a roar of pain.

"You think you're entitled to your property when you're not paying any of the bills?" she said, escaping around the back of the sofa into the freedom of the hallway.

He hobbled out to follow, pointing at her as his neck and face turned red in the effort to maintain the volume and control of his voice. "This was all your stupid idea in the first place."

"No one held a gun to your head."

"What was the alternative? To have you crying and moping around the place every day?"

"Me moping? *Me* moping? I'm so sick of *you* moping around I could scream."

It was the worst of their fights for almost a full year. It led them from room to room, where they tried simultaneously to escape the sound of each other's voices and make their own voices heard. No space was big enough to contain the depth of their resentment of each other.

"I knew you'd fall apart as soon as this stupid quiz ended," he told her. "If you haven't got any friends, that's nothing to do with me. And you know why you haven't got any friends? Because you're a needy, clingy—"

"*You're* the reason I don't have any friends. You're a boring, useless shell of a person. Do you hear me? A *shell*. And you've taken all I loved about being here—you've stamped all over it and *ruined* it."

The letter lay discarded somewhere on the floor, and after Jaime had fled into the humid stairway of the building ("Leave me alone. I mean it, Luke. Leave me *alone!*"), the fight chased them outside as Luke followed her down the stairs and out the front door.

He jogged behind her as she hurried away on the damp pavement under a spray of summer rain. "Everything might not have been perfect," he said over her shoulder, "but I was settled, I was stable. Nothing's ever good enough for you."

"Stable?" Jaime spun around. "Things were not 'stable.' You were about to leave me to go back to Keswick," she hissed. "Do you think I've forgotten what you said about being 'swallowed' by me?"

"I said I was unhappy. If you want to spin that into some sort of soap opera for whatever abandonment issues you're having or whatever, then that's your own problem."

He was a liar and a hypocrite and a leech. But more than that; he was cruel. She was stunned by it.

And to add to her humiliation she started crying—red, ugly, breathless crying—when she had resolved not to. "You're never going to marry me, are you? You're never going to get me a ring or save for a deposit or anything. So just go back to Keswick. Just go back and live with your mum and leave me the fuck alone."

There was nothing left to say after that, so they returned to the flat, weak and shaking and vulnerable in their rain-soaked clothes; Jaime realized she was still wearing candy-striped pajama bottoms and her fleece-lined slippers. But in their desperation to flee out of the door of the flat, neither of them had remembered their keys. So they had no choice but to stand at the front door and wait in silence for their downstairs neighbor to answer the buzzing of her intercom.

"Oh, hello," Jaime said, when her crackling answer came to their aid. "I'm afraid we've locked ourselves out. Do you happen to have our spare key so we can—"

"Listen," came her hard, spitting voice, "I've got your key, but if you think I'm going to let your screaming ruin my weekend then you've got another think coming. Is that clear?"

CHAPTER THIRTY-THREE

Question: *What poem by Henry Lawson begins "The fields are fair in autumn yet, and the sun's still shining there"?*
Answer: The Things We Dare Not Tell

The employment support officer's name was Sally, and she smiled in a stretched line that didn't show any of her teeth. Donna sat with her in an empty conference room in the Icon Marketing offices on the Monday after the semifinal—the same conference room where she'd had the humiliating meeting with Bernard Cope.

With her tanned legs crossed at the ankle under a shin-length plaid skirt, Sally smoothed her blonde fringe away from the outrageous length of her thick, black eyelashes, telling Donna she was here to "facilitate" her "working environment" in any way that suited Donna's "needs."

"Well, what 'needs' do you mean?" Donna wanted to know.

"Anything that best allows you to happily operate at work. But let's talk about your life outside of work for a moment, Donna. Do you have a good support system in place? Family? Friends?"

"Well—I was doing this quiz tournament thing, with some friends. That was fun to—you know—blow off steam."

"Interesting. And does a hobby help you feel more positive?"

"Why do you say 'hobby' like that? Like it's trivial? It was actually really . . . Anyway, I'm not doing it anymore, so it's not important."

"Why aren't you?"

"Why aren't I what?"

"Doing the quiz tournament with your friends?"

"Because we lost."

"Was that upsetting for you?"

Donna shrugged. "Can we sort of stop talking about it now?"

Sally flipped a page in her notebook and gathered her breath. "Why don't you tell me about the time off you had last year, Donna?"

"Would you stop saying my name like that?"

"I wasn't aware I was—"

"Anyway, that's personal information."

"It simply helps me in—"

"I was tired, alright? Haven't you ever needed a holiday?"

"I believe right before the . . . holiday, there was an incident in the kitchen where you—"

"Alright, look." Donna stood up so swiftly, with such a forceful push from her arms, that her chair careened up onto two legs before tumbling onto its side. And Sally reared back in horror—her hand clutching the collar of her shirt and her mouth forming a pert, innocent "O"—as the chair rocked on the floor as if it were a fatally wounded animal.

Donna should have said sorry, but the urgency to leave devoured her. She left the conference room without saying anything, holding both her hands to the sides of her face so no one could see her shame or her panic.

*　　*　　*

"Well, what do you mean she's not coming home? Where did she go?"

"I don't know." Arthur lay on his back on the sofa, blowing malted milk balls inches into the air before they bounced off the stream of his breath and rolled away, smearing chocolate onto the cushions. "She just said she wasn't coming home, that's all."

"Arthur." Bryony caught a suspended candy in her fist and pulled him up by his arm.

"Wha-at?"

"Listen to me. Explain it to me properly."

Arthur slouched over his knees and emitted a deep sigh of annoyance or boredom. "We met at the lower-form gates as usual, and she just said she wasn't coming home, and said would I be alright by myself."

"And then what?"

"She just walked off."

"Where? What direction?"

"I don't know."

The next forty minutes were full of frantic phone calls to the parents of Lydia's friends. And all these people, in their clueless dawdling, may have found it strange that Bryony's voice had taken on a tone of such panic, but they didn't have daughters who cut off their hair with kitchen scissors and who screamed at their mothers that they "never listened."

". . . Well, I don't think so, Bryony, but let me ask—*Keesha!* Did you walk back with Lydia today? Well, are you sure? . . . No, I'm afraid, I don't know, Bryony. But, listen, she'll turn up soon . . ."

". . . Hm, well, she doesn't always walk home with Arthur, does she? Surely she goes up to the shops sometimes, or maybe . . ."

". . . Honestly, Bryony, try to relax. Is Glen with you? Have you called him?"

But she couldn't call Glen, who was at the Rose with Jonesy. He would be furious. What sort of mother didn't know where her own daughter was?

At six-thirty, three hours after Arthur had come home alone, Bryony was pacing the kitchen in tight circles, gnawing at the knuckles of her hand; each ringing sound of teenage laughter had her running to the window. Eventually, she slung on her jacket and told Arthur that she would try not to be long.

"You call me if anything happens, alright? Or if Lydia comes back. Do you have mine and Dad's mobile numbers in your—? Good. Now, don't *do* anything, OK?"

Arthur slumped deep in the armchair, looking half the size that he had the night after parents' evening, when he'd astonished her by how much he had grown. He could have been three or four years younger than he was. He had a kiwi-sized bruise on his shin (and where had that come from?) and he badly needed a haircut.

"Are you alright?"

Arthur only flicked his dark gaze to her and away again. "Suppose so. Will you be back soon? Will Dad?"

Bryony stooped down to his dangling feet; the strap of her shoulder bag flopped over his skinny ankle. Well, *would* he always forgive her? Or was he only a year or two behind Lydia in the thin wearing of whatever "unconditional" love was supposed to mean? She didn't know how to have that conversation with him. All she could do was promise herself she would have it another time (and hadn't she promised that before?) and assure him that she'd be back as soon as she could.

She shut herself in Glen's van and didn't even fasten her seatbelt until she found herself jolted forward, having braked suddenly at a crossing. An amused group of teenage girls giggled behind their hands as she studied them intently over the steering wheel. None of them were Lydia.

In Bryony's agitated and endless loops of the roads surrounding the school, Crystal Palace Park and the Triangle, the clock raced forward to seven . . . seven-twenty . . . seven-thirty-two . . . seven-forty-five . . . Eventually she pulled over, under the large shade of a tree, to breathe heavily onto the steering wheel. She composed herself for a minute to call Arthur—" Any sign of her yet? . . . What about Dad? . . . Alright, I'll be home soon, OK?"—before letting her forehead press helplessly against the driver's seat window. What was she supposed to do—call the police? And what was she supposed to say? Would they call child services? Would they take Lydia away in some nondescript car to live with someone who could clearly love her better and with more patience than Bryony could?

Then on the passenger seat, her phone began to ring; it was her parents' home number.

"Mum?"

"Bryony—what on earth's happened?"

"Did Arthur call you?"

"No. Did you know Lydia came here all the way by train? From London?"

"Lydia's there? With you?" Bryony bent into her knees, holding her breath as her juddering, silent sobs bounced her head against the steering wheel. "Is she alright?" she said into the footwell.

"Well, of course she's alright. Your father told her he'd take her back home, but she just started—I don't know—crying about a teacher at school and said that you and Glen were . . . Have you and Glen been fighting?"

"Well, never mind all that now." Bryony regained a controlled tone of authority: Lydia was OK; she wasn't in the back seat of some strange man's car or hitchhiking down the A22 with her school blazer tied around her waist. "Look, I'm coming over to get her, OK?"

"Fine." The sound of Win's indignant inhale of breath filled Bryony's ear. "You know, perhaps if you paid more attention to your family and stopped gallivanting down the pub for quizzes, you wouldn't be dealing with a runaway. How did you allow things to get this bad, Bryony? It's unacceptable."

"I'm not 'gallivanting,' Mum. Anyway, all that's over now. Just let me talk to Lydia, alright?"

When Lydia's small, terse voice came on the phone, trying to sound more grown-up than she was, Bryony pinballed from anger to pleading and back again.

"What do you think you're doing, taking off like that?"

"I don't care."

"*I* care. And you're coming home—tonight."

She scoffed. "No, I'm not."

"That wasn't a question. Why are you doing this, Lydia? Please."

"I *hate* you. I hate *both* of you."

The words punched through Bryony's chest, leaving her wrestling for breath. She was silent for a full minute, but it didn't seem to matter, as Lydia appeared to have left the phone call anyway. Her mother's voice came on again.

"Well, that went as well as I'd expected it to go," Win said.

Bryony swiped her tears away, then gripped the steering wheel in a fury until her fingers ached. "Listen—you know what?" she said. "She can stay with you. If she hates being here so much that she ran away, then she can stay there." The only problem was, Bryony wasn't sure if she was saying it because it was best for Lydia or because she simply couldn't cope with any more contempt from her. She felt completely unequipped to parent her way through it.

"Well, that's fine," Win said. "She's outside with your father now, and—oh look—they're starting up the barbecue." And in the peaceful silence that followed, Bryony imagined her mother to be looking out through her French doors and onto the far-reaching, flowered garden, where Lydia might be swaying on the swing seat, secured to a branch of her mother's colossal cherry tree. And perhaps Win was smiling on the other side of the glass, signaling to her granddaughter that there was no need to worry; she was taking care of everything.

"And here you are, abandoning your responsibilities again, Bryony," Win said. "I just never thought you would abandon your own daughter."

CHAPTER THIRTY-FOUR

Question: *Which superhero has a vulnerability to Kryptonite?*
Answer: *Superman*

Two weeks after the semifinal, Harry's life had begun to resemble normality once again. He no longer avoided eye contact with himself in the mirror each morning by staring solidly at his mouth while he brushed his teeth. Occasionally a wave of humiliation hit him, when a flash of streetlight or the headlights from a passing car would send him back to sitting under the ceiling lamps in the Five Bells, hearing Jude's voice and seeing Vivienne and his mother's small, disappointed faces. But it was alright: he had learned the trick of holding his breath and pressing the crescents of his fingernails into the palms of his hands until the feeling passed, and it always did. He would get on with his day, sometimes not thinking about that evening for hours at a time. The problem was that he had not seen Vivienne again since. He had called her, but she'd cut him off after a few minutes of brief, terse conversation. And he supposed that was alright too: she'd need a little time to digest the whole business with his mother. It can't have been pleasant having to break the news to an anxious, ageing woman in the middle of a crowded pub.

"I just don't understand why you did it, Harry. God, I was mortified."

"I'd just lost my job, alright? She didn't need to hear about you dumping me too."

"Don't you dare blame me. I'm not the one who caused all this."

Well, but she had, hadn't she? Vivienne had been the one to leave him, freshly unemployed, in the shame of signing on for jobseeker's allowance and having to admit to everyone that he was thirty-one years old and had lost everything.

"Look, I just didn't want to upset her, alright? And then it just went on and on, and I never got around to it."

"'Never got around to it'? Oh, Harry, you know what you are? You're like some big child, and I don't think you'll ever grow up."

Well, alright. Maybe he would and maybe he wouldn't. But in the awkward teatime of that Sunday after the semifinal, his mother had turned out to be more understanding than he'd have predicted. She'd even let him know, over the cantankerous scrape of her knife and fork, that he was forgiven, but that Vivienne was not.

"I'm tougher than all that nonsense," she had said, and she had knocked his knee with her own under the table. "You think I don't know about breakups? I didn't try to hide it when your dad left us. I wasn't ashamed."

"No, I know."

"Good riddance to him, I said. Wasn't worth my spit. And I can't say much for Vivienne either. She's always been a snob. You're too good for her."

"What are you talking about? You always said you loved her."

"Well, I didn't want to upset you, did I?"

"I didn't want to upset *you*."

"How about we pack all this in then? This upsetting each other business, eh?"

And in Harry's stunned discovery that someone could not be captured by Vivienne's enchantment, as he silently chewed and swallowed his boiled carrots, his mother unleashed her most surprising advice of all.

"Don't ever be desperate for someone to love you," she'd said. "It'll get you nowhere." And her mouth tightened in such a self-righteous scowl that it was easy to believe she could take on anything—ex-husbands, ex-girlfriends and every dripping tap that Harry couldn't fix anyway.

Now, on this pleasantly warm Tuesday, he felt almost at ease. Rays of sun came reflecting through Kingsley's large windows, Vivienne might only need another day or two to come round, and he was meeting Donna for a drink at lunchtime. Despite everything, he was looking forward to seeing her, and his mouth was already watering at the thought of a cold glass of cider outside on a sun-warmed pub bench. He had not seen Donna since the semifinal, but she and the others had offered him brief and sympathetic hugs before they parted ways on the street, where behind them the Five Bells still rang in celebration for the Civil Servants. They may have needed more time to fully forgive him, but the silent press of their embraces seemed to say *Well, OK, let's just try to move on now, shall we?* It may have been the only thing that allowed him to get out of bed the next morning.

Now he turned his attention to the task at hand—checking the property brochure PDFs to approve them to print. It might be dull work, but in the efficiency of his inspection—this one a two-bedroom, that one with an en suite . . . a hundred square meters . . . balcony . . . communal garden—it was easy to tie up a good job and tell Darren it was done well ahead of time.

"Thanks, Harry. Listen—wait a minute—do you fancy coming out with me to Millen Road later? Viewers are looking for a renovation project, and I'd bet they'd like to hear what you have to say on the place. You know—what you envision. Bloody thing's been on the market for a year."

"Sure. Sounds good. Thanks, Darren."

And Ashton, who had been trying to rouse interest in the big Millen Road house among his own clients for a number of months, had heard the entire exchange. No sooner had Darren closed the door to his office than Ashton's almighty hand was clamping down on Harry's shoulder.

"Word in the kitchen, mate?" he said into Harry's ear.

In the small kitchenette, a cupboard-sized room consisting of a sink, a kettle, a fridge and shelves of jumbled mugs and plates, Ashton towered over Harry to reach his WORLD'S BEST BOYFRIEND mug. It came down in the clasp of his hand, from where his large veins snaked down his wrist and disappeared under the cuffs of his shirt. Harry had no choice but to crumple into the kettle's billowing steam.

"Now I don't need to tell you about overstepping your mark here," Ashton said, leaning against the worktop. "It's embarrassing, alright?" And his tilting pink face displayed the look of someone commiserating over something out of their control.

"Well, it's Darren who's asked me, Ashton. Not like I can refuse, can I?"

"Actually," Ashton said, proceeding to go about the makings of a cup of instant coffee. "I think you'll find you can."

"Look, mate, I'm not here to—"

"I don't give a fuck what you're here to do," he said, serenely circling a teaspoon inside his mug. "I'm just telling you the way it is. Nice tie, by the way."

"What?"

"Nice tie. You've got a lot of nice ties." Ashton dropped the teaspoon into the sink. "So let's both understand something—you keep your ties to yourself, keep your hands off my properties, and we won't have a problem. Alright?"

Donna tilted her face to the sun. "Superman pose," she said, "for confidence; I saw it on a TED talk. Now, listen—hands on hips, stand with your feet hip-width apart. Now lift your chest—no . . ." Annoyed, she rearranged his limbs. "Come on, do it properly. This is two minutes of your life, Harry—lift your chest. Come on."

Harry copied Donna's pose, and he had to admit her commitment to it made her look the picture of determination: she was tall and proud, in some sort of dramatically billowing patterned skirt, with her chin lifted in conviction and her blonde hair streaming out behind her in the breeze. But the other people in the pub garden had started to incline their heads toward them and give them curious looks of bemusement. And the most remarkable thing was that Donna didn't even seem to notice.

She side-eyed him. "Like you mean it."

He lifted his chest and chin until his neck began to ache with the effort. He was turning red. "Now what? Am I supposed to feel something?"

"You spend two minutes doing a power pose—don't worry, I'm counting, you can sit down in a minute—you spend two minutes doing a power pose and it can radicalize your confidence levels. When we feel scared, we cower, we make ourselves small. You don't need to do that. You are good at what you do, and Ashton is a prick. Got it?"

A few seconds passed, in which Donna's face went serious. She slunk out of the pose and took off her sunglasses. He saw how tired she looked—her eyelids were tender and puffy.

"I'm leaving," she said suddenly.

"What?"

"I'm leaving London. The country, actually."

Harry's arms fell to his sides. His heart turned cold. "What about—what about your job?"

Donna waved her hand. "Politics," she said.

"Where are you going?"

"India." She started to pull at the tendrils of her hair. "It's the spiritual capital of the world. Four major religions were—"

"What the . . . Why?"

"Harry, you sound like a bonehead—'What? Where? Why?'—because I'm not sticking around for the inevitable. That's why. And with the Quiz League over . . . well. I have a flight early Sunday morning."

"The inevitable what?"

"Everything going to shit—that's what's inevitable. Come out with me Saturday night. Say goodbye. I'm just going to pack my suitcase and head out, get an early coach or something."

Harry could have imagined it, but he thought her bottom lip wobbled.

"Only if you want to," she said.

He took her by the shoulders and she stiffened, looking down at his hands, annoyed. "You know what you're doing," he insisted. "You're chucking it all in. Don't."

"That's not it at all, Harry. Don't you think it's good to get away from the grind? Re-center yourself?"

"Don't talk bullshit."

"Come with me," she said. "To India."

"Do you hear yourself? Seriously, do you hear yourself, Donna?"

"We both hate our jobs; we both hate the people we work with. We've got no ties or anything. Why the hell not? We have fun together, don't we?"

"Well—yes, but I can't take off to India. I have my job. I have Vivienne. You need to speak to someone."

"I hate my life, Harry." In her pale, listless eyes was a vacant and dark unhappiness.

"Are you listening to me at all, Donna? You need to speak to someone, because you're sounding pretty insane right now."

She opened the arms of her sunglasses with a snap and jabbed them onto her nose. "That was a low blow, Harry." She sat down again. "Well, forget it. Forget I said anything. If you want to stay here and chase Vivienne around then I suppose you have to get that out of your system."

Harry sat glumly opposite her. He couldn't think of anything to say, but he knew one thing: the strength of his concern for Donna had taken him by surprise.

She folded her arms on the table to lean across to him. "You'll never change, will you? God forbid you ever open yourself up to anything outside the walls of the estate agents or the pub."

He was reminded of Vivienne calling him a "big child" over the phone ("I don't think you'll ever grow up"). Well, alright—but maybe this was what growing up looked like. He couldn't allow anything else to distract him from getting his life back in order. He had gone along with Donna's whim in the whole Quiz League business and look how that had ended.

Before they parted ways on the street, Donna lowered her sunglasses to look with squinting revulsion at the front of Kingsley & Co., before saying, "Maybe see you Saturday then? I'll let you know where."

"You're not really leaving, are you?"

"Of course I am." And she walked away, her blonde hair flashing in the stripes of sunlight and shadow on the pavement.

Later, in the office, just before it was time to leave with Darren for Millen Road, he spent two minutes locked in a cubicle of the bathroom, standing astride in Superman pose in front of the toilet bowl. "Sure, Darren. Let's head out. Let's get an offer on this place," he whispered, fearing someone would come into the bathroom and hear him—and he prayed to God if it had to be someone, it wasn't Ashton.

Out in the office, Darren was slipping on his suit jacket by the door, signaling that it was time to go. As Harry passed behind Ashton, who hunched over his desk with all the muscles in his back tensed, he buttoned up his jacket and stepped out with Darren into the sunshine.

CHAPTER THIRTY-FIVE

Question: *What is the system of springs and shock absorbers by which a vehicle is supported on its wheels?*
Answer: *Suspension*

"Hi Donna, take a seat."

Outside Tess's window, a sunlit crest of cloud appeared to form a halo around her head.

"You know Mark from HR? Good. Now—I'll just get to it, alright? Pending an investigation of gross misconduct for the incident with your employment support officer, we have no choice but to suspend you. You will receive full pay and benefits."

Tess laced her hands together, and Donna sat trying to absorb her words. She was going to lose her job. She might have booked the ticket to India, but she wasn't really going to go, was she? Even when she'd hit the payment button, stiff with defiance, a bigger part of her had assumed some matter of importance might prevent it or someone would talk her out of it. But Harry had tried, hadn't he? And she—the neurotic wreck that she was—had shut him down. And as if Harry ever would have abandoned Vivienne to escape across an ocean and live in Donna's chaos. She'd tempted fate, and it had called her bluff.

"Well, I knocked over a chair," Donna said. "It was an accident." She should have apologized to Sally, but she'd walked out like an obstinate, arrogant child.

"I'm afraid the nature of the incident isn't entirely clear. You'll find the details and terms of the suspension here." Tess slid a sealed envelope across the desk, which Donna tore open.

. . . In accordance with the Company's formal discipline procedure . . . your suspension is to enable us to conduct a thorough . . . failure to comply with these instructions may in itself constitute . . .

Donna replaced the letter on the desk. She held on to her thighs in an effort to stop both her hands and her knees trembling. "Well, Tess—and Mark, I suppose—that's a nice letter and everything, but you can't just sack me."

"This is not a termination, Donna."

"So, I quit. I hand in my notice, or whatever. How's that?"

"Oh, Donna." Tess slipped off her glasses, tossing them in front of her where they skittered across the desk top. She pinched the bridge of her nose, her eyes closed against what looked like the formation of a troubling headache. "Why can't you see we're trying to help you? Can't you see that at all?"

Donna was unable to confront Tess's tired face. "Well, alright. But you can't. So, I think it's best we both left it there, don't you?"

So they left it there. Donna had imagined striding out of that place with her head held in a mature expression of long-suffering tolerance and dignity, clutching a cardboard box of belongings, like they did in the movies. But the scant contents of her desk—a William Boyd novel, a silver necklace with a broken clasp and a two-year-old postcard from Lottie (¡Hola hermana!)—all fitted neatly into a canvas shoulder bag. It was as though she had always held herself poised for flight.

And when she arrived home, after she had slung the meagre canvas bag onto the unswept floorboards and stood for a long time at the front door, pinching the bridge of her nose, she saw an envelope on the floor addressed to Bernadette. Inside, a starched card, made from some expensive kind of linen paper, proclaimed:

LOFT

WELCOMES DONNA MARCH

GUEST OF BERNADETTE MCCABE

*   *   *

At six-thirty on Friday, Jaime arrived home late from her day at Print-Pro. She arched her tired spine as she hung up her bag and kicked off her shoes. She had just enough time for a quick nap and a light dinner, before she had to—

"Luke?"

When the sound of the swinging door chain ceased, she'd noticed the absence of any sound at all. No incessant commentary or revving from the motorsport channel, or jangle of soundtrack from a video game, or the phlegmy rattle of Luke clearing his throat. He was not in the living room, where the television was dark, the coffee table was bare and even the sofa didn't show the sagging indentations of use. Nor was he in the bedroom, where the bed was made. In the kitchen, the cord of his laptop adaptor snaked around the table legs, but his laptop wasn't there. On top of the table, an opened letter announced a "final demand" from We Pay Today—*You have failed to comply with the terms of the default notice* . . .

What did this mean? What were they going to do to her? And she was sorting it out, wasn't she? Another two or three paydays and it wouldn't be a problem. But he had seen this letter and gone off somewhere in a bad mood—probably to wander listlessly around the park, regretting ever asking her to marry him at all.

It occurred to her that today was the last working day of June, and her wages from both PrintPro and the supermarket should have landed tidily in their joint account this morning. She dug out her phone: she would log on now, pay off this particular bill and then she could tell Luke that—But wait . . . her account still showed a balance well into her overdraft. That couldn't be right. And when she scrolled down to the deposits and withdrawals, she became caught in a sensation of sickening suspension. The solid feeling of the kitchen tiles beneath her socks disappeared and her head swam in the rumble of passing buses and tinkling mugs swaying on the mug tree.

The account showed the deposit of her wages and then an immediate withdrawal of fifteen hundred pounds to the bank account of *Mr. Luke P. Myers.*

She dashed through to the bedroom, where she wrenched open the wardrobe doors and all of the drawers in Luke's dresser. What was this? Was he trying to teach her a lesson? That she couldn't handle their money and so he would take it all from her? But then, if that was the case—if that was all he was trying to prove—why had he taken all of his clothes?

* * *

"Hi, Vivienne? It's me . . . Hi. Listen, things've got a bit weird, haven't they? Ever since the . . . Well, I wondered if you wanted to meet me for dinner. There's stuff we need to figure out, don't we? How's tonight? Can you get away? . . . Oh, well, sure. Of course. How about an early one on Saturday, then? I might have to meet up with a friend later . . . Well, that sounds great. I'll book a table, about six-thirty? . . . Oh, I know, Viv, I know; there's a lot to talk about."

Harry ended the phone call. It's what he wanted, wasn't it? To talk Vivienne round and pretend the whole semifinal fiasco had never happened. But the optimism or relief he should be feeling wasn't surfacing. He kept thinking about Donna ("I hate my life, Harry")—the thought of her on a plane to India, suspended in the air, being carried away from everyone who knew her and cared about her. And what would happen to her in India if she continued to spiral away? Should he try to call a doctor or something, or get in touch with her family—whoever and wherever they were?

Oh, get a grip, he told himself, taking a steadying breath and sitting down at his computer. He just needed to book a table for himself and Vivienne and focus on that. Focus on things he could fix.

* * *

"What do you mean, he's gone? . . . I can't even . . . You mean he's taken all of it?"

"What's going on?" Glen said, muting the television. "It's gone ten, for crying out loud. Is it Lydia?"

"Hold on just a second," Bryony said into her phone before holding it away from her ear. "It's Jaime. Luke's just . . . disappeared or something—taken all their money."

Glen jabbed the remote control, heaving a sigh. The television blared to life.

Guilt stabbed in the base of Bryony's throat. She had hoped that the space left in Lydia's absence might allow them both to breathe, to find some sort of territory for forgiveness. But instead Glen had been so spitting angry at her that he'd been unable to look her in the eye for two full days. Now, almost two weeks later, Lydia was still at her mother's—leisurely completing the work her school had sent her after Bryony had called them to explain the "family crisis," having barbecues and doing whatever else it was they did—and, other than hauling her into the car like a tantruming toddler, Bryony didn't know how to get her back, physically or any other way. Her mother was right; she was a terrible parent—still as unequipped as a teenager.

Bryony went out into the hallway, closing the living-room door behind her.

"Jaime, what's going on? . . . Listen, you have to calm down. I can't—Tonight? Well, I'm not sure that's a good . . . Oh, Jaime, look, of course I care. It's only . . . Well, alright then . . . yes, come on over as soon as you—you know—need to."

When Bryony came back into the living room, Glen was sitting stiffly in the flickering glow of the television, drumming the remote against his knee. "When are you going to start putting us first, huh?" he asked her. "You've chased Lydia away. When are you going to stop trying to fix everyone else's problems?"

Oh, because I can't fix my own! she wanted to rage at him. Because if she could help Jaime it might, somehow, mean that she wasn't as awful a person as everyone thought she was. Wasn't it obvious? Couldn't he even understand something as simple as that? But she only faced the wall and bit down hard on her lip until the swelling urge to cry had subsided.

CHAPTER THIRTY-SIX

Question: *What is the meaning of* prozek, *the Slovenian word from which the name of the sparkling wine prosecco is derived?*
Answer: *Path through the woods*

The problem with Donna's suitcase was that it was old and tattered and made of cheap polyester, and it was filled with the sort of clothes not welcome at Loft. From the new and unworn clothes still hanging from her wardrobe door (she had just *known* the perfect opportunity would arise to wear these things), she selected the outfit most appropriate for Loft and for continuing on to a brave and wistful flight to Mumbai: a blue calf-length cotton-cashmere ribbed dress and a wool-blend blazer. With box-fresh white tennis shoes (she had checked Loft's dress code) and the layering of the best jewelry she owned, anyone on the plane, and in Loft for that matter, might assume she was some European heiress on a summer excursion.

But she'd have to stash the suitcase somewhere out of sight—surely Loft had an ample cloakroom? The other problem was the rising sense of panic that simmered somewhere at the bottom of her ribcage and periodically threatened to ascend all the way up her throat and through her brain, where it held every promise of paralyzing her. In those moments, all she could do was lean heavily against the nearest wall or tube handrail to whisper compassionately to herself—"You're OK, you're OK, you're OK"—until the moment had passed.

Loft turned out to be an arrangement of wide and abundant rooms in the basement of a handsome Georgian townhouse, fronting the narrow pavement of a fast, chaotic roadside that was still ringing with traffic at seven in the evening.

"Then why is it called Loft," Donna enquired of the top-hatted doorman, "if it's in a basement?"

"Well, it's ironic, isn't it?" he said with a curl of his clean-shaven top lip, while he discreetly chewed a cud of gum.

After she had deposited her shameful suitcase with the cool, high-cheekboned hostess, she stood hesitantly at the bar of gold-veined calacatta marble—"Oh, I'll have a prosecco—no, wait, make that champagne"—sipping at the fizzing brim of her drink under a brass dome, laser-cut with the exquisite patterning of a Moroccan lamp.

"Excuse me," the barman said sharply when she had reached up to touch it, and then shook his head with the patient tolerance of a weary parent. And this sent her into another interlude of climbing dread.

Still clutching her champagne, she pushed her way through a terrarium-like parlor of palms and embroidered velvet chairs and crisp, pressed tablecloths until she found herself in a sickly pink bathroom, lined in curtains of gauze that billowed to the floor. There she bent over the scalloped quartz sink, where behind her in the mirror, two or three bejeweled women were taking photographs of themselves draped over a quilted chaise longue. As soon as she had recovered, she texted Harry.

> Flight at 6.30 a.m. Getting coach to airport at 4ish. I'll be at Loft until then. Come.

She wasn't entirely sure how she would get him inside, but no matter—she'd work that one out later.

* * *

Jaime sat deep in the sofa cushions of Bryony's living room, a wad of damp tissues clutched in her hands.

"And I just don't understand how anyone could *do* this to someone they're supposed to love," she was saying to Bryony, who was beginning to flag after the long emotional course of the afternoon. "To someone they're supposed to marry. I mean, everyone has fights, but to just *leave*? And take all their *money*? And the ridiculous part—the really ridiculous part—is that all that money is *mine*."

Jaime had arrived at Bryony's door soon after their phone call last night, a damp, swollen-eyed whirlwind of injustice and heartbreak, who teetered between trembling fury and grief-stricken collapse. She had slept and then risen early on Saturday for a shower, and Bryony hoped she would have regained some composure, perhaps channeling her suffering into something practical—calling her landlady to discuss breaking their contract or calling the bank to shut down the joint account—but by Saturday evening Jaime still appeared frozen in the grip of panic. Glen and Arthur had even shut themselves upstairs for the majority of the day to escape the sorrow that engulfed every room she was in.

"I mean, honestly, Jaime," Bryony said now, placing a consoling hand on Jaime's knuckles. "I know this is awful—just awful—but come on, is he worth all this? Is he worth this much unhappiness? He's been exploiting the situation for—"

"Bry." Glen stood in the doorway, unsmiling. "Can you come into the kitchen for a minute?"

He paced the kitchen with his arms folded. "This is getting a little much. Can't you see that? Shouldn't we be focusing on getting Lydia home?"

"Glen, I—" Bryony lowered her voice and quietly shut the kitchen door. "I don't know how to tell her to leave. I know we need to, but—"

"Don't we have enough on our plate right now? You can't be her only friend in the world. Listen." He stopped pacing to take both of her arms in an awkward, clinging grasp. "I know you're sorry about Lydia, but I've had enough."

He was asking her to send Jaime home. But all Bryony could see was Jaime's face collapsing into a sobbing crumple of betrayal. And it wouldn't bring about Lydia's forgiveness, would it? It would only mean she'd let another person down.

"That's the thing—I think I *am* her only friend. And I can't just chuck her *out*."

"You're Lydia's only mum."

"Well, it seems like she's better off without me."

Glen let go of her arms. "I'm going to go stay with Jonesy and Karen tonight," he said; all the emotion in his voice was gone.

"You're *leaving* me?" Her voice cracked in alarm—so now he was better off without her too.

"I'm not 'leaving' you. I just need some bloody space. I'll be back tomorrow, alright?"

*   *   *

"So sorry I'm late, Harry. I had to stop by the post office, and then Maria called: she's got a new job at the Wellcome Collection—how exciting is that?"

"Oh yeah. Well done, her."

Harry had looked for a restaurant on the South Bank, but the contemporary bars and restaurants were a concrete-and-glass mystery to him. They all served "small plates" or "bottomless brunches" or "a trio of desserts," with menus that defied logic and eye-wateringly expensive wine lists. He had booked a table at a place that declared themselves "Scandinavian style" (the Scandinavians appreciated the simple things in life, didn't they?), for a dinner with minimum fuss but with enough class to impress Vivienne. But when he reached the tall-windowed dining area, with its uncomfortable, angular furniture and oversized light fixtures, a cool, heavy-lidded waiter had asked if he was interested in one of their "sundowners." Harry had quickly said no in a panic, not even knowing what "sundowners" meant. And the place didn't look romantic. It was too wide and bright for one thing, like an office canteen, and its windows would only illuminate the sheen of grease across his nose and forehead.

So that was the first part that hadn't gone to plan. The second part was that Vivienne didn't look like she had made much of an effort. She was wearing rumpled jeans and her hair had been hastily thrown into a fraying ponytail. She had even brought several bags of shopping with her, which she dropped at her feet under the table, as though she had only stopped by on her way to do something else.

"This is . . . nice," she said, as her finger grazed the menu. "Ooh, sundowners—yum!"

Harry stole a glance at his phone. Still nothing from Donna—where would she be going and why hadn't she texted him? He balanced the phone on his knee to tap out a message. If he could just speak to her properly, maybe he could talk her out of this whole stupid thing.

Where are you? Are you still going out?

"What's wrong?" Vivienne was looking at him expectantly.

"Nothing. Don't worry, it's nothing."

Vivienne looked happy enough, didn't she? And wasn't it more important that she was relaxed and carefree enough around him to not have to dress up all the time? What sort of a relationship would they have if it relied on the need for darkened, exotic restaurants or the time it took to put on a face of makeup and an elaborate dress? She was here. So perhaps everything could still be salvaged.

*   *   *

There was Sabrina, with a gleaming fall of chestnut hair and white teeth too large for her pursing mouth, who was getting married in a week, an angular, pouting model called Romy in a plaid catsuit, and another girl called Anna or Amber, whose dad had been a DJ at Studio 54. Someone had a cocktail served with a "fragrance"—a rose encapsulated in a copper container, which, when opened, revealed a wafting spill of perfumed dry ice and gave way to a cascade of Ahhhs across the tables.

"Well, and I mean Enzo will be in Sweden until Thursday," Sabrina was saying, "so I won't even *see* him till Friday. I guess I'm not sure whether to just—you know—hold off, or have a last—"

"So this is your *hen* party? Well!" Donna was on her sixth (or was it seventh?) glass of prosecco—no, wait, champagne—and she almost upset her glass bringing a slapping palm down on her knee. "We must get you another . . . something. What are you drinking? It's on me."

"That's awfully sweet of you, but we have a tab."

And where was Harry? Didn't he care that she was leaving tomorrow? (And was she really going through with it?) Well, whatever—honestly, *whatever*—these glossy-haired, clipped-voiced women, with their tabs and gold-buckled handbags, would give Donna the send-off she deserved, if only the features of their slick, smiling faces would stop blurring and dancing in front of her eyes. But if she were really happy about it, then why couldn't the bubble of anxiety in her stomach be quashed? Why couldn't she stop wringing her hands in dread?

"Tell me," she said to Sabrina after a waiter had come obediently to replenish her glass. "Why do you want to get married? Most people are better off on their own, don't you think?"

*   *   *

In the softening light of the evening, Bryony and Jaime had curled into the living room—Jaime in the armchair, looking small and vulnerable in its deep seat and Bryony on the sofa with her ankles tucked underneath her. Bryony had put on some new crime drama, with an intricate twisting plot that she couldn't follow. Arthur had escaped upstairs again, and Glen had tossed clean underwear and his toothbrush into a backpack and left for the night.

Nothing she said or didn't say seemed to leave the slightest impression on Jaime. She gazed into space, seeming like she was listening, but then she would start talking about something completely unconnected to the thread of the conversation.

"What you need to do is start thinking about the lease on your flat," Bryony was saying. "I know that might seem painful, but you need to stop paying all that rent."

Jaime frowned, looking momentarily lost. "The thing is, Bry . . . look, you're going to think . . . well, you're going to think I'm crazy, but I've really got myself into a mess."

Bryony sighed and rubbed at her aching temples. "I know it seems like a mess now, Jaime. But people break up all the—"

"No, I don't mean that." Jaime shuffled forward in her seat, pink with embarrassment. "I've had a bit of money trouble—with some payday loans. You know the type? I was having such a headache covering all the bills and Luke was always so . . . Anyway, I think I owe something like two thousand pounds, and oh God, it might even be more. And I never even told Luke about it until we got this *awful* letter, and I think that might be why he finally . . ." Jaime fell silent. She yanked down her cuffs to cover her hands and the neckline of her top up to hide her mouth, as though to shield as much skin as she could in shame.

But Bryony couldn't help but see Jaime's astounding resemblance to Lydia in the throes of one of her angst-ridden outbursts; it ignited a savage flare of anger in her heart, where everyone, always, sought out something soft and weeping and compassionate.

*　　*　　*

"So what's Enzo do, then? You know, when he's in Switzerland or Sweden or wherever? I'm out of a job, you see. And, listen." Donna upended her empty glass. "Can I get another one of these things?"

"Well, he's a consultant for—"

"Oh, I see—I see. And let me guess: you're the cool girlfriend—well, *wife*—who stays at home and . . . Do you know, I've really got the worst headache."

Stark uplights dappled the palms and ferns of the terrarium room in neon green. They cast grotesque silhouettes on the molded ceiling and flashed off columns of glass, casting painful flares into Donna's eyes.

"Are you alright? Would you like a glass of water? Shall I get a— what was your name again?"

"Donna."

"Oh, how pretty. Like Donna Summer."

The green-lit portrait of Sabrina lurched and swayed in her vision. "Do you think it's funny—do you really think it's funny to make fun of someone's name?"

"Oh, I—"

"No, listen. Listen—I've really had enough of people like you—"

"Donna? Donna, is that you?"

A spindly, familiar figure with a rope of dark hair, scintillating in a dress of iridescent sequins, appeared in front of her. It was Bernadette.

"Donna, what are you doing here? Are you alright? You look sort of—you don't look well at all."

*　　*　　*

Over plates of smoked pork meatballs and a wild mushroom tart, Harry took Vivienne's hand. In blinking alarm, she wiped her mouth on her napkin.

Harry licked his lips; his tongue felt dry and shriveled. "Sorry about all the business at the pub," he said, without quite knowing why he was apologizing again. "To tell you the truth, it was a really rough night. We all took it hard."

Vivienne released her hand from his. "I don't see any reason to be so morose about the whole thing, Harry. It's just a pub quiz."

Harry hurriedly chewed and swallowed his mouthful of food. For God's sake—hadn't he told her, time and time again, how important it had been to him? Would it really hurt her to care? Did she even listen? For the first time since they had come together again, he fixed her with a challenging stare. "Why did you bother coming to watch, then?" he said.

Vivienne blinked at him. "I was just trying to be positive. You were like a nervous little puppy. And then you just . . . well, never mind. It was just embarrassing, that's all."

"I already said I was sorry—twice. What more do you want me to say?"

"Not about your mum. The whole thing. I didn't see why you were so . . . Look, it doesn't matter, alright?" Vivienne resumed slicing the crust of her tart. "Let's just finish our food."

"No, come on. Why I was so what?"

She thrust down her knife and fork and pushed her plate away. "Alright. If you really must know—I didn't see why you couldn't even get a single question right. It was a disaster. I was sitting there wondering if you were really that uneducated. I wondered if we had anything in common at all."

Uneducated. Christ—she *was* a snob. She didn't even know he'd looked at the fucking clipboard. How scathing—how belittling— would her reaction have been then? He had come clean and tried to do the right thing, but he knew even if he told her this—even if he tried to explain—she wouldn't say anything different. He was never going to be good enough for her.

"Well, my teammates have forgiven me, Viv. I don't see why it's so hard for you to do the same. Do you enjoy looking down on everyone this much or is it just me?"

She held onto her stomach as though she might be sick. "Well, as long as we're being honest with each other." She looked away to the tall windows, where a spindly pair of trees were bending under a gathering breeze. "Ashton's asked me to marry him and I suppose I've said yes. I guess it's time to—you know—I guess it's time to stop mucking about."

"Great." Harry jolted out his chair and checked his phone. The message to Donna still sat pending on his screen. It hadn't gone through. Where was she? And what was he even doing here, while somewhere outside this overpriced, pretentious restaurant, one of his best friends, lost and in pain, was becoming unreachable?

He took a last look at Vivienne, perched on her chair, as poised and self-possessed as ever. But her face, illuminated by the dying slants of sunlight, was a rigid contortion of resentment and bitterness. Well, he wanted to tell her, join the fucking club.

*   *   *

Bryony knew she wasn't really angry at Jaime. She was angry at Glen and Lydia and her mother, and the person she was most angry at was herself. But the problem was there was no one else here to take the brunt of it. She got to her feet. "Jaime, that's—two thousand pounds?"

Jaime's eyelashes brimmed with fresh tears. "Do you think Luke could ever forgive something like that?"

"Well, honestly? I mean, yes, I can understand why he'd be really disappointed by all this. Do you know the interest rates on those things? And what did you do when you first started to miss payments? Did you just ignore it?"

"I know. Look, I know, alright? Do you think you could . . . well, give me some help or something? I don't know what to do. If Luke had just—"

"Oh my God. If I hear Luke's name one more time I'm going to scream. I don't need any more children, Jaime. I've got enough problems with the first ones, thank you. Did you even remember that Lydia ran away? You're just—it's completely thoughtless."

Jaime's mouth twitched in startled pain. "Alright—alright. But don't talk to me about 'thoughtless.' At least I didn't get pregnant at seventeen. At least I got my degree before I was irresponsible enough to have a couple of kids."

Bryony backed away in hurt. "You know how important it was to me to get my degree. You know it still is."

"Then why aren't you doing it instead of just talking about it all the time?"

Bryony leaned into the wall and rested her head against the cool plaster. "Look, Jaime—I think you should go, alright? I just . . . well, I think you should stay somewhere else tonight."

"Well, good. I do too."

Jaime hesitated, her dark eyes glinting around the dimly lit living room, perhaps waiting to see if Bryony would change her mind. But then she scrambled out of the armchair and upstairs to retrieve her things, before she swung out of the front door without saying goodbye.

"Jaime, wait," Bryony said, her trembling hand held to her mouth, but she knew she hadn't said it loudly enough for Jaime to hear. She sat down in the armchair, still warm and sagging from the impression of Jaime's body, and bent her head down into her lap.

CHAPTER THIRTY-SEVEN

Question: *What emergency procedure word was conceived as a distress call in the early 1920s by Frederick Stanley Mockford?*
Answer: *Mayday*

"Just give me my fucking suitcase, alright?"

"We really need your ticket, madam. You would have been issued it when you—"

"Well, no one issued me a—Look, it'll be the one that doesn't fit in, OK? Because I'm not fucking rich. It's not a Gucci or a—it'll be the disgusting one in the corner. That should be simple enough, shouldn't it?".

Outside the tall Georgian windows of the lobby the sun was setting. Donna had stumbled up the basement stairs, with Bernadette trailing behind her. ("Wait, Donna. *Wait!*") She must have fallen somewhere because the heels of her hands stung; when she looked down at them they were skinned with grazes. And now, upstairs, above the series of frightening and garish underground rooms, Donna's phone issued an urgent series of pings.

Where are you? Are you still going out?
Donna come on why is your phone off? Call me

I'm home now. Call me soon as you get this
You ok? Just let me know if you're ok

"Look," Bernadette was saying to the hostess. "I really need to get her home. Can't you see she needs to go home? Can you just go back there and find her suitcase? Can I?"

"I'm afraid . . ."

Her phone hadn't had any signal. Look how worried Harry was. Look how upset she had made him.

You're just like him.

There was too much to fix; it was too hard and too humiliating. There were too many people who would never forgive her. And why should they?

You're just like him.

She felt sick. And just as she wondered if she would vomit, the hot, sour liquid came spilling out of her mouth of its own accord, splashing onto her hair and down onto the lobby's polished floor.

"OK!" The hostess was shrilling. "OK! Let me just—"

Donna's suitcase was thrust into her thighs, and she spun away, out of the door, with Bernadette's sharp voice behind her.

"Donna, let me just—"

"Oh, just leave me alone, will you!"

You're just like him.

If someone had been watching from the other side of the narrow pavement outside Loft, where a series of taxis and buses and a rocketing motorbike darted past, they would have seen the wheels of Donna's suitcase become entrapped on the high doorstep, and Donna yanking with all her weight to free it. And if their gaze had flickered away for just a moment, they might have missed it—not seeing whether her hands had simply lost their grip or whether she let go, pitching her body in a backwards arc over the darkening pavement and into the flashing surge of traffic on the road.

* * *

The sound of his vibrating phone woke Harry from sleep. He groped for it, squint-eyed and with a buzz in his ears, murmuring a dry-throated, "What is it? Donna?"

"Is this Harry?" a woman's voice wobbled. There was shouting in the background. "Do you know Donna March? I have her phone here and you'd been texting her tonight."

"Hang on." Frowning, Harry hoisted himself up and sat on the edge of the bed rubbing his eyes. "Well, what's . . . I know Donna, yeah. What's going on?"

"She's been taken to University College Hospital. She was—we were just coming out of a club and—well, she's had an accident. She fell into the road and—Do you have her parents' number or anything?"

"Is she OK?"

"Oh, I don't know. I don't know. They've just taken her."

CHAPTER THIRTY-EIGHT

Question: *Plain, self-raising, whole wheat, 00, semolina, and rye are types of what?*
Answer: *Flour*

"So she's had a CT scan—which apparently was clear, no skull fractures or anything like that. But she was unconscious for a long time, so they have to watch for an . . . internal bleed, I think? Something like that. Anyway, she had a nasty break—her arm—she needs surgery for that tomorrow. I mean, other than that she's having a psychiatric review. It's not quite clear what state she was in when she—Sorry, I know this is a lot. Are you OK? Your breathing sounds sort of funny."

Bryony paced the carpet of her living room, listening to Harry's voice on the phone. "Where are her parents?" she said.

Harry sighed. "She doesn't want her mum to come. And her dad is . . . unavailable."

"Well, when can we come and see her?"

"Tonight if you want. Visiting hours are six till eight. I'll just give Jaime a call, and you guys can—"

"Harry, I . . . oh, Harry."

"I know, Bry. But let's just focus on getting her better, OK? Let's just be there for her. All of us."

"Yes, alright." She was immeasurably touched by Harry's earnestness; she couldn't let him off the call until she'd said so. It was important—wasn't it?—to tell people how you felt at times like these. "And Harry?" she said, wrapping both hands around the phone. "You did a really good thing being there for Donna like that. She's lucky to have you. Well, we all are."

For the remainder of the morning, Bryony tried to busy herself, but there were no more dishes to soak or clothes to fold or crevices to dust free of cobwebs. And when she tried to bake a loaf of banana bread (you could bring these things into hospital, couldn't you?), the packet of flour split as she took it down from the cupboard, sending white billowing clouds down over her head, over the kitchen worktops and down onto the floor.

"Oh—*fuck!*"

Scooping up the stuff with a wad of damp paper towel created a thick coating of gluey paste over every surface. She should have vacuumed it up—of course she should have—wasn't it obvious? Couldn't she even do a simple thing like clean up a spill of fucking flour?

She gave in to the urgency to kneel on the kitchen floor with her head against a cabinet door, taking several deep, steadying breaths. This is why Lydia couldn't stand to be here—because there was an exposed rage and resentment in everything she did. If she'd only been the kind of mother to find contentment in baking banana bread and to do it impeccably, not the kind to constantly seek something that was missing. Lydia could tell what kind of mother she was, and what if she'd been able to tell since she was a little girl, and now nothing would make her believe that Bryony still loved her? And worse: what if she did believe it, but it simply wasn't enough?

Glen came in from the garden. "What's going on?"

And even then she couldn't pull herself off the floor; she was crying so hard that it sapped all the strength from her limbs. "Oh, I was just—I just spilled a—look, I'm sorry, alright? What do you expect me to do about it?"

"Hey, alright, I was just—"

Bryony brought up a hand to shield her eyes but her hand trembled no matter how hard she tried to steady it.

"What's wrong?"

"Donna—from the pub quiz—she's in hospital. And I'm a terrible . . ." She swallowed the catch in her throat. "I'm a terrible mother."

"Listen, sit down, OK? Here—look, here's a chair. You want some water or something?"

Shedding plumes of flour, Bryony pulled herself up from the floor and sank onto the dining chair. She accepted a warm glass of water from Glen.

"You're not a terrible mother," he said. "And what's happened to Donna?"

"She fell into the road—and she—she might've done it to herself. Look, I don't expect you to care about her or anything, I just—"

"Well, come on—I'm not a monster. And Lydia will come home. She just needs to cool off."

"Away from me, you mean. You've been saying it for months. I didn't do any of this to hurt anyone, Glen. Sometimes I'm so . . . sometimes I just don't want to do this anymore, because there are no right answers. Everything I do or don't do is wrong. And I know you hated the Quiz League—"

"I didn't hate the Quiz League." Glen pinched the bridge of his nose. "I just thought you preferred it to being with us."

"You get to go to work and out with Jonesy *and* be a dad. And it was the only thing I did where I felt like something other than being a boring old, mediocre mum. And now it's gone."

Glen knelt down in front of her, putting his warm, tanned hand on her floury thigh. His sparse eyebrows furrowed together.

"Did you know," she said, "I spoke to the school on Friday and Lydia's sent in all her bloody homework? She even did an extra Geography assignment and—"

"Well, that a good thing, isn't it?"

"No. It just proves my mother right." Her hands tightened around the water glass.

"She's just not playing up for Win because Win's not her mum. Come on, you know that. It's—you know—a novelty. Look," he said, wandering into the kitchen to inspect the garden through the open window. "I think we've been pretty hard on each other for a long time now, don't you?"

Bryony unearthed a box of tissues from a debris of mail, textbooks, and newspapers and blew her nose. "Well, yes. I know that." Under his bristled jaw and the creases beginning to appear across his forehead, she tried to see the pimpled boy from the cinema buried under the weather-roughened tanned skin and stray chin whiskers. "The problem is that I don't know who we are without the kids. I don't know who I am either. How are you supposed to be happy if you don't even know that?"

The rub of honesty might have been too much for him. He brushed at the hairs on his forearms, as though to smooth away the shiver of a cold breeze, and his mouth made an odd shape of emotion. "Maybe we can sort of just try to give each other a break," he said.

Bryony nodded. Who knew what that looked like right now? But it seemed important to agree. He hadn't said that they could be happy again, but maybe there wasn't much more to expect. And Glen wouldn't be trying, would he? He wouldn't be fetching her a glass of water and offering her a chair if he didn't . . . well, if he didn't love her anymore.

"Why don't you go upstairs and have a shower or something?" he said. "I'll sort this."

"Well, but you'll have to use the vacuum. Don't try to—"

"Yeah, yeah, alright. I know."

"Thanks, then. Thank you."

After she'd shampooed the flour out of her hair and eyebrows in a hot shower, she sat, wrapped in a towel, on her bed for a long time, inspecting the ageing, veined redness of her feet. And then her phone rang; she stared in bewilderment at the name flaring on the screen: JUDE.

"Jude?" She padded quietly to the door and closed it so Glen wouldn't hear. "Look—no, let me speak first, please—I don't think it's appropriate for you to be calling me, do you? We said all we had to say at the—"

"Bryony, would you listen? I'm not calling about any of that."

"Oh." Bryony felt a prickle of embarrassment over her bare skin. Would she ever stop humiliating herself in front of this man? "Well, what is it then?"

"I just got a call from Priya."

"Oh?"

"The Civil Servants have been disqualified for cheating, Bry—one of them saw the sodding clipboard I left in the toilets and confessed the whole bloody thing."

"Well, alright. What's that got to do with me?"

"Oh, Bry. For someone so clever you're not very bright, are you? It means—if you want it—the Quizzy Peppers have a place in the final."

CHAPTER THIRTY-NINE

Question: *What are the four humors of Hippocratic medicine?*
Answer: *Black bile, yellow bile, phlegm, and blood*

Jaime stood at the door to Donna's ward, chewing her knuckles. Her stomach churned and writhed under her ribs, and her hands hadn't stopped shaking since Harry had called her yesterday. And then the news from Bryony: they were back in the final. As elating as this would have been a few days ago, this morning she couldn't get out of bed without first winding herself around a pillow and waiting patiently for a knot of dread to unfurl in her belly. All she had been able to do since Luke left was try to desperately hold her brains together.

She stood rubbing her temples. The sounds of Bryony and Harry's urgent exchanges echoed across the glossy, linoleum floor and the smell of lime-scented disinfectant was giving her a headache.

"Are you sure that's what Jude said?"

"Of course I'm sure."

"Well, when is it? Are they delaying it or—"

"Nope. It's still scheduled for Thursday. I suppose they don't want to—"

"So they *really* cheated? What scumbags."

"Well, listen, my point is—what do we do about telling Donna?"

Harry rapped on the window ledge in agitation; the yellowish tint of its pane turned the blue sky an acid green. "We have to tell her," he said. "The only reason it all happened is because of her."

Bryony nodded. "Shall we go in?"

Behind the bay curtain, Donna was lying on the bed, small and pale.

Jaime shuffled to Donna's side and lowered herself into one of the chairs. She wanted to take Donna's hands, but the taped skin around the complicated-looking cannula looked red and swollen and the other arm was set in a cast. Instead she held onto the waffle blanket.

Donna's face was gray, lips pale and cracked, her eyes swallowed by a blossom of purple.

"Hi," she said with a sigh. "Silly me, eh? Draw the curtains, will you? Thanks.'

"Oh, Donna." Jaime's voice wobbled in a surge of regret.

"Come on. *I'm* the one in a hospital bed. Heard Luke ran off, though. Sorry about that."

And for some reason this struck Jaime as absurdly funny, and she could not stop an eruption of laughter. She covered her mouth. "I'm sorry," she said, shaking her head. "That's not funny."

"His loss," Donna said. The effort to keep up her usual vigor seemed to exhaust her. She lay still, seeming to be limited to the quick movements of her eyes or the slight turn of her head on the pillow.

Bryony, meanwhile, efficiently skittered around the bay. She adjusted the angle of Donna's bedside light, poured a cup of water from the plastic jug on the swiveling table and waited patiently while Donna slowly sucked it through a paper straw.

"You must let us contact your parents," Bryony said with a frown. "They have a right to know."

Donna wagged her fingers, a weakened version of her usual dismissive wave. "No. I don't want anything like that."

"Well, at least—"

"I said no." Donna lowered her eyes. "So I suppose Harry's told you all about the psychiatrist, then."

"A little,' said Bryony. "I think it's very sensible, don't you?"

Donna shrugged one shoulder. "He's got a ridiculous moustache."

"Well, that hardly matters."

"Alright, so I suppose he has some interesting things to say," Donna said. "It's just so . . . well, inconvenient, all this mental health business."

"But, Donna," Jaime insisted. "If you think—I mean, you absolutely must—"

"I didn't say I wouldn't, OK? Just don't get all sentimental about it or anything. What's been happening while I've been stuck in here anyway?"

Bryony's face turned pink and she held a hand to her cheek. She flicked a look at Harry.

Donna's eyes flitted restlessly between them. "What's going on?"

"Well—look." Harry folded his arms, leaning back into his chair. "Before we start, you have to promise to keep calm, OK?"

"Keep calm about what?" Even in Donna's frailty, her voice rang loud and commanding across the curtained space. "Would someone tell me what's happened?"

"Jude called Bryony yesterday," Harry said in an even voice. He could have been one of Donna's doctors, explaining the delicate nature of a medical procedure. "The Civil Servants—the team we lost to in the semifinal—have been disqualified. They found Jude's clipboard in the men's and cheated—actually cheated. So that means—"

"We're in the final?"

Harry spoke carefully. "That's what Jude said."

"I'm discharging myself." And Donna frantically searched left and right, inching herself up on her elbows and glancing in annoyance at the tangles of tubes and the cumbersome cast on her arm.

Harry stood up. "Absolutely not—"

"Oh, what are you going to do?" Donna sneered. "Are you going to try and stop me?"

Harry stalked around Donna's bed in an agitated, teeth-gritting loop. "You can't discharge yourself, Donna. You're not well."

Ignoring him, Donna implored Bryony. "What did you say? To Jude. What did you tell him?"

"There's a lot to consider here. It's not just you, Donna. Luke's gone too, remember? We're potentially a team of only three, and we—well, we . . ."

Donna stared hard at Bryony. "We what?"

"Well, Harry saw the answers too," Bryony said, folding her arms with a defensive lift of her chin. "Doesn't anyone remember that?"

"We did not *cheat*," said Jaime, and she had begun to pace against the curtain with Harry to dispel her nervous energy. "We very deliberately *didn't* cheat. And that's why we lost. We did the right thing."

"Wait," Bryony said, remaining still amid the dizzying circling of the others around Donna's hospital bed. "This thing is on Thursday— *this* Thursday."

"Oh, well, I'll be fine by then," Donna said, but there was no mistaking the tremor of exhaustion in her voice.

"No," Harry said. "No way. You need to *stop* this, Donna."

"You're being entirely dramatic, Harry. It's hardly as if I'm—"

"No."

"Look—can someone press the call button? I'll just speak to my doctor and—"

"*You're having surgery tomorrow!*" It was the first time any of them had heard Harry raise his voice, and it cast all their eyes downwards in an embarrassed silence.

The curtain snapped away on its hooks and the face of a frowning nurse appeared. "Can you please keep your voices down? Now, please?"

Donna's small, colorless face was still for a moment before it started to crumple and turn red. Her hand, dragging her IV line behind it, came up to hide her eyes, but her stretched, quaking lips and her gritted white teeth could be seen behind the hanging, snaking tubes.

Harry sprang to Donna's side, his tentative hands seeming not to know where to touch her: every part of her body was sore or bandaged. He touched the ends of her golden hair instead.

Donna's hand fell from her face. "I don't need my arm to do a pub quiz," she said. "I just want—I wanted to go." Her voice sounded so different; the vulnerabilities of tears had stripped away all its harshness. There was no way for her to stem her running nose and so Harry reached over and mopped it like an infant's, tucking her hair behind her ears.

At this tenderness, heat rose behind Jaime's eyes and in the walls of her throat: she missed Luke. But as soon as the thought entered her head, she knew it wasn't true—not entirely. She just wished she could have someone who would wipe her nose and smooth back her hair, and fuss around her when she wasn't well. That person wasn't Luke.

"This was *my* quiz," Donna was saying. "It was *mine*." She pointed her fingers to her chest, behind the cumbersome yard of fabric that secured her casted arm.

Harry nodded. "I know."

"Don't you understand?" She gripped Harry's fingers. "It's the only thing I . . ." and suddenly she looked lost. Terror gripped the features of her tear-streaked face. "Everything else I just chucked away, like you said. Don't you get it? It's the only thing I've ever—I'm a *Quizzy Pepper*."

"You'll always be a Quizzy Pepper."

Bryony touched Jaime's elbow and flicked a nod to the parting in the curtains. "Let's go get a cup of coffee or something."

And downstairs in the ground-floor canteen, circling her cup of weak tea with the plastic stirrer, Bryony laid her hand close to Jaime's on the Formica table. "I've never been broken up with," she said.

Adrift in her thoughts over Donna, Jaime shook her head. "What do you mean?"

"Glen was my first boyfriend and then that was that. So I don't know what it feels like." Bryony sipped her tea. "I might have pretended I did, but it was all just condescending rubbish and . . . well, I'm sorry, that's all. It must feel awful and very, very painful, and I'm sorry." Bryony's kind, serious face was full of remorse. "Glen and I—we're not doing so well and Lydia still isn't home. And I think it's going to take a lot of long, hard work to make things better again, if they can be made better at all."

"Oh, don't say that. Of course they can."

"Well, I don't know. It feels like all we've ever been are parents. That's all we *have* ever been. I suppose sometimes I start acting like everyone's mother, but you didn't need me to be your mother. You just wanted me to listen to you and I didn't."

"Oh no, Bry. And I didn't mean any of those things about you getting pregnant and your degree." She grabbed Bryony's hand. "I was—I was feeling very angry. At myself and everyone else." Bryony had a dry callus on the ball of one knuckle. Where would she be if she lost Bryony as well as Luke? She couldn't bear to contemplate it.

"No, you were right. I've been blaming everyone else, you see? And there's no one who can sort it out other than me. But listen." Bryony lifted up Jaime's hand and knocked it gently on the table's surface for emphasis. "There are lots of things you can do here: debt consolidation, you can get a flatmate to pick up the other half of your rent, or even get a bank loan to pay off the debt—the interest will be so much more manageable."

"You don't need to help me. It's not your job and I've been so stupid."

"Of course I'll help you, Jaime. Of course I will."

And how could Jaime stay angry at her? All Bryony had ever tried to do was make sure Jaime was safe and happy and listened to. She wasn't sure she had provided the same—she had tried—but all the days had bled together in an exhausting knot of wheeling supermarket stock, ringing up poster tubes on the till and searching tiredly through bank statements for answers that weren't there. All against the backdrop of Luke's derision and indifference.

"Bryony, I'm . . . I'm so glad I met you. I keep thinking if all this had happened with Luke last year I would have been well and truly . . . well, you know—on my own. So—thank you, I guess."

In the haste of their arms coming around each other, Jaime's half-cup of lukewarm coffee spilled across the table.

"Oh—look at that—"

"Stupid, that was my fault—"

And in the confusion of their shy apologies and quickness to grab napkins, Jaime started to laugh again, as inappropriately as she had done upstairs on Donna's ward.

"I don't know what's wrong with me," she said. "I'm just so relieved Donna is OK. I keep laughing at really stupid . . . I'm like, look at that, I just spilled a cup of coffee everywhere, and it all seems terribly funny." She looked down into her lap. "When Harry called me, I thought Donna was—I thought Harry was going to say she was—"

"No, I did too. It's alright, I thought so too." Bryony's sad profile was pensive and her voice was filled with concern. "What are we going to do about the final?"

"I don't know. Doing it without Donna seems unimaginable." Jaime covered her mouth with her fingers. "Poor Donna. And Luke is such a . . . he's such a shit. Do you know, I messaged him yesterday—about Donna? And alright, I know I probably shouldn't have, but I suppose I thought he ought to know or something. But he didn't even reply."

Bryony squared her shoulders, throwing back a gulp of tea. "Well, I think it's clear by now that Luke only cares about himself."

"And I'll tell you something else." Jaime's hands balled tight into fists. "I'm glad Luke's lost his chance of getting any of that prize money, because he never would have deserved any of it. He would've spent it on Chinese takeaways and video games. Maybe Donna can have his share, to make her feel better, or maybe you and Glen can—" Suddenly her heart came alive. "Why not ask Glen?"

"Ask Glen what?"

"To sub in—for the quiz."

"Are you joking? He's always hated that I've done it. No—he would never—"

"Well, maybe he feels—I don't know—left *out* or something. Do you guys spend any time together? It might be nice."

Bryony sucked at the inside of her cheek. "Well, alright. I can ask him."

CHAPTER FORTY

Question: *Performed by Cliff Richard, what song was the British entry for the Eurovision Song Contest in 1968?*
Answer: *"Congratulations"*

It wasn't until Harry encountered Ashton at work again on Tuesday that he realized he hadn't spoken to Vivienne in three days. Even a week ago, three days without hearing from her would have catapulted him into a spiral of anguish and self-loathing, where he would have circled the rooms of his flat, hoping to find an explanation through the furious pacing of his feet.

One of the sales progression assistants swung past Ashton's desk early that morning. She grabbed his suit shoulders and gave him an affectionate little shake. "Heard the news!" she shrilled, her black-lined eyes flaring wide. "Congratulations!" And Harry had blinked at them for a full minute, while Ashton beamed the full wideness of his smile, before he realized they were talking about Ashton's engagement to Vivienne. He had been so consumed with Donna—thoughts of her small, blonde head sinking into the stiff hospital pillow in whatever hopelessness she felt—that he had entirely forgotten. And for the remainder of the morning, as a string of colleagues swept past to continue congratulating Ashton, he kept bracing himself for a collapse into heartbreak—but it didn't come. And as he sat through one exclamation of delight after another, sipping at his cooling tea, he realized why: he felt good about himself. He had been there for Donna—he had leapt out of bed and scrambled into his twisted clothes and into a cab to find her at the hospital, where he had stayed for twelve troubling hours. The thought of going into the final of the Quiz League without her left him cold, but he knew they could win it, just like they were meant to before his obsession with Vivienne had ruined everything. And he didn't need the praise of Vivienne, or Jude's clipboard, or even Donna's scare tactics to do it. Who else was going to calm their nerves, keep them cool, and answer the football questions? He was indispensable.

And then, right before lunchtime, Darren had "good news" for him.

"Good news. Got that offer on Millen Road. Honestly, mate, couldn't have done that without you. I mean—opening up that kitchen diner; changing that useless walk-in to an en suite . . ." He kissed the tips of his fingers. "All perfect. Genius really. Sellers even held out for a pinch below asking, and they got it." All Darren's white teeth gleamed when he laughed. "Now, about that commission . . ."

Harry shifted uncomfortably in his chair, pressed against the wall in the tight space allowed by Darren's sprawling desk.

"I know I said we'd split it if we got these guys, but I just . . ." Darren squinted and smacked his lips in a feign of careful thought. "I just worry it sends the wrong message, you know? For the other juniors. But you keep at it, alright? You'll get there in no time."

"I see."

"And listen—Ashton's got something on Thursday evening, too. Down on Fox Hill. Nice little place."

"Suppose I won't be getting commission on that either, will I?"

"Well, Harry." Darren smoothed the back of his hair with the flat of his hand. "It's policy. You can understand a thing like that, can't you? My hands are tied." And he encircled his wrist with the loop of his thumb and fingers to show what a deeply inflexible situation he was in.

"Well. Afraid I can't make it Thursday, Darren. Got something important on."

"You'll have to talk to Ashton about it, mate."

And Harry did. When he didn't find Ashton swinging in his chair and chewing on his biro at his desk, it gave Harry an elated spasm of pleasure to discover that he was in the kitchenette, covertly picking at one of his nostrils while he waited for the kettle to finish its boil.

"Can't make Fox Hill Thursday," Harry said, softly cuffing the doorframe. "Got better things to do." But as he swung away, intending to leave as quickly as he had come, Ashton called out after him.

"Your decision, mate. Won't be able to keep you on if you don't."

Harry came back to the door, all the muscles in his jaw tensed.

"We don't have any need," Ashton said, "of someone who's not interested in doing the job."

"Ashton, that's—"

"Oh, what—it's unfair? I don't give a shit. Be there at seven or don't bother coming in again."

"Well, I'm out of here, then."

Ashton plucked up his WORLD'S BEST BOYFRIEND mug and laughed, showing the slick pink of his tongue. "Not so fast. You got to work notice, mate."

Harry clung to one side of the doorframe as he launched the other hand in a tremendous slap at Ashton's bastard mug—"I don't have to work notice; I'm still on probation, *you prick*"—and it tumbled out of Ashton's feeble grip, fracturing into three jagged pieces in the sink. "Have a great wedding, yeah? Much love to the bride." And Harry strode away, looking back to see Ashton's slack mouth opening and closing stupidly, his hand still suspended in the air.

Harry wandered the park after that, having to take off his jacket in a disbelieving sweat. Oh my God, he said to himself again and again, passing under the colossal shadow of the sports center and out to where the noise of a playground full of children cut into his eardrums. Oh my God, I just quit my job.

"What are you doing here?" Donna said when Harry arrived at the hospital an hour before visiting time ended. "Why aren't you at work?"

Her elbow had been pinned in surgery that morning, held against her body in a fresh sling, and Harry noted the faint purple bruises under her eyes were yellowing.

"I quit," he said.

"Oh. Well—good."

"You don't have to feel sorry for me."

"I don't"

"I'm free." He sat back in the chair next to Donna's bed, stretching the length of his neck in a loud and refreshing sigh. "I'm bloody free. My mum is going to go spare—*again*—and I've got no money, but I'm just not unhappy about it, so I'm not going to pretend I am."

"Are you even listening to me?" Donna produced a weak smile that weighed on his heart. "I said *good*. And don't lie to your mum again. You should tell her."

"Absolutely not."

"Jesus Christ, Harry. Have you learned nothing?"

And then she stayed unusually quiet for the remainder of his visit. She didn't even mention the Quiz League as they stared dimly at an episode of *The Office* on the little television, suspended on its mechanical arm over her bed. Yesterday, before they'd said goodbye, she had sat hard-faced through Jaime and Bryony's suggestion that Glen sub in for the final. "Well, he can substitute Luke," she had said. "He's not substituting *me*."

When the consultant had come by on his rounds—smoothing down his ketchup-stained tie and picking at something in his teeth as he flipped through her notes—he had muttered something about her psychiatric evaluation and then slunk away somewhere into the sterilized smells of the ward, behind the billowing curtains.

Donna didn't expand on it, so Harry didn't ask, and when it was time for him to go, he slipped on his windbreaker and stamped a kiss on her forehead.

"Listen, I'll call you when I've heard about Glen, alright?"

"Why bother?"

"Don't start all that."

"I could still discharge myself, you know," she warned darkly. "They say I could be out of here on Friday. And well, what's one day sooner?"

"Well, I thought we talked about this?"

"The psychiatrist thinks I have bipolar disorder," she said suddenly.

With his hands in his pockets, Harry sat down on the edge of her bed. "He said that? Like, for definite?"

"He said it bears the hallmarks."

"What else did he say? What does it mean?"

"Well, I sort of lost track, to be honest. Mood stabilizers, lithium, talking therapy—which sounds sort of . . . you know . . . awful."

"OK. Well, look. It's alright," he said, even though he didn't really know if it was alright. He didn't know anything about it.

"Is it? I was under the impression it was a bit shit." She covered her face and started to cry. He'd seen her cry more in two days than in the whole seven months of knowing her.

He came forward to hug her but she wriggled away in a panic. Her bare skin was hot.

"I'm sorry, Harry. It's not that I don't want you to—it's not that I don't appreciate . . . you know."

"I know. You're alright."

"Listen. Can you call my mum? Can you tell her to come? And Lottie—that's my sister. Look, I have their numbers right here. And can you sort of do it before I change my mind?"

"Of course."

She pulled the little television closer to her face, to stab at its complicated array of buttons. "Thanks, but I really don't want to talk about it anymore."

And over the phone, Donna's mother—her voice an older version of her daughter's, aged by smoking or grief or hardship—started to cry too.

"You mean she—is she . . .? Oh, God."

Harry didn't tell her the details of the accident or about the psychiatric evaluation—he simply assured her that Donna would be fine—but he got the impression that she was crying over something more than a broken elbow.

And whatever the longstanding reasons Donna had had for putting off that phone call, the bravery she had shown in asking Harry to do it, and in awaiting surgery and a psychiatric evaluation and missing the—he sucked in a breath—missing the Quiz League . . . well, it made him feel like a coward. And maybe it was the sounds of Donna's mother's grief over the phone too, that made him take out his phone and dial his own mother's number.

"Mum? . . . Hi, yeah, everything's fine. Well, actually—actually it's not totally fine. You see—well, you see, I just quit Kingsley. And I really don't want you to worry about me. I don't want you to . . . Well, look, I was just really unhappy, you know. I sort of hated it and everything about it and I . . . well, I'm sorry if you're disappointed in me, Mum. I promise I'll . . . The point is I don't want to lie to you again, Mum . . . What was that? . . . Oh . . . Oh, well, that's—thanks, Mum. That's really—you know, I love you, too."

$$* \quad * \quad *$$

"You said you didn't want to come home, Lydia. What did you expect her to *do*? Come over there and drag you?"

Bryony was coming out of her bedroom with the Birkbeck prospectus cradled to her chest when she heard Glen speaking. Following his voice, she peered through a gap in Lydia's bedroom door, finding Glen sitting on her single bed facing away from her, a fresh blue T-shirt stretched over his broad back, revealing a strip of his sun-reddened neck.

"Well, of course she wants you home—we all do . . . Alright, well, your grandmother's never been the easiest person to deal with and—OK, but you're under her roof now so I suppose you just have to put up with it or . . . well, or you come home. You say the word, and we'll come and pick you up and—Oh, don't be daft, of *course* she loves you. Now, listen . . ." Glen began to wag his finger as though Lydia were in the room with him. "Your mother is the most hardworking, caring person I could have ever hoped to meet. She'd do anything for you and Arthur. Are you listening? She's got a heart as big as—Well, yes, I know, but we all go a little nuts sometimes, don't we? And your mother's also entitled to go a little nuts . . . Well, alright. I love you too . . . Everything'll get back to . . . well, it will get better."

Bryony swallowed, her lungs and throat full. He had never said anything like that to her, but when had she said anything similar to him? And then Glen's back started to tremble and he dipped his graying head into his hands; he was crying. She stepped back then, feeling like an intruder on his private sadness. If he wanted to come out and cry with her then he would have. She lowered her eyes, stepped back from the door, and tiptoed quietly down the carpeted stairs.

A few minutes later, recovered but with a mottled, scrubbed face, Glen came trotting into the living room, where Bryony had positioned herself at the coffee table, hunching with a sharpened pencil over a notebook.

"What's this?" he asked.

"I'm working on the personal statement for my application form," she said, without meeting his eyes.

Glen plucked up the glossy prospectus on the page Bryony had folded open.

"Applied Public History," he recited, wandering across the rug. "Is this the one, then?"

She nodded, gnawing at the ragged edge of her thumbnail.

"'Led by the Center for the History of People, Place and Community at the Institute of Historical Research, this course enables learners to develop transferable approaches to their own local history and heritage interpretation.' Hm, well."

"Well, what?"

"Sounds sort of practical, doesn't it?"

"I thought so."

"Well." He rested his hands on his hips. "Good luck with it all, then. I suppose I better see about changing my hours. You know, to make it all work out."

He towered over the coffee table, long enough for her to see the incremental changes of his face from a decisive little frown to a slight tremor of his lips. And before Bryony could wonder whether he'd push her away or laugh it off, she sprang from the sofa and encircled her arms around his neck. His own arms came around her with ease.

"Thank you," she said into the clean smell of his shirt.

"Well," Glen said with an embarrassed cough over her shoulder. "I do—you know—want you to be happy and everything."

Last night, lying in bed, she had practiced all the ways in which she might ask Glen about the quiz final, until her lips started to move silently in conviction: "We can't possibly do this without you, Glen . . . it's just one night; a couple of hours tops . . . it's ten thousand pounds!" But all of those imaginings had ended with his scornful grunts or his derisive and cold "No, thanks," leaving her bashful with rejection. And yet she had to ask him, so she'd better ask him now before she lost her nerve.

"Glen?" she started, and lifted her head away from his chest to stare steadily at his shaven chin. "There's something I wanted to ask you. I heard yesterday that we're back in the Quiz League—the final actually." She chanced a glance up at his eyes, to find them curiously searching her face. "And well, Luke's gone and Donna's still in hospital. We can hardly play just the three of us." God, her heart was drumming. "And I know it's just a stupid little—I know you hate it, but I wanted to know—I was wondering if you might consider . . ."

"Consider what?"

"I was wondering if you wanted to join us tomorrow night. In the final. Join me."

It felt important that she face him properly now, so she did. And there was no scornful frown; he only looked bewildered. He cleared his throat and sat down on the sofa, shaking out the newspaper to drape it over his crossed knee.

"Well, alright," he said. "I'm pretty good at these things, you know."

"You are." She had to turn away, pretending to clear her notebooks from the table.

CHAPTER FORTY-ONE

Question: *What is the sequel to Lewis Caroll's* Alice's Adventures in Wonderland?

Answer: Through the Looking-Glass, and What Alice Found There

Donna twisted a clutch of stiff hospital blanket in her fist as she waited for the call to connect.

"Harry? It's me . . . Oh, I'm fine. Really, I'm fine. I just wanted to say good luck tonight. And listen, I want you to go for it, OK? Don't doubt yourself or anything; take risks and all of that; no regrets, alright? . . . Good, because I want you to forget all that semifinal business; it doesn't matter. And will you tell the others? Will you tell them good luck from me? . . . Alright. And tell them—well, give them my love and everything, won't you? Especially Jaime. Will you tell her she's going to be brilliant? And will you call me after? . . . Good. And can I just—is Glen there? Put him on a sec, will you? . . . Glen? Hi, Glen— nice to meet you. Listen, this is very important. First, don't answer straight away, alright? Not even if you think you know the answer. Not even if you're *sure* you know the answer, got it?"

After Glen had listened studiously, sounding dazed, and then disconnected from the call, Donna eased out of bed for the sole purpose of looking at her face in the mirror that hung above the sink and the industrial pump of antibacterial handwash. She'd been making a habit out of it since she'd been shut up in here, trying to spot any small pieces of evidence that might indicate all was not lost.

Here was her wheat-colored hair, no longer clinging to her skull, since she had showered that morning with the help of a broad and patient nurse. The purple bruises under her eyes had yellowed, and pale rosettes of pink had appeared on her cheeks—though maybe it was just warm in here. It was easier to fixate on her mouth, on the familiar crookedness of her bottom teeth and the pale slice of her bottom lip, rather than look into her eyes. What if she saw hatred there, or worse, indifference? Best to focus, instead, on the small signs of health returning to her body—proof that it was not a body dying.

A twitch at the curtains caught her eye. A tight-knuckled hand split the opening so that the fabric quivered in its grip, and the pale, meek face of a blonde, freckled woman peered inside.

"Donna?"

Relief came in an unexpected rush of warmth and nerves and dread.

Donna drew back the curtain, arranging her face into a benign smile of welcome. You couldn't, after all, expect these things to come easily.

"Hi, Mum. Thanks for—you know—thanks for coming."

The visit went as awkwardly as Donna had expected. Her mother was tearful and imploring ("Why didn't *you* call us? Are we really that unbearable?"), sweeping her up into an embrace in which Donna remained stiff and uncertain. And Lottie was quiet, chewing on the cuff of her sleeve like a child, her overtalkative bravado absent, which was unnerving; Donna preferred her the way she usually was. But they had brought a new set of soft jersey pajamas and a cotton robe for Donna to change into, to be free of the starched hospital gown.

"Well, look, I ought to just tell you, alright?" Donna said, once they had settled into a somewhat comfortable arrangement around the bed, taking boiling sips of weak hot chocolate from the vending machine. "The thing is . . . well . . ." She drew a breath. "I have bipolar disorder. That's what the doctor thinks, anyway. So that's that." Unexpectedly (because she had predicted she would get through this with minimum emotion), hot tears swarmed in her eyes. Her chest and nose felt flooded with them. "Just like Dad," she said, wiping her nose on the back of her fingers, causing her cannula to shift and sting.

"Oh, Donna." Her mum's tired face fell into something that almost looked like relief. "Are you really surprised this has happened? Did you think you could just ignore it? What did you think would happen?"

"Well, I don't know. I suppose I just hoped it would go away."

"You have to get on top of this, Donna, or it'll—it'll just . . ." Her mother swerved her thin body away, pressing her fingers to her lips.

"So I guess you won't want anything to do with me either now, will you?"

"That's not true."

"Well, why would you? He's awful. He's awful, and I'm awful too."

Lottie plucked a new round of tissues from the box on the swivel table and bundled them into her mother's lap. "You're not awful," she said. "And neither is he. He's just not well."

"What's the difference?"

Her mother's face turned pink, her cheeks quivering in an eagerness to be understood. "The difference is he never took any responsibility for it," she said. "He had everyone behind him, he had *choices*, and he made the *wrong* ones. He never kept up with his medication or his appointments—any of it. And it's not that he couldn't—he just didn't want to. He just didn't care. And he hasn't changed—that's why he is where he is."

"I don't know if I can do this." Donna was breathless; her mum may have been assuring her that, with all the right methods, anyone could master this, but instead it just sounded overwhelming. How was it any way to live your life? Her dad had once been strong and capable, hadn't he? He had been funny and warm and—*normal*. And then it had hit him, or crept up on him or whatever it did.

"It's going to follow me forever, isn't it?" she asked them fearfully. "Always over my shoulder, like something about to grab me. How can I ever trust myself again? How can I trust anything I do or think or say?"

Her mother sprang to the side of her bed and clutched Donna's hand. Her skin was cold and paper-dry. She couldn't remember the last time she had touched her mother's hands. "You have us. You have all your friends."

"Dad had us, didn't he? Well, didn't he?"

"Now listen to me." Her mum stood up and loomed over the side of the bed, and Donna allowed herself to be taken by the shoulders and gently shaken like a disobedient toddler. "You've spent too long pretending you know it all, pretending no one else knew what they were talking about. You never listened to me. You never listened to Lottie."

"What do you care? You don't have to visit him; you don't have to think about him anymore."

"All I do is *think* about him, Donna. Do you think I don't—do you think I don't miss him?"

Donna's face grew hot under her mother's tearful accusations; a graze on her forehead began to sting with the rush of blood. But at the same time there was a comfort in being told what to do. Is this what it felt like, to be taken care of? It felt like relief. And she hadn't felt that— maybe ever. She was tired. That was all. She was so tired.

"It's going to be hard work," her mother continued. "And I won't always understand what you're going through, but you don't have to be like him. You *decide* you're not going to be—do you hear me?"

And in their trembling, tearful faces, Donna understood that she *was* like him. It had felt easier to push them all away, so she was free to sink into whatever was happening to her alone, free of the burden of caring about anyone; freeing anyone else of the burden of having to care about her. But what her dad had perhaps not understood was that they had never been free of him—they never would be. They'd carry the blame and the regret with them forever, a weight locked around their necks that pulled them into stooping resentment. Every anxious visit spent at Meadow Hall. Every gathering around a Christmas dinner table where an empty chair sat without a place setting.

Alright, she found herself thinking as her mother's arms slid from her shoulders and collapsed around her, so what now? She didn't want to end up in Meadow Hall. She didn't want to lead her mother into despair and have Lottie hate her, or have her friends turn away from her, or lose her job. She wanted to be like everyone else: to wake up in the morning and not be afraid.

"OK." She nodded. "OK, I can try." And from the swivel table she rooted for the page of notes she had scribbled down after her meeting with the psychiatrist, in the hope it all might begin to make sense. She laid it in her mother's hands. "So, here's the medication he's suggested," she began, pointing with a shaking finger. "And then there's two hours of therapy once a week, maybe twice. And then—"

Her mum grabbed her hand to stop its tremor. "Just one thing at a time, alright?"

Donna nodded, her vision swimming. "If you could . . . you know—help me."

"We will. Of course we will."

CHAPTER FORTY-TWO

Question: *In Scotland and Ireland, what word would describe a narrow valley?*
Answer: *Glen*

Glen stepped into the warm sunlit pub, with its shabby wallpaper and well-trodden carpet. It smelled of warm pints and perspiration—everyone had ambled off the overheating trains from work and piled in through the double doors. Lively jangles of laughter ricocheted across the room, and everyone was moving everywhere at once—jogging to the bar, turning around in their seats and yelling, or telling jokes that required sweeping gestures of their arms.

He thought he might swing by the bar, order a draught of Amstel, and stand there, tall and proud, in the admiration of Bryony's mysterious friends, saying things like, "Of course. Happy to step in. Should be a bit of fun." But there wasn't time to stand around talking to anyone; there wasn't even time to get a drink. He and Arthur were hurried in by Bryony and steered to a narrow table in front of the bar, where Bryony, Harry, and Jaime started to anxiously explain, while wagging their hands and tripping over their own sentences, the rules. Bryony had already done this the previous evening, but in the glare of their anxiously talking faces, he didn't have the heart to say so.

"I mean, Bryony's basically brilliant at everything," Harry was saying, waving a sloshing pint of Magners cider. He was slight in build and shorter than Glen had expected, but with a classically handsome face and curly hair that tumbled in carefree, fashionable waves around his ears and forehead. But the tension of the evening—of the last few months perhaps—had rendered him a little too gaunt and shaken.

"But history especially," he said. "She knows *everything*. But you must know that already."

Clearly pleased, Bryony's cheeks turned pink. "Well, and art questions have to go to Jaime. I don't think she's ever got one wrong."

"Entertainment and sports rounds," Jaime said, twisting her fingers at the pocketed waist of her denim dungarees. She wouldn't meet Glen's eyes, maybe in embarrassment at the day and night she had spent wandering around his house in tears. "Music, TV—you know, anything like that—Harry's pretty good at those. Unless—I mean—unless you're pretty good at all that yourself."

The whole business was set up like some kind of quiz show. Seemed pretty simple. What did they all get so worked up about? Get the question wrong and it went to the opposing team—first team to fifty points wins. No problem.

And then Harry strode over, holding up a mobile phone. He stopped close to Jaime's ear to say something that made her face blush with pleasure. And then Harry thrust the phone at Glen. Confused, Glen put it to his ear. "Hello?"

"Glen? Hi, Glen—nice to meet you. Listen, this is very important. First . . ."

Apparently this was Donna, the one in hospital, the one who, perhaps in abandon or sadness or stupidity, had ended up in a road accident in Mayfair at the weekend. And Glen tried to listen to her, because the sound of her commanding voice told him how critical it was that she be listened to, as though he may be some sort of trainee doctor entrusted with life-saving surgery or a civilian tasked with diffusing a bomb.

Harry brought him a warm lager and Glen devoured half of it in three deep swallows. Was the crowd getting thicker or noisier? Every few minutes the squeal and creak of the door hinges announced more people pouring inside. Well, alright, maybe it was starting to feel a little claustrophobic in here, which could easily make someone nervous. And maybe the thought of not knowing any of the answers—because what if he didn't?—was sort of intimidating. Was this what Bryony had disappeared into, month after month? Had the lights always been this bright and hot? And had there been this many people, all looking down on her curiously and shouting to each other across the room?

Jaime, restlessly fingering her eyelashes, sat down on one side of him and Bryony sat on the other. He checked frequently on the stern concentration of her profile. She looked completely composed, and then a flash of bright happiness came into her face as she spotted Arthur in the audience. He stood, not entirely interested, thumbing a Nintendo Switch, under the protective arm of a red-haired, slope-browed woman who was apparently Harry's mother. Bryony swung out of her chair to squeeze her arm and smile in an exchange of pleasantries while holding her hair behind her ear. And then she stooped down to Arthur—who with his long, awkward limbs was fast requiring no stoop at all—and swept his dark hair off his forehead to stamp him with a kiss.

When she settled back into her seat, a freckled, brawny man with an important-looking clipboard approached them.

He nodded at the empty chair next to Harry.

"What happened to Donna?" the man asked. "And the guy with the glasses?"

"Donna's in hospital," Bryony informed him without meeting his eyes.

"Oh. Is she alright?"

"She will be. And Luke . . . well, Luke's not around anymore. This is my husband, Glen."

"Good. That's . . . I'm glad. Good luck, mate—Glen, I mean. Glad to have you here."

The man retreated, frowning over his clipboard and signaling to an Indian woman with an iPad. She came warmly up to them to shake Glen's hand.

"Good of you to step in—Glen, is it?"

Glen turned red under her powerful stare. "Oh, well, sure. I mean, it's a pleasure."

She nodded down the table at the others. "We'll be starting in five minutes," she said, and moved on to the opposing team on the other table.

"That's who we're playing," Bryony said to him. "The Mile End High Club. Donna was always worried about them."

"What, these jokers?"

The Mile End High Club were a complete party of five, all wearing red T-shirts bearing their printed team name in white and blue. And they radiated confidence in everything they did—the casual way they lounged in their chairs, their assured laughter as they smiled at and chatted with each other, and the entirely unembarrassed way they wore their silly T-shirts.

"We should have worn something special—a team color or something, to boost morale," Jaime said, peering around Glen's back at the red wall of them.

"They've had a month to get ready for this," Bryony said. "We've had three days."

"Wouldn't catch me dead in matching outfits," Harry said. "Donna'd be howling. God, I wish she was here." He took a deep, steadying gulp from his pint glass.

Bryony smiled, flicking her eyes around playfully. "She would have made some joke about them looking like Union Jacks."

Everybody managed a chirrup of nervous laughter, and then, it appeared, it was time to get going. Glen licked his dry lips, wishing he'd had time for another pint, as Jude bounced up in front of them and called between his two cupped hands for the crowd to "quiet down." Glen's stomach clenched unexpectedly, and he searched under the table for Bryony's knee. She gripped his fingers with her cold hand.

"I'll warn you," Jude said enticingly, strutting in front of the bar with a knowing smile. "There'll be some surprises here tonight. Because what would a final be without some twists and turns?"

But there wasn't time to wonder what he meant, or to worry about it, because then he was introducing the Mile End High Club as "the team with the fastest win record in the entire League," and then the Red Hot Quizzy Peppers as "here by unfortunate circumstances— regrettably a depleted team of four."

In the disappointment of their introduction and the coin toss in favor of the Mile End High Club, the match began.

"First round—Sport . . ."

The Mile End High Club were smooth and efficient. They answered quickly, and they passed without any hesitation, sprinkling their responses with extra crowd-pleasing nuggets of their knowledge. And when their answers were incorrect they moved on, unconcerned, with no little frowns of self-chastisement and no frustrated gestures of their hands.

"I believe the answer is lacrosse, Jude."

"Correct! Julian, who was the first boxer to beat Muhammad Ali?"

"Joe Frazier—and that was in 1971."

"Correct! Jessie, how many regulation strokes are there in swimming?"

"Five?"

"I'm sorry . . ."

Jessie rolled her eyes in good humor. "I'll get it next time." She winked.

Though usually regarding himself as a good sportsman, Glen quickly grew tired of their smug voices. But the Red Hot Quizzy Peppers held their own, even through their stumbling and stuttering answers and fumbling passes.

"Jaime, how long is the total distance of a marathon?"

"Twenty-six . . . oh, uh . . . twenty-six-point-two miles?"

"Correct! Harry, how many players are on a baseball team?"

"Pass to . . . uh . . . pass to Bryony?"

"Nine, I think?"

"Correct! Glen, which British cyclist's first Olympic gold was won at the 2008 Beijing games?"

Glen broke out in a hot prickle of panic when Jude announced his name, and even though his first answer was too scrambling—"Oh . . . guy with the sideburns . . . whatshisname? Bradley Wiggins!"—it was, at least, correct. Underneath the table, Bryony gripped his knee.

The Mile End High Club finished the first round ahead by three points. And, during the short break between rounds, as Jude and the woman with the iPad conferred on some matter of importance, Glen caught the first fracture in their red armor. The tall man on the end of the table—a man called Elliott, whose loose jeans revealed a bunched glimpse of his *Avengers* underpants—blotted his brow with a napkin and muttered something. Charlotte—the cool, blonde woman by his side—touched his arm in concern, but Elliott shook her away in annoyance.

"Are you having a good time?" Bryony asked him.

"Sure." He swiped his upper lip where a bead of moisture had gathered.

"You look a little stressed."

"Not at all. No worries."

"Oh, you had all those Olympic questions completely covered," Jaime said. "Good to have another sports guy around now that . . . well, now that Luke . . ."

And Glen clapped a hand down on her shoulder, gathering his breath before he bellowed, "He's a tosser!," knowing it would be the right thing to say, and that it might even ease the tension all round.

Jaime blinked rapidly, with a wobbling smile of belief. It might have spurred her on—Glen was sure that it had—because in the next round (Culture), she reeled off a series of answers for obscure art questions that Glen could barely comprehend. All the hesitancy of the first round seemed to melt away as, with expressions of complete ease, Harry, Bryony, and Glen passed to her time and time again.

"Harry, name the extravagant period of art and architecture prevalent in Europe during most of the seventeenth century."

"Pass to Jaime."

"The Baroque period."

"Correct! Bryony, which other painter is often associated with Françoise Gilot?"

"Pass to Jaime."

"Picasso."

"Correct! Glen, who was the first living person to have their art displayed in the Louvre?"

"Oh, uh . . . pass to Jaime?"

"Georges Braque."

"Correct!'

The round ended with a long and loud cheer, perhaps meant for Jaime alone, but she hid her mouth with a drink of iced Coke. The Quizzy Peppers were on twenty-four points, the Mile End High Club on eighteen. Glen pounded his foot with the rhythm of the applause, his jaw thrust out in fearlessness—this stuff was easy.

But then Jude announced "General knowledge!" in a sobering voice, and, either side of him, Jaime and Bryony sagged over the table.

"Always so tricky," Bryony muttered.

But he didn't have time to ask what she meant before the first wave of questions started.

"Jaime, what is the capital of Finland?"

"Pass to Bryony."

"Helsinki."

"Correct. Harry, what does IPA stand for?"

"Indian Pale Ale?"

"Correct. Bryony, which five colors make up the Olympic rings?"

"Pass to Glen."

It was the first time anyone had passed to him, and in its unexpectedness he realized he had forgotten the question already. "Sorry, can you—can you say that again?"

Jude repeated the question, and Glen hoped that he'd heard correctly, because he was too embarrassed to ask again.

"Blue, yellow, red . . . black . . . and green?"

"Correct." And then, of course, it was his turn again. "Glen, how many valves does the heart have?"

"Four!" He had shouted in the relief of knowing the answer.

"Correct . . ."

His heart was hammering so loudly in his ears and his throat that if someone passed to him again now he wouldn't even be aware of it. Surely they had this round in the bag. And if they could see out this round then there was every reason to hope they would—

"I'm sorry . . ."

Jaime had been beaten on a question that had something to do with Winston Churchill. Under the delighted voices of the Mile End High Club, who had snatched the round from them, Glen sat in a slowly building dismay as the Quizzy Peppers' lead of thirty to eighteen fell away and the round ended at thirty to thirty-two.

Round four began. "The Tudors," Jude announced. Relieved whispers came from Jaime and Harry, and underneath the table,

Bryony's fingers closed around his own. In that moment, with her eyes alive and a fervent grin stretched across her face, she looked no different from the fifteen-year-old he had met at the cinema in Tunbridge Wells who had dunked her hand unapologetically into his cardboard bucket of popcorn as one side of her face lit up with the film trailers— "I'm Bryony. You want some Skittles?" And he had to admit he felt pretty confident too: Arthur had been obsessed with the Tudors for months. But first they had to wait for the Mile End High Club's run to end.

"Julian, who is known as the Nine Days' Queen?"

"Lady Jane Grey—later known as Lady Jane Dudley."

Glen squeezed his knuckles. This joker could eff off.

"Correct! Penny, who was Henry the Eighth's first wife?"

"Anne Boleyn."

"I'm sorry . . ."

They had scored six points. And he might have felt sorry for Penny—who looked as regretful and sick as a little girl who'd eaten too much birthday cake—except he'd known that answer himself, and smugly thought it was pretty silly for her not to have.

Jude turned to them. "Red Hot Quizzy Peppers. Harry?"

"Pass to Bryony."

"Catherine of Aragon."

"Correct! Bryony, what food did Sir Walter Raleigh bring back to England from the New World?"

"Potatoes."

"Correct! Glen, what is the surname of Elizabethan mariner and explorer Sir Francis—what?"

"Pass to Bryony."

"Sir Francis Drake."

"Correct. Jaime, the Wars of the Roses was an ongoing battle between which two royal houses?"

"Pass to Bryony."

"Lancaster and . . . York?"

"Correct. Harry, who was the first Tudor king?"

"Pass to Bryony."

"Henry the Seventh."

"Correct. Bryony, Henry the Eighth married Anne of Cleves, largely on the basis of a portrait painted by which artist?"

"Pass to Jaime."

"Hans Holbein."

"Correct. Glen, who served as chief minister to King Henry the Eighth from 1534 to 1540?"

Glen slapped the table so hard that it stung. "Thomas Cromwell."

"Correct!"

It was the conclusion of the round—the Quizzy Peppers were on thirty-nine and the Mile End High Club on thirty-eight—and it wasn't until then that Glen became aware of the small, shouting voice of Arthur, who was waving his Nintendo Switch in the air, his stick arms flailing with abandon. And no wonder these people thought Bryony was so astonishing. No wonder she disappeared off every week, beaming. They all thought she was marvelous. And crikey, she was, wasn't she? In shame, he thought back to last Christmas, when he'd sulked over the family trivia book the morning after her first quiz, resentful (and maybe ashamed) of feeling as though she could surpass him—that she could easily leave him behind.

She must have seen that he was looking at her funnily then, because she leaned in close to his ear. "Thank you for . . . well, you know," she said.

"Don't worry about it."

"You're doing brilliantly. I just wish—I wish Lydia was here. Not that she would have wanted to come."

"I know, love. She'll come home soon."

After the applause had subsided, Jude dropped his clipboard to his side, his jaw held tense as he scanned the audience with delicious anticipation.

"I said there'd be some surprises here tonight," he said. "Please listen carefully, because the next round will be a wipeout round."

The whispers of the audience fell silent.

"Each team will be asked a question, after which you can confer and then nominate one team member to give your answer. If the answer is correct, your team will gain ten points. If the answer is incorrect, you will lose ten points. Or you can pass the question to the other team, and your points will remain intact."

Stunned, they all sat back. Had they heard that right? "So if we get it right, we'd win?" Harry asked.

"Not quite," Bryony said. "We'd get to forty-nine, and they'd get to forty-eight. So if we also got the next question right after that, we'd win."

Jude stepped forward, his clipboard held aloft. "Red Hot Quizzy Peppers, are you ready for your wipeout round question?"

Harry answered that they were.

"November this year will mark the fiftieth anniversary of which Beatles album?"

They turned their chairs inwards, bending their heads low to whisper furiously at one another.

"Well, alright," Bryony said. "I don't know this—do you?"

Jaime covered her mouth with her fingers. "I have *Abbey Road*—what year was that?"

Harry was staring down at the tight grip of his fingers on each of his kneecaps, his mouth in a little gape of disbelief. That was the look of a man who couldn't believe his luck. Harry knew the answer. Glen was certain of it.

"Harry," he said. "Go on, mate. What do you reckon?"

Harry looked up blinking. "It might be the *White Album*. It was on the news—I watched it with Mum. I remember, because back in the third match I called us the Fab Four—like the Beatles—I forgot Luke, and Donna found it funny. I remembered that when I saw it on the news."

Glen wagged a pointed finger at him. "I think he's right, you know."

"You don't even like the Beatles," Bryony said. "You say they're overhyped."

Harry rubbed his hands together. In the silence of the room, Glen could hear the swish of his dry palms passing over each other. He had the impression Harry might never be certain of anything.

"We should just pass," Bryony said finally. "It's too risky."

Jaime nodded vigorously, looking relieved. "If we don't know it for sure, I think that's the right thing to do."

Harry cleared his throat, studying his hands. A little crease appeared between his eyebrows. "Well, I don't know. I'm pretty sure."

"Well, it's a big decision," Bryony said. "It could lose us the—"

"It's the *White Album*." Suddenly Harry straightened, his expression clear of uncertainty. "That's the answer. And look, I know I've never been exactly . . . well, knowledgeable or anything, and I know I've let us all down before, but that's the answer. And I want you to trust me."

"Well, of course we *trust* you, Harry," Bryony said, and then turned to Jaime. "What do you think? We should all be in agreement here."

Jaime had pulled the cuffs of her sleeves down to cover her fisted hands. "Alright," she said. "I trust you. Let's do it."

"Are we all happy, then?" Bryony said, and after a succession of hesitant nods, they scraped their chairs back into position.

"So, we . . . uh . . . we think it's the *White Album*," Harry said. "That the answer is the *White Album*."

In an agonizing minute that might as well have been an hour, Jude shuffled over to the woman with the iPad and bent his head low, whispering.

He straightened and walked back to the center, his face betraying nothing. "The album was self-titled '*The Beatles*,' he said, "but colloquially known as the *White Album*. That is the correct answer, putting the Red Hot Quizzy Peppers on forty-nine points."

The audience exploded. Bryony shook Harry's shoulder, who was staring wonderingly into his lap with a smile of disbelief, and shouted something in his ear.

The host continued. "Mile End High Club, are you ready for your wipeout question?"

"Yes," said Penny.

"Which city in the world has the most diversity in terms of language?"

For all of ten seconds, the Mile End High Club swayed and shook and nodded their heads together, until Penny faced Jude and raised her voice. "Is it New York City?"

"That is the correct answer. That puts the Mile End High Club on forty-eight points. Alright, folks, next round: World History."

Glen heard the intake of Bryony's breath. Her hand gripped his knee.

"Glen, we left off with you. What land was called Caledonia by the Romans?"

Glen smiled. Under the table he gave Bryony's knee a little shake, and then leaned back with his arms behind his head.

"Pass to Bryony," he said.

CHAPTER FORTY-THREE

Question: *In Greek mythology, what did the goddess Nike personify?*
Answer: *Victory*

Donna's phone didn't ring until nine o'clock. The cold remnants of a hospital canteen chicken casserole had been left congealing on her plate, pushed away on the swivel table. And when Harry's name flashed up on her screen, the phone skittered over the surface in an urgent vibration. Donna swiped to answer the call with slick, sweating fingers.

"Donna!" There was shouting in the background. There were whoops and hollers and the sound of a breaking glass. Harry was shouting. "Donna, are you there?"

"Yes—yes, I'm here."

"We won," Harry said. "We won."

Donna brought her trembling fingers to her mouth. "Oh my God. What?"

"We won. Donna, I wish you could—hang on—wait. Wait right there, OK?"

The call cut off, leaving Donna in torturous quiet. Where, exactly, did he think she would go? Soft murmurs and coughing came from behind her bedside curtains; somewhere a blood pressure cuff hissed and softly beeped. How could the ward be sleepily continuing on after this? How could people be dozing against their pillows and the nurses lazily sharing a plate of biscuits?

It took almost an hour for Harry to reach the hospital. When he thrashed through the curtain, his overjoyed face in frantic motion, Donna was pacing restlessly at the foot of her bed, stiff and high-shouldered in anticipation, her arm held painfully in her sling against her chest as it jiggled with every turn of her socked heels on the linoleum floor. Harry rushed at her, swallowing her into the fold of his arms. His hair, either from sweat or rain, was a mass of damp curls sliding against her cheek.

"Ow—mind my arm."

"Sorry—sorry. The matron's given me ten minutes. Shh—listen, or she'll chuck me out. Look, here . . ." And from his jacket pocket he produced a heavy brass medal fastened on a loop of blue ribbon. On a circle the size of her palm, an engraved star bore the insignia of a question mark and the embossed words: THE LONDON PUB QUIZ LEAGUE. It was a cheap old thing, probably purchased from the internet; it was one of the most precious things she had ever held.

"Oh, wow—this is hilarious," she whispered.

"We all got one."

"It looks like a sheriff's badge or something. Where're the others?"

"Getting completely sloshed down the Five Bells. They wanted to come but they wouldn't have let us all in."

"I bet it was amazing. Was it amazing?"

Gesticulating with his hands high in the air and swiping his hair back from his forehead to hold his head in amazement, Harry talked quickly and in disbelief. "There was a bit near the end—a wipeout round. You had to answer a question right or you'd lose all your points. It was mad. And, oh my God, I knew the answer—it was a stupid Beatles question I'd seen on TV with Mum, and I knew it. And I was sitting there thinking . . ." He clasped and squeezed her hands. "You told me to go for it, and I did."

"I wish I'd been there." She shook her head. "But look—you should go back. You should be celebrating."

"It wasn't the same without you." He took the medal from her hands and lifted it over her head, and when his fingers slid down the ribbon on either side of her neck, he gave it a surprising little tug, pulling her face to his until his warm mouth was on hers for just a moment. Just a moment and then it was over—if it hadn't been for the apologetic knit of Harry's eyebrows and what he said afterwards, Donna might have told herself she'd imagined the whole thing.

"I'm sorry. That was a stupid thing to do."

"No, it's OK."

"You don't need me coming in here and—"

"No, listen, Harry, really it was—"

"Making everything weird or—"

"*Harry.* Please. Would you shut up a minute?"

"Sorry."

Donna flipped her hair out of the necklace of ribbon, using the excuse of having to adjust it beneath the collar of her pajamas to not meet his eyes. "Did you mean it?" she asked.

"I just . . . well, I just really missed you."

"I said, did you *mean* it?"

His lovely face fell still. "Yes. I meant it."

"Alright. Well, I need to get better, OK?" She weighed the heavy brass disc in her palm, rubbing her thumb over the polished question mark. "But I'm glad you meant it."

CHAPTER FORTY-FOUR

Question: *What is the biblical name for sulfur, said to symbolize eternal damnation?*
Answer: *Brimstone*

Bryony and Glen stepped out of Glen's van and onto the scrape of her parents' graveled driveway. After the astonished celebrations of the previous night, in which they had clasped hands and hugged and blinked brightly and disbelievingly into each other's eyes as though they were seventeen again, Bryony had slid decisively out of bed this morning and dialed her mother's number to speak to Lydia.

"Lydia," she'd said, and her voice had not betrayed any waver of regret or doubt, even as she'd paced the length of the kitchen in nervousness. "I want you to come home—today. And, oh, look, Lydia, I'm not saying that to order you around or pretend I know best or anything like that. I'm saying it because I miss you—we all do—and I'm sorry. I'm sorry for being shouty and forgetting things and arguing with Dad all the time and not listening to you. We'll do better, OK? I just want you to come home."

And after that breathless speech, Bryony had stopped at the window, gulping for air, as she'd heard Lydia's small and trembling little sigh of relief.

"Well. OK."

And outside her parents' house, as she straightened the collar of her cotton blouse, worn to suggest all her capabilities as an adult, she'd said to Glen, "Do you want to make sure Lydia's all ready? I want to speak to my mother."

Before she'd even knocked on the door, it opened and Win was standing on the door mat, graceful, tall, and straight in her neat, pastel-colored clothes, her gray hair blow-dried and fortified with hairspray. She didn't say hello; instead she stepped aside to let them into the house. Folding her hands at her waist, she asked, "How was the traffic?" and Bryony said it had been fine.

"Lydia's upstairs. In Bryony's old bedroom."

"Thanks. I'll just—I'll let you two . . ." Glen kicked off his muddied trainers and disappeared upstairs without finishing.

In the living room, an array of tea things had been set out on the glass-topped table, under a frothy arrangement of pink peonies cut from the garden.

"Please, sit down," Win said formally. "I'm afraid it's awfully warm in here." She went about the complicated turns and snaps required to unlock the French doors and then pushed them open to allow in the cool air from the garden. "There, that's better,' she said, but Bryony felt confronted by a wave of heat.

"How's she been?" Bryony untangled the twisted strap of her bag from her arm and tossed it onto the sofa.

"Fine. Will you have some tea?"

"No, thank you."

Win sighed, with a terse shake of her head that wobbled the loose skin of her jaw, showing how tirelessly patient she could be in the face of the unreasonable. She extended a hand to indicate Bryony to sit. Bryony sat down and reluctantly poured from the teapot, just to have something to do with her hands.

Win could have taken the seat next to Bryony. She could have taken Bryony's hands into her lap and squeezed them in an effort to "talk this through properly." But instead she settled into one of the wing chairs opposite, a higher, straighter seat, from which to glare down onto Bryony.

"I was expecting some gratitude—for having taken Lydia in. It's an imposition, after all. We do have lives of our own. Don't you think everyone's had enough of it? Do you *know* how upset Lydia's been?"

"I know I've made a lot of mistakes."

Win sat back in her chair. "You aren't even aware where Lydia is or what she's doing at any hour of the day. She was able to leave school and get on a train here without you even knowing about it.

"I just agreed with you, Mum. I'm not arguing with you."

"You didn't know anything about being a mother when you were seventeen and you're still struggling now. Yet again, your father and I have to—"

"You and Dad don't have to *do* anything. Glen and I don't require your help."

Win lifted her chin. "You've always required our help."

Bryony's head sank onto her hands. She raked her fingers back and forth against her scalp. Win may have had the impression that Bryony had started to cry; she swiftly crossed the room to sit next to her on the sofa and bent her head low to implore Bryony with her outstretched hands. She smelled of freesias and breath mints.

"Where did we go wrong?" Win said. "You had everything you ever wanted. You had everything going for you. What did we do wrong?"

Bryony lifted her head, peering into her mother's anxiously lined face. "Well, you've always been like this, for a start—arrogant, contemptuous, impossible to please."

Win reared back, her mouth trembling as it opened and clamped shut again. "We've always supported you. We've always made sure you're happy."

"Only on your terms, though. Even back when I was applying to Durham—"

"You *wanted* to go to Durham."

"I did!" Bryony held her jaw tense to keep her voice from wavering. "I did."

"I never heard you decline anything. You needed a house to raise Lydia."

"I know that, Mum, and we're grateful. I just don't want it thrown back in my face every time I do anything wrong. Why did everything have to come with strings attached?"

Win stood up and went to stand by the threshold of the garden where, on the patio, a twirling fall of white petals circled around the sun loungers. The light fabric of her trousers rippled in a breeze. "For years I've been looking for the point in time when I could have prevented it," she said, still gazing out at the garden. Her head wobbled on her tall neck. "I've looked and I've looked, and I've never been able to find it. It's always been a mystery to me. And I suppose I'll die without ever understanding it."

The sounds of birdsong floated into the silence of the room, and above their heads the first brimstone butterflies began their fluttering, entrapped dance against the skylight.

"You're never going to forgive me, are you?" said Bryony.

Win hugged her elbows against her body, looking frail. "Forgiveness doesn't change the past, Bryony."

"Then I suppose we'd better be going. Thank you for having Lydia."

Upstairs, in the silence of the plush carpet and heavy curtains, Bryony found Lydia sitting on the bed with Glen at her side. Bryony's old room was now a guest room, stripped of the old posters and cork board of silly letters from school. The duvet cover and pillowcase were unfamiliar too—a crisp, white expanse, sewn with rows of seed pearls. It was as though she'd never lived there.

Lydia was wearing an unfamiliar blue sundress that Bryony knew she would never have chosen, and Bryony could smell her chewing gum and strawberry body spray. It had been almost three weeks since she'd seen her.

"Are you ready to go home?" By Lydia's feet was her school backpack and a department-store paper bag, probably containing a few new clothes and a toothbrush, urgently purchased by her mother when she'd shown up with nothing but her school uniform.

"Are you going to get a divorce?" Lydia asked suddenly. "When Keesha's parents got a divorce, she had to talk to this awful woman about who she loved most—her mum or her dad—"

"They don't ask you that," Glen said, with his large, reassuring hands coming up to rest on Lydia's narrow shoulders. "I bet they asked her who she wanted to live with."

"Isn't that the same thing?"

"No, not at all," Bryony said. "Sometimes it's to do with school, or . . . Anyway, we're not getting a divorce." She peered at Glen. What if he said they might? Or something more gently noncommittal like, "Well, me and your mum have a lot to sort out." But his serious face did not betray a flicker of doubt.

"Of course we're not," he said.

Bryony could have sunk to the carpet and wept, but she hid the relief on her face by picking up the bag of clothes and swinging the backpack onto her shoulder. "Come on," she said. "Let's all go home. We have a lot to talk about, don't we?" As Glen reversed from the driveway, her mother stood straight-backed against the front door, her mouth held in a small rosebud of civility. Through the windscreen, Bryony waved an outstretched hand to her. Win's head bobbed on her tall neck as she briefly raised her own hand before bringing it to her face to brush her top lip. She lowered her chin and averted her eyes.

CHAPTER FORTY-FIVE

Question: *The Latin* ego te absolvo *is said by Roman Catholic priests during the Sacrament of Confession and translates to what?*

Answer: *I forgive you*

"Have you got a minute? Mind if I come in?"

On a bright Saturday in August, Jaime opened the door to see Donna standing on her doorstep, holding a rectangular, bubble-wrapped package under one arm. Her other arm was strapped in a structured black sling, out from which peeked the edges of her lumpy white cast. And after Jaime had let her inside and led her upstairs into the flat's living room, Donna had stood looking small and lost on the rug, staring and blinking around the place, seemingly at a bookcase with a meagre collection of unimpressive paperbacks, of the type often said to be "trash." Jaime had to fight the impulse to tear the books down from the shelf where they could not be seen, but Donna said nothing at all. She had always appeared so tall and magnificent, with her elegantly tousled hair and clomping boots and sharp, blue glare, but now her face was scrubbed of makeup, her hair was pulled back into a ponytail, and her cropped acid-wash jeans and oversized T-shirt left her looking skinny and in an uncertain hover of nerves.

She smiled meekly at Jaime and asked, "How've you been?"

"Oh, you know—OK. Are you alright?"

"Well . . ." Donna briefly lifted her cast. "It's all fun and games here. Listen, I'm having a clear-out. My flatmate moved out and . . . well, I brought you something."

Inside the bubble-wrapped package that Donna handed over was a framed pencil sketch of a hook-nosed, jacketed woman in a black dress. And in the corner was the circular stamp of what Jaime knew to be the signature of Toulouse-Lautrec. Jaime stood with it at arm's length, blinking and shaking her head. She reached around to hold all the damp hair off the nape of her neck, as though the heaviness of it stopped her thinking clearly.

"Is this real?"

Donna waved her hand. "It's just a lithograph."

"Like an original?"

"Well, yes. I thought you might like it."

"Oh, Donna." And Jaime was going to decline it—she knew she was—but she was already wandering from wall to wall, holding the frame up against different falls of light. She may as well commit to memory what a Toulouse-Lautrec would have looked like in her living room. She came back to stand in front of Donna.

"I really can't—"

"Of course you can."

"No, really—"

"Well, look, Jaime, if you don't want it, it's going down the charity shop. So."

"Why don't you sell it?"

"I don't want to sell it." Donna folded her arm over her stomach, underneath her sling. Her face turned pink. "I want you to have it, because I don't know anyone else who would like and deserve it more."

"Oh, well, Donna, that . . ." Jaime didn't know what to say.

"Listen, Jaime." Donna's small blonde head jerked as she swallowed. "I've been really awful to you, for a really long time, and I'm very sorry."

"You don't have to—"

"No, I knew you'd say that. And you should really demand better for yourself, Jaime. You didn't deserve any of it."

"I thought you just found me incredibly annoying or something."

Donna looked down at her sandaled feet, maybe in an effort to minimize the exposure of her embarrassed face. "Everyone was annoying. Everyone and everything. Not just annoying, but hateful. It's a pretty awful world to live in when you think like that—it's destructive and ugly and . . . well, it's terribly deceptive. But it didn't have anything to do with you. I just used you as an easy target or something crappy like that."

"I'm sorry I called you a horrible person, at that cocktail bar."

"I didn't come here for an apology swap. And to be honest, I don't deserve it."

"But you weren't well."

"Well, I know. But that's not an excuse. So how about you just let me say sorry and take this picture and we have that be it, OK?"

"OK. Well, thank you."

"I'd like to be friends."

"Me too. And not just because you give me priceless artworks."

Donna's face erupted into a smile. "Well, good, because I don't have any more."

Jaime placed the frame gently against the wall, and in the rustle of the bubble-wrap scrunched tightly in Jaime's hands, they both stepped back to admire it. When she looked at Donna's pensive face, it was at peace. If this had been Bryony, Jaime would have thrown her arms around her dear neck, but Donna didn't look like a girl that wanted to be hugged. And she almost wished she didn't feel so desperately sorry for Donna too, because Donna was also a girl who would never want anyone to pity her.

"Shame your flatmate's moving out," Jaime said.

"Oh, that's OK. She's well shot of me, honestly."

"What are you going to do?"

"I'm not sure yet. I'm on disability pay—for now, at least—so I'm just going to take my time. Think things through. What about you? Are you staying here?"

"Oh no—I don't think I could stand to. I've given my notice. Going to look for a flat share or something. And then I can—you know—finally stop those twilight shifts. You want a cup of tea or something?"

"Oh no." Donna slung her hand on her hip. "I was just on my way to Gipsy Hill. Got a date with a psychiatrist."

"Oh. Well, good luck with it."

"The guy's OK. I like him. Well, anyway . . . see you." Donna let herself out, and from the kitchen window Jaime could watch her for a minute as she weaved down Gipsy Hill and slid out of sight. Jaime was pleased with the dignity of that conversation. It had been mature and free of any silly outbursts of bitterness. It was the kind of conversation that unfurled all her joints and ligaments; she felt content.

After Donna had left, Jaime occupied herself with the routine of a lonely person, pretending that the rituals and obligations to take care of yourself—and take care of yourself properly—took up quite enough time, thank you very much. Each task had to be performed methodically and purposefully to fill these hours of loneliness. Or rather she should refer to it as something mature like "solitude," because, to her surprise, she didn't mind it. She woke up in the morning and took care of herself. She didn't have to worry about anyone else. It was a relief. And, as it turned out, she was pretty good at taking care of herself.

First the laundry, which needed untangling (because bed sheets and long-sleeved shirts always became tightly entwined in everything else), and that could easily take up an hour. And then it was time to face her online bank accounts, which had, unexpectedly, become one of the favorite parts of her week. What had started as an exercise in self-punishment had quickly become proof of her ability to cope. The prize money had gone straight to the loan debts, and, with Bryony's help, a low-interest bank loan had taken care of the rest. Everything made sense on a bank statement: there was nothing to betray you—if the credits didn't exceed the debits then you simply had to readjust the balance. And if you didn't achieve that one month, the next month would always allow you another stab at getting it right. There were untold advantages to a solitary's person's bank statement too—here was her gas and electric bill, markedly dropped now only accommodating one person, and there was the weekly food shop, which did not allow for takeaways when there were fresh vegetables in the fridge. Nothing would be squirrelled away for gaming equipment and she had long cancelled the sports channel subscription. She was fine.

And when her mother rang her, as she had taken to doing twice a week now, Jaime told her she was fine too.

"I'm fine, Mum. Really."

"Alright, love. Well—I've put some shortbread in the post, and they were giving away free sachets of washing powder at the shop this week. I popped those in too."

"Thanks, Mum."

"Saw Luke in town this week."

"Oh, you did?"

"Slinking around the chip shop with whatshisname—boy from school—Stratten Cooley."

"Well, he can do what he likes, I suppose."

Jaime feigned a yawn and told her mother she was tired and wanted to get some sleep, but after she'd put down the phone, the flat intercom buzzed.

"Alright if I come up?" the voice said. It was Luke.

The shock of hearing his voice gave her that drifting sensation again, as though the floorboards had dissolved under her feet. What was he doing here? And what could he possibly want?

Jaime buzzed him through and opened the front door to allow him inside before she'd even stopped to consider whether she wanted that. She ran to the bathroom to check her face in the mirror and found it wildly staring back at her; she wasn't even wearing any makeup. Oh, she knew if she saw his face she would cry.

And she did. His face, pink and bloated from a day of travelling on the train in the hot weather, and when he touched her shoulder to console her, it took all the self-possession she had not to collapse against his chest. When she had composed herself enough to speak, she said he'd better come into the living room and sit down.

"I'm sorry the place is such a mess," she said, except that it wasn't.

Luke didn't sit down, but wandered in aimless circles, as though he were a prospective tenant inspecting the place for rent.

"Congratulations on winning the League, by the way," he said.

"How did you hear about that?"

"Looked it up online."

Then Jaime remembered. "You never—didn't you get my message about Donna?"

"Oh, yeah. Yeah, I did."

"Why didn't you say anything?"

"Well, I'd just left, hadn't I? I was still angry with you."

"I was angry with you too. I still took the time to let you know. Donna was your friend, and I . . ." She had been about to say, "was your girlfriend," but the "was" still stung.

"But she's fine now?"

Jaime nodded.

"Listen, Jaime, I—I'm sorry. For leaving without saying anything. For taking the money."

She sniffed, holding her arms tightly around her waist as though to keep the contents of her stomach inside. "Well, the money thing in particular was sort of low."

"I suppose I felt entitled to it. You were at least still working, and I had nothing coming in. Besides, I thought you'd been—you know—dishonest."

"Well, alright. If you've just come here to blame me or something, then I don't think—"

"No. No, I haven't. I just wanted to explain it, was all."

"Alright."

"So, how have you been?"

"Fine. You?"

"Fine."

"You got a job up there yet?"

"No."

"Oh. You don't have a job." Jaime started to laugh, and even to her it sounded cruel and mocking. Well, so what? He'd complained about London since the day they'd arrived. He'd wanted to go back home, certain his happiness lay there, and now—now that he'd followed through—he was no better off. And he'd betrayed her in the process; she hoped he was satisfied.

"Not exactly easy in Keswick. It's not exactly a thriving metropolis or anything."

"Then why did you want to go back?"

"Oh, I don't know, Jaime." He started to pace around the room with his hands in the pockets of his ugly brown corduroys. "Maybe I didn't want to go back. Maybe I just didn't want to be here anymore."

"Well, that's nice. That's very nice of you."

"I'd like to come back."

"What, here? To the flat?"

"Well, not to the flat. Somewhere else, maybe. To another flat or maybe even Manchester or Birmingham or . . . well, anywhere."

She remembered having asked him the same thing—perhaps she had even suggested the same places. She even remembered thinking what a good idea it was.

"You could transfer your shifts at the supermarket," he said. "And don't they have branches of PrintPro in other—you know—cities?"

The idea drained all the warmth from her body. "Well, that's a lot to think about," she said, and she let her gaze rest on the lithograph leaning against the wall. She thought of Donna's perceptive and serious face. ("You should really demand better for yourself, Jaime.")

Luke followed her gaze. "What's that?"

"A lithograph. By Toulouse-Lautrec."

"Who?"

"Never mind."

Luke dipped his head, as though to inspect his shoelaces. "And about the Quiz League," he said. "The prize money."

"What about it?"

"What happened to my share?"

"We split it between the four us. That's fair, isn't it?"

"Oh." His nostrils flared in a sharp sniff, and Jaime's stomach tightened.

"Oh, what?"

"Well, no, it doesn't seem fair."

"Excuse me?"

"I went through five rounds of that thing and contributed as much as everyone else."

Jaime squinted at his boyish, entitled face, and the way he blinked at her expectantly. She saw now that his polo shirt was ironed with sharp creases down the sleeves and that the collar had been pressed. And obviously his mother had done that for him. She had laundered his shirts and his underwear and bought the shampoo that had freshly washed his hair. Had this child even fastened his own buttons or bought his train ticket or tied his own shoelaces?

"Did you come back here to get the prize money?"

He blinked at her. "Well, for us—not just for me."

"I think you should go, Luke. Thanks for the offer, but no."

"Well, shouldn't we at least—"

"No. We shouldn't."

CHAPTER FORTY-SIX

Question: *Which chemical element has the symbol Au?*
Answer: *Gold*

On a luminous September afternoon in Donna's flat, in the long shadows of the curbside trees, a spate of summer showers splattered the windows with raindrops of gold. Jaime had given noticed on her flat'in Gipsy Hill and was moving in with Donna, into Bernadette's vacated, echoing room. Outside on the pavement, Donna heard the wrench of Glen's van door, and the shouting calls of him, Harry, and Bryony navigating the heavy lifting of one of Jaime's possessions.

Donna was packing clothes destined for the charity shop into a plastic trash bag. "What have they got down there?' Jaime reached up on tiptoe to peer out of the window and down onto the street. She had swept her freshly washed hair into a ponytail to reveal her round, innocent face. "I think it's a chair or something."

Donna had continued to purge her belongings: books of the kind to coach your "mind, body and spirit," expensive clothes that had no purposeful wear, the DIY materials for the chimney breast. A jangling set of enameled bangles, stolen from a department store twenty years ago.

"Well, don't worry," Jaime had said, when she inspected the crumbling plaques of plaster on her arrival, prodding her finger into the powdery mortar between the yellow bricks. "We can fix this up—the landlord won't ever notice."

Now Harry and Glen, sweating with the lifting and hauling of furniture and packed boxes, were barreling through the front door, gritting their teeth and frowning in the effort to heave a linen wing chair across the living room. Bryony followed, shouting wincing instructions over their heads.

"Wait—wait—watch out for the *wall*!"

"Mind the corner, mate—up on the left."

"Wait . . . OK, got it. Where'd you want this thing?"

Jaime held her arms wide to present a sunlit patch of floor. "Oh, here by the window would be nice, don't you think?"

"Sure," Donna said, as Harry and Glen lowered the thing to the floorboards and a plume of dust from the upholstery was released into the air.

Harry, with a ring of perspiration at the neck of his T-shirt, stood for a while at the window. Donna was captivated by his long, pensive gaze as he scratched the damp curls at the nape of his neck. On the street below, a woman on a bike fled past with a ring of her bell, and a teenaged boy was pulled by a barking dog past a chain of parked cars.

Well, what was Harry thinking in these quiet moments to himself? And why—after two months—wouldn't he make his move? She was getting better, wasn't she?

The last two months had been nothing but routine and obligation—physical therapy for her arm, psychiatric appointments, and diligent, unchallenged adjustments to her medication. And Harry had been there too, the evening when she'd sat with the first dose of it held in her lap, in the tight grip of fear. (What if she could never be free of these things? What if they turned her into someone else?) He had gathered her against his chest as she'd swallowed the candy-like pink and white capsules in the refuge of his deodorant-scented T-shirt, and stayed with her ear against his chest until she heard the lazy gentleness of his voice.

"Fancy a pizza?" In the cheerful sounds of the television, she'd expected to see his eyebrows drawn in pity or concern, but there was only a patient benevolence in his slow-blinking eyes as they wandered over the room.

"Alright," she had said, while thinking, with her heart drumming under her shirt, that she didn't want to be without him.

Now, Jaime offered a round of tea, which she efficiently made and brought into the living room on a neat little tray, with the polite smile of a proud hostess.

Harry peered at Donna over his scalding mug as he took his first delicate sip. "Drink at the pub?"

"Oh." Donna's throat closed. "Yeah?"

"Need a shower first," he said, but then he looked over at Jaime, Bryony, and Glen—"Up for it, guys?"—and Donna's lungs deflated.

"I got to go get the kids," Glen said, the keys to his van jangling in his palm as he took Bryony by the shoulder. "But I'll see you back at home later, love." And he stamped a kiss on her cheek.

Donna hunched down into the sofa and drew her knees protectively against her chest. What was wrong with him? What was wrong with *her*? Or had the half-kiss on the hospital ward faded so swiftly from his memory? Had he even "meant it" at all? For God's sake—it was as if they were thirteen years old.

They agreed to meet at the Five Bells at four o'clock, and she hastily excused herself to her bedroom to change from her dusty clothes, with Jaime glancing worryingly after her. Would these sorts of glances of concern always follow her now, whenever she was simply in a sulk? It was enough to have her mother and Lottie calling almost every day to probe into her recovery (and she never failed to answer either). I'm fine, she wanted to tell her—it's just a run-of-the-mill case of heartache.

*   *   *

"Hi. This Harry West?"

Harry scrubbed his damp hair with a towel. "Yep, that's me."

"Harry, good to be in touch. Name's Callum Bailey. I'm calling from Hunters—we had a joint agency on the Millen Road house with Kingsley? Heard the sale was down to you." Callum's voice was deep and rich, like a host on a radio station that played sophisticated jazz. "That was nice work."

Harry balled up the towel in one hand and tossed it on the sofa. "Well, it wasn't just . . . well, OK, sure—yes. I made that sale."

"We were sorry to have missed out, but, listen—heard you left Kingsley, and I wondered if you'd like to come down to Hunters for an interview next week? Position for senior agent's just come up—think you'd be a great fit."

"Wow—yeah, I'd love to." Harry winced at his own eagerness, before thinking, the hell with it—Callum had called *him*, hadn't he? "Sure, Callum," he added. "That sounds terrific."

They settled on Tuesday morning. Callum said he was looking forward to it, that he couldn't wait for Harry to "meet the team." Ordinarily Harry might have run through everything that could go wrong—his suit wouldn't be sharp enough, there'd be a stain of dripped egg yolk on his shirt, his handshake would be limp and unconvincing—but he didn't think any of those things. He wandered into the steam-filled bathroom, just to look at himself in the fogged mirror. "You've just got yourself a job," he said to his reflection.

The first person he wanted to tell was Donna, and his heart responded with a quickening flurry. It seemed as though her recovery was successfully steady—her bouts of laughter never descended into cruelty, and her focus didn't stray into fixation or obsession. Donna could hide a lot of things in the babble of her happy voice, but he knew her well enough—didn't he?—to tell the difference between her authenticity and the barriers she could build around herself. He was sure of it. The problem was, every time an opportunity arose to come out with his long-practiced invitations ("Hey, Donna, shall we grab a drink, just you and me?," "Hey, listen, you free this weekend?"), he retreated, too nervous of her reaction. He might have only one opportunity to do it right and at the acceptable time, or he could ruin everything. She may well regard him with a frowning roll of her eyes and say something like, "Didn't I say I needed more time, Harry?" But how much time were you supposed to allow for something like this? It wasn't something you could google (and he'd tried). And it didn't stop him lying in bed, his mind wandering to the night they had spent in his flat after that first pub quiz, or of lacing the medal ribbon around her neck on the hospital ward, compelled to kiss her. Whenever he saw her afterwards, his face grew hot with shame. Don't be a creep, he had to warn himself.

And over their damp, wooden table at the Five Bells, after the sweet, celebratory taste of Harry's first sip of Aspall cider, Donna was the first person he told.

"Sounds like they were really impressed with you," she said, and her face was nothing but sincere as she took a long drink of fizzing lemonade and wiped her mouth. "Who knew that shitty place would lead to something like this?"

"Well, thanks." He ducked his face into his drink again. The sweet intensity of her attention, sitting in a spaghetti-strapped summer dress the color of plums, was enough to swell all the walls of his heart.

"Have you told your mum? She's going to be so proud of you."

"Not yet—I'll call her tomorrow. I know she's not sitting around worrying about it or anything. And I just wanted to . . . well, I wanted to tell you first. And listen, if you're around Tuesday, maybe we could—"

"What's this?" Bryony cut him off as she strode over to the table from the bar with Jaime, holding a pair of wine glasses aloft.

Harry gave Donna a brief smile of apology, but he couldn't tell whether she understood what he was sorry for as she tucked her hair behind her ears and proudly announced, "Harry's got a job interview next week." And in their joyful cries, Harry's ears burned pink.

"Well, that's amazing news, Harry. Congratulations."

"I knew something would turn up! Oh, well done!"

"And you see that poster over there?" Bryony pointed with the hand that held her glass. "There on the far window—it's the call for entries for the Quiz League. You see their logo?"

"Oh my God, yes!" Jaime's face came alive. "We have to defend the title."

"Count me in," Donna said. "I'm owed a final, aren't I?"

"Christ," Harry said. "Barely recovered from this year."

With the swing of her knee, Donna gently knocked his leg under the table. "Don't be ridiculous. It's not till December, anyway."

And Bryony was the first to solidify their plans, along with the achievements of the day, with her glass poised high above their heads. "Well, here's to the Quizzy Peppers," she said, "and to Donna's wonderful new flatmate, *and* to Harry's new job—Shh, of course you'll be offered the job, Harry, don't ruin my toast."

And in their warming cheers and the congratulatory clink of their glasses that sounded over the chatter and mumble of the pub, Harry knew he'd never felt so at ease.

At six o'clock, Bryony headed off to start dinner, and Jaime needed to drop her keys back at the estate agents before they closed.

"Bye, then," they called—"Bye!"—with promises to see each other again soon.

When Harry and Donna reached where they would part on Anerley Road, they slowed the brisk bounce of their walk and Harry pulled Donna into a brief one-armed hug. He inhaled the fresh watermelon that could have been the scent of her hair or perfume or chewing gum.

"Well, good luck at the interview then," Donna said. "I'm sure you'll smash it."

"Thanks."

"Alright, then."

"Alright. See you."

He turned on his heel, and he thought he heard her sigh, but when he wheeled around again, she was trotting quickly away, her arms folded around her waist. Through the black railings of the park, the golden evening light cast rippling stripes of shadow over her ducked head as she walked.

For God's sake. Had he come through the last year of self-loathing and fear, only to be crippled by this stupid and pointless hesitancy? Hadn't it cost him enough already? And didn't Donna—brave, funny, complicated Donna—deserve better than any of this?

He called out—"Donna? Hey, wait a minute!"—and he jogged up to her. "Sorry—I just . . . well, I just wanted to say that I . . ." Christ, he couldn't breathe. "Well, I guess I was waiting for some sort of perfect— you know—*moment* or something, or maybe I'm just scared shitless. But I mean, *wherever* we are is . . . well, pretty perfect already really, you know? Because *you're* there. In the Bells or just sitting around or out here on the pavement. And what's really scary is that one day I'll walk away, and it'll be gone for good. That you'll have met some six-foot gym guy who wears skinny jeans and who *actually* asked you out. So listen—if you haven't changed your mind or anything—you free for dinner tomorrow night?"

Donna's lips parted in an expression that was both bewildered and delighted. "I—yes."

"Cool. It's a date."

They stood in the fading rays of sunlight, all at once shy and laughing and relieved, as their two pairs of hands found each other and held on.

CHAPTER FORTY-SEVEN

Question: *What is the section or speech at the end of a book or play that serves as a comment on or a conclusion to what has happened?*
Answer: *Epilogue*

On an early morning at the beginning of October, Bryony laid the post on the coffee table, waiting for the house to come to quiet. Upstairs Lydia, running late for school, thundered across her bedroom floorboards: "Mum, have you seen my—oh, I got it, don't worry! Oh, and what about—no, I found it!" Arthur waited in the hall in his new shoes, scratching at an insect bite on his elbow, shouting up at his sister to hurry up. Glen wandered around the kitchen, sucking toast crumbs from his fingers and stacking the breakfast bowls and mopping up a spill of cereal, going about the routine of getting ready for work, just like the day before. And at times like these she occasionally found herself thinking: Well, why Glen? Why me? Why not anyone else on the planet? But just hearing his contented little sighs and mumbles and his socked feet creaking the floorboards underfoot filled her with a deep sense of comfort, of everything being how it should be. She might not ever be the type of person to believe in anything as childish as a "soulmate" or that someone could be "her person," but why *not* Glen? Why *not* her? Couldn't you choose your person just as much as them being given to you?

When he came into the living room to hand her a mug of tea, he kissed her temple, saying, "You told them yet?"

She smiled up at his proud face. "I'm calling Jaime now."

And once Lydia and Arthur had jostled each other out of the front door, Bryony picked up the phone and dialed Jaime's number.

"Jaime? Hi, it's me . . . Hi! How's the flat? You settling in alright? . . . Oh, that's great. Because you know you can always—you know—let me know if you need anything . . . Good . . . Oh, Lydia's great. Really, she—she's really turned a corner. I think we all have. But anyway, the post just came and I heard from Birkbeck. I got in . . . I know! Honestly, my hands are still shaking. I just got the—you know—the letter this morning, and . . . Well, that's very– that's very sweet of you, Jaime. Thank you . . . Well, that sounds great. Hold on, let me just . . . *Glen! Glen, did you want to go to the quiz on Thursday?* . . . That's perfect, Jaime, we'll be there. You'll ask Donna and Harry? . . . Good. I can't wait."

ACKNOWLEDGEMENTS

My most sincerest thanks to Laura Williams and Sherise Hobbs for their enthusiasm, insight and guidance. And all at Headline, Alcove Press and Greene & Heaton

I am indebted to the most wonderfully supportive, talented, funny and critically minded writing group, the Writer's Tears: Pete Sherlock, Rhiannon Barnsley, Jo McClean, Nicola Venning, Dave Telford, Melanie Reynard, Becky Brynolf, Lucy Bamforth, Daisy Pfeil, Rute Évora-Jauad, and Elise Summers. They have become such treasured friends and this book would not exist without them.

I also owe gratitude to readers and friends who backed this book from its early drafts, notably Babs Ward, April Hilton, and Marnie Riches. And, of course, my wonderful mum, Susan Farnsworth.